THE CHILDREN'S HOUR

Caravan of Fun

A BOOK TO GROW ON

Consultant Editor for
Caravan of Fun

HELEN DEAN FISH
Editor and Author

CONSULTANT EDITORS FOR THE CHILDREN'S HOUR

CAROL RYRIE BRINK
Author
Newbery Prize Winner

JULIA CARSON
Author and Biographer

IRVING CRUMP
Editor and Author

HELEN DEAN FISH
Editor and Author

WILHELMINA HARPER
Anthologist, Librarian
Redwood City, California

WILLIAM HEYLIGER
Author,
Editor of Literature for Youth
The Westminster Press

SIDDIE JOE JOHNSON
Children's Librarian
Dallas Public Library

CORNELIA MEIGS
Author and Teacher
Newbery Prize Winner

NORMA RATHBUN
Chief of Children's Work
Milwaukee Public Library

MABEL L. ROBINSON
Author, Associate Professor
Columbia University

MARGARET JONES WILLIAMS
Director of Elementary Education
Cornell College, Iowa

THE CHILDREN'S HOUR

MARJORIE BARROWS, *Editor*

Caravan of Fun

MATHILDA SCHIRMER
Associate Editor

DOROTHY SHORT
Art Editor

THE SPENCER PRESS, INC. • *Chicago*

Acknowledgments

The editor and publishers wish to thank the following publishers, agents, authors, and artists for permission to use and reprint stories, poems, and illustrations included in this book:

APPLETON-CENTURY-CROFTS, INC., for "The Casting Away of Mrs. Lecks and Mrs. Aleshine" by Frank R. Stockton, with illustrations by George M. Richards. Copyright, 1933, D. Appleton-Century Company, Inc.

BRANDT & BRANDT for "A Nautical Extravaganza" from *Random Rhymes and Odd Numbers* by Wallace Irwin, published by The Macmillan Company, copyright, 1906, by The Macmillan Company; and "The Won't-Pick-Up-Toys Cure" from *Mrs. Piggle-Wiggle*, first volume, by Betty Bard MacDonald, published by J. B. Lippincott Company, copyright, 1947, by Betty Bard MacDonald.

CONSOLIDATED BOOK PUBLISHERS for "Bertram and the Lion" and "Bertram and the Musical Crocodile" by Paul T. Gilbert; and illustrations by Rosemary Buehrig, Clarence Biers, and Marilou Wise.

CURTIS BROWN, LTD., for "Jonathan Bing" from *Jonathan Bing and Other Verses* by Beatrice Curtis Brown, published by Oxford University Press of New York, copyright, 1936, by Beatrice Curtis Brown.

DOUBLEDAY & COMPANY, INC., for "The Ransom of Red Chief" from *Heart of the West* by O. Henry, copyright, 1907, by Doubleday & Company, Inc.; and "The Elephant's Child" from *Just So Stories* by Rudyard Kipling.

HARCOURT, BRACE AND COMPANY, INC., for "The Huckabuck Family" from *Rootabaga Pigeons* by Carl Sandburg, copyright, 1922, by Harcourt, Brace and Company, Inc.; and "The First Day of School" from *The Moffats* by Eleanor Estes, copyright, 1941, by Harcourt, Brace and Company, Inc.

HENRY HOLT AND COMPANY, INC., for "The Ship of Rio" from *Collected Poems* by Walter de la Mare. Copyright, 1920, by Henry Holt and Company, Inc. Copyright, 1948, by Walter de la Mare.

HOUGHTON MIFFLIN COMPANY for "Elizabeth Eliza's Piano" and "The Lady Who Put Salt in Her Coffee" from *The Peterkin Papers* by Lucretia P. Hale, with an illustration by H. I. Bacharach; and "The Ruggleses' Christmas Dinner" from *The Birds' Christmas Carol* by Kate Douglas Wiggin.

ALFRED A. KNOPF, INC., for "Freddy the Detective Solves a Mystery" from *Freddy the Detective* by Walter R. Brooks, copyright, 1932, by Walter R. Brooks, with illustrations by Kurt Wiese; and "The Big Baboon," "The Gnu," and "The Yak" from *The Bad Child's Book of Beasts* by Hilaire Belloc, copyright, 1931, by Hilaire Belloc.

J. B. LIPPINCOTT COMPANY for "Mrs. Goose's Rubbers" from *Mrs. Goose and the Three Ducks* by Miriam Clark Potter, copyright, 1936, by Miriam Clark Potter; "Cake for Company Dinner" from *Oh, Happy Day* by Miriam Mason, copyright, 1939, by J. B. Lippincott Company; and "The Old Woman and the Tramp" from *Fairy Tales from the Swedish* by N. G. Djurklou, copyright, 1920, by J. B. Lippincott Company.

LITTLE BROWN AND COMPANY for "Mr. Popper and Captain Cook" from *Mr. Popper's Penguins* by Richard and Florence Atwater, copyright, 1938, by Richard and Florence Atwater; "The Panther" and "The Rhinoceros" from *Many Long Years Ago* by Ogden Nash, copyright, 1933, by Ogden Nash; "The Tale of Custard, the Dragon" by Ogden Nash, copyright, 1936, by Ogden Nash; and "Eletelephony" from *Tirra Lirra* by Laura E. Richards, copyright, 1918, 1930, 1932, by Laura E. Richards.

MACMILLAN COMPANY OF CANADA for Canadian permission to reprint "The Elephant's Child" from *Just So Stories* by Rudyard Kipling; and illustrations by John Tenniel for Lewis Carroll's "The Lobster Quadrille" and "The Walrus and the Carpenter."

MACMILLAN AND COMPANY, LTD., OF LONDON for illustrations by John Tenniel for Lewis Carroll's "The Lobster Quadrille" and "The Walrus and the Carpenter."

OPEN ROAD, THE YOUNG PEOPLE'S MAGAZINE for "You Never Saw Such an Egg" by Russell Carpenter.

RAND McNALLY AND COMPANY for "Fun" from *The Jolly Jingle Picture Book* (*Rimskittle's Book*) by Leroy F. Jackson, copyright, 1926, by Rand McNally and Company.

ST. MARTIN'S PRESS, INC., for illustrations by John Tenniel for Lewis Carroll's "The Lobster Quadrille" and "The Walrus and the Carpenter."

SCOTT, FORESMAN AND COMPANY for illustrations by John Merryweather for Ogden Nash's "The Panther" and "The Rhinoceros."

STORY PARADE, INC., for "Oscar, the Trained Seal" by Mabel E. Neikirk and "The Camel Is A Mammal" by Peter Wells.

THE VIKING PRESS, INC., NEW YORK, for story and illustrations from "The Case of the Cosmic Comic" and "Homer Price and the Doughnuts" from *Homer Price* by Robert McCloskey, copyright, 1943, by Robert McCloskey; "Serapina Proves Herself" from *The Story of Serapina*, by Anne H. White, copyright, 1951, by Anne H. White, with illustrations by Tony Palazzo.

ANN WATKINS, INC., for "The Magic Glass" from *The Spider's Palace* by Richard Hughes, copyright, 1932, by Richard Hughes. Originally published by Harper and Brothers.

A. P. WATT & SON and Mrs. George Bambridge for "The Elephant's Child" from *Just So Stories* by Rudyard Kipling.

EDWARD WADE DEVLIN for "The King's Wish."

HELEN AND ALF EVERS for "The House the Pecks Built" and "Mr. Scrunch" by Helen and Alf Evers, with illustrations by Helen Evers, originally published by Rand McNally and Company.

JOSEPHINE LOFTING for story and illustrations from "The Crazy Story of Dizzy Lizzie" by Hugh Lofting, first published in *Child Life Magazine;* "Dr. Dolittle Meets a Londoner in Paris" by Hugh Lofting, (J. B. Lippincott Company, Philadelphia); "Dr. Dolittle and the Pushmi-Pullyu" from *The Story of Dr. Dolittle* by Hugh Lofting, J. B. Lippincott Company, publisher.

JOHN DUKES McKEE for "The Tillyheehee," first published in *Child Life Magazine.*

CLIFFORD MEIGS for "Maybe" by Mildred Plew Meigs.

MRS. BRIDGET O'CONNELL for "How to Tell Wild Animals" by Carolyn Wells.

THOMAS C. O'DONNELL for "The Pink Giraffe" first published in *Child Life Magazine.*

RAY ST. CLAIR for "The Cannery Bear" first published by Story Parade, Inc.

JOHN GEE for illustrations for Carl Sandburg's "The Huckabuck Family."

WALTER V. ROUSSEFF for illustrations by Minnie Rousseff for Edward Wade Devlin's "The King's Wish," and Richard Hughes' "The Magic Glass."

Great pains have been taken to obtain permission from the owners of reprint material. Any errors that may possibly have been made are unintentional and will gladly be corrected in future printings if notice is sent to the Spencer Press, Inc.

Contents

Ogden Nash

THE TALE OF CUSTARD, THE DRAGON

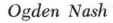

Belinda lived in a little white house,
With a little black kitten and a little gray mouse,
And a little yellow dog and a little red wagon,
And a realio, trulio, little pet dragon.

Now the name of the little black kitten was Ink,
And the little gray mouse, she called her Blink,
And the little yellow dog was sharp as Mustard,
But the dragon was a coward, and she called him Custard.

Custard the dragon had big sharp teeth,
And spikes on top of him and scales underneath,
Mouth like a fireplace, chimney for a nose,
And realio, trulio, daggers on his toes.

Belinda was as brave as a barrel full of bears,
And Ink and Blink chased lions down the stairs,
Mustard was as brave as a tiger in a rage,
But Custard cried for a nice safe cage.

Belinda tickled him, she tickled him unmerciful,
Ink, Blink, and Mustard, they rudely called him Percival,
They all sat laughing in the little red wagon
At the realio, trulio, cowardly dragon.

Belinda giggled till she shook the house,
And Blink said, "Weeek!" (which is giggling for a mouse),
Ink and Mustard rudely asked his age
When Custard cried for a nice safe cage.

1

Suddenly, suddenly they heard a nasty sound,
And Mustard growled, and they all looked around.
"Meowch!" cried Ink, and "Ooh!" cried Belinda,
For there was a pirate, climbing in the winda.

Pistol in his left hand, pistol in his right,
And he held in his teeth a cutlass bright,
His beard was black, one leg was wood;
It was clear that the pirate meant no good.

Belinda paled, and she cried, "Help! Help!"
But Mustard fled with a terrified yelp,
Ink trickled down to the bottom of the household,
And little mouse Blink strategically mouseholed.

But up jumped Custard, snorting like an engine,
Clashed his tail like irons in a dungeon.
With a clatter and a clank and a jangling squirm
He went at the pirate like a robin at a worm.

The pirate gaped at Belinda's dragon,
And gulped some grog from his pocket flagon.
He fired two bullets, but they didn't hit,
And Custard gobbled him, every bit.

Belinda embraced him, Mustard licked him,
No one mourned for his pirate victim.
Ink and Blink in glee did gyrate
Around the dragon that ate the pirate.

Belinda still lives in her little white house,
With her little black kitten and her little gray mouse,
And her little yellow dog and her little red wagon,
And her realio, trulio, little pet dragon.

Belinda is as brave as a barrel full of bears,
And Ink and Blink chase lions down the stairs.
Mustard is as brave as a tiger in a rage,
But Custard keeps crying for a nice safe cage.

Rudyard Kipling

THE ELEPHANT'S CHILD

ILLUSTRATED BY *Keith Ward*

I N THE High and Far-Off Times the Elephant, O Best Beloved, had no trunk. He had only a blackish, bulgy nose, as big as a boot, that he could wriggle about from side to side; but he couldn't pick up things with it. But there was one Elephant—a new Elephant—an Elephant's Child—who was full of 'satiable curiosity, and that means he asked ever so many questions. *And* he lived in Africa, and he filled all Africa with his 'satiable curiosities. He asked his tall aunt, the Ostrich, why her tail feathers grew just so, and his tall aunt, the Ostrich, spanked him with her hard, hard claw. He asked his tall uncle, the Giraffe, what made his skin spotty, and his tall uncle, the Giraffe, spanked him with his hard, hard hoof. And still he was full of 'satiable curiosity! He asked his broad aunt, the Hippopotamus, why her eyes were red, and his broad aunt, the Hip-

4

popotamus, spanked him with her broad, broad hoof; and he asked his hairy uncle, the Baboon, why melons tasted just so, and his hairy uncle, the Baboon, spanked him with his hairy, hairy paw. And *still* he was full of 'satiable curiosity! He asked questions about everything that he saw, or heard, or felt, or smelt, or touched, and all his uncles and his aunts spanked him. And still he was full of 'satiable curiosity!

One fine morning in the middle of the Precession of the Equinoxes, this 'satiable Elephant's Child asked a new fine question that he had never asked before. He asked, "What does the Crocodile have for dinner?" Then everybody said, "Hush!" in a loud and dretful tone, and they spanked him immediately and directly, without stopping, for a long time.

By and by, when that was finished, he came upon Kolokolo Bird sitting in the middle of a wait-a-bit thornbush, and he said, "My father has spanked me, and my mother has spanked me; all my aunts and uncles have spanked me for my 'satiable curiosity; and *still* I want to know what the Crocodile has for dinner!"

Then Kolokolo Bird said, with a mournful cry, "Go to the banks of the great gray-green, greasy Limpopo River, all set about with fever trees, and find out."

That very next morning, when there was nothing left of the Equinoxes, because the Precession had preceded according to precedent, this 'satiable Elephant's Child took a hundred pounds of bananas (the little short red kind), and a hundred pounds of sugar cane (the long purple kind), and seventeen melons (the greeny-crackly kind), and said to all his dear families, "Good-bye. I am going to the great gray-green, greasy Limpopo River, all set about with fever trees, to find out what the Crocodile has for dinner." And they all spanked him once more for luck, though he asked them most politely to stop.

Then he went away, a little warm, but not at all astonished, eating melons, and throwing the rind about, because he could not pick it up.

He went from Graham's Town to Kimberley, and from Kimberley to Khama's Country, and from Khama's Country he went east by north, eating melons all the time, till at last he came to the banks of the great gray-green, greasy Limpopo River, all set about with fever trees, precisely as Kolokolo Bird had said.

Now you must know and understand, O Best Beloved, that till that very week, and day, and hour, and minute, this 'satiable Elephant's Child had never seen a Crocodile, and did not know what one was like. It was all his 'satiable curiosity.

The first thing that he found was a Bi-Colored-Python-Rock-Snake curled round a rock.

"'Scuse me," said the Elephant's Child most politely, "but have you seen such a thing as a Crocodile in these promiscuous parts?"

"*Have* I seen a Crocodile?" said the Bi-Colored-Python-Rock-Snake, in a voice of dretful scorn. "What will you ask me next?"

"'Scuse me," said the Elephant's Child, "but could you kindly tell me what he has for dinner?"

Then the Bi-Colored-Python-Rock-Snake uncoiled himself

At this, the Elephant's Child said, "Led go! You are hurtig be!"

very quickly from the rock, and spanked the Elephant's Child with his scalesome, flailsome tail.

"That is odd," said the Elephant's Child, "because my father and my mother, and my uncle and my aunt, not to mention my other aunt, the Hippopotamus, and my other uncle, the Baboon, have all spanked me for my 'satiable curiosity—and I suppose this is the same thing."

So he said good-bye very politely to the Bi-Colored-Python-Rock-Snake, and helped to coil him up on the rock again, and went on, a little warm, but not at all astonished, eating melons, and throwing the rind about, because he could not pick it up, till he trod on what he thought was a log of wood at the very edge of the great gray-green, greasy Limpopo River, all set about with fever trees.

But it was really the Crocodile, O Best Beloved, and the Crocodile winked one eye—like this!

"'Scuse me," said the Elephant's Child most politely, "but do you happen to have seen a Crocodile in these promiscuous parts?"

Then the Crocodile winked the other eye and lifted half his tail out of the mud; and the Elephant's Child stepped back most politely, because he did not wish to be spanked again.

"Come hither, Little One," said the Crocodile. "Why do you ask such things?"

"'Scuse me," said the Elephant's Child most politely, "but my father has spanked me, my mother has spanked me, not to mention my tall aunt, the Ostrich, and my tall uncle, the Giraffe, who can kick ever so hard, as well as my broad aunt, the Hippopotamus, and my hairy uncle, the Baboon, *and* including the Bi-Colored-Python-Rock-Snake, with the scalesome, flailsome tail, just up the bank, who spanks harder than any of them; and *so*, if it's quite all the same to you, I don't want to be spanked any more."

"Come hither, Little One," said the Crocodile, "for I am the Crocodile," and he wept crocodile-tears to show it was quite true.

Then the Elephant's Child grew all breathless, and panted,

7

and kneeled down on the bank and said, "You are the very person I have been looking for all these long days. Will you please tell me what you have for dinner?"

"Come hither, Little One," said the Crocodile, "and I'll whisper."

Then the Elephant's Child put his head down close to the Crocodile's musky, tusky mouth, and the Crocodile caught him by his little nose, which up to that very week, day, hour, and minute, had been no bigger than a boot, though much more useful.

"I think," said the Crocodile—and he said it between his teeth, like this—"I think today I will begin with Elephant's Child!"

At this, O Best Beloved, the Elephant's Child was much annoyed, and he said, speaking through his nose, like this, "Led go! You are hurtig be!"

Then the Bi-Colored-Python-Rock-Snake scuffled down from the bank and said, "My young friend, if you do not now, immediately and instantly, pull as hard as ever you can, it is my opinion that your acquaintance in the large-pattern leather ulster" (and by this he meant the Crocodile) "will jerk you into yonder limpid stream before you can say Jack Robinson."

This is the way Bi-Colored-Python-Rock-Snakes always talk.

Then the Elephant's Child sat back on his little haunches, and pulled, and pulled, and pulled, and his nose began to stretch. And the Crocodile floundered into the water, making it all creamy with great sweeps of his tail, and *he* pulled, and pulled, and pulled.

And the Elephant's Child's nose kept on stretching; and the Elephant's Child spread all his little four legs and pulled, and pulled, and pulled, and his nose kept on stretching; and the Crocodile threshed his tail like an oar, and *he* pulled, and pulled, and pulled, and at each pull the Elephant's Child's nose grew longer and longer—and it hurt him hijjus!

Then the Elephant's Child felt his legs slipping, and he said through his nose, which was now nearly five feet long, "This is too butch for be!"

8

Then the Bi-Colored-Python-Rock-Snake came down from the bank, and knotted himself in a double-clove-hitch, round the Elephant's Child's hind legs, and said, "Rash and inexperienced traveler, we will now seriously devote ourselves to a little high tension, because if we do not, it is my impression that yonder self-propelling man-of-war with the armor-plated upper deck" (and by this, O Best Beloved, he meant the Crocodile), "will permanently vitiate your future career."

That is the way all Bi-Colored-Python-Rock-Snakes always talk.

9

So he pulled, and the Elephant's Child pulled, and the Crocodile pulled; but the Elephant's Child and the Bi-Colored-Python-Rock-Snake pulled hardest; and at last the Crocodile let go of the Elephant's Child's nose with a plop that you could hear all up and down the Limpopo.

Then the Elephant's Child sat down most hard and sudden; but first he was careful to say "Thank you" to the Bi-Colored-Python-Rock-Snake; and next he was kind to his poor pulled nose, and wrapped it all up in cool banana leaves, and hung it in the great gray-green, greasy Limpopo to cool.

"What are you doing that for?" said the Bi-Colored-Python-Rock-Snake.

" 'Scuse me," said the Elephant's Child, "but my nose is badly out of shape, and I am waiting for it to shrink."

"Then you will have to wait a long time," said the Bi-Colored-Python-Rock-Snake. "Some people do not know what is good for them."

The Elephant's Child sat there for three days waiting for his nose to shrink. But it never grew any shorter, and, besides, it made him squint. For, O Best Beloved, you will see and understand that the Crocodile had pulled it out into a really truly trunk same as all Elephants have today.

At the end of the third day a fly came and stung him on the shoulder, and before he knew what he was doing he lifted up his trunk and hit that fly dead with the end of it.

" 'Vantage number one!" said the Bi-Colored-Python-Rock-Snake. "You couldn't have done that with a mere-smear nose. Try and eat a little, now."

Before he thought what he was doing the Elephant's Child put out his trunk and plucked a large bundle of grass, dusted it clean against his forelegs, and stuffed it into his own mouth.

" 'Vantage number two!" said the Bi-Colored-Python-Rock-Snake. "You couldn't have done that with a mere-smear nose. Don't you think the sun is very hot here?"

"It is," said the Elephant's Child, and before he thought what he was doing he schlooped up a schloop of mud from the banks of the great gray-green, greasy Limpopo, and slapped it on his

head, where it made a cool schloopy-sloshy mud-cap all trickly
behind his ears.

" 'Vantage number three!" said the Bi-Colored-Python-Rock-
Snake. "You couldn't have done that with a mere-smear nose.
Now how do you feel about being spanked again?"

" 'Scuse me," said the Elephant's Child, "but I should not
like it at all."

"How would you like to spank somebody?" said the Bi-Colored-Python-Rock-Snake.

"I should like it very much indeed," said the Elephant's
Child.

"Well," said the Bi-Colored-Python-Rock-Snake, "you will
find that new nose of yours very useful to spank people with."

"Thank you," said the Elephant's Child, "I'll remember that;
and now I think I'll go home to all my dear families and try."

So the Elephant's Child went home across Africa frisking
and whisking his trunk. When he wanted fruit to eat he pulled
fruit down from a tree, instead of waiting for it to fall as he used
to do. When he wanted grass he plucked grass up from the
ground, instead of going on his knees as he used to do. When
the flies bit him he broke off the branch of a tree and used it
as a fly-whisk; and he made himself a new, cool, slushy-squshy

11

mud-cap whenever the sun was hot. When he felt lonely walking through Africa he sang to himself down his trunk, and the noise was louder than several brass bands. He went especially out of his way to find a broad Hippopotamus (she was no relation of his), and he spanked her very hard, to make sure that the Bi-Colored-Python-Rock-Snake had spoken the truth about his new trunk. The rest of the time he picked up the melon rinds that he had dropped on his way to the Limpopo—for he was a Tidy Pachyderm.

One dark evening he came back to all his dear families, and he coiled up his trunk and said, "How do you do?" They were very glad to see him, and immediately said, "Come here and be spanked for your 'satiable curiosity."

"Pooh," said the Elephant's Child. "I don't think you peoples know anything about spanking; but *I* do, and I'll show you."

Then he uncurled his trunk and knocked two of his dear brothers head over heels.

"O Bananas!" said they, "where did you learn that trick, and what have you done to your nose?"

12

"I got a new one from the Crocodile on the banks of the great, gray-green, greasy Limpopo River," said the Elephant's Child. "I asked him what he had for dinner, and he gave me this to keep."

"It looks very ugly," said his hairy uncle, the Baboon.

"It does," said the Elephant's Child. "But it's very useful," and he picked up his hairy uncle, the Baboon, by one hairy leg, and hove him into a hornets' nest.

Then that bad Elephant's Child spanked all his dear families for a long time, till they were very warm and greatly astonished. He pulled out his tall Ostrich aunt's tail feathers; and he caught his tall uncle, the Giraffe, by the hind leg, and dragged him through a thornbush; and he shouted at his broad aunt, the Hippopotamus, and blew bubbles into her ear when she was sleeping in the water after meals; but he never let anyone touch Kolokolo Bird.

At last things grew so exciting that his dear families went off one by one in a hurry to the banks of the great gray-green, greasy Limpopo River, all set about with fever trees, to borrow new noses from the Crocodile. When they came back nobody spanked anybody any more; and ever since that day, O Best Beloved, all the Elephants you will ever see, besides all those that you won't, have trunks precisely like the trunk of the 'satiable Elephant's Child.

FUN

Leroy F. Jackson

I love to hear a lobster laugh,
Or see a turtle wiggle,
Or poke a hippopotamus
And see the monster giggle,
Or even stand around at night
And watch the mountains wriggle.

13

Laura E. Richards

ELETELEPHONY

Once there was an elephant,
Who tried to use the telephant—
No! no! I mean an elephone
Who tried to use the telephone—
(Dear me! I am not certain quite
That even now I've got it right.)

Howe'er it was, he got his trunk
Entangled in the telephunk;
The more he tried to get it free,
The louder buzzed the telephee—
(I fear I'd better drop the song
Of elephop and telephong!)

14

Miriam Clark Potter

MRS. GOOSE'S RUBBERS

ILLUSTRATED BY *Ruth van Tellingen*

ONE day Mrs. Goose could not find her rubbers. She looked in the same old place in the dark hall closet, and she looked under the bed, and she looked on the back porch; but she could not see them. So she went to Mrs. Pig's house and knocked at the door. When Mrs. Pig came to see who was knocking, Mrs. Goose said: "Have you seen my rubbers?"

"Of course I haven't seen your rubbers, Mrs. Goose," Mrs. Pig told her. "They wouldn't be at my house, would they?"

"I don't know," said Mrs. Goose. "I just thought they might be."

Then she went to Mrs. Squirrel's house and knocked at the door. When Mrs. Squirrel came to let her in, Mrs. Goose said, "I just came to see if you had seen my rubbers."

Mrs. Squirrel was making a nut-patty pudding. "No, I haven't seen them," she said. "Did you think they were *here?*"

"I didn't know," sighed Mrs. Goose. "I just thought they might be."

Then Mrs. Goose went home. She looked under the stove, she looked behind the door, she looked up on the clock shelf, she looked in the wastepaper basket, she looked in the icebox, but she could not find her rubbers.

Just then Mrs. Sheep went by.

"Oh, Mrs. Sheep," called Mrs. Goose; "have you seen my rubbers?"

Mrs. Sheep stopped by the fence. "Why, no, I haven't seen your rubbers," she said. "Where do you usually keep them?"

"In their same old place in the dark hall closet," said Mrs.

15

Goose. "But they are not there."

Mrs. Sheep thought for a minute, and then she said, "Why do you want your rubbers, anyway, Mrs. Goose? "It's sunny!"

"Well, it might rain tomorrow," Mrs. Goose replied, "and then I'd want them."

"That's right," said Mrs. Sheep. "Come to think of it, I don't know where *my* rubbers are, either. I'd better go home and look them up." And she hurried on.

Still Mrs. Goose could *not* find her rubbers. She looked in the teakettle, she looked on the back stairs, she looked in the bread box, she looked under her pillow, and then she got a ladder and climbed up on the roof and stared all around; but her black eyes did not spy them anywhere.

"Dear me, dear me," she sighed, "where can my rubbers *be?*"

Then she ate her supper and went to bed. Next morning when she woke up, rain was coming down—*drip, drip, drip,* on the roof. "Oh, it *is* raining today," said Mrs. Goose, "and I've got to go to market, and I haven't found my rubbers, and I'll get my poor feet all wet!"

She got up and made her bed and ate her breakfast. She dusted her house; and then she just *had* to go to market. The rain was coming down in big bursts and splashes and there were puddles all over the sidewalk.

"I *must* find my rubbers!" thought Mrs. Goose. And she looked and looked in all the same places, but they did not turn up. "Well," she sighed, "I shall have to go without them. That's *what!*" And she put on her coat and bonnet, took her big green umbrella from its place in the dark hall closet, and started out. She shut the door behind her, locked it with the tiny key, and stepped out on her porch. Then she put her big green umbrella up.

"Plop! Plop!" Two big somethings hit her on the head and almost knocked her bonnet off. They fell down on the porch behind her. "What can they be?" thought Mrs. Goose. She turned around and looked at them. They were her rubbers!

"I must have put them inside my umbrella," said Mrs. Goose. "Oh, now I remember! I put them there so they would not be lost. But it would have been a good deal better if I had put them back in their same place, in the dark hall closet."

Then she put her rubbers on and went splashing along through the puddles on her way to market.

Helen and Alf Evers

THE HOUSE THE PECKS BUILT

ILLUSTRATED BY *Helen Evers*

MR. PECK was a carpenter, and a good one, too. But he was very poor. So he and his wife, Mrs. Peck, with their daughter, Bertha Peck, their son, Albert Peck, and the dog and the cat, all lived way out in the country in a little house with only one room. But the house was neat and clean, and all the family were very proud of it because it was the smallest house in the world.

Then people began to find out what a good carpenter Mr. Peck was and to hire him to build houses for them. So he began to make more money.

One night when he came home he said, "I must have a bedroom of my own, where I can lie down and rest before dinner without getting in my wife's way while she is cooking."

Then Albert said, "I want a bedroom, too."

And Bertha said, "So do I."

And Mrs. Peck, who was busy popping corn, said, "I can't hear what it is that all of you want but if you are going to have one, I want one, too."

So Mr. Peck, with the help of Mrs. Peck and Bertha and Albert, built four bedrooms.

One day, when all the bedrooms were finished, Mr. Peck came home, very tired and hungry. He brought some fish for Mrs. Peck to fry for dinner.

But Mrs. Peck said, "If I fry those fish here in this room where we cook and eat and spend our evenings, I'll never be able to get the odor out of the curtains."

So Mr. Peck said, "Very well, my dear. I'll build you a kitchen, and while I'm at it I'll build a dining room, too."

Then Albert Peck said, "Father, I think it would be nice if I had a room where I could play with my electric train without having people stumbling over it."

And Bertha Peck said, "If Albert has a room for his train I want one for my dolls."

So Mr. Peck, who liked to make his family happy, said, "Very well, besides the kitchen and the dining room we'll build a trainroom and a dollroom."

And as Mr. Peck was now no longer just a carpenter but a prosperous builder he added, "I need an office for my business, so I think I'll build that at the same time."

So all the Peck family got to work, and in a few weeks the new rooms were finished.

Then one day some of Mrs. Peck's friends came in to play cards, and after they had left Mrs. Peck thought how nice it would be to have a cardroom where she could entertain her friends.

When Mr. Peck came home she mentioned it to him.

Then Albert Peck said, "I'd like a room where I can play ping-pong with *my* friends."

And Bertha Peck said, "It would be nice if I could have a sewing room where I could make clothes for my doll."

Mr. Peck said, "Well, I was just about to build myself a study, so I don't see why we can't build the cardroom, the ping-pong room, and the sewing room at the same time."

So with the help of Mrs. Peck, Albert and Bertha, Mr. Peck added all these rooms to the house, as well as four or five more

bathrooms and—a dressing room for Mrs. Peck, as a surprise, because it was her birthday.

By this time the Peck house filled the whole lot, so Mr. Peck bought all the land around it, to have more room for a garden.

One morning Mr. Peck said to Mrs. Peck, "It seems to me that our bedrooms are entirely too small. I think that we should build some new ones."

"That would be fine," said Mrs. Peck. "We could use the old ones for storerooms."

So all the family helped, and the new bedrooms were built.

Then one day Mr. Peck lost the book he was reading, and he said, "We really need a library, where we can keep all our books in order."

So he built a library, and at the same time he added a small greenhouse for Mrs. Peck, who was very fond of flowers, and a music room where Albert and Bertha could practice their piano lessons without disturbing anyone. And since Mr. Peck was very rich by this time he put up a billiard room for himself, too.

A short time after this, Mrs. Peck had a letter from her Cousin Hattie, whom she hadn't seen for years. So she invited her and her seven children to visit. After she had sent the letter, Mrs. Peck realized that she didn't have a single guestroom. So she talked to Mr. Peck about it.

And Mr. Peck, who was very fond of Cousin Hattie, said, "Very well, my dear. I'll put all my men to work, and if you and the children can help we'll have the eight guestrooms up in a week."

So in a week the eight guestrooms were finished—just an hour before Cousin Hattie and her seven children arrived.

After Cousin Hattie had been at the Pecks a few days she said, "You know, I think it's strange that with such an enormous house you haven't a sun porch. I find mine so convenient."

When Mr. Peck heard this, he set his men and his family to work building four sun porches—one for each of the Pecks—and at the same time, because there was some lumber left over, a gymnasium for Albert and Bertha.

20

This brought the house to the edge of the Peck property, so Mr. Peck bought a great deal more land, just in case he should ever want to add more rooms.

It wasn't long before the Pecks *did* build again. This time it was a breakfast room, a banquet hall for Mr. Peck to entertain his business friends in, a ballroom—because Bertha was studying dancing—and a small observatory, as Albert and Bertha were much interested in the stars.

The Pecks went on like this for several years, building constantly. There was never a day when masons and carpenters and painters weren't working somewhere on the house.

At last the Peck house became famous as the largest house in the world. It rambled on for miles, down valleys and up hills.

Crowds came from the city on week ends to see the house, and the railroad ran special excursions on the Fourth of July and on Labor Day at one dollar for the round trip.

The Pecks were very proud of their house. Mr. Peck liked to tell the tourists that there were many rooms in it which he hadn't entered for years.

Albert Peck was very proud of himself because he had taken some of his Boy Scout friends on a two-week trip through the

house. All the boys carried rations and bedding and camped out in whatever room they happened to be in. They were lost for two days once, but succeeded in finding their way out with the help of a compass.

But the Peck family were beginning to find out that, although their house was something to be proud of, it was a little hard to live in.

It took Mrs. Peck several hours to reach the kitchen from her bedroom in the morning. And when Bertha and Albert wanted to play in the gymnasium they had to take some sandwiches and milk with them, because they couldn't possibly get there and back between breakfast and luncheon.

Mr. Peck made maps of the house and bought roller skates for all his family. That helped a good deal, especially when sweeping, but not enough.

Then Mr. Peck built a road around the house, so that whenever any of the Pecks wanted to go to a distant room they could drive.

When Mrs. Peck gave a dinner party she found it best to take her guests from the living room to the dining room by train, as the dining-room door was close to the railroad station in the next town.

Little by little Mr. Peck, Mrs. Peck, Bertha and Albert, and the dog and the cat, became more and more tired, because they had to keep traveling all day long.

Then one night, as the Pecks were sitting in their living room without enough energy to read or to talk, Mr. Peck broke the silence.

"I have been thinking very hard, my dear," he said to Mrs. Peck, "and I believe I have found a way to make all of us happy again. The trouble is that our house is so large we have to spend most of our time traveling from one room to another. Now, if we tore down all of it except one room . . ."

"It would be wonderful!" exclaimed Mrs. Peck, her face shining with happiness. "Think how easy things would be if I could cook and serve dinner and see my friends all in the same room!"

"I haven't played with my train for a year," said Albert, his chin quivering, "because it's too far away."

"And I've hunted and hunted but I can't find my dollroom," said Bertha tearfully.

So the next day all the Pecks set to work tearing the house down. It took many months of hard work, but at last there was nothing left of the largest house in the world except the one room with which it had started.

All the Pecks were very proud of their house. More tourists than ever came to see it, because it was now famous as the smallest house in the world.

Mr. Peck liked to tell the tourists that the house was so simple he could get up, eat breakfast, and get to work with his eyes shut.

Mrs. Peck would chime in with, "The house is so easy to run that I can get all my housework done in an hour a day."

Albert and Bertha Peck became so healthy and happy that they grew over a foot in one year.

But one night when Mr. Peck came home he said, "I must have a bedroom of my own, where I can lie down and rest before dinner without getting in my wife's way while she is cooking."

Then Albert said . . .

(If you want to know what Albert said, and what Bertha said, and what Mrs. Peck said, turn back to the beginning and read the story all over again.)

23

Edward Wade Devlin

THE KING'S WISH

ILLUSTRATED BY *Minnie Rousseff*

I T WAS at breakfast that King Peramund made his surprising remark. Queen Amalia was drinking her chocolate and peeling her egg, just as she did every morning, and so was quite unprepared when the king put down his napkin and said quietly, "I have been thinking lately that it would be nice if I could learn to fly."

"Good gracious!" exclaimed the queen. "Whatever for?"

"Well, my dear," said the king, "there are several reasons. One is, that it would be faster and more comfortable than riding in a coach; another is, that it would be something that not every king can do; a third is, that I could go straight in at my window without having to climb all those stairs; and best of all, it would be fun."

"Oh!" said Queen Amalia, and there was silence for a moment. "Well, and how do you propose to go about it?"

"Really, my dear, you must give me time to think it over," said the king. "It is only an idea of mine. I don't know if it can be done, but I shall certainly find out."

As far as Queen Amalia was concerned, that ended the affair. But not with King Peramund! Immediately after breakfast he locked himself in his study, and an hour later emerged inky but triumphant, with the following written on a long piece of paper:

KING PERAMUND IV TO HIS LOYAL SUBJECTS:

"WHEREAS we have Decided that it would be to our Ad-

24

vantage and the Edification of our Loyal Subjects if we were to learn the difficult Art of Flying;

"WE THEREFORE DECREE that if any Person or Witch Whatsoever shall possess the Power to teach us this Art, he shall inform the Prime Minister at once, who will give said Person or Witch Whatsoever Reward he shall Demand."

This he gave to the prime minister, who wrote it out correctly and hung it on the palace gate.

Early next morning the entrance bell rang loudly, and upon the gate being opened, a lady of peculiar appearance presented herself and said that she had come in answer to his Majesty's proclamation.

She was gingerly conducted into the presence of King Peramund and entered the throne room just as His Majesty, who had arisen but a moment before, was struggling with the top button of his waistcoat. Seeing her come in, he left it undone and carelessly placed one hand across it.

The unprepossessing lady bowed stiffly and said in a voice like the breaking of dried branches, "I have come to teach you to fly."

The king jumped up, exclaiming, "Have you really?" Then he sat down and said in a very dignified voice, "We are interested." Then he jumped up again and cried, "Come, don't lose a moment!"

The lady pursed her lips and stared at him so long that he shuffled. At last she said, "You agree to pay me anything I ask?"

"Anything, anything!" cried Peramund, dancing with excitement.

But the lady still stared at him, and said slowly, "You have seriously considered what you are doing?"

"Pooh!" cried the king, "there is nothing to consider. Come, begin at once!"

"Very well," said she, "I have warned you. Remember that, when the worst happens."

"But what have you warned me against?" asked the king uneasily.

"That," said the lady, "you will soon see. Are you ready?"

25

"Er—yes," said the king nervously. Then he threw his head back and said, as a king should, "Yes!"

At that, the witch waved her stick over his head and uttered a long word which I had better not try to spell. "Now!" she said, "I shall ask for my reward. I demand that you give your eldest daughter to the dragon that lives in the bright blue hill!"

"But, good gracious!" cried the king, "I can't possibly do that, because—"

"Ah!" said the witch furiously. "So kings don't keep bargains! Well, witches do, and I shall keep mine too well for your liking!"

With which she gave a shrill whistle, leaped onto her stick, and sailed out of the window. The king was rather startled, but concluded that this was the usual way for such persons to take their leave. Her last words disturbed him somewhat, but she had said he could fly, and that was the main thing.

He climbed onto the throne, bent his knees, and jumped, directing himself toward a large tapestry at the other end of the room. To his delight he rose gracefully into the air, and found himself clinging to the top of the tapestry. Releasing his hold, he glided gently down, bounced off the floor, and glided gently up again. Then he pushed away from the wall and sailed through an open window and out over the palace yard. When he looked down, he gasped and shut his eyes and flew hurriedly back to the window ledge. He stood there for a moment to recover and then ventured forth on a short circular flight. When he had gathered sufficient courage, he rose above the rooftops, his sword dangling behind him and his cloak billowing in the wind. He circled one or two chimney pots, to the annoyance of the pigeons, and then he flew off over the town.

Some time later Queen Amalia was peacefully having her morning cup of chocolate in bed. The sun was streaming through the open window, and the pigeons were talking softly on the eaves. Suddenly a monstrous black shadow swooped across the window and in flew King Peramund. The queen screamed and dived under the covers; but soon she emerged and gazed at him in speechless wonder.

"Whatever shall I do?" wailed the king, flying in small circles above her bed.

"What *do* you mean?" cried the queen, more amazed than ever.

"Don't you see?" moaned his Majesty. "I have started to fly, and I don't know how to stop!"

At this the Queen burst into shrieks of laughter, which so upset the king, that he darted out of the window again and flew miserably round and round the highest tower of the palace.

Here he was found some time later by the prime minister and the queen, who by this time fully realized the seriousness of the situation. When he saw them he shouted, "What shall I do? Tell me something to do!"

As he drew near, Queen Amalia cried, "Hold on to the weather vane!"

So the king clutched the large golden rooster as he flew by; there was a terrific crash, and off he sailed, hugging it to his bosom. He dropped it into the moat and flew back. "Whatever am I to do?" he moaned. "I can't fly round here forever!"

"I daresay you *could*, Your Majesty," said the prime minister. "It's *stopping* you which is so difficult."

27

After that the king flew round in silence for a time. Then Queen Amalia, like the thoughtful person she was, fetched him his coat and muffler and gaiters. It was really very funny to see him putting them on in the air, and when he had done so he looked like a huge bumblebee going round and round the tower. The queen then declared that she would have her bed moved up onto the parapet, and live there with her unhappy husband. But this the king nobly forbade her to do. On her alone rested the fate of the country, he said, and she must take his place. At this everyone wept.

That night the moon came up and gasped with surprise at seeing King Peramund floating around the tower of his palace. When it went down, it had to peek over the treetops for a last look at him. And soon the sun came up and blinked at him in amazement. The sun and moon came up and went down many times; but King Peramund stayed up all the time.

He snatched food that the queen held out to him, and he slept by flying on his side. At night men-at-arms were posted round the parapet, so that if he came too close in his sleep, they could push him gently away again.

He had his amusements, for he could always review the army from the air. And he made many aërial tours across his kingdom, when he was always acclaimed loudly by his subjects, who gathered in the fields and cheered and waved handkerchiefs. But at night he always returned to the tower.

The townspeople would bring their lunches in a hamper and sit on the grass beneath the palace walls to watch him flying. Some even slept there at night, when the king could be seen as a large, dark shape, circling round the tower against the stars.

All this time everyone was trying to find the witch, but from the start everyone felt that it was hopeless, for witches are noted for turning themselves into owls or rabbits, or even for vanishing.

As a matter of fact, the lady in question had gone off at the invitation of the king of a neighboring country to turn somebody he didn't like into a hoptoad.

But they did catch her when she came back after doing this.

And very exciting it was, for she turned herself into all manner of unpleasant things. But the king's brave soldiers held her firmly by her right ear and her left thumb (which is the only way to catch witches), and off they went with her to the king's palace. They took her up into the tower and showed her the awful plight that King Peramund was in. The king flew down at once, and implored her to disenchant him. But she was very sulky and only said, "Kings don't keep bargains. Witches do."

"But my good woman!" cried the king. "Don't you see that I couldn't possibly give you what you asked? You asked that I give my eldest daughter to the dragon, and as it happens I haven't got a daughter at all. Only you went off in a huff before I could tell you so!"

"Oh!" said the witch. "I see. That makes quite a difference, so now I will disenchant you."

King Peramund flew over the parapet—the witch said an unspellable word—and his Majesty settled as lightly as a feather upon the stone floor—and stayed there!

After that he had to learn to walk all over again. But he could never walk in a straight line; for, you see, he had circled about the tower from right to left, and was so wound up that way that he never became completely unwound.

Richard and Florence Atwater

MR. POPPER AND CAPTAIN COOK

ILLUSTRATED BY *Robert Lawson*

CAPTAIN COOK is a penguin who has been given to Mr. Popper by Admiral Drake, the South Sea explorer. Here is one of Mr. Popper's funny adventures.

VERY reluctantly, Janie and Bill had to leave Captain Cook and go to school. Mrs. Popper was busy in the kitchen, rather belatedly doing the breakfast dishes; and while she dimly realized that the penguin was going in and out the refrigerator pretty frequently, she thought nothing of it at first.

Meanwhile Mr. Popper had abandoned his telephoning and was now busy shaving and making himself neat in honor of being the owner of such a splendid bird as Captain Cook.

But the penguin, though thus neglected for the moment, was by no means idle.

With the unusual excitement, and having to go to market earlier than usual, Mrs. Popper had not yet got around to straightening the house. She was an excellent housekeeper. Still, with two children like Janie and Bill and a husband with such untidy ways, there is no denying the fact that she had to pick up the place rather frequently.

Captain Cook was now attending to the picking up.

Into the corners of every room he prowled and poked and pecked with a busy thoroughness; into every closet he stared with his white-circled eyes; under and behind all the furniture he crowded his plump figure, with little subdued cries of curiosity, surprise, and pleasure.

And each time he found what he seemed to be looking for, he picked it up in the black end of his red beak, and carried it,

30

waddling proudly on his wide, pink feet, into the kitchen, and into the icebox.

At last it occurred to Mrs. Popper to wonder what on earth the busy bird was up to. When she looked, she could only scream to Mr. Popper to come quickly and see what Captain Cook had done now.

Mr. Popper, himself looking rather remarkable, as Mrs. Popper noticed later, joined her in staring with astonishment into the refrigerator.

Captain Cook came up, too, and helped them look. "*Ork, ork,*" he said with triumph.

Mrs. Popper laughed, and Mr. Popper gasped as they saw the results of Captain Cook's trips through the house.

Two spools of thread, one white chess bishop, and six parts of a jigsaw puzzle . . . A teaspoon and a closed box of safety matches . . . A radish, two pennies, a nickel, and a golf ball. Two pencil stubs, one bent playing card, and a small ash tray.

Five hairpins, an olive, two dominoes, and a sock . . . A nail-file, four buttons of various sizes, a telephone slug, seven marbles, and a tiny doll's chair . . .

Five checker pieces, a bit of graham cracker, a parchesi cup, and an eraser . . . A door key, a buttonhook, and a crumpled piece of tinfoil . . . Half of a very old lemon, the head of a china doll, Mr. Popper's pipe, and a gingerale cap . . . An inkbottle cork, two screws, and a belt buckle . . .

Six beads from a child's necklace, five building blocks, a darning egg, a bone, a small harmonica, and a partly consumed lollipop. Two toothpaste lids and a small red notebook.

"I guess this is what you call the rookery," said Mr. Popper. "Only he couldn't find any stones to build his nest with."

"Well," said Mrs. Popper, "those penguins may have heathen ways at the South Pole, but I declare I think this one is going to be quite a help around the house."

"*Ork!*" said Captain Cook, and strutting into the living room, he knocked over the best lamp.

"I think, Papa," said Mrs. Popper, "that you had better take Captain Cook outside for a little exercise. Good gracious, but

31

you're all dressed up. Why, you look almost like a penguin yourself."

Mr. Popper had smoothed down his hair and shaved off his whiskers. Never again would Mrs. Popper have to reproach him for looking as wild as a lion. He had put on a white shirt with a white tie and white flannel trousers, and a pair of bright tan, oxblood shoes. He had got out of the cedar chest his old black evening tailcoat, that he had been married in, and brushed it carefully, and put it on, too.

He did indeed look a little like a penguin. He turned and strutted like one now, for Mrs. Popper.

But he did not forget his duty to Captain Cook.

"Can I have a few yards of clothesline, please, Mamma?" asked Mr. Popper.

Mr. Popper soon found that it was not so easy to take a penguin for a stroll.

Captain Cook did not care at first for the idea of being put on a leash. However, Mr. Popper was firm. He tied one end of the clothesline to the penguin's fat throat and the other to his own wrist.

"*Ork!*" said Captain Cook indignantly. Still, he was a very reasonable sort of bird, and when he saw that protesting did him no good, he recovered his customary dignity and decided to let Mr. Popper lead him.

Mr. Popper put on his best Sunday derby and opened the front door with Captain Cook waddling graciously beside him.

"*Gaw,*" said the penguin, stopping at the edge of the porch to look down at the steps.

Mr. Popper gave him plenty of clothesline leash.

"*Gook!*" said Captain Cook, and raising his flippers, he leaned forward bravely and tobogganed down the steps on his stomach.

Mr. Popper followed, though not in the same way. Captain Cook quickly got up on his feet again and strutted to the street ahead of Mr. Popper with many quick turns of his head and pleased comments on the new scene.

Down Proudfoot Avenue came a neighbor of the Poppers,

Mrs. Callahan, with her arms full of groceries. She stared in astonishment when she saw Captain Cook and Mr. Popper, looking like a larger penguin himself in his black tailcoat.

"Heavens have mercy on us!" she exclaimed as the bird began to investigate the striped stockings under her housedress. "It isn't an owl and it isn't a goose."

"It isn't," said Mr. Popper, tipping his Sunday derby. "It's an Antarctic penguin, Mrs. Callahan."

"Get away from me," said Mrs. Callahan to Captain Cook. "An anteater, is it?"

"Not anteater," explained Mr. Popper. "Antarctic. It was sent to me from the South Pole."

"Take your South Pole goose away from me at once," said Mrs. Callahan.

Mr. Popper pulled obediently at the clothesline, while Captain Cook took a parting peck at Mrs. Callahan's striped stockings.

"Heaven preserve us!" said Mrs. Callahan. "I must stop in and see Mrs. Popper at once. I would never have believed it. I will be going now."

"So will I," said Mr. Popper as Captain Cook dragged him off down the street.

Their next stop was at the drugstore at the corner of Proudfoot Avenue and Main Street. Here Captain Cook insisted on looking over the window display, which consisted of several open packages of shiny white boric crystals. These he evidently mistook for polar snow, for he began to peck at the window vigorously.

Suddenly a car wheeled to the near-by curb with a shriek of its brakes, and two young men sprang out, one of them bearing a camera.

"This must be it," said the first young man to the other.

"It's them, all right," said the second young man.

The cameraman set up his tripod on the sidewalk. By this time a small crowd had gathered around, and two men in white coats had even come out of the drugstore to watch. Captain Cook, however, was still too much interested in the window exhibits to bother to turn around.

"You're Mr. Popper of 432 Proudfoot Avenue, aren't you?" asked the second young man, pulling a notebook out of his pocket.

"Yes," said Mr. Popper, realizing that his picture was about to be taken for the newspaper. The two young men had, as a matter of fact, heard about the strange bird from the policeman, and had been on their way to the Popper house, to get an interview, when they saw Captain Cook.

"Hey, pelican, turn around and see the pretty birdie," said the photographer.

"That's no pelican," said the other, who was a reporter. "Pelicans have a pouch in their bills."

"I'd think it was a dodo, only dodos are extinct. This will

34

make an elegant picture, if I can ever get her to turn around."

"It's a penguin," said Mr. Popper proudly. "It's name is Captain Cook."

"*Gook!*" said the penguin, turning around, now that they were talking about him. Spying the camera tripod, he walked over and examined it.

"Probably thinks it's a three-legged stork," said the photographer.

"This bird of yours—" said the reporter. "Is it a he or a she? The public will want to know."

Mr. Popper hesitated. "Well, I call it Captain Cook."

"That makes it a he," said the reporter, writing rapidly in his notebook.

Still curious, Captain Cook started walking round and round the tripod, till the clothesline, the penguin, Mr. Popper and the tripod were all tangled up. At the advice of one of the bystanders, the tangle was finally straightened out by Mr. Popper's walking around the tripod three times in the opposite direction. At last, Captain Cook, standing still beside Mr. Popper, consented to pose.

Mr. Popper straightened his tie, and the cameraman snapped the picture. Captain Cook shut his eyes, and this is the way his picture appeared later in all the newspapers.

"One last question," said the reporter. "Where did you get your strange pet?"

"From Admiral Drake, the South Pole explorer. He sent him to me for a present."

"Yeah," said the reporter. "Anyway, it's a good story."

The two young men jumped into their car. Mr. Popper and Captain Cook continued their walk, with quite a crowd following and asking questions. The crowd was getting so thick that, to escape, Mr. Popper led Captain Cook into a barber-shop.

The man who kept the barbershop had, up to this time, been a very good friend of Mr. Popper's.

It was very quiet in the barbershop. The barber was shaving an elderly gentleman.

Captain Cook found this spectacle very interesting, and in order to get a better view, he jumped up on the mirror ledge.

"Good night!" said the barber.

The gentleman in the barber's chair, his face already white with lather, half-lifted his head to see what had happened.

"*Gook!*" said the penguin, flapping his flippers and reaching out his long beak toward the lather on the gentleman's face.

With a yell and a leap, the gentleman rose from his reclining position, left the barber's chair, and fled into the street, not even stopping for his coat and hat.

"*Gawk!*" said Captain.

"Hey," said the barber to Mr. Popper. "Take that thing out of my shop. This is no zoo. What's the idea?"

"Do you mind if I take him out your back door?" asked Mr. Popper.

"Any door," said the barber, "as long as it's quick. Now it's biting the teeth off my combs."

Mr. Popper took Captain Cook in his arms, and amid cries of "*Quork?*" "*Gawk!*" and "*Ork!*" made his way out of the shop and its back room and out a door into an alley.

Captain Cook now discovered his first back stairway.

Mr. Popper discovered that when a penguin has found steps going up somewhere, it is absolutely impossible to keep him from climbing them.

"All right," said Mr. Popper, panting up the steps behind Captain Cook. "I suppose, being a bird, and one that can't fly, you have to go up in the air somehow, so you like to climb stairs. Well, it's a good thing this building has only three stories. Come on. Let's see what you can do."

Slowly but unwearyingly, Captain Cook lifted one pink foot after another from one step to the next, followed by Mr. Popper at the other end of the clothesline.

At last they came to the top landing.

"Now what?" inquired Mr. Popper of Captain Cook.

Finding there were no more steps to climb, Captain Cook turned around and surveyed the steps that now went down.

Then he raised his flippers and leaned forward.

Mr. Popper, who was still panting for breath, had not supposed the determined bird would plunge so quickly. He should have remembered that penguins will toboggan whenever they get a chance.

Perhaps he had been unwise in tying one end of the clothesline to his own wrist.

At any rate, this time Mr. Popper found himself suddenly sliding, on his own white-clad stomach, down the three flights of steps. This delighted the penguin, who was enjoying his own slide just ahead of Mr. Popper.

When they reached the bottom, Captain Cook was so eager to go up again that Mr. Popper had to call a taxi, to distract him.

"432 Proudfoot Avenue," said Mr. Popper to the driver.

The driver, who was a kind and polite man, did not laugh at his oddly assorted passengers until he had been paid.

"Oh dear!" said Mrs. Popper, when she opened the door to her husband. "You looked so neat and handsome when you started for your walk. And now look at the front of you!"

"I am sorry, my love," said Mr. Popper in a humble tone, "but you can't always tell what a penguin will do next."

So saying, he went to lie down, for he was quite exhausted from all the unusual exercise, while Captain Cook had a shower and took a nap in the icebox.

Charles Dickens

THE MAGIC FISHBONE

ILLUSTRATED BY *Marilou Wise*

T HERE was once a king, and he had a queen. They had nineteen children and were always having more. Seventeen of the children took care of the baby; and Alicia, the eldest, took care of them all. Their ages varied from seven years to seven months.

One day the king was going to the office, when he stopped at Mr. Pickle's, the fishmonger's, to buy a pound and a half of salmon not too near the tail.

The king then went on towards the office in a melancholy mood, for payday was such a long way off, and his children were growing out of their clothes.

Just then a rich-looking old lady came trotting up.

"King Watkins the First, I believe?" said the old lady.

"Watkins," replied the king, "is my name."

"Listen. You are going to the office," said the old lady.

It instantly flashed upon the king that she must be a fairy, or how could she know that?

"You are right," said the old lady, answering his thoughts. "I am the good Fairy Grandmarina. Listen! When you return home to dinner, politely invite the Princess Alicia to have some of the salmon you bought just now. Then she will leave a fishbone on her plate. Tell her to dry it, and to rub it, and to polish it, till it shines like mother-of-pearl, and to take care of it as a present from me."

"Tell the Princess Alicia," said the fairy, "that the fishbone is a magic present which can only be used once; but that it will bring her, just once, whatever she wishes for, provided she wishes for it at the right time."

The . . . coarse apron flew away, and she appeared exquisitely dressed.

With those words, Grandmarina vanished, and the king went on and on, till he came to the office. There he wrote and wrote and wrote, till it was time to go home.

Then he invited the Princess Alicia, as the fairy had directed him, to eat some salmon. And when she had enjoyed it very much, he saw the fishbone on her plate, and he delivered the fairy's message, and the Princess Alicia took care to dry the bone, and to rub it, and to polish it, till it shone like mother-of-pearl.

And so, when the queen was going to get up in the morning, she said, "Oh, dear me, dear me, my head, my head!" and then she fainted away.

The Princess Alicia was very much alarmed when she saw her royal mamma in this state, and she rang the bell for Peggy, which was the name of the lord chamberlain. But remembering where the smelling-bottle was, she climbed on a chair and got it; and after that she climbed on another chair by the bedside, and held the smelling-bottle to the queen's nose; and after that she got some water and wet the queen's forehead; and, in short, when the lord chamberlain came in, that dear old woman said to the little princess, "I couldn't have done it better myself!"

But that was not the worst of the good queen's illness. Oh, no! She was very ill indeed, for a long time. The Princess Alicia kept the seventeen young princes and princesses quiet, and dressed and undressed the baby, and made the kettle boil, and heated the soup, and swept the hearth, and poured out the medicine, and nursed the queen; for there were not many servants at that palace for three reasons: because the king was short of money, because a raise in his salary never seemed to come, and because payday was far off.

But on the morning when the queen fainted away, where was the magic fishbone? Why, there it was in the Princess Alicia's pocket! She had almost taken it out to bring the queen to life again, when she put it back, and looked for the smelling-bottle.

After the queen had come out of her swoon, the Princess Alicia hurried upstairs to tell a secret to her friend the duchess.

People thought she was a doll, but Alicia knew she was really a duchess.

"Alicia," said the king, one evening, when she wished him good night.

"Yes, Papa."

"What is become of the magic fishbone?"

"In my pocket, Papa."

"I thought you had lost it?"

"Oh, no, Papa!"

"Or forgotten it?"

"No, indeed, Papa."

And so another time the little snapping dog, next door, made a rush at one of the young princes, and he put his hand through a pane of glass, and bled, bled, bled. Then the seventeen other young princes and princesses saw him and screamed themselves black in their seventeen faces all at once.

But the Princess Alicia put her hands over all their seventeen mouths, one after another, and persuaded them to be quiet

because of the sick queen. And then she put the wounded prince's hand in a basin of cold water.

Then she said to two chubby-legged princes, "Bring me in the royal rag-bag: I must snip and stitch and cut and contrive." So these two young princes tugged at the royal rag-bag, and she made a bandage, and it fitted beautifully; and so when it was all done, she saw the king, her papa, looking on by the door.

"Alicia."

"Yes, Papa."

"Where is the magic fishbone?"

"In my pocket, Papa."

"I thought you had lost it?"

"Oh, no, Papa!"

"Or forgotten it?"

"No, indeed, Papa."

After that, she ran upstairs to the duchess, and told her what had happened, and told her the secret over again; and the duchess shook her flaxen curls and laughed with her rosy lips.

41

Well! and so another time the baby fell under the grate, and it gave him a swelled face and a black eye.

The way the poor little darling came to tumble was that he was out of the Princess Alicia's lap just as she was beginning to peel the turnips for the broth for dinner; and the way she came to be doing that was, that the king's cook had run away that morning with her own true love, who was a very tall but very tipsy soldier.

Then the seventeen young princes and princesses, who cried at everything that happened, cried and roared. But the Princess Alicia (who couldn't help crying a little herself) said, "Hold your tongues, you wicked little monkeys, every one of you, while I examine the baby."

Then she examined the baby, and found that he hadn't broken anything, and she held a cold cloth to his poor dear eye, and he presently fell asleep in her arms.

Then she said to the seventeen princes and princesses, "I am afraid to let him down yet, lest he should wake and feel pain; be good and you shall all be cooks."

They jumped for joy when they heard that, and began making themselves cooks' caps out of old newspapers. So to one she gave the salt-box, and to one she gave the barley, and to one she gave the herbs, and to one she gave the turnips, and to one she gave the carrots, and to one she gave the onions, and to one she gave the spice-box, till they were all cooks, and all running about at work, she sitting in the middle smothered in the great coarse apron, nursing baby.

By and by the broth was done; and the baby woke up, smiling like an angel, and was trusted to the sedatest princess to hold.

When the broth came tumbling out, steaming beautifully, and smelling like a nosegay good to eat, they clapped their hands. That made the baby clap his hands; and that, and his looking as if he had a comic toothache, made all the princes and princesses laugh.

So the Princess Alicia said, "Laugh and be good; and after dinner we will make him a nest on the floor in a corner, and he

42

shall sit in his nest and see a dance of eighteen cooks." That delighted the young princes and princesses, and they ate up all the broth, and washed up all the plates and dishes, and cleared away, and pushed the table into a corner; and then they in their cooks' caps and the Princess Alicia in her apron danced a dance of eighteen cooks before the angelic baby.

And so then, once more the Princess Alicia saw King Watkins the First, her father, standing in the doorway looking on, and he said, "Where is the magic fishbone, Alicia?"

"In my pocket, Papa."

"I thought you had lost it?"

43

"Oh, no, Papa!"

"Or forgotten it?"

"No, indeed, Papa."

The king then sighed so heavily, and seemed so low-spirited, that the seventeen princes and princesses crept softly out of the kitchen, and left him alone with the Princess Alicia and the angelic baby.

"What is the matter, Papa?"

"I am dreadfully poor, my child."

"Have you no money at all, Papa?"

"None, my child."

"Is there no way of getting any, Papa?"

"No way," said the king.

"Papa," said she, "when we have tried very hard, and tried all ways, we must have done our very, very best. And when we have done our very, very best, Papa, and that is not enough, then I think the right time must have come for asking help of others."

This was the very secret connected with the magic fishbone, which she had found out for herself from the good Fairy Grandmarina's words, and which she had so often whispered to her beautiful and fashionable doll, the duchess.

So she took out of her pocket the magic fishbone that had been dried and rubbed and polished till it shone like mother-of-pearl; and she gave it one little kiss and wished it was payday. And immediately it was payday; and the king's salary came rattling down the chimney, and bounced into the middle of the floor.

Immediately afterwards the good Fairy Grandmarina came riding in, in a carriage and four (peacocks), with Mr. Pickle's boy up behind, dressed in silver and gold, with a cocked hat, powdered hair, pink silk stockings, a jewelled cane, and a nosegay.

The Princess Alicia embraced her; and then Grandmarina turned to the king, and said rather sharply, "Are you good?"

The king said he hoped so.

"I suppose you know the reason now why my goddaughter

here," kissing the princess again, "did not apply to the fishbone sooner?" said the fairy.

The king made a shy bow.

"Ah! but you didn't then?" said the fairy.

The king made a shyer bow.

"Any more questions to ask?" said the fairy.

The king said no, and he was very sorry.

"Be good, then," said the fairy, "and live happy ever afterwards."

Then Grandmarina waved her fan, and the queen came in most splendidly dressed; and the seventeen young princes and princesses came in, newly fitted out from top to toe, with tucks in everything to admit of its being let out.

After that, the fairy tapped the Princess Alicia with her fan. The smothering coarse apron flew away, and she appeared exquisitely dressed, like a little bride, with a wreath of orange blossoms and a silver veil.

After that, the kitchen dresser changed of itself into a wardrobe, made of beautiful woods and gold and looking glass, which was full of dresses of all sorts, all for her and all exactly fitting her. After that, the angelic baby came in running alone, with his face and eye not a bit worse, but much the better.

A little whispering took place between the fairy and the duchess; and then the fairy said out loud, "Yes, I thought she would have told you." Grandmarina then turned to the king and queen, and said, "We are going in search of Prince Certainpersonio. The pleasure of your company is requested at church in half an hour precisely."

So she and the Princess Alicia got into the carriage; and Mr. Pickle's boy handed in the duchess, who sat by herself on the opposite seat; and then Mr. Pickle's boy put up the steps and got up behind, and peacocks flew away with their tails behind.

Prince Certainpersonio was sitting by himself, eating barley-sugar, and waiting to be ninety. When he saw the peacocks, followed by the carriage, coming in at the window he knew something unusual was going to happen.

"Prince," said Grandmarina, "I bring you your bride."

The moment the fairy said those words, Prince Certainpersonio's face left off being sticky, and his jacket and corduroys changed into peach-bloom velvet, and his hair curled, and a cap and feather flew in like a bird and settled on his head. He got into the carriage by the fairy's invitation and smiled at the duchess, whom he had seen before.

The marriage in the church was ever so beautiful! The duchess was bridesmaid and looked on at the ceremony from the pulpit, where she was propped up by the cushion of the desk.

Grandmarina gave a magnificent wedding-feast afterwards. The wedding-cake was delicately ornamented with white satin ribbons, frosted silver, and white lilies, and was forty-two yards round.

When Grandmarina had drunk a toast to the young people, and Prince Certainpersonio had made a speech, and everybody had cried, "Hip, hip, hip, hurrah!" Grandmarina announced to the king and the queen that in the future there would be eight paydays every year, except in leapyear, when there would be ten.

She then turned to Certainpersonio and Alicia, and said, "My dears, you will have thirty-five children, and they will all be good and beautiful. Seventeen of your children will be boys, and eighteen will be girls. They will never have the measles and will have recovered from the whooping cough before being born."

"It only remains," said Grandmarina in conclusion, "to make an end of the fishbone."

So she took it from the hand of the Princess Alicia, and it instantly vanished, before it could possibly be snapped up by the little pugdog next door.

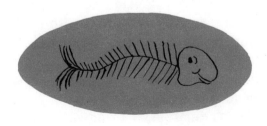

Carl Sandburg

THE HUCKABUCK FAMILY

ILLUSTRATED BY *John Gee*

JONAS JONAS HUCKABUCK was a farmer in Nebraska with a wife Mama Mama Huckabuck, and a daughter, Pony Pony Huckabuck.

"Your father gave you two names the same in front," people had said to him.

And he answered, "Yes, two names are easier to remember. If you call me by my first name Jonas and I don't hear you then when you call me by my second name Jonas maybe I will.

"And," he went on, "I call my pony-face girl Pony Pony because if she doesn't hear me the first time she always does the second."

And so they lived on a farm where they raised popcorn, these three, Jonas Jonas Huckabuck, his wife, Mama Mama Huckabuck, and their pony-face daughter, Pony Pony Huckabuck.

After they harvested the crop one year they had the barns, the cribs, the sheds, the shacks, and all the cracks and corners of the farm, all filled with popcorn.

"We came out to Nebraska to raise popcorn," said Jonas Jonas, "And I guess we got nearly enough popcorn this year for the popcorn poppers and all the friends and relations of all the

47

popcorn poppers in these United States."

And this was the year Pony Pony was going to bake her first squash pie all by herself. In one corner of the corn crib, all covered over with popcorn, she had a secret, a big round squash, a fat yellow squash, a rich squash all spotted with spots of gold.

She carried the squash into the kitchen, took a long, sharp, shining knife, and then she cut the squash in the middle till she had two big half squashes. And inside just like outside it was rich yellow spotted with spots of gold.

And there was a shine of silver. And Pony Pony wondered why silver should be in a squash. She picked and plunged with her fingers till she pulled it out.

"It's a buckle," she said. "A silver buckle, a Chinese silver slipper buckle."

She ran with it to her father and said, "Look what I found when I cut open the golden yellow squash spotted with gold spots—it is a Chinese silver slipper buckle."

"It means our luck is going to change, and we don't know whether it will be good luck or bad luck," said Jonas Jonas to his daughter Pony Pony Huckabuck.

Then she ran with it to her mother and said, "Look what I found when I cut open the yellow squash spotted with spots of gold—it is a Chinese silver slipper buckle."

"It means our luck is going to change, and we don't know whether it will be good luck or bad luck," said Mama Mama Huckabuck.

And that night a fire started in the barns, cribs, sheds, shacks, cracks, and corners where the popcorn harvest was kept. All night long the popcorn popped. In the morning the ground all around the farmhouse and the barn was covered with white popcorn, so it looked like a heavy fall of snow.

All the next day the fire kept on and the popcorn popped till it was up to the shoulders of Pony Pony when she tried to walk from the house to the barn. And that night in all the barns, cribs, shed, shacks, cracks, and corners of the farm, the popcorn went on popping.

In the morning when Jonas Jonas Huckabuck looked out of the upstairs window he saw the popcorn popping and coming higher and higher. It was nearly up to the window. Before evening and dark of that day, Jonas Jonas Huckabuck, and his wife Mama Mama Huckabuck, and their daughter Pony Pony Huckabuck, all went away from the farm saying, "We came to Nebraska to raise popcorn but this is too much. We will not come back till the wind blows away the popcorn. We will not come back till we get a sign and a signal."

They went to Oskaloosa, Iowa. And the next year Pony Pony Huckabuck was very proud because when she stood on the sidewalks in the street she could see her father sitting high on the seat of a coal wagon, driving two big spanking horses hitched with shining brass harness in front of the coal wagon. And though Pony Pony and Jonas Jonas were proud, very proud all that year, there never came a sign, a signal.

The next year again was a proud year, exactly as proud a year as they spent in Oska-

49

loosa. They went to Paducah, Kentucky, to Defiance, Ohio; Peoria, Illinois; Indianapolis, Indiana; Walla Walla, Washington. And in all these places Pony Pony Huckabuck saw her father, Jonas Jonas Huckabuck standing in rubber boots deep down in a ditch with a shining steel shovel shoveling yellow clay and black mud from down in the ditch high and high over his shoulders. And though it was a proud year they got no sign, no signal.

The next year came. It was the proudest of all. This was the year Jonas Jonas Huckabuck and his family lived in Elgin, Illinois, and Jonas Jonas was watchman in a watch factory watching the watches.

"I know where you have been," Mama Mama Huckabuck would say of an evening to Pony Pony Huckabuck. "You have been down to the watch factory watching your father watch the watches."

"Yes," said Pony Pony, "yes, and this evening when I was watching father watch the watches in the watch factory, I looked over my left shoulder and I saw a policeman with a star and brass buttons, and he was watching me to see if I was watching father watch the watches in the watch factory."

It was a proud year. Pony Pony saved her money. Thanksgiving came. Pony Pony said, "I am going to get a squash to make a squash pie." She hunted from one grocery to another; she kept her eyes on the farm wagons coming into Elgin with squashes.

She found what she wanted, the yellow squash spotted with gold spots. She took it home, cut it open, and saw the inside was like the outside, all rich yellow spotted with gold spots.

There was a shine like silver. She picked and plunged with her fingers and pulled and pulled till at last she pulled out the shine of silver.

"It's a sign; it is a signal," she said. "It is a buckle, a slipper buckle, a Chinese silver slipper buckle. It is the mate to the other buckle. Our luck is going to change. Yoo hoo! Yoo hoo!"

She told her father and mother about the buckle. They went back to the farm in Nebraska. The wind had been blowing and blowing for three years, and all the popcorn was blown away.

50

"Now we are going to be farmers again," said Jonas Jonas Huckabuck to Mama Mama Huckabuck and to Pony Pony Huckabuck. "And we are going to raise cabbages, beets, and turnips, we are going to raise squash, rutabaga, pumpkins, and peppers for pickling. We are going to raise wheat, oats, barley, rye. We are going to raise corn such as Indian corn and kaffir corn—but we are *not* going to raise any popcorn for the popcorn poppers to be popping."

And the pony-face daughter was proud because she had on new black slippers, and around her ankles holding the slippers on the left foot and the right foot, she had two buckles, silver buckles, Chinese silver slipper buckles. They were mates.

Sometimes on Thanksgiving Day and Christmas and New Year's, she tells her friends to be careful when they open a squash.

"Squashes make your luck change good to bad and bad to good," says Pony Pony.

THE TILLYHEEHEE

John Dukes McKee

Oh, the giggly, wiggly Tillyheehee,
Lives in a queer little cave by the sea.
He has a pink bow tied under his chin,
Just at the place where his whiskers begin,
And horn-rimmed glasses, not for his sight,
But to make him look witty, pretty, and bright.
He lives upon gumdrops, pickles, and tea,
And little blue jellyfish, fresh from the sea.
He has a merman to tickle his nose,
Another his ears and another his toes.
And he laughs and giggles and wiggles all night,
And chuckles and roars until it gets light.
Then he wraps up his head in his overgrown tail
And sings him to sleep with a musical wail.
And if *you* ever pass this cave by the sea,
Won't you tickle the nose of the Tillyheehee?

Helen and Alf Evers

MR. SCRUNCH

ILLUSTRATED BY *Helen Evers*

MR. JASPER SCRUNCH was a very famous inventor. Kindness shone from his pink face, which was set off by white hair and whiskers. But Mr. Scrunch was clever as well as kind. So he had spent his life inventing thousands of machines to help people and to make them happier. His machines made it easier for people to work, easier for them to play, and even easier for them to do nothing at all.

Mr. Scrunch invented a Dresser and Undresser. This clever machine, which looked like a comfortable chair, could take off or put on the clothes of anyone sitting in it, in a few seconds. It could also sew on missing buttons, mend tears, and remove spots and stains while it dressed or undressed.

This machine was sold all over the world, except in those uncivilized places, such as the South Sea Islands, where people don't wear enough clothes to make it worth while.

Mr. Scrunch was also the inventor of a sled which could coast uphill even faster than it could downhill.

A few more of Mr. Scrunch's inventions were a self-making bed, a rocking chair which rocked itself, and, for *very* lazy people, a game-playing machine, which played baseball, tennis, cards, or croquet for them.

All these inventions made Mr. Scrunch very rich.

But Mr. Scrunch worked so hard at inventing things to keep other people from working that he became very tired. His friends insisted that he take a vacation.

So the inventor bought a quiet little farm, on a quiet little road near a quiet little village, and went there to take a long rest. When Mr. Scrunch reached the farm, he hired two men to do the farm work. Then he sat down on the steps and did nothing at all for ten whole minutes.

As Mr. Scrunch sat on the steps, doing nothing, he saw four little pigs racing round and round the barn. One of the pigs was always last, because he had such short legs. Mr. Scrunch felt very sorry for this pig.

So he coaxed the pig into the house with a bowl of milk and a banana. Then, while the pig was busy eating, Mr. Scrunch thought hard and invented something to help the short-legged pig run faster. The invention was remarkably simple. It was just four little stilts with straps to hold them in place.

First, kind Mr. Scrunch tested the stilts himself. It was so much fun that he hated to take them off.

Then he put the stilts on the pig. Away went the little pig, tumbling down at every step. Down went chairs and tables, lamps and pictures.

And down went Mr. Scrunch. The pig raced faster and faster as he learned how to manage the stilts. At last he vanished through the open door.

Mr. Scrunch sat on the floor, a picture frame around his neck and a lamp cord wound around his legs.

"Dear me!" he murmured. "That worked altogether too well, but never mind, it has given me a *tremendous* idea."

"All these years," said Mr. Scrunch unwinding the lamp cord, "I have been inventing things to help people, but I have never thought of making inventions to help animals do their work and enjoy their play. Someone must do it," he said solemnly, "and that someone will be me."

So the inventor removed the picture frame from his neck and started right in inventing.

First he invented prettier and more comfortable hats for the horses to wear in hot weather.

Then he invented an automatic fly swatter to save the horses the trouble of swishing their tails all day in hot weather. As the swatter revolved, it produced a gentle breeze which kept the horses cool, even on the hottest day.

Mr. Scrunch hated to see the hens sleeping at night clinging to their hard roost. So he invented comfortable beds with soft pillows for them.

He invented little sails for the ducks to use on the pond, so that they would not have to work so hard at swimming.

Mr. Scrunch made clean white bathtubs for the pigs. He thought that it would be so much nicer for them to bathe in these, instead of in the mud puddles they had used before.

And finally Mr. Scrunch invented a grazing machine for Belle, the old cow.

For a long time Mr. Scrunch had felt sorry for cows, because they had to work so hard grazing. It didn't seem right to him that cows should spend most of the day with their faces practically on the ground, tugging away at the grass and sometimes picking up insects, thorns, sand, or even stones, by mistake.

So Mr. Scrunch invented a machine, something like a lawn mower, with a fan in front and a basket on top, to be strapped to Belle. As Belle walked, the mower cut the grass, the fan

blew everything but the grass away, and all Belle had to do was to eat from the basket right in front of her mouth.

But when the horses had their hats and automatic fly swatters they had so little to do, when they were in the pasture in the summer, that they just couldn't stand it.

So they jumped over the fence into Mr. Scrunch's fine cornfield and ate and ate cornstalks, until they became very sick.

Then the veterinary had to come and cure them with some bitter medicine.

When the hens tried their new beds they found them so comfortable that they couldn't get up in the morning and get to work laying eggs, although they wanted to very much.

When the ducks were fitted out with their sails a breeze came up, and they just whirled round and round the pond like tops until they became dizzy.

And the pigs refused to use their tubs at all because they thought that mud was much better than clean water for bathing.

And Belle, the cow, loved the old way of grazing and hated Mr. Scrunch's grazing machine so much that she became angry and raced across the fields, kicking her heels in the air, with Mr. Scrunch after her.

She crossed the road and raced right through the poppies and roses in Mrs. Green's garden, leaving a smooth path behind her and chopped-up flowers flying through the air.

On she went through Mr. Jenkins' vegetable patch, mowing

down the neat rows of carrots and lettuce.

And on she raced across the lawn where Mrs. Anderson had spread her best tablecloths and napkins to bleach in the sun.

The chopped-up bits of white cloth swirled in the air around Belle like snowflakes in a blizzard.

At last, with a crash that could be heard for miles, Belle

smashed the grazing machine against a stone wall. Then she felt much better.

Mr. Scrunch came up, puffing and panting. First he paid Mrs. Green, Mrs. Anderson, and Mr. Jenkins, who had arrived full of anger and threats, for the damage done by the grazing machine.

As he led Belle home, Mr. Scrunch patted her affectionately.

"Dear me," he murmured. "This is all too bad, but never mind, it has given me an idea for a tremendous invention to help animals."

For days Mr. Scrunch slaved away at his invention, hardly stopping to eat or sleep. It looked like an immense box, with a sort of coffee mill on top. When it was finished he put it in the barnyard and called all the animals together.

Mr. Scrunch took the stilts from the pig, the sails from the ducks, the beds from the henhouse, the bathtubs from the pigs' yard, and the hats and automatic fly swatters from the horses. He put them all, one by one, in the top of the machine. Then he pressed a button.

There was a sighing, wheezing noise from inside the machine. A little puff of blue smoke popped out, hovered over the machine for a moment, and slowly sailed away.

This was all that was left of Mr. Scrunch's inventions for animals.

"Hurrah," cried Mr. Scrunch, "for the last and best of my inventions for animals—Scrunch's Universal Uninventor for Useless Inventions!"

Then Mr. Scrunch put one arm around Belle and the other on one of the horses. A chicken flew to the top of his head and a happy duck to his shoulder, while a pig rubbed his side against the inventor's legs.

"At last," said Mr. Scrunch in a voice made unsteady by emotion, "at last I have invented something that has helped all of you and made you happy. All my work has not been in vain."

And then kind Mr. Scrunch, with a smile on his face, went to the house, sat down on the steps, and did nothing at all for a long, long time.

Mabel E. Neikirk

OSCAR, THE TRAINED SEAL

ILLUSTRATED BY *Clarence Biers*

OSCAR and Mr. Zabriski were on their way
to a big fair in California. Oscar was a trained seal. He was
going to do circus tricks at the fair, and Mr. Zabriski was going
along to take care of him.

"Now, how shall we go?" asked Mr. Zabriski when they
planned the trip. "Shall we go by air, by water, or by land?"

"By air, by water, or by land," repeated Oscar. "What kind
of traveling is that?"

"Why, you silly seal!" replied Mr. Zabriski. "By air means
flying, of course. Would you like to go in an airplane? By water
means on a boat, and by land means on a train. I think perhaps
the train would be best."

"None of them are any good," remarked the seal. "I couldn't
take my bathtub on a plane. Now, could I?"

"No, I suppose not," his master replied. "It would be too
heavy."

"And s'pose I got seasick on the boat, and I can't go on the
train—"

"Well, why not?" he was asked.

"Just because, just because," said Oscar convincingly, "and
anyway, I want to ride in a truck."

58

Mr. Zabriski was an agreeable man, and he always tried to please Oscar, so they started off across the country in a Ford truck, Mr. Zabriski sitting in front driving, and Oscar riding in back, taking baths all the way. When the truck went over a bumpy road, the water swished and splashed, and Oscar would roll about in his tub, diving and swimming and making seal noises. It was a great lark. Oscar pretended that his tub was an ocean. But so many waves splashed out that the floor of the truck dripped like an ice wagon, and they had to stop at almost every gas station for water.

Mr. Zabriski would drive up to a station and say to the attendant, "Will you please put some water in my car?"

Then he and Oscar would chuckle because the man always went to the front of the car and seemed surprised when he found the radiator full.

"You've plenty of water, sir," he usually said.

"I mean I need water for the tank in the back of my truck," Mr. Zabriski would explain.

Then the man would go around and almost fall over backward in his surprise, because Oscar always stuck out his head and shouted, "Boo!"

They had lots of fun for two days, and then they had lots of trouble, because Oscar's bathtub sprung a leak. They filled it up and they filled it up, and the leak kept getting worse and worse.

Finally, Mr. Zabriski stopped the truck, and he and Oscar got out and sat down beside the road to think.

"Now we *are* in a jam," groaned Mr. Zabriski. "We simply must get to California. The people at the fair are looking for us even now."

"We can't go by plane. There's no airport here," grumbled Oscar.

"And we can't go by boat. There's no water," Mr. Zabriski added. He put his head in his hands, and Oscar put *his* head in his flippers, and they began to think.

Then suddenly, a loud "Whoo-oo-oo!" screeched through the air, and looking up, they saw a column of black smoke shooting

to the sky, and they heard the roar and puff-puff of a big steam engine rushing nearer every minute. The seal jumped up.

"We've got to go by train," he shouted. "And here it comes. Grab your baggage and make it snappy!"

They made a dash for it. There wasn't even time to buy tickets. They called to the station-master to take care of their truck, and they climbed on board. Mr. Zabriski rode in the Pullman, but Oscar had to ride in the baggage-car.

"You arrange for my bath," he whispered when they parted, and Mr. Zabriski said that he would see what he could do.

Now the train on which they were riding was a very fine one, streamlined, of course. There were observation and club cars in which you could read or watch the country flying by, and there was a dining car. You could sit at a table and eat turkey dinners with cranberry sauce and ice cream while you looked out of the window. There were large dressing rooms and even a bathroom with a big tub. A man called a porter made the passengers comfortable. He gave them pillows for their heads when they were tired, and footstools for their feet, and he put clean towels in the bathroom.

Mr. Zabriski called the porter. "My seal wants a bath."

"Can't be done! Can't be done!" said the porter crossly. "This isn't a circus train. This is a first-class passenger train."

"You're right. This *is* a very fine train, and that's a very nice bathroom, and all the better, because my seal *must* have a bath. He's used to it," said Mr. Zabriski firmly. Then he put his hand into his pocket and gave the porter two shiny quarters.

"That's all right. That's all right. I'll fix it up. Thank you, sir," the porter answered at once, grinning when he saw the nice, new money. "*Sure*, your seal can have a bath. Now when we get to the next station, and everybody is looking out of the windows, then's your chance. For if anyone saw a seal going through the car, they'd have fits! Yes, sir!"

Mr. Zabriski agreed that was an excellent plan. The train began to slow up, so he hurried to tell Oscar. And when all the passengers were looking out at the people on the platform, Oscar slid quietly down the Pullman aisle to the bathroom and nobody saw him at all.

In a jiffy, Mr. Zabriski had drawn a big tub full of cold water, and Oscar dived in.

"Are you all right?" Mr. Zabriski asked.

"Fine," replied the seal. "This is keen. You go and have a smoke."

So everything was fixed up. Mr. Zabriski was enjoying a cigar in the club car and Oscar was enjoying his bath. Mr. Zabriski thought that the porter was watching the bathroom and the porter thought that Mr. Zabriski was watching, but no one was there except Oscar, splashing about in the tub.

By and by, a young lady passenger said to her friend, "It's awfully hot, isn't it? I think I'll take a bath and see if I can get cooled off." She gathered up her toilet articles and went down the aisle. Opening the bathroom door, she started in, but hastily backed out with a terrible shriek.

"Oh-o-o-o!" she screamed. "Help! Help! Save me! Save me!"

All the people jumped from their seats and came crowding around her. "Save you from what?" asked a man anxiously.

"There's a bear in the bathroom," the frightened girl cried. "I saw his trunk—oh-o-o-o! Oh-o-o!"

"Stop it!" said the man sharply. "Bears don't have trunks. I'll look."

He opened the door cautiously and stuck in his head, and just then Oscar rolled over with a tremendous splash, throwing water in every direction; and the man shut the door with a *bang!*

"It's a w-w-w-*whale!*" he sputtered, mopping water out of his eyes and nose and hair and off his new necktie. "I saw his long neck."

"I knew it was a ferocious animal," cried the young lady. "I knew it! Just listen to him barking!"

"Fiddlesticks!" an old lady spoke up. "Are you both crazy? There aren't any whales or bears in that bathroom. I'll bet it's a cat. You're both so scared you don't know what you are saying. Who ever heard of bears with elephants' trunks on their noses, or of whales with their heads on top of giraffes' necks? Ridiculous! And as for barking, it might very well be a dog. I'll call it."

She began: "Here, kitty, kitty, kitty. Nice doggy. Come, Fido. Come here, sir!" She turned the knob ever so carefully, and peeked through the crack.

"Mercy me!" she exclaimed. "It's a whole Noah's Ark and a flood, too." And she slammed the door shut just as fast as she could while rivers of water came running along the floor and out into the corridor.

By this time everybody was greatly excited. A crowd had gathered around the bathroom door, and some of the people were trying to peek through the keyhole.

"Oh-o-o-o!" the young lady kept on screaming.

"Ring for the porter!" someone yelled.

63

"Yes, the porter! The porter! Call him," several people cried all at once. The men rumpled their hair in their excitement, the women twisted their handkerchiefs into thin strings. And they all rang their bells for the porter.

He came running, and Mr. Zabriski came, too.

"I'll lose my job," muttered the porter.

"They'll put us off the train," Mr. Zabriski worried out loud, "and then how'll we get to California?" But suddenly an idea flashed into Mr. Zabriski's head. As he reached the end of the car near the bathroom, he jumped up on a seat and raised his hand for silence.

"La-dies and gen-tle-men," he shouted. "Quiet. Pl-ease! I have a surprise for you. We have with us today, Oscar! Oscar, the *famous* trained seal! And what is he going to do, my friends? He is going to perform his circus tricks for your entertainment."

"Hurrah! Hurrah! Yip-ee!" cried the passengers.

"He has been limbering up in his bath," called Mr. Zabriski, "and now, if you will all be kind enough to take your places in the club-car, the show will be ready to begin in a few minutes."

"Three cheers for the seal," the passengers shouted, and they all rushed for the club-car, each one trying to be there first in order to get a seat in the front row.

Then Mr. Zabriski opened his suitcase, and hurriedly put on his pink velvet suit, and his shiny black silk hat, and he and Oscar entered the club-car. Mr. Zabriski cracked a whip while Oscar did all sorts of marvelous tricks. He balanced colored balls on his nose, he wheeled a baby buggy, he danced, and he even sang, "Yankee Doodle."

The people clapped their hands and cried for more, and more, and more, and they slapped each other on the back. And the conductors of the train were so pleased because everyone was having such a good time, that they decided to have a party. They sent the porter to the dining-car for refreshments, and everybody had cinnamon toast, and chocolate cookies, and tea. Mr. Zabriski had some, too.

And Oscar, what did *he* have? Why, a nice big fish.

Richard Hughes

THE MAGIC GLASS

ILLUSTRATED BY *Minnie Rousseff*

THERE is a little boy I know who always looks very carefully in wastepaper baskets, "because," he says, "you never know what valuable things you may find, that some silly grownup has thrown away."

One day he found what looked like the glass off the end of an electric torch. "That will make a most useful magnifying glass," he said, and put it in his pocket.

That night he woke up; and not being able to get to sleep again he thought he would look at a few things through his glass. The first thing he looked at was a wooden rabbit lying on the end of his bed; but the strange thing was, that, when he looked through the glass instead of the toy, what he saw was a real live rabbit, sitting up on its hind legs and wobbling its nose at him! Then he took the glass from his eye: and lo and behold, it was only a wooden one again.

"This *is* a funny glass," thought the little boy.

Then he looked through it at a china duck there was on the mantelpiece: and, sure enough, there was a real duck, which would have jumped down on to the floor if he hadn't taken the glass from his eye and turned it back into china again.

By this time the little boy was so excited with his glass that he got out of bed and crept down to the room where his father and mother were lying asleep. "For," he thought, "if it turns toys into real, I wonder if it turns real people into toys?" And he put it to his eye and looked at his father and mother. And so it was: they were immediately wooden Mr. and Mrs. Noah out of the Ark. To make sure, he took a pin, and keeping the glass firmly over his eye he tried to stick his mother. But it

wouldn't go in, for she was now quite hard: it only scratched a little paint off. Then he took the glass away, and they were his mother and father again. But just to make sure he stuck the pin in again. This time it went right in, and his mother sat up with the most awful yell.

"You naughty boy!" she said. "What are you doing out of bed? And *what* did you stick a pin into me for?"

"I'm awfully sorry, Mother," he said, "but I thought you were Mrs. Noah! You were, a minute ago, you know!"

"Mrs. Noah?" said his mother. "Stuff and nonsense! You must have been dreaming! Go back to bed at once."

So he went back to bed, and soon was asleep. In the morning when he went to school, he put the glass in his pocket. . . .

When he got to school he forgot about the glass till halfway through the lessons, when he took it out of his pocket and looked at the mistress through it. Immediately she turned into a golliwog.

The little boy was not very surprised, but you may imagine all the other children were! They made such a noise in their astonishment that the headmistress came into the room, and hearing her coming he slipped the glass back into his pocket.

"Now then, children!" she said, "what's all this noise?" (It wasn't a very nice school.)

"The mistress has just turned into a golliwog!" shouted the children.

"Nonsense!" said the headmistress, who was a very cross old woman; but just then the little boy looked at the mistress again, and turned her again into a golliwog.

"Good gracious me! What's this?" said the headmistress, and went up to take hold of the golliwog: but when she got close, of course, the little boy could see her through the glass too, and immediately she turned into a Dismal Desmond.

At that, of course, the children were awfully pleased, and wanted to have them to play with: but the little boy said no, they mustn't go near or they'd all be turned into dolls, and all the other children said how clever the little boy was to have

done it. So he kept on looking at them until lesson time was over; and then he went home.

That night, when he was in bed, his mother remembered his trousers wanted a button sewed on, so she came upstairs and fetched them, and then she found the glass in his pocket, and took it downstairs with her.

"What a funny glass," she said, and put it to her eye, and looked at herself in the looking glass.

That was a most awful thing to happen: for not only did she turn into wooden Mrs. Noah immediately, but the glass simply became a painted glass in Mrs. Noah's eye. And so she would have to stay, because the wooden Mrs. Noah, of course, couldn't move, and as long as she didn't move she was staring at herself in the looking glass, and, as long as she stared at herself, Mrs. Noah she would stay.

As a matter of fact she was Mrs. Noah all night, and still Mrs. Noah when the maids came down in the morning to sweep the room.

"There's that naughty boy left one of his toys in the drawing-room," they said, and went to move it: but as soon, of course, as they moved it away from the looking glass it turned back into a person.

"Good gracious!" they said. "It's the Mistress!"

And she rubbed her eyes, and said she felt very sleepy because she had sat up all night. Meanwhile the glass rolled away into a corner, and happened to stop just in the mouth of a mouse-hole, and no one thought of it any more.

That afternoon the little boy's mother had a whole lot of people coming to tea. They were very stiff and grand people that the little boy didn't like at all; but all the same he thought he would creep downstairs and have a look at them. So he did and watched them from where he couldn't be seen. But the little boy wasn't the only inquisitive one. Just at the same moment the little mouse came up his hole, and thought he would have a look at them too: and across the hole was the magic glass, so he looked through that.

Immediately all the people turned into the funniest lot of

dolls you have ever seen: Dutch dolls and wax dolls and rag dolls, and even china ornaments. And that wasn't all. There were some pictures on the wall which the mouse could see, too: and while the real people turned into toys, the people in the pictures all stepped down into the room, in their funny old-fashioned dresses, and started to eat the tea. At that the little boy was so pleased that he laughed and clapped his hands, and the noise frightened the mouse, who ran away into the back of his hole, and so all was as before.

But presently the mouse came back and thought he would have another look. Just then the little boy's father came in from the office, and was standing in the drawing-room door when all the people turned into toys again, and the pictures started once more coming out of their frames. Meanwhile, the mouse was so excited he kept turning round to tell the other mice what he was seeing, and then looking back, and then turning round again, so that the boy's father was nearly astonished out of his wits, seeing them turn from people into toys and toys into people again as fast as the wink of an eye. But at last the mouse went away: and then they all stayed people, and when the tea-party was over went home as if nothing had happened.

But the little boy's father was really rather frightened. "There's something magic about this house," he said to himself; and as soon as he could he found another house, and they all went to live in that and left the old one empty.

But no one noticed the magic glass sticking in the mouth of the mouse-hole: and if someone else comes and lives in that house, and the mouse comes up his hole to have a look at them, I suppose the same thing would happen to them!

69

Walter de la Mare

THE SHIP OF RIO

There was a ship of Rio
    Sailed out into the blue,
And nine and ninety monkeys
    Were all her jovial crew.
From bos'un to the cabin boy,
    From quarter to caboose,
There weren't a stitch of calico
    To breech 'em—tight or loose;
From spar to deck, from deck to keel,
    From barnacle to shroud,
There weren't one pair of reach-me-downs
    To all that jabbering crowd.
But wasn't it a gladsome sight,
    When roared the deep-sea gales,
To see them reef her fore and aft,
    A-swinging by their tails!
Oh, wasn't it a gladsome sight,
    When glassy calm did come,
To see them squatting tailor-wise
    Around a keg of rum!
Oh, wasn't it a gladsome sight,
    When in she sailed to land,
To see them all a-scampering skip
    For nuts across the sand!

And nine and ninety monkeys were all her jovial crew.

Laura E. Richards

A LEGEND OF LAKE OKEEFINOKEE

There once was a frog,
And he lived in a bog,
On the banks of Lake Okeefinokee.
And the words of the song
That he sang all day long
Were, "Croakety-croakety-croaky."

Said the frog, "I have found
That my life's daily round
In this place is exceedingly poky.
So no longer I'll stop,
But I swiftly will hop
Away from Lake Okeefinokee."

Now a bad mocking-bird
By mischance overheard
The words of the frog as he spokee.
And he said, "All my life
Frog and I've been at strife,
As we lived by Lake Okeefinokee.

"Now I see at a glance
Here's a capital chance
For to play him a practical jokee.
So I'll venture to say
That he shall not today
Leave the banks of Lake Okeefinokee."

So this bad mocking-bird,
Without saying a word,
He flew to a tree which was oaky;
And loudly he sang,
Till the whole forest rang,
"Oh! Croakety-croakety-croaky!"

As he warbled this song,
Master Frog came along,
A-filling his pipe for to smokee;
And he said, " 'Tis some frog
Has escaped from the bog
Of Okeefinokee-finokee.

"I am filled with amaze
To hear one of my race
A-warbling on top of an oaky;
But if frogs can climb trees,
I may still find some ease
On the banks of Lake Okeefinokee."

So he climbed up the tree;
But alas, down fell he!
And his lovely green neck it was brokee;
And the sad truth to say,
Never more did he stray
From the banks of Lake Okeefinokee.

And the bad mocking-bird
Said, "How very absurd
And delightful a practical jokee!"
But I'm happy to say
He was drowned the next day
In the waters of Okeefinokee.

FREDDY is a pig with ideas. He likes
to play detective. Here is one of his
adventures that starts when Mrs. Winnick comes to see him.

Walter Brooks

FREDDY THE DETECTIVE
SOLVES A MYSTERY

ILLUSTRATED BY *Kurt Wiese*

MRS. WINNICK was a widow who
lived down by the edge of the
woods. In her day she had been
as pretty a young rabbit as you could wish to see, but since
the loss of her husband the cares of providing for a large
family had taken every bit of her time and energy. She took no
part in the gay social life of the other animals in the neighborhood, and they seldom saw her, though they were good to her,
and one or other of them was always taking a fresh head of
lettuce or a couple of carrots down to her, for they suspected
that she and the children did not always get enough food.

"Oh, Mr. Freddy," she burst out, "it's about Egbert. He's
disappeared, and whatever I shall do I don't know. He was always such a good boy, too—kind and helpful, and willing to
look after the baby. With the other children it's play, play,
play all day long, but Egbert—" And she began to cry. . . .

"Come, come," said Freddy briskly. "Just tell me all about
it, and we'll see what can be done. I'm sure it's not as bad as you
think. Now, do you want me to help you find Egbert?" And as
she nodded tearful assent, "Well," he continued, "let's get at the
facts. Let's see—Egbert. He's your eighth oldest, isn't he? Or
ninth?"

"Twelfth," she replied, "and always such a good—"

73

"Yes," said Freddy quickly. "And when did you last see him?"

After asking a good many questions Freddy got Mrs. Winnick's story. The night before Egbert had taken several of the children up through the woods to Jones's Creek to get some watercress. At nine o'clock the children had come home without him. They had not found any good watercress, and Egbert had said that he would go farther down the creek to a place he knew where there was sure to be some, but that they must go home, as it was their bedtime, and their mother would worry. Mrs. Winnick had put the children to bed and had presently gone to bed herself. But this morning Egbert's bed was empty. He had not come home, and nothing had been seen or heard of him since.

Freddy consoled the weeping widow as best he could. "I'll get to work on it right away," he said, "and meanwhile don't worry. I'll soon have Egbert back for you. By the way, who sent you to me?"

"It was the children," said the rabbit. "They'd heard about your setting up to be a detective, and they wanted me to come and see you. Not that I have any faith in it—excuse me, sir. But you haven't been at it very long, have you?"

"No," Freddy admitted, "but there always has to be a first time, doesn't there? Even Sherlock Holmes made a start once, didn't he? Don't you worry, ma'am. I've made a deep study of the subject, and there isn't an animal in the country that knows more about detecting than I do. Why, I've read a whole book about it."

Mrs. Winnick seemed satisfied with this and went off home, stopping after every three or four hops to cry a little and blow her nose. Freddy wasted no time, but set out at once for the creek. He found the watercress bed which Egbert had visited with his little brothers and sisters, then went slowly on downstream, keeping a sharp lookout for any signs of the missing rabbit. Once he saw where some wintergreen leaves had been nibbled, and once, in a sandy place, he saw the plain imprint of a rabbit's foot, so he knew he was on the right track. And then where the stream widened out, just before it took a bend

round to the right to join the river, he found another big bed of cress, and in the swampy shore a large number of rabbit's footprints.

Freddy had been happy when he started out. Mrs. Winnick's visit had cheered him up a lot. Here was a new problem. He would solve it and prove to his friends that he was a real detective after all. But now this problem was just as bad as the other one. What was he going to do? These were Egbert's footprints all right, but what good did they do him? There ought to be some clue that he could follow up. There always was in the Sherlock Holmes stories. "You can't solve a case without clues," he muttered unhappily. "These might be clues to Sherlock Holmes, but to me they're just a lot of footprints." And he sat down on the bank to think.

He was thinking so hard that for some time he did not see a small rabbit who hopped down out of the woods to the cress bed, picked a few stalks, then hopped back up among the trees. The rabbit had made several trips before Freddy suddenly caught sight of him.

The rabbit hadn't seen Freddy either, and when the pig started up suddenly, he dodged quickly behind a bush.

"So *you're* the one who made all those footprints in the mud here, are you?" said Freddy.

"Yes, sir," came a small anxious voice from behind the bush. "Isn't it all right, sir?"

"Sure it's all right," said the pig. "Come out; I won't hurt you. I'm looking for a rabbit about your size. Haven't seen one around, have you?"

The rabbit hopped timidly out. "No, sir," he said. "Who was he, sir?"

"Ah," said Freddy mysteriously, "*I'm* the one to be asking the questions. I'm a detective. Just you answer up briskly, young fellow. Haven't seen any other rabbits around, eh?"

"No, sir—"

"No other footprints in the mud when you came here?"

"I don't think so, sir. You see, I—"

"How long have you been here?"

"Since last night, sir. You see, I came to get some watercress, and as I was —"

Freddy stopped him. "That's enough," he said severely. "Please just answer the questions I ask you, without adding anything of your own. Just answer yes or no. You heard no unusual noises?"

"Yes, sir—I mean no, sir," said the rabbit, who was getting confused.

"What do you mean—'yes, sir, no, sir'?" said Freddy. "Please give me a straight answer. Did you or did you not hear any unusual noises?"

"No, sir—I mean—" The rabbit gulped. "—no, sir."

"Good," said the pig. "That's the stuff; a straight answer to a straight question. And—ha, h'm—let me see—" He hadn't found out anything, and yet he couldn't think of any more questions to ask. "Well, ah—what are you doing here anyway?"

But the rabbit didn't answer. "Come, come," said Freddy sharply. "Answer me! What are you—"

But the rabbit interrupted him by bursting into tears. "You told me to answer yes or no," he sobbed, "and you can't answer that question yes or no. I c-came here to get watercress, an' I was just going home an' I found a little bird with a hurt wing, an' I thought I ought to stay with it, an' I know my mother'll worry, b-but I don't like to leave the bird all alone, an' now you come an' ask me a lot of questions I don't know the answers to, an'—" Here he broke down entirely and cried so hard that he got the hiccups.

Freddy was a kind-hearted animal, but he had been so absorbed in asking questions in a thoroughly detective-like manner that he hadn't really noticed that he was frightening the rabbit so badly that the poor little creature couldn't give him any information even if he had it to give. In this Freddy was more like a real detective than he realized. Some detectives will ask a simple question like "What is your name?" in so frightening a voice that the person he asks can't even remember whether he has a name or not.

"There, there," said Freddy, patting the rabbit on the back, "I'm sorry I scared you. It's all right. Where is this bird?"

"Up in a hollow behind that tree," hiccuped the little animal.

"All right," said Freddy. "I'll look after him for you. You run along home. I've got to find this other rabbit I was telling you about, but first I'll see that the bird is taken care of. Run along and tell your mother not to worry any more."

The rabbit wasted no time, but trotted off, still crying, and hiccuping occasionally, and Freddy went in search of the bird. He found it presently—a fledgling wood thrush, too young to talk yet. Beside it was a small heap of watercress which the rabbit had evidently been trying to feed it.

"Tut, tut," said Freddy. "Feeding an infant like that watercress! He'll be sick. And he's hidden here so that his mother couldn't possibly find him. That rabbit has a kind heart, but he certainly isn't very bright." He picked up the little thrush carefully in his mouth and carried it, fluttering feebly, out into an open space, then went back into the bushes and sat down. In five minutes there was a rush of wings, and the mother thrush alighted beside the hungry fledgling and began consoling him with little chirps. Freddy slipped away without waiting to be thanked.

"Now," he said to himself, "for Egbert. Though how in the world I'm to find him I don't know. But I've *got* to or I'll never dare to show my face in the farmyard again. I wish I'd never tried to be a detective, that's what I wish!"

On a chance he decided to go a little farther down the creek, at least as far as the hermit's house, a deserted cabin which stood on the other side of the stream. Perhaps some of the waterside animals might have seen the missing rabbit.

But he had not gone far before something drove all thought of Egbert from his mind. There were sounds coming from the hermit's house. Shouts and rough laughter and occasional pistol shots. What a chance for a detective! Freddy crept forward; then, finding that the bushes on the opposite bank were too high to permit him to see what was going on, he plunged into the water, swam quietly across, and worked his way up toward the house. And this is what he saw:

Hanging from the limb of a tall tree in front of the house was a swing made of two ropes and a board for a seat. A big man with a cap pulled down over his eyes, and his coat collar turned up, was swinging in long, dizzy swoops. He had a revolver in his hand, and at the top of his swing, when he was level with the top of the house, he would shoot the revolver and try to hit the chimney. A smaller man was sitting in a rocking chair on the porch. He wore a black mask over his face, and no cap, and was knitting busily away at a woolen muffler.

Pretty soon the big man stopped swinging. "Come now, Looey," he shouted. "It's your turn now."

The small man shook his head. "No, Red, I must get this muffler done. We'll both want to wrap up warm tomorrow night; we'll be out late."

"Oh, come on," said Red. "Take a couple of shots anyway. Bet you can't beat me. I got two out of seven."

The other got up rather unwillingly. "Well, all right. But you have got to promise to be more careful. I worry about you all the time. You remember that last bank we robbed; it was a rainy night, and you didn't wear your rubbers, and you caught a bad cold."

"Yes, yes, Looey," Red replied. "I'll be careful. Come on, now. Into the swing."

"You'll have to push me, Red," said Looey, taking a large revolver from the pocket of his coat. He seated himself in the

78

swing, and the big man started him swinging. Higher and higher he went, until at each push Red was running right under him. Then when he was high enough, he aimed the revolver, and bang! a brick flew from the chimney.

"Hooray for Looey!" shouted Red. "A bull's-eye! Shoot again!"

Freddy, peering out from his hiding-place, was so excited he could hardly breathe. Here was real work for a detective, and no mistake. For these men were certainly robbers. And if he could capture them, his name as a detective was made.

But just then, as Looey was whizzing for the tenth time up into the treetops, one of the ropes broke; he let go his hold and went up in a great curve like a rocket, then came hurtling down through the foliage and into the very bush behind which Freddy was hiding.

He wasn't hurt, for the bush had broken his fall, and he picked himself up immediately, and his eye fell on the amazed pig. Freddy did not wait to see what would happen. With a squeal of fright he bolted.

"A pig! Quick, Red, a nice fat pig!" shouted Looey, and started after him, the other robber close behind. There was much shouting and a great banging of revolvers, and two or three bullets whizzed past Freddy's head, but he was a good runner and in a very few minutes had left them far behind.

He ran on for a while, then sat down to rest under a beech

tree—and realized suddenly that he didn't know where he was. The woods on this side of the creek extended for many miles. If he could find the creek, he would be all right—but he did not know where the creek was. And the day was cloudy; he could not tell his direction from the position of the sun. "Well, I suppose the best thing to do is to keep on going," he said to himself. "May meet a squirrel or a jay who can tell me where I am." And he started on.

But though he walked and walked, he met no one, and there was no sign of the creek. He had just about decided that he would have to stay out all night when he noticed some footprints. "H'm, someone been along here not many minutes ago," he said. "Looks like a pig, too. Wonder what another pig is doing in these woods. I guess I'll follow them and see if I can catch up."

So he went on, following the footprints, until he came to a place where the other pig had sat down to rest before going on. There was the plain print of a curly tail in the leaf mold under a beech tree. Freddy sat down too, and then suddenly something about the place seemed familiar to him. This beech tree, those bushes over there—"Why, this is where I sat down to rest myself a long time ago! Those are my own footprints I've been following!"

This realization made him feel very foolish, as well it might, for it *is* rather silly for a detective to try to shadow himself. Still, he realized that all he had to do was to follow those footprints *backward* instead of forward, and he would come out by the hermit's house. Which he did, and presently he heard the sound of voices.

But this time he did not stop to see what the robbers were doing. He gave the house a wide berth, jumped into the creek, swam across, and in a few minutes more was back on familiar ground.

"I'll just stop in and see if anything has been heard of Egbert," he said to himself. So he turned down toward the Widow Winnick's home. Half a dozen small rabbits were playing about on the edge of the woods as he came up, and one of them called down the rabbit-hole: "Mother! Mr. Freddy's here!"

Almost at once Mrs. Winnick's head popped up through the opening. But it was a changed Mrs. Winnick that beamed happily at him.

"Oh, Mr. Freddy!" she cried. "How can I ever thank you? My Egbert! You found him for me!"

"But," stammered the bewildered Freddy, "I didn't—" And then he stopped. For one of the little rabbits who were standing around him in a respectful and admiring circle hiccuped, and said politely: "Excuse me." And Freddy saw it all. Of course! That rabbit had been Egbert all the time!

He recovered himself just in time. Oh, don't thank me, Mrs. Winnick. Don't thank me," he said rather grandly. "It was nothing, I assure you—nothing at all. Indeed, I am very grateful to you for having sent me down in that direction, for I have made some very important discoveries. However, I am glad Egbert got back safely. All the other children are well, I hope. Good, good; I am very glad to hear it. Good evening." And he went on homeward.

"Well," he said to himself, "I guess as a detective I'm not so bad after all. Restored a lost child to his mother and discovered a band of robbers, all in one day! Huh, Sherlock Holmes never did more than that, I bet."

FREDDY, disguised as a man, now hunts up those robbers.

It was nearly dark in the woods, though above him the tree-tops were bright green and gold in the light of the setting sun. Since he could not swim the creek in his men's clothes, to get to the hermit's house he had to cut through the woods to the bridge and then walk back on the other side. He walked on his hind legs, because he felt that he needed all the practice he could get if he was to make anybody think he was a man. But the trousers bothered his legs, and he stumbled over roots and tripped over vines and fell into holes until, long before he reached the creek, he was so bruised and hot and out of breath that he sat down on a log to rest. "My goodness," he said to himself, "I'm glad I'm not a man! How they ever manage to

81

do anything or get anywhere in all these clumsy hot clothes I can't imagine! Lords of creation, they call themselves! Humph, I'd rather be a pig any time."

Pretty soon he got up and went on again, and at last he reached the bridge. On the farther side of the bridge a narrow, grassy road ran off to the left toward the hermit's house. Freddy followed it. He began to feel rather nervous, but he was a brave pig and he had no thought of turning back.

By this time it was dark. The windows in the hermit's house were lighted up, but they were so dirty that Freddy couldn't see what was going on inside. He could hear music, however—someone was playing the harmonium, and a man's voice was singing. The song was "Sweet and Low," but both singer and accompanist were going as fast as they could, and they were never together for more than one note. The singer would be ahead, then the player would put on a burst of speed and pass him, only to get behind again when he stopped to take breath.

Freddy thought this was the funniest singing he had ever heard, and he went up to the front door and peeked through the keyhole just as the song came to an end. The big man, who was sitting at the harmonium, was wiping sweat from his forehead. "You won that time, Looey," he was saying, "but it's the chords in that second part that slow me up."

"I'll race you on 'Boola Boola,'" said Looey.

"No you won't either," said Red. "You always win on that because you leave out about six 'Boolas,' and I can't keep track when I'm playing. Let's take something where all the words aren't alike. Let's do 'Annie Laurie.' One, two, three—go!"

The noise was terrible. If you don't believe it, try singing "Annie Laurie" as fast as you can. Freddy couldn't stand it any longer, and he rapped on the door.

The musicians were going so fast that they couldn't stop for about four bars. Then there was a moment's silence, followed by the clump of heavy shoes, and the door was flung open. Freddy touched his cap and bowed politely.

"My gosh, what's this?" said Red. "Come in, young feller. What can I do for you?"

Freddy stepped inside. The room was lit by three kerosene lamps, but the lamp chimneys were so dirty that they gave very little light, and he felt reasonably sure that if he kept his cap on, they wouldn't know he was a pig. Nevertheless he was scared when they both came close to him and squatted down with their hands on their knees and stared at him.

At first they didn't say anything. They stared at him for a minute, then stood up and stared at each other, then squatted down and stared at him again.

"Well, I'll be jiggered!" said Red.

"So'll I!" said Looey. "He's a—what do you call those little men—a wharf, isn't it?"

"A dwarf," said Red. "You ought to know that, Looey."

"Well, wharf or dwarf, what does it matter what we call him? The point is, what does he call himself? What's your name, guy?"

Freddy pointed to his mouth and shook his head.

"He's dumb," said Looey. "What good's a dumb dwarf? Let's throw him out and go on with the music."

Freddy had in his pocket the chart that he had prepared, but although from long practice in handling books and papers he had got so that he could use his forefeet almost as if they were hands, he was afraid that if he took it out and gave it to them they would see that he had hoofs instead of hands, and would realize that he was a pig.

83

Fortunately at this moment Red said: "Wait! I've got an idea!"

"I hope it's better than the one you had last Thursday," said Looey.

"This is a good one," said Red. "Listen, this dwarf is little, and he's dumb. That means he can get in places where we can't get in, and that he can't tell anybody about it afterwards. How about that back window in the Centerboro National Bank?"

"Gosh!" exclaimed Looey. "That *is* an idea!" He turned to Freddy. "Say, dwarf, would you like to make a lot of money?"

Freddy nodded enthusiastically.

"Fine! You come with us and do just what we tell you to, and we'll give you fifty cents. Come on, Red, get your things on." And almost before he knew what had happened, Freddy was walking back up the dark road with one of the robbers on each side of him.

He hadn't had a chance to show them his chart, and he hadn't the least idea what sort of adventure he was in for now. "Something pretty shady, I bet," he said to himself. "But no use worrying. I'm in with them now, and if I can't catch them after this, I'm a pretty poor detective."

At the bridge they stopped, Red dove into the bushes, and pretty soon there was the sputter of an engine and he drove out into the road in a badly battered open car. Red hoisted Freddy in, and they started off in the direction of Centerboro. Nothing was said on the way. Both the robbers had on raincoats, black masks, and rubbers, and carried pistols in their hands. Looey had hard work driving with the pistol in his hand, and once when he had to shift gears, it went off. It was pointed at the windshield when it went off, and Freddy was surprised not to see the glass fly to pieces, but Looey only laughed.

"We don't carry loaded pistols when we're at work," he explained; "it's too easy to have an accident."

As they drove down Main Street, Freddy saw that there were lights in all the stores, just as the sheriff had told him there would be. They slowed up when they came to the bank, and he saw a watchman sitting on the front steps with a gun across his knees. But he paid no attention to them as they turned into the alley next to the bank.

Looey stopped the car in the alley, and they all got out. Red took a stepladder out of the back seat and put it against the bank wall under a small window. "There you are," he said. "They don't bother to lock this window because it's too small for anybody to get through. But you can get through, and when you're inside, we'll throw this sack in after you, and all you have to do is stuff all the money into the sack, throw it out, and then come out yourself. See?"

Freddy saw all right. He saw that he was going to be a robber in spite of himself, and there was nothing else to do. But he had reckoned without the stepladder. Climbing the back stairs at the farm with Mr. Bean's trousers on had been bad enough, but this was hopeless. He scrambled up three steps, then caught his left foot in his right trouser leg, stumbled, squealed, and Freddy and the ladder and Looey came down with a crash on the cobblestones of the alley.

At once the night was full of noise. Windows went up, police whistles blew, men ran out into the streets and began shouting and firing off their guns. Looey scrambled to his feet, tossed Freddy into the car, and climbed in beside him as Red started up the engine. With a roar they dashed out of the alley and up Main Street at full speed. Half a dozen cars swung out into the street behind them as they dodged and twisted to avoid the men who tried to stop them. Red drove magnificently; he almost seemed to dodge the bullets that were fired at them, for none of them hit the car. In less than a minute they were thundering back up the road on which they had come into town, with the pursuit streaming out behind them. In a few minutes more they came to the bridge and crossed it; then Red put on the brakes so quickly that they were all nearly flung through the windshield, swung the car round, snapped off the lights, and drove into the bushes where the car had been hidden before.

One by one the pursuing cars flashed past their hiding-place.

When the last one had gone by, the two robbers climbed slowly out of the car.

"You can go on back where you came from, dwarf," said Looey in a disgusted voice.

"You ought to be ashamed of yourself," said Red. "Now we haven't got any stepladder, all on account of you. I was going to put up fresh curtains in the living room tomorrow, but how I'm to do it without a stepladder I don't know."

"Go on," said Looey, "Beat it. We don't want anything more to do with you. You haven't got any more sense than a pig."

Freddy grinned to himself in the dark; then he took the paper out of his pocket and handed it to Red.

"What's this?" said the robber. He lit a match to look, then called in an excited voice to his companion: "Look, Looey, he's got a map of that farmer's place—the one that lives across the creek—and it shows where his money is hidden."

They bent over the paper, lighting match after match to examine it. "Map of Mr. Bean's barn, showing location of hidden treasure," it said at the top, and under this Freddy had drawn a chart of the barn, but from one of the box stalls he had drawn a long arrow, at the end of which was written: "Under the floor of this stall is hidden a box containing ten thousand dollars in gold."

The robbers were greatly excited. "This is what he came to give us," said Looey. "Maybe he ain't such a bad dwarf after all." He turned to Freddy. "I'm sorry I said that about your being a pig. Are you sure the money is there?"

Freddy nodded emphatically.

"It's worth trying," said Red. "But, just the same, I ain't taking any chances. We'll take this fellow to the house and tie him up while we go over and see if the money's there. If it is, all right; we'll give him his share. But if it ain't—" He glared at the detective. "Well, he'll regret it, that's all."

This didn't suit Freddy at all, but there was nothing else to be done. They took him back to the hermit's house and tied him in a chair and then set out—on foot, this time, as there would be too many people looking for their automobile on the road.

Freddy was almost in despair. He had made no arrangements for the capture of the robbers. If they went to the barn, they would find nothing in the box stall but a dozen or more animal prisoners. If they came back empty-handed a second time this evening, what would happen to him? To think about it made his clothes feel even more tight and uncomfortable than they already were.

But he didn't think about it long, for the robbers had not been gone more than a minute when there was a movement in a dark corner of the room, and a tiny voice said: "That you, Freddy?"

"Cousin Augustus!" exclaimed Freddy. "Gosh, I'm glad to hear your voice! Gnaw these ropes through, will you, like a good fellow? I've got to get to the farm before those fellows get there or I'll miss an important capture."

Cousin Augustus's teeth were sharp; in a very few minutes Freddy was free and had thrown off his disguise. "Ha," he exclaimed, "this feels like something! Now I'm equal to anything! But I wonder if I can get there before they do. Tell me, Gus, is there any bird round here that you could wake up and get to take a message to Jock?"

"Sure," said the mouse, "there's a wren lives under the eaves of the porch. I'll just slip up and take a peek in his nest and see if he'll go."

Cousin Augustus wasted no time. In two minutes he was back, accompanied by a very sleepy and rather cross wren, who, however, when he realized that it was Freddy, the renowned

87

detective, who wanted his help, was only too anxious to oblige.

"Fly over and wake up Jock or Robert," said Freddy, "and tell them to clear all the prisoners out of the second box stall right away. Tell 'em they mustn't waste a second. There are two robbers coming over there, and I want them to get into that stall without any difficulty. Tell Jock to get all the other animals up and have them hide in the barn and keep quiet until the men get in the stall. I'll be there before there's anything else to be done."

The wren repeated the message to be sure he had it straight, and flew off, and then Freddy dashed down to the creek, dove in and swam across, and galloped off through the woods toward the farm. It was much easier going on four feet than it had been on two, and it wasn't long before he reached the pasture. From there on he went more carefully, and by the time he reached the barn he was creeping along like a shadow.

Faint sounds came from the barn, and now and then a light flickered and was gone again. The robbers were there, then! Freddy slipped inside and into Hank's stall. "Hello, Hank," he whispered. "Everything going all right?"

"Far as I know," said Hank. "Though what it all means is beyond me. Just a few minutes ago Jock and Robert and Mrs. Wiggins came in here and made all the prisoners go into one stall, and then they hid—they're over there in the corner—and then two men sneaked in, and it sounds as if they were tearing up the floor. What's it all about anyway?"

But there was no time to explain. Freddy tiptoed across the floor to the door of the stall. Sure enough, there were Red and Looey, working by the light of an electric torch, heaving at a plank in the floor. With great caution Freddy pushed the heavy door slowly shut and dropped the peg into the hasp.

The robbers heard nothing, and Freddy made no noise, for he had a reason for letting them go on with their work. He went over to the corner where his friends were hiding.

"I guess you can come out now," he said. "We've got 'em safe and fast. This is a great night's work! But what I've been through since I left here you wouldn't believe!"

He started to tell them the tale of his adventures, but suddenly there was a great rattling at the door of the stall. The robbers had found out that they were locked in.

Jock laughed. "Let 'em just try to get out!" he said. "That door will hold an elephant. Anyway I sent down for Peter, in case anything should go wrong. He can handle 'em all right."

Freddy started to go on with his story, when they heard a car drive into the yard, and a loud voice shouted: "Hey, farmer! Wake up!"

"I know that voice," said Freddy. "It's the city detective. Well, let's see how many robbers he's caught tonight!"

The animals went to the barn door. A light had sprung up in an upper window, and pretty soon Mr. Bean's head, in its red nightcap with a white tassel, was poked out into the night.

"Stop raisin' all that rumpus, or I'll come down and take my horsewhip to ye!"

"I want to know if you've seen an open car go by here in the past hour," shouted the detective.

"I got something better to do at night than to sit up and watch for open cars," said Mr. Bean. "Now go 'long about your business. I won't have my animals woke up an' disturbed this way."

"I'm huntin' for two robbers in an open car!" shouted Mr. Boner.

"Well, I ain't two robbers in an open car," replied the farmer. "I'm a self-respectin' citizen in a nightshirt, an' what's more, I got a shotgun in my hand, and if you ain't gone in two minutes—"

Just then another car drove into the yard, and the sheriff got out. Mr. Bean's manner changed as soon as he recognized the newcomer. "Oh, how d'e do, sheriff?" he said. "Who is this feller? Friend of yours?"

The sheriff explained. They were combing the countryside for the two robbers who had been frightened away while trying to rob the Centerboro bank, and they wondered if Mr. Bean had seen or heard anything of them.

"I been in bed for three hours," said the farmer. "But there's

Freddy comin' across from the barn. Looks like he might have somethin' to show you. Now I'm goin' back to bed. Look around all you like, but for goodness' sake be quiet about it. I want them animals to get their sleep." And he shut down the window.

Meantime Freddy had come up to the sheriff. He raised a foreleg and waved it toward the barn.

"What is it, Freddy?" asked the sheriff. "You know somethin', I bet."

"Oh, that pig again!" exclaimed the disgusted detective. "Come along, sheriff, there ain't anything here."

"Not so fast," replied the sheriff. "I'm goin' to see." And he followed Freddy to the barn and up to the door of the stall, which was still being shaken by the imprisoned robbers.

"H'm," said the sheriff, lugging out his big pistol. "Looks like you'd caught something this time. Stand aside, animals." And he pulled out the peg.

The door gave way suddenly, and out tumbled Looey and Red.

"Stick up your hands!" said Mr. Boner, stepping forward. And as the discomfited robbers backed up against the wall with their hands in the air, he turned to the sheriff. "There's your prisoners, sheriff," he said dramatically. "I knew they were here all the time. That's why I stopped in here in the first place."

"Yeah?" said Looey. "Is that so! Well, let me tell you something. It wasn't you that caught us, city detective. You couldn't catch a lame snail."

"No back talk from you!" exclaimed Mr. Boner angrily. "If it wasn't me that caught you, who was it?"

"It was a little feller in a checked cap, if you want to know," said Looey. "And if all you detectives was as smart as him, you'd have caught us long ago."

"Here's your 'little feller,'" said the sheriff, pushing Freddy forward.

"There you go with your pig again," snorted the disgusted Boner. "I drove into this barnyard to look for 'em, didn't I? And they're here, ain't they? Well, then, who caught 'em? And who's going to believe that a pig could have done it?"

90

"The pig done it," said the sheriff doggedly, "and the pig ought to get the credit, *and* the reward!"

Looey and Red were staring at Freddy in amazement. "A pig!" exclaimed Red. "My gosh, Looey, a *pig*!"

"Pig, all right," replied Looey wearily. "Gee, we're a hot pair of robbers. Caught by a pig!" And then as Mr. Boner started in again to argue that it was he that should get the reward, Looey added: "Well, take us away and lock us up. Anywhere where we won't have to listen to this guy talk any more."

Mr. Bean, in his long white nightshirt and carrying a lantern, had appeared a few moments earlier in the barn door. "Trying to take the credit from my animals, is he?" he muttered. "We'll soon fix that." And he put his head outside and called softly: "Peter! Get rid of this fellow for us, will you?"

"And I want to tell *you* something too, Mr. Sheriff," Mr. Boner was saying. "You ain't done anything on this case, any more than your friend the pig has, and I'm going to give my own story of the capture to the newspapers, and don't you try to stop me. They're going to say that Mr. Montague Boner, the famous detective, was successful in putting an end to the depredations in upstate banking circles last night. With his brilliant capture of the two—"

Here he stopped, and abruptly, for something rough and furry had rubbed up against him. He turned to look. Peter, the

91

bear, was standing on his hind legs beside him, his mouth wide open, his arms spread out, looking twice his size in the flickering lantern-light.

Mr. Boner opened his mouth almost as wide as Peter's, and out of it came a long yell. Then he dashed for the door. He yelled as he reached the yard, and he continued to yell as he turned out of the gate and dashed off up the road, with Peter loping along easily a few feet behind him. The animals crowded to the door; they could see nothing, but they could hear those diminishing yells dying away in the direction of Centerboro, until at last through the calm night they came back as a thin thread of sound, like the whine of a mosquito. And presently that was gone too, and there was silence.

"Thank you, Mr. Bean, and animals all," said the sheriff. "I'll be getting along now. I'll be up in the morning, Freddy, to have you show me where all that stolen money is. I'll bring the reward with me. Come along, you two. Couple o'nice cells all made up for you, with clean towels and flowers in the vases and everything. Night, all."

Mr. Bean said good night; then he turned to the animals. "Now don't sit up talking half the night," he said gruffly. "Lots of time to go over it all tomorrow. I'm proud of you, Freddy." He patted the pig clumsily on the shoulder. "Good night." And he stumped off toward the house.

Lewis Carroll

THE LOBSTER QUADRILLE

"Will you walk a little faster?"
said a whiting to a snail,
"There's a porpoise close behind us,
and he's treading on my tail.
See how eagerly the lobsters
and the turtles all advance!
They are waiting on the shingle—
will you come and join the dance?
Will you, won't you, will you, won't you,
will you join the dance?
Will you, won't you, will you, won't you,
won't you join the dance?

"You can really have no notion how delightful it will be
When they take us up and throw us, with the lobsters out
 to sea!"
But the snail replied, "Too far, too far!" and gave a look
 askance—
Said he thanked the whiting kindly, but he would not join the
 dance.
 Would not, could not, would not, could not, would not join
  the dance.
 Would not, could not, would not, could not, would not join
  the dance.

"What matters it how far we go?" his scaly friend replied.
"The further off from England the nearer is to France.
There is another shore, you know, upon the other side.
Then turn not pale, beloved snail, but come and join the dance.
 Will you, won't you, will you, won't you, will you join the
  dance?"
 Will you, won't you, will you, won't you, won't you join the
  dance?"

Ray St. Clair

THE CANNERY BEAR

ILLUSTRATED BY *Esther Friend*

Once there was a bear who loved canned
salmon. Nothing else tasted good to him—honey, fresh fish, or
any of the other things that bears usually eat.

He had tried to get along by helping himself to cans of
salmon which the village people kept on their pantry shelves,
but he got into trouble too often. Housewives whacked him
with broom handles when they caught him, and they usually
did catch him because he was too big to get away quietly.

Then, too, his conscience bothered him. He was probably
stealing—and besides, he could not get as much canned salmon
as he needed.

So he gave this up. He got himself a job in the local salmon
cannery where they needed help so badly that they would hire
anyone, human or not.

"Now," he thought the first morning, "I am at the place where
all the canned salmon comes from. I can get enough for once."

But everybody worked so fast that the bear had no chance
to pause for a quiet bite of canned salmon. If he stopped for
just a moment his work piled up, and the foreman spoke sharply
to him.

He had a hard enough time to keep up with the humans because his new overalls were too tight for him to move freely, and his necktie choked him. He fell behind quite a bit at first until he happened to notice that the humans wore shoes only on their hind feet; so he removed the new shoes from his front paws. This helped, but he still felt discouraged at the end of the day.

As he rode his bicycle home from work that night he thought about his troubles. He ached in every muscle, and all four feet were blistered from the shoes. He was so tired that he fell off his bicycle even oftener than usual. His necktie still choked him, but he could not get it off.

Worst of all, he had not been able to get more than five or six cans of salmon. "I wish—," he thought, "I wish—" But he did not know what he wished because he was too tired to think. All he wanted was enough canned salmon, without all this trouble.

He dropped off to sleep as soon as he entered his cave, without even oiling his bicycle or trying once more to get his necktie off.

He dreamed that a little fuzzy bear flitted into his cave.

"Who are you?" he asked.

"I am a fairy bear!" she answered.

"I don't believe it!" he replied. "There is no such thing as a fairy bear, and besides, I'm dreaming!"

"That's right!" she agreed, smiling, "you *are* dreaming, and there *is* no such thing as a fairy bear. But here I am!" She tapped him lightly on each shoulder. "And I am going to grant your dearest wish."

"I still don't believe it," the bear insisted. "But suppose it is true, and you do get me a couple of cases of canned salmon. Will I get into trouble?" He had heard of what happens to people who get their wishes granted.

"Oh, dear no!" she exclaimed. "You are a good bear and you have already earned your wish." With that she vanished and the bear went on sleeping.

Next morning he felt much better. His rest had done him good, and some time during the night his necktie had come loose by itself so he could breathe. Also, though he did not know it, his overalls had split up the back. His shoes still hurt, but no more than could be expected seeing that they were on backwards.

He looked for the cases of canned salmon the fairy had promised, but they were not to be seen. "There is no such thing as fairies or magic!" said the bear firmly and went off to work.

That day went off fairly well. He was able to eat thirteen cans of salmon, hardly a mouthful really, but enough to keep his spirits up. His feet did not hurt too much, but a queer feeling in his shoulders bothered him.

"Lumbago?" he thought. "I must put liniment on them tonight."

So before he went to bed he rubbed his shoulders with some stove oil that a peddler had sold him as powerful liniment. Then he fell asleep.

He dreamed the little fairy bear flew into his cave again. She wrinkled her nose. "What's that awful smell?" she demanded.

"Liniment," the bear replied. "On my shoulders."

"Liniment nothing!" snapped the fairy bear. "That is common, old, smelly stove oil. Let me wipe it off." She cleaned him up with a pawful of grass. "What is the matter with your shoulders?" she asked.

"I got lumbago," he explained.

"Don't you worry about those shoulders," the fairy bear said. "They are doing fine!" Then she disappeared.

The bear really felt good next morning, better than he had for weeks. "It must be good luck," he thought, "to dream the same dream twice."

He was so gay that he forgot his bicycle. He skipped and leaped so lightly that his feet scarcely seemed to touch the ground.

Then he noticed that his feet were *not* touching the ground. "It can't be!" he exclaimed—but it was. He was really flying, and he could feel his shoulder muscles working the new wings. They were invisible, so he could not see them, but they were there!

"Wings!" he thought. "What do I want with wings? Who ever heard of a flying bear? I want canned salmon, not wings!" He sat down beside the path to think.

Suddenly the little fairy bear appeared before him. "Very nice!" she smiled. "A perfect fit."

"I'm dreaming again!" bellowed the bear. "And in broad daylight! This is all very nice indeed, but where's my canned salmon?"

The fairy bear chuckled. "I forgot to tell you about your Radar," she said.

"Never mind the Radar!" exclaimed the bear. "How about my salmon?"

"The Radar is important!" the fairy bear explained. "It is right on top of your head. You know what a Radar is, I suppose?"

"Yes, of course," shouted the bear. "But what about my canned salmon—"

"It works," the fairy bear continued, "just like any other Radar. You won't have any trouble with it." And she vanished.

The bear rubbed his nose. "I'm a flying bear," he wailed, "like nothing anybody ever heard tell of. Besides that, I've got a Radar outfit on top of my head—and nobody ever heard of that *either*." He sighed loudly. "I'm a freak, and my feet still hurt—and all because I wanted a little canned salmon."

Then he remembered that the wings and the Radar were invisible. At least nobody could see that he was a freak. So he went to work after all and managed to get eleven cans of salmon for his lunch. "I wish," he thought, "that I did not like canned salmon so much. It is such a nuisance working in the cannery!"

As he ate, he listened to the foreman talking to his assistant. "If that fishing fleet won't get here with its load until morning," he heard the foreman say, "I'll have to send everybody home. If it is only an hour or so out, I'll keep them here. I wish I knew!"

The bear thought for a moment about Radar and wings; then he said slowly, "I think I can find out for you."

The foreman understood enough Bear to follow this. "Go ahead," he said. "I hope you can!"

So the bear climbed the stairs to the roof. Then he flapped his wings and took off toward the sea, working his Radar. As plain as anything he saw the fleet headed in. He could even see the scales on the fish, and he saw that there was a huge catch.

He had to repeat the news several times to the foreman before he could understand the Bear talk, but at last he got the idea. "I don't know how you can be so sure," the foreman said, "with the fleet still two hours out. But I haven't any other information—so I'm going to take a chance on you. I'll keep the workers here, and I'll even put in a call for extra help. For your sake," he added, "I hope you are right."

So for two hours the bear and the foreman paced the floor. Neither said anything, but they were both thinking, and while the foreman chewed his fingernails the bear gnawed his paws.

At last the foreman said, "If you turn out to be right, I will pay you three cases of canned salmon every day to tell me when the fleet will come in and how big the catch is. Maybe you have some kind of instinct."

"I got a Radar," the bear explained.

"I don't understand Bear talk very well yet," said the foreman. "It sounded like something about a Radar. . . ."

And then the fleet arrived, with a huge load of fish, so the foreman did not finish the sentence. Instead, he clapped the bear on the back and shouted, "Here is your salmon, my boy. You did a good job! I'll call a truck to get it home for you."

The bear sighed deeply and grinned all over his face. "That fairy bear!" he thought gratefully.

Aloud he said, "Don't bother."

He pulled a case of canned salmon lovingly toward him.

"I'll eat it here."

Laura E. Richards

THE QUEEN OF THE ORKNEY ISLANDS

Oh! the Queen of the Orkney Islands,
She's traveling over the sea;
She's bringing a beautiful cuttlefish,
To play with my baby and me.

Oh! his head is three miles long, my dear,
His tail is three miles short.
And when he goes out he wriggles his snout,
In a way that no cuttlefish ought.

Oh! The Queen of the Orkney Islands,
She rides on a sea-green whale.
He takes her a mile, with an elegant smile,
At every flip of his tail. . .

Oh! the Queen of the Orkney Islands,
She dresses in wonderful taste;
The sea-serpent coils, all painted in oils,
Around her bee-you-tiful waist.

Oh! her gown is made of the green sea-kale;
And though she knows nothing of feet,
She can manage her train, with an air of disdain,
In a way that is perfectly sweet.

Oh! the Queen of the Orkney Islands,
She's traveling over the main.
So we'll hire a hack, and we'll take her straight back
To her beautiful Islands again.

Paul T. Gilbert

BERTRAM AND THE LION

ILLUSTRATED BY *Clarence Biers*

ONCE there was a little boy named Bertram. And he lived on Elm Street in a red house with a green roof. And he had a baby brother named Sam. Baby Sam had a nursemaid, and *her* name was Julia Krause. Julia was sixteen years old and was very pretty. She could draw pictures, and she knew no end of stories. Bertram liked her very much.

One night, after he had eaten seven slices of mince pie, Bertram had a bad dream. He dreamt that a lion was trying to crawl into bed with him. It was a regular nightmare. And because he couldn't get back to sleep again, Julia had come in to comfort him.

She had turned on the light, and now, perched on the foot of his bed in her pink pajamas, like a little Harlequin, she was telling him a story. She was telling him about Androcles and the Lion.

"And then," Julia was saying, "circus day came around. And in the morning there was a parade, with elephants and gold band wagons and a steam calliope and everything. So people came from miles around and brought their little boys and girls. And they had red lemonade and peanuts and balloons."

"Did they feed any peanuts to the elephants?" asked Bertram.

"Sure, they did," said Julia. "Bushels of them. Pop! Right into their greedy red mouths. Then, after the bareback riders and the acrobats had got through performing, the circus man said, 'All right, Androcles, you can go in and tame that lion now.'

"And Androcles said, 'Don't I get a whip or anything?' So the circus man gave him a little penny switch, and shoved him out into the ring, and laughed."

"That wasn't very nice, was it?" said Bertram.

102

So Bertram took the lion home.

"Of course it wasn't nice. But wait until you hear what happened." And Julia went on to tell him how the lion bounced out with his mouth open and made for Androcles with a roar that sent cold chills down his spine.

"Then, just as Androcles thought he was going to be bitten, the lion fawned on him and licked his hands. It was the very same lion whose paw he had taken a thorn out of when he was a runaway slave, living in a cave in the mountains. The king was so pleased that he let Androcles go, and Androcles and the lion lived together in the cave and became friends."

"Golly!" said Bertram sleepily. "I think it would be keen to have a lion you could be friends with."

"I don't know about that," said Julia, poking her toes into her little bedroom slippers which had fallen off. "Androcles lived a long time ago, and lions may have changed since then. Of course you might find one who would be chummy if you pulled a thorn out of its paw, but I wouldn't count on it too much. If I had my choice, I'd rather have a kitten."

"Aw, kittens are girls' pets," said Bertram. "Lions are lots nicer." Then he yawned and Julia, turning out the light, went back to her own bed.

Well, the next day Bertram was playing that he was a runaway slave. There was a little cave in the side of a hill back of his house, and he had fixed it up with a rag rug and magazine pictures on the wall, as Androcles had done.

It was almost suppertime when Bertram heard an awful yowling outside. He was scared a little at first, but he peeked out, and there, not ten feet away, he saw a great, big, yellow lion. The lion was limping along on three legs and holding up one of his front paws. He was yowling and groaning like everything.

"What's the matter?" asked Bertram. "Have you got a thorn in your paw?"

"Yes," said the lion. "A great, big one. Pull it out. It hurts something awful."

"Well, don't you bite then," said Bertram. And the lion crossed his heart.

103

"This is going to hurt a little," said Bertram, "but you mustn't cry." So he took the lion's paw in his lap and pulled out a perfectly nasty sharp thorn. The lion said, "Ouch!" but didn't bite. Then Bertram put a dandelion leaf over the wound and tied it up neatly with his clean pocket handkerchief.

The lion fawned on Bertram and began to lick his hands. Then he stood up on his hind legs and licked Bertram's face. Only Bertram didn't like that very much because the lion's tongue was sticky.

"Now we are friends," said the lion, "and if you love me as I love you, no knife can cut our love in two. Do you live here in this cave?"

"No," said Bertram. "I just play here. I live in a house. That house over there with the green roof."

"All right," said the lion. "I'll go home with you and we can live together. Won't that be nice!"

So Bertram took the lion home. He found an empty drygoods box and put some hay in it and nailed some slats across it. "There," he said, "that's your cage."

But the lion didn't like his cage. He wanted to live upstairs in the house. But Bertram's mama, when she heard about it, shook her head. "I don't quite approve of your keeping a lion in the house," she said. "Lions are so apt to bite. He might bite Baby Sam."

"Oh, he won't bite," said Bertram. "He's a tame lion, and

anyway, he's crossed his heart. Haven't you, lion?" And the lion said he had.

"Well, just to be on the safe side," said Bertram's mama, "I insist on his wearing a muzzle. Even if he only bit in play, he might tear your pants, and then I'd have to mend them, I suppose. As if I didn't have enough to do already."

So Bertram bought a muzzle at the dime store and put it on the lion. The lion said, "You'll take this off, of course, when we sit down to eat?"

"You mean at the table?" said Bertram.

"Why not? You're not going to treat me like a dog, are you? Me—your best friend!"

Bertram's mama grumbled a little, but she set an extra place at the supper table for the lion—opposite Baby Sam. Bertram's daddy wasn't there, of course, or he wouldn't have had it. He had gone to Omaha on business.

"I'm glad to see," said the lion, after he had tucked his napkin under his chin, "that my friend is eating his spinach. Spinach is good for him."

"That's what I keep telling him," said Bertram's mamma.

"I think he wants a second helping," said the lion.

"No, I don't," said Bertram. But he got the second helping just the same.

Then the lion noticed that Bertram was picking at his meat. He was picking all the fat off and eating only the lean.

"See here, my little friend," said the lion. "That won't do at all. You eat that fat—every bit of it and lick the platter clean."

"But it's all cold," protested Bertram, who just hated fat.

"That doesn't make any difference," said the lion sternly. "Do as you're told."

So Bertram had to eat the cold fat, and it simply spoiled his supper.

When bedtime came, the lion made a fuss about going down to his cage. "I want to sleep with my little friend," he said. "It will be lots chummier than sleeping in a cage, and we can tell each other stories. Besides, I have bad dreams when I sleep alone."

Then Bertram remembered his bad dream, which seemed as if it now were coming true. But he was afraid the lion might get mad and forget his promise if he crossed him. So—very reluctantly—he gave the lion one of his daddy's nightgowns, and after they had brushed their teeth, the two piled into bed, and Bertram's mamma tucked them in. However, the lion snored so loudly that Bertram couldn't sleep. And a flea bit him. And the lion kept rolling over and pulling off all the covers.

When Bertram's mamma came to make the bed next morning,

she said, "See here, if you're going to let that lion sleep with you, you'll have to wash him. Look at this bed! Just look at it! All full of hair and sand and burrs."

So Bertram took the lion down to the basement and put him in the laundry tub and gave him a good scrubbing. But the lion wiggled and squirmed and carried on so when Bertram tried to wash his ears that he slopped water all over him, and soaked him to the skin.

"Now let's play something," said the lion, after Bertram had changed his clothes. "Let's play parchesi or something."

Bertram got out the parchesi board, and they began to play, only the lion didn't play fair. He made a fuss every time Bertram sent one of his men home. And he'd take the man and put it back on the board again. And so, of course, he always won. The lion won seventeen games in succession.

"This isn't any fun," said Bertram. "You cheat. It's no fair when you win all the time."

"It is, too, fun," said the lion. "It's more fun than I've had in a dog's age. It's your turn to shake first." And the lion handed Bertram the dice box.

Well, they might have gone on playing all the afternoon only George Fish came over and yoo-hooed for Bertram. But the lion went out on the front porch and said, "What do you want?"

And George said, "I want Bertram."

"Well, you can't have him," said the lion. "He's playing parchesi with me, and I'm his chum. Go away or I'll bite you."

"I won't," said George Fish. "Go away yourself."

Then the lion bounced up in the air and made for George Fish with a *yowl*. George turned and ran. He ran as fast as his fat legs would carry him. And all the people cried, "Look out!" and climbed up lamp posts. But George's mamma saw him coming and opened the door just in time for him to tumble in head first before the lion could grab him. It was a mercy!

Bertram had hidden the parchesi board, and when the lion came back, he said, "I've got to do my homework."

"Oh, all right," said the lion. "Then I'll look at your picture book."

107

So Bertram began to study his arithmetic, and the lion got down one of his favorite picture books and turned the pages with his tongue and got them all sticky. And when Bertram tried to take the book away from him, the lion made a fuss.

"You're a fine friend!" said the lion. "Can't a fellow even look at your book?"

"I'm not going to be friends any more," said Bertram, "if you treat my nice new picture book like that."

Bertram was disgusted with the lion, only he didn't know how to get rid of him. At suppertime the lion made Bertram eat more spinach and fat. And when they went to bed, the lion snored again and pulled off all the covers. The next morning Bertram had a cold.

Then, that very afternoon, he came down with the measles. Bertram's mamma sent for the doctor, but the lion wouldn't let him come into the room. "He'll give him nasty medicine," he said, "and make him stick out his tongue and say 'Ah.' You leave my little friend alone."

And every time Bertram's mamma or Julia Krause tried to get into the room, the lion shooed them away too.

So the doctor said, "Well, I guess he's got measles all right. Measles are going around now something awful. Keep him in a dark room and give him plenty of spinach but no pie. And here are some pills. Give him one of these three times a day."

At first they didn't know how to get the pills to Bertram. But finally Julia Krause thought of a way. She took Bertram's little toy locomotive and wound it up and put the pills in the tender. Then she tied a string to the locomotive and ran it in, and Bertram took one of the pills and felt better. Then Julia put Bertram's spinach on a little wagon with spool wheels—it was Baby Sam's wagon—and tied that to the locomotive. And the locomotive pulled it in.

But Bertram got lonesome without anybody but the lion to keep him company. "I want Julia Krause," he said. "I want her to tell me a story."

But the lion said, "*I'll* tell you a story. I'll tell you a story about Jack-a-Nory, and now—"

"But I don't want *that* story," said Bertram. "That's Mother Goose. I'm not a baby. I want one of Julia Krause's stories—the one about the Oyster Mayor or the Duchess."

"Oh, all right," said the lion. "I'll tell you another about his brother—"

"I don't want that one either," said Bertram. And he began to kick and cry. And Julia Krause peeked in and felt so sorry for him that she cried too.

"Oh, I wish you'd go home where you belong, you old lion," sobbed Bertram. "I hate you, and you're just a horrid old donkey, so there."

But the lion only fawned on him and licked his hands.

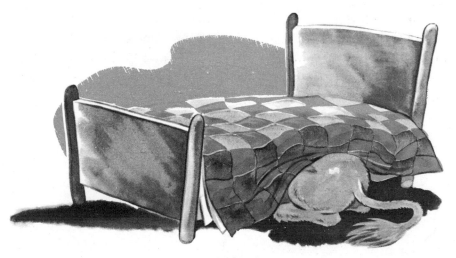

Well, you'd never guess what happened. The very next day the lion came down with the measles and my, but didn't he make a fuss! He wanted Julia Krause to tell him a story, but she wouldn't.

Then the doctor came and felt his pulse and made him stick out his tongue and say "Ah!" And then he said, "Plenty of spinach, but no fresh meat of any kind, *and no pie*. And give him a tablespoonful of sulphur and molasses every half hour."

Now sulphur and molasses is about the nastiest medicine anybody can take. So when the lion saw the medicine and smelled it, he crawled under the bed and tried to hide like a naughty little boy. But Julia Krause pulled him out by the tail and held his nose while she poured the sulphur and molasses down his throat. And *how* the lion screamed and yowled and acted up!

Then Julia put Bertram to bed in the spare room and gave him ice cream.

After a while both Bertram and the lion got well. And the lion came and poked his nose into the spare room and made a face at Bertram and said, "All right for you! That's what I get for being nice to a squirmy little pollywog like you. You go and give me the measles, and I can't have any pie, and I have to take that awful medicine. Bah! I'm mad at you. I think you're an old meanie."

And with that, the lion stalked majestically out of the house. But Bertram only laughed. That night Julia sat on the foot of his bed again, telling him a story.

"And so the Oyster Mayor said that if I'd teach him some of my cat's cradles, he'd take me to the codfish ball. And then—"

But Bertram was asleep.

Ogden Nash

THE RHINOCEROS

The rhino is a homely beast,
For human eyes he's not a feast.
Farewell, farewell, you old rhinoceros,
I'll stare at something less prepoceros!

Ogden Nash

THE PANTHER

The panther is like a leopard,
Except it hasn't been peppered.
Should you behold a panther crouch,
Prepare to say OUCH.
Better yet, if called by a panther,
Don't anther.

Thomas C. O'Donnell

THE PINK GIRAFFE

The pink giraffe lives in a tree,
　The upper part, I mean;
His legs are down with you and me,
　The rest is in between.

THE OLD WOMAN AND THE TRAMP

ILLUSTRATED BY *Ruth van Tellingen*

THERE was once a tramp, who went plodding his way through a forest. The distance between the houses was so great that he had little hope of finding a shelter before the night set in. But all of a sudden he saw some lights between the trees. He then discovered a cottage, where there was a fire burning on the hearth. How nice it would be to roast oneself before that fire and to get a bite of something, he thought; and so he dragged himself towards the cottage.

Just then an old woman came towards him.

"Good evening, and well met!" said the tramp.

"Good evening," said the woman. "Where do you come from?"

"South of the sun, and east of the moon," said the tramp; "and now I am on the way home again, for I have been all over the world with the exception of this parish," he said.

"You must be a great traveler, then," said the woman. "What may be your business here?"

"Oh, I want a shelter for the night," he said.

"I thought as much," said the woman; "but you may as well get away from here at once, for my husband is not at home, and my place is not an inn," she said.

"My good woman," said the tramp, "you must not be so cross and hard-hearted, for we are both human beings, and should help one another, it is written."

"Help one another?" said the woman. "Help? Did you ever hear such a thing? Who'll help me, do you think? I haven't got a morsel in the house! No, you'll have to look for quarters elsewhere," she said.

Reprinted by permission of the publishers, J. B. Lippincott Company from *Fairy Tales from the Swedish* by N. G. Djurklou. Copyright, 1920, by J. B. Lippincott Company.

But the tramp was like the rest of his kind; he did not consider himself beaten at the first rebuff. Although the old woman grumbled and complained as much as she could, he was just as persistent as ever and went on begging and praying like a starved dog, until at last she gave in, and he got permission to lie on the floor for the night.

That was very kind, he thought, and he thanked her for it.

"Better on the floor without sleep, than suffer cold in the forest deep," he said; for he was a merry fellow, this tramp, and was always ready with a rhyme.

When he came into the room he could see that the woman was not so badly off as she had pretended; but she was a greedy and stingy woman of the worst sort, and was always complaining and grumbling.

He now made himself very agreeable, of course, and asked her in his most insinuating manner for something to eat.

"Where am I to get it from?" said the woman. "I haven't tasted a morsel myself the whole day."

But the tramp was a cunning fellow, he was.

"Poor old granny, you must be starving," he said. "Well, well, I suppose I shall have to ask you to have something with me, then."

"Have something with you!" said the woman. "You don't look as if you could ask any one to have anything! What have you got to offer one, I should like to know?"

"He who far and wide does roam sees many things not known at home; and he who many things has seen has wits about him and senses keen," said the tramp. "Better dead than lose one's head! Lend me a pot, grannie!"

The old woman now became very inquisitive, as you may guess, and so she let him have a pot.

He filled it with water and put it on the fire, and then he blew with all his might till the fire was burning fiercely all round it. Then he took a four-inch nail from his pocket, turned it three times in his hand and put it into the pot.

The woman stared with all her might.

"What's this going to be?" she asked.

"Nail broth," said the tramp, and began to stir the water with the porridge stick.

"Nail broth?" asked the woman.

"Yes, nail broth," said the tramp.

The old woman had seen and heard a good deal in her time, but that anybody could have made broth with a nail, well, she had never heard the like before.

"That's something for poor people to know," she said, "and I should like to learn how to make it."

"That which is not worth having, will always go a-begging," said the tramp.

But if she wanted to learn how to make it she had only to watch him, he said, and went on stirring the broth.

The old woman squatted on the ground, her hands clasping her knees, and her eyes following his hand as he stirred the broth.

"This generally makes good broth," he said; "but this time it will very likely be rather thin, for I have been making broth the whole week with the same nail. If one only had a handful of sifted oatmeal to put in, that would make it all right," he said. "But what one has to go without, it's no use thinking more about," and so he stirred the broth again.

114

"Well, I think I have a scrap of flour somewhere," said the old woman, and went out to fetch some, and it was both good and fine.

The tramp began putting the flour into the broth, and went on stirring, while the woman sat staring now at him and then at the pot until her eyes nearly burst their sockets.

"This broth would be good enough for company," he said, putting in one handful of flour after another. "If I had only a bit of salted beef and a few potatoes to put in, it would be fit for gentlefolks, however particular they might be," he said. "But what one has to go without, it's no use thinking more about."

When the old woman really began to think it over, she thought she had some potatoes, and perhaps a bit of beef as well; and these she gave the tramp, who went on stirring, while she sat and stared as hard as ever.

"This will be grand enough for the best in the land," he said.

"Well, I never!" said the woman; "and just fancy—all with a nail!"

He was really a wonderful man, that tramp! He could do more than drink a sup and turn the tankard up, he could.

"If one had only a little barley and a drop of milk, we could ask the king himself to have some of it," he said; "for this is what he has every blessed evening—that I know, for I have been in service under the king's cook," he said.

115

"Dear me! Ask the king to have some! Well, I never!" exclaimed the woman, slapping her knees. She was quite awestruck at the tramp and his grand connections.

"But what one has to go without, it's no use thinking more about," said the tramp.

And then she remembered she had a little barley; and as for milk, well, she wasn't quite out of that, she said, for her best cow had just calved. And then she went to fetch both the one and the other.

The tramp went on stirring, and the woman sat staring, one moment at him and the next at the pot.

Then all at once the tramp took out the nail.

"Now it's ready, and now we'll have a real good feast," he said. "But to this kind of soup the king and the queen always take a dram or two, and one sandwich at least. And then they always have a cloth on the table when they eat," he said. "But what one has to go without, it's no use thinking more about."

But by this time the old woman herself had begun to feel quite grand and fine, I can tell you; and if that was all that was wanted to make it just as the king had it, she thought it would be nice to have it just the same way for once, and play at being king and queen with the tramp. She went straight to a cupboard and brought out the brandy bottle, dram glasses, butter and cheese, smoked beef and veal, until at last the table looked as if it were decked out for company.

Never in her life had the old woman had such a grand feast, and never had she tasted such broth, and just fancy, made only with a nail!

She was in such a good and merry humor at having learnt such an economical way of making broth that she did not know how to make enough of the tramp who had taught her such a useful thing.

So they ate and drank, and drank and ate, until they became both tired and sleepy.

The tramp was now going to lie down on the floor. But that would never do, thought the old woman. "Such a grand person must have a bed to lie in," she said.

116

He did not need much pressing. "It's just like the sweet Christmastime," he said, "and a nicer woman I never came across. Ah, well! Happy are they who meet with such good people," said he; and he lay down on the bed and went asleep.

And next morning when he woke the first thing he got was coffee and a dram.

When he was going the old woman gave him a bright dollar piece.

"And thanks, many thanks, for what you have taught me," she said. "Now I shall live in comfort, since I have learnt how to make broth with a nail."

"Well, it isn't very difficult, if one only has something good to add to it," said the tramp as he went his way.

The woman stood at the door staring after him.

"Such people don't grow on every bush," she said.

THE YOUNG LADY'S EYES

Edward Lear

There was a young lady whose eyes
Were unique as to color and size;
   When she opened them wide,
   People all turned aside,
And started away in surprise.

117

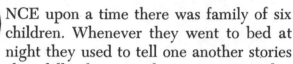

Hugh Lofting

THE CRAZY STORY
OF DIZZY LIZZIE

ILLUSTRATED BY THE AUTHOR

ONCE upon a time there was family of six children. Whenever they went to bed at night they used to tell one another stories to pass the time till they fell asleep. In the summer months, when the daylight was long, they held what they called "The Longest Story Competition"—to see who could tell the longest story. It was a great success and was won by the oldest of the boys.

Then they had many other competitions: for The Most Thrilling Story; for The Funniest Story; for The Saddest Story; and for The Shortest Story.

Finally competitions had been won and prizes received by all the children—except the youngest girl. She had won nothing, and there did not seem to be any competition left to invent.

But one night when the children were talking it over in bed she said, "I know of one. And I bet you all I win it."

"What is it?" asked the others.

"It's the Craziest Story Competition," said the youngest. "Let's see who can tell the craziest story."

But the rest wouldn't go in for such a contest, for they prided themselves on being sensible. Nevertheless the youngest held it anyway and gave herself the prize. And because none of the others had a story to tell that night they listened to hers.

And this is the tale she told:

There was once a little girl and her name was Dizzy Lizzie. The way she got this name was rather peculiar: at school the geography teacher was explaining to the class how the earth revolved about the sun.

"Oh," said Lizzie, "does the earth spin round?"

"Certainly," said the teacher.

118

"Which way does it spin?"

"From left to right," the teacher told her.

"Ah," cried Lizzie, "now I know what makes me so dizzy. I never could spin that way without feeling funny in the head."

And always after that they called her Dizzy Lizzie.

Lizzie just loved to be crazy.

"People," she used to say, "who are never crazy don't know what they miss. Myself, I get no end of pleasure out of being crazy—especially after a big meal. Anybody can be just sensible. But to be interestingly crazy is a great gift. I often think that is the surest sign that I am a remarkable woman. Most of the great women in history were somewhat crazy. Why, look at Cleopatrick: she swallowed a pearl worth a fortune. I never did anything as crazy as that—though to be sure I did swallow a pearl shirt button once."

Occasionally Lizzie, when her parents were away, gave what she called crazy parties. She sent out invitation cards—and on them was written: *Dizzy Lizzie at Home this afternoon. Refreshments will be served in the woodshed at four o'clock. Everybody Welcome (except mad dogs and sensible people).*

These parties were very gay affairs. Everybody acted in the craziest way he could think of. The guests arrived in wheelbarrows and drank tea standing on their heads.

One of Dizzy Lizzie's hobbies was making maps. She had a place she called her "studio"—it was really a linen closet. And here she made maps of all sorts of things. Her atlas was quite different from most. It contained such pages as, "Map of my Toy Box"; "Map of my Doll's Bathroom"; "Map of my Father's Face," etc. She was a very unusual girl.

Dizzy Lizzie was a butcher's daughter, and for pets she had two little hot dogs which she always took everywhere with her, tied on the end of a string. She called them Soss and Sidge.

She also had a brother, called Aloysius the Awkward. He was a very peculiar boy—indeed the whole family was rather odd. When Aloysius was very young he stepped on his tongue. That shows how awkward he was. Curious people often would ask him how it happened, and he would say, "Oh, it was a hot day.

119

My tongue was out, hanging around loose, you know. We were playing shop. And while serving a customer I stepped on it. That's all."

Besides being very awkward Aloysius was also very idle. He hated even the work of putting on his clothes in the morning and taking them off at night. One day he met a sailor who had pictures of anchors tatooed on his arms. This gave Aloysius an idea. He got the sailor to tatoo a collar and tie on his neck for him, and socks on his ankles, so he wouldn't have so much trouble dressing in the morning. He wanted to have a coat and pants done that way too. But the sailor said he would find it rather cold in winter.

Aloysius also hated having his ears washed. And it was he who invented linen ears that you could take off and send to the laundry to be cleaned, the same as collars and cuffs.

As I have told you, Dizzy Lizzie loved to be crazy. But her parents didn't care for it. She had often asked them to allow her one crazy day a week, but they wouldn't listen to her. And for this reason, because they would never let her be as crazy as she liked, Lizzie was always trying to lose her parents. But every time she got away from them somebody always told them where she was and she would be found and brought home.

However, one day, after trying for years to lose her parents, she succeeded—by an accident which led her through many strange adventures. This is how it happened:

Lizzie and Aloysius were returning from school. Their home lay at the foot of the hill. From the top they saw their parents leaving the house to go shopping in the town.

"Ah!" said Lizzie. "After they've gone we can have a nice crazy time. Let's get behind that tree till they are out of sight."

But in trying to hurry behind the tree, Aloysius tripped over his own hair, which was very long, and went rolling down to the bottom of the hill. There he knocked his head against his own doorstep, and all the mathematics he had learned that day at school were spilled all over the road. The parents then told Aloysius and Lizzie to come with them, and the two children had to go shopping with their mother and father.

120

Now Lizzie had a loose tooth. She was always wondering when it would come out. Aloysius had a tooth missing in the front and he could whistle very loud through the hole where it used to be. Lizzie wanted to be able to whistle like that too. A dozen times a day she would look into the mirror to see if her tooth was any looser. She spent so much time doing this that her mother put her mirror up against the ceiling where Lizzie couldn't reach it. Then Lizzie used to look at her tooth through a telescope.

Well, on this walk through the town the parents went into a shop to buy something and left the children to wait outside.

"I wish," said Lizzie to Aloysius, "I knew some way to get this tooth out without its hurting me. Father won't pull it for me—he says it isn't loose enough yet—even though it's a first tooth. How did you ever manage to get yours out, Aloysius?"

"It's quite simple," said her brother. "You tie a string around it. Then you fasten the other end to the handle of a door, sit down, and get someone to slam the door for you. And the tooth is jerked out as easy as anything."

"Oh," said Lizzie, "I think I'll try that."

"I've got a string in my pocket," said Aloysius. "I'll tie it on for you."

Her brother fastened the string firmly about her tooth. Then they looked around for a door to tie the other end to.

"We can't use the shop door. Mother and Father might see us," said Aloysius.

But just at that moment a stagecoach came down the street and stopped before the shop to let a passenger alight.

"Why not fasten it to the coach door?" whispered Lizzie.

"Good idea!" said Aloysius.

And creeping up behind the carriage, so he would not be seen by the driver, he tied the string to the door-handle.

"Now," he said to Lizzie, "you sit down in the road and I'll slam the door."

But before Lizzie had time to sit down the coach started off.

Now her father had been right: her tooth wasn't nearly loose enough to come out yet. And it held fast. And presently poor

Lizzie found herself being dragged along the road, fastened to a stagecoach by her front tooth.

She squealed a loud squeal, and Aloysius shouted. Then two lady passengers looked out of the window and *they* screamed. That made the horses take fright, and suddenly they bolted and went galloping down the road like wild fire.

At first Lizzie ran behind the coach trying to keep up. But presently, as the horses went faster and faster, her feet left the ground altogether. And at last she was just sailing along on the wind, like a rag tied to the end of a string.

The driver did his best to stop the runaway horses, but they were thoroughly frightened and they went on for miles and miles. Goodness only knows how far Lizzie would have traveled but for the next town. There, going round a sharp turn at the far end of the market place, she caught hold of the top of a signpost and clung for all she was worth. The coach tore madly on without her. With a jerk, Lizzie's tooth came out and followed it—leaving Lizzie on the post.

Before she got down she read the writing on the sign and found that she had traveled twenty miles. Also she found that

122

she could now whistle beautifully, the same as Aloysius.

"Well," she said as she slid down to the ground and started off to explore the town (she had never been abroad before), "it was a rough ride but I've lost my tooth—*and* I've lost my parents. Now I can be as crazy as I like."

The town which Lizzie had come to was inhabited by two races of people, the Shrivelkites and the Hiccupheimers. The Shrivelkites were little shriveled up, dwarfish people, rather like small dried apples to look at. They did not amount to much. By far the larger portion of the population were the Hiccupheimers. These were not so strange to look at but very peculiar to listen to. For hundreds of years this people had been afflicted with hiccups. Although visitors found it very odd, they themselves had long since got used to it and treated it as quite an ordinary thing. They had made a language out of hiccups. They even had hiccup operas.

Lizzie had many adventures in this town, but the greatest of them came about through her meeting with the cross-eyed family. While going through the market place she met a small cross-eyed boy who said to her, "What makes your neck so long?"

"It isn't long," said Lizzie. "You're cross-eyed."

"I know that," said the little boy proudly. "All of my family are cross-eyed. But your neck *is* long—the longest I ever saw. Why don't you tie a bow in it?"

Then Lizzie put her hand up to her neck and found that what the little boy had said was true: it was twice as long as it used to be.

"Oh, well," she said, "I suppose it got stretched. I've just had an adventure with a coach. Goodness! It *is* long, isn't it? Never mind. All the better. I won't be so easily recognized. I have escaped from my parents."

"By coach?" asked the little boy.

"Well, yes—by coach and string. I wanted to be crazy, and my parents wouldn't let me. Do you like being crazy?"

"Oh, yes," said the little boy, looking more cross-eyed than ever, "I just *love* it."

"Fine!" said Lizzie. "Then let's be crazy together. But first I must have something to eat. I'm hungry."

"Well, come to have tea with us," said the little boy. "My family will just be sitting down to it now."

So Lizzie went off and had tea with the little boy's family. They were, as he had told her, all cross-eyed like himself. They had curious, twisting corkscrew stairs to their houses because they couldn't see straight to go up ordinary ones. But they were very nice people. There were five children altogether, and the smallest one was very tiny. She walked about the table munching a large crumb during the meal. And she was always falling into her father's teacup. Lizzie, the only member of the party who wasn't cross-eyed, had to fish her out with a teaspoon.

After a large meal (they had ham and eggs and jam tarts and all sorts of things that Lizzie liked) she felt in a perfectly splendid mood for craziness, and she and the little boy went off seeking adventures. They began by having a bet with one another—that they should go outside the town and climb every tree they met. This they did and had a good deal of fun over it. But finally they came to an enormously high tree. The little boy couldn't climb this, but Lizzie went right to the top of it. Standing in the fork of the branches, she got a splendid view of the sea. But when she started to come down she found that her foot was stuck in the fork. She tugged and tugged but she couldn't get it free. So the little boy, seeing that she was stuck, went and told his father. His father came, bringing the Mayor with him; and the Mayor brought the Town Engineer.

"Dear me!" said the father gazing up into the tree. "The steeple jack will have to carry up her meals to her till we can think of a way to get her down."

"Cut the tree down and carry her home in it," said the Mayor.

"No, no," said the Engineer. "The tree would be too heavy if you did chop it down. There's only one way to get that child out: bend the top of the tree down—with ropes—and let it snap back upright again. She will then be thrown clear out of it into the sea. Have a boat waiting to pick her up and she can be brought safely to shore."

Well, that was what they did. But the tree was very strong, and great numbers of workmen and ropes and pulleys were required to bend the top of it down. And when at last they did let it go, it snapped back with such force that Lizzie was sent on another journey even longer than the one by coach. She was sailing out to sea, right over the boat which was waiting for her, on and on and on.

Lizzie's parents, who had followed her in the next coach, arrived at the town just as Lizzie left it. The Mayor said he was sorry he could not tell them where their daughter was. When last seen, he said, she was traveling through the air towards the next country, which lay some thirty miles across the sea to the westward.

Lizzie after her experience with the coach was almost getting used to traveling through the air. But on this journey she went at such a speed she hardly had time to think at all. In the middle of her flight she bumped into a wild goose who was flying home after his summer vacation.

"Good gracious!" cried the goose rubbing the shoulder of his wing with his foot. "Why don't you look where you're going?"

"How can I?" said Lizzie, "when I don't even know where I'm going."

Indeed she was for the first time beginning to feel that she would like to *find* her parents again. Her voyages and experiences were getting a little too crazy—even for her. And she determined that as soon as she struck solid earth she would set about making her way home.

But alas! more adventures and stranger ones yet awaited her. When she finally began coming down she saw that she was falling into the middle of a large town situated on an island. In fact she landed exactly in the center of the market square. Now it happened that workmen were repaving the square at this moment. And they were using an enormous roller, drawn by six teams of horses, to make the paving smooth and firm. Unfortunately Lizzie landed right in front of this enormous roller; and before anyone had time to pick her up or stop the horses the roller passed right over her and rolled her out flat.

Of course, as soon as people realized what had happened, there was tremendous excitement. A policeman rushed up and asked Lizzie for her name and address to put in his notebook. But poor Lizzie had been so flattened that even her voice had been squashed out of her—together with her name and address and everything else she had ever remembered.

People gathered around in crowds, wondering what ought to be done. And presently the king of the island, hearing the commotion, came out of his palace to see about it. And with him came his Foreign Secretary.

"Goodness gracious!" said the Secretary. "Just look at that! She reminds me of the pressed flowers I used to keep in an album as a boy. What shall we do with her, Your Majesty?"

"She looks to me," said the King, "like a foreign child. We had better put her in an envelope and send her back to her parents by mail."

So an envelope was brought and Lizzie was folded up like a sheet of note paper and put inside.

"I will write a letter to her father and enclose it," said the King. "She will be Spanish by the looks of her. Bring me my Spanish pen."

Now this king had a very remarkable set of pens. They had been given him by a famous magician. Anybody who possessed these pens did not have to have any education at all. He did not even have to know how to write. For each pen wrote letters in a different language. You merely had to *think* your message and hold the pen on the paper, and it wrote it down in French or Greek or what not, according to the pen you chose.

But the stupid Foreign Secretary, still thinking about his pressed flower album, made a mistake; and instead of bringing the King the Spanish pen, he brought the Persian pen. And then of course His Majesty's letter was written in Persian and a Persian address was put on the envelope. And after a postage stamp had been stuck on Lizzie, she was dropped in the letter box outside the General Post Office of the town. And that is how our heroine (who was now more anxious than ever to get back to her parents) started off on another journey by mail which carried her even farther away from her mother and father than she was already.

127

HUGH LOFTING

In Persia, Dizzy Lizzie was delivered at the palace of a very extraordinary gentleman, known as Pussywillow Pish-Tush, the Persian Philanderer. She was pushed under the front door of his palace by the postman early in the morning.

Pussywillow was probably the oddest man in Asia. His father had been a merchant prince and he was enormously, fabulously rich. He was so rich that the pigs of his farms had diamond rings in their noses instead of iron ones. His palace was as big as a town and he had a great number of servants and retainers. He loved new things of any kind. And having many, many friends he was always receiving presents.

When he opened Lizzie's envelope at breakfast and looked inside he gave a little gurgle of pleasure and rang a gold bell that stood on the table. The bell was answered by his Grand Vizier, Ali Boobi.

"Boobi," said Pussywillow, "some good friend has sent me a present of a new kind of balloon. It seems to be in the shape of a child. But it needs to be blown up. Take it to the Master of the Revels and have him pump it up for me, please. I will play with it on the terrace after breakfast."

"Very good, your Excellency," said the Grand Vizier. And he put Lizzie back in her envelope and took her away.

128

Then Lizzie was blown up with an air pump by the Master of the Revels. She got bigger and bigger, and rounder and rounder and rounder, and still he went on pumping. But just before she thought she was going to burst he stopped.

Although she was now enormously large, Lizzie felt very light and airy. She began to dance. But the first spring she took, she bumped her head against the ceiling and then came down to the floor very, very slowly—just like a balloon.

"Dear me!" she thought. "I must be careful. I don't seem to weigh more than a feather."

She was taken out on to the Terrace. And after breakfast Pussywillow came to play with her. While he was bouncing her up and down imagine his astonishment to find that his new balloon talked!

"Be careful of the wind," said Lizzie. "A sudden gust of wind could easily blow me over the palace wall."

"Good gracious!" cried the Persian Philanderer. "The balloon speaks! This is something very new. Were you sent me by the Empress of China?"

"No," said Lizzie. "I was sent by a mistake. They meant to mail me back to my parents. I'm not a balloon. I'm a real person."

"By the Prophet's beard!" gasped Pussywillow. "I had no idea—tell me, how does it feel to be blown up?"

"Sort of light in the head and crazy in the feet," said Lizzie; "otherwise very pleasant."

"But how did you get so flat?" asked the Philanderer. "So you could fit into an envelope?"

"I ran away from my parents—or rather I got pulled away by a coach; and after many adventures I was run over by a big roller and flattened. Oh, look out! Hold me, here comes the wind!"

But before Pussywillow could catch her, the wind suddenly pushed Lizzie over and rolled her down the terrace like a straw hat. The Philanderer ran after her; but another, stronger, gust of wind swept her up into the air and she sailed over the palace roof like a piece of thistledown. Then Pussywillow called

for his tame storks and sent them up after her. And it required
six of them to drag her back to earth.

"It's very embarrassing," said Lizzie when she had been
returned to the terrace, "to get blown away in the middle of
conversation like that. I'm afraid you'll think me an awfully
frivolous person."

"Oh, not at all," said the Philanderer. "Anyway, I like frivolous people. Sit down here and hold on to the seat. Would you
like a piece of string to tie yourself down with? No? All right.
Now tell me: Why did you wish to get away from your
parents?"

"They wouldn't let me be crazy," said Lizzie. "I tried to get
them to allow me one crazy day a week. But they wouldn't
do that."

"What peculiar people!" said Pussywillow. "Here we have
no objection to craziness whatever. Make yourself thoroughly
at home. I have several thousand children of my own. They are
at their lessons now. But when the comic arithmetic class is
over you will see my children—and you will hear them."

"When the *what* class is over?" asked Lizzie.

"The comic arithmetic class," the Philanderer repeated. "My children found the old-fashioned mathematics rather dull. So I hired a Chinese comedian to liven it up a bit. He teaches the multiplication tables by drawing pictures and telling funny stories about them. You'd be surprised to find how much they learn that way."

"Are the children allowed to make all the noise they like?" asked Lizzie.

"Yes," said Pussywillow. "But only in certain parts of the palace—and only certain kinds of noises. This terrace for instance is called the Titter Terrace. It was built specially for children who titter. Inside the big dome on the top floor you will find the Giggling Gallery—where the children can run around and giggle all they like. And beyond the stables at the bottom of the garden you will find the Yelling Yard where the noisiest can go and let off steam whenever they wish. Yes, I believe in children having a good time. The only thing I can't stand is children who whine. And for them we have the Whine Cellar, underneath the icehouse. There whining children are put till they have learned to make some more cheerful kind of noise and then they are let out. You'd better have my Chief Silkworm take you round the establishment and show you everything. By the way, are you bothered by nightmares at all?"

"Yes, I am sometimes," said Lizzie.

"Drop in on the Head Nursery Physician. You will find his office in the left wing of the Children's Dormitory Building. He will give you a few of his Comic Dream Pills. You will find them excellent."

"What are they for?" asked Lizzie.

"To give you cheerful dreams instead of nightmares," said Pussywillow. "I believe in encouraging the sciences. I got this physician to work out a special pill which would produce comic dreams—even for people who had very little sense of humor. They are very popular with the children. You will often hear them giggling all through the night after taking them."

So later in the day Lizzie was introduced to the Philanderer's three thousand children and found them very good company. She was taken over the whole of the enormous palace by the Chief Silkworm who wore silk pyjamas on all of his sixteen legs. She was shown all the sights, including Pussywillow's gigantic thoroughbred Chinese wolfhound. This creature was so well-bred and haughty that he was too proud even to wag his own tail. He had another little dog to wag it for him whenever he wanted to show that he was pleased. Before going to bed Lizzie took one of the Nursery Doctor's Comic Dream Pills and spent a most amusing night. When she awoke in the morning her ribs were quite sore from laughing at the funny dreams she had had.

She found very little inconvenience from being so light and flimsy, after she once got used to it. But she was always careful, when the wind was strong, to hang on to something so she wouldn't be blown away.

On the first morning, however, when she took her bath she discovered a curious thing: she couldn't sink. She just bobbed about on the top of the water like an empty paper bag. And it was through this that she invented the bath-anchor. She wore it round her waist, tied to a silver chain, to weight her down. For that was the only way she could get wet all over.

She usually took her bath-anchor with her when she went bathing in the sea beyond the palace walls. But one day, when several of the children rushed into her room and invited her to go bathing, she ran off with them and forgot to take it with her. It had been a calm day. But no sooner had she jumped into the surf than a squall came up; and before she had time to call for help she was being wafted out to sea on the surface of the water. She was blown right down the Persian Gulf, across the Indian Ocean, round the Cape of Good Hope, and all the way home to her own country.

Her parents, who had given her up for lost, were overjoyed at her return. So was Aloysius the Awkward. He had not whistled since she had left, sorrowfully blaming himself that his advice about the loose tooth had caused his sister's tragic disappearance. He put on a clean pair of linen ears to celebrate her return. In fact the whole family was so delighted to see her

that Lizzie thought this would be a good time to ask for something. And what do you think she asked for? The same old thing—one crazy day a week. And to her great surprise her parents gave in. Secretly they were afraid that if they didn't she would go away again.

"All right," said her father. "Every Tuesday you can be crazy. But only on the condition that you are strictly sensible the rest of the week."

When this and the story of her adventures got to be known among the children of the town, Lizzie became a great heroine. Other parents soon followed the example of her mother and father; and finally Crazy Day was observed by everybody as a regular thing.

And it is said that on account of this custom the people of that town became famous in time for their sensibleness. There were two reasons for this: one was that they had been allowed to work off their craziness as children; and the other that as grownups they were compelled to stop working and take a thorough rest one day a week. For on Tuesdays the noise was so great in that country that mothers and fathers had to descend into what were called Parent Cellars. There were soundproof underground passages where the parents played dominoes with one another while the children celebrated Crazy Day, that great institution which was given to the world by Dizzy Lizzie.

Beatrice Curtis Brown

JONATHAN BING

Poor old Jonathan Bing
Went out in his carriage to visit the King,
But everyone pointed and said, "Look at that!
Jonathan Bing has forgotten his hat!"
(He'd forgotten his hat!)

Poor old Jonathan Bing
Went home and put on a new hat for the King,
But up by the palace a soldier said, "Hi!
You can't see the King; you've forgotten your tie!"
(He'd forgotten his tie!)

Poor old Jonathan Bing,
He put on a *beautiful* tie for the King,
But when he arrived an Archbishop said, "Ho!
You can't come to court in pyjamas, you know!"

Poor old Jonathan Bing
Went home and addressed a short note to the King:

> *If you please will excuse me*
> *I won't come to tea;*
> *For home's the best place for*
> *all people like me!*

134

R BUEHRIG

Lucretia P. Hale

ABOUT
ELIZABETH ELIZA'S PIANO

ILLUSTRATED BY *Mary Miller*

ELIZABETH Eliza had a present of a piano.

They decided to have the piano set across the window in the parlor, and the carters brought it in and went away.

After they had gone the family all came in to look at the piano; but they found the carters had placed it with its back to the middle of the room, standing close against the window.

How could Elizabeth Eliza open it? How could she play it?

Solomon John proposed that they should open the window. Then Elizabeth Eliza should go round upon the piazza and open the piano. Then she could have her music-stool on the piazza and play upon the piano there.

So they tried this; and they all thought it was a very pretty sight to see Elizabeth Eliza playing on the piano, while she sat on the piazza with the honeysuckle vines behind her.

It was very pleasant, too, moonlight evenings. Mr. Peterkin liked to take a doze on his sofa in the room; but the rest of the family liked to sit on the piazza. So did Elizabeth Eliza, only she had to have her back to the moon. But when the fall came, Mr. Peterkin thought the air was too cold from the open window, and the family did not want to sit out on the piazza.

Elizabeth Eliza practiced with her cloak on; but she gave up her music in the evenings, the family shivered so.

One day, when she was talking with the lady from Philadelphia, she spoke of this trouble.

The lady from Philadelphia looked surprised, and then said, "But why don't you turn the piano round?"

One of the little boys pertly said, "It is a square piano."

But Elizabeth Eliza went home directly, and, with the help of Agamemnon and Solomon John, turned the piano round.

"Why did we not think of that before?" said Mrs. Peterkin. "What shall we do when the lady from Philadelphia goes home?"

Betty MacDonald

THE WON'T-PICK-UP-TOYS CURE

ILLUSTRATED BY *Matilda Breuer*

H
UBERT was a very lucky little boy whose grandfather always sent him wonderful toys for Christmas. Hubert's mother said that his grandfather sent him these marvelous presents because Hubert was such a dear little boy. His father said that it was to make up for that awful name they had wished on him. Hubert was named for his grandfather. His full name was Hubert Egbert Prentiss.

Hubert liked the presents his grandfather sent him, but who wouldn't? He had an electric train with track that went four times around his bedroom and into the closet and out again and had seven stations and every signal there was and two bridges and a snow shed. He also had a Little-Builder set so large that he could build regular office buildings, and a great big wagon full of stone blocks made into shapes so that he could build big stone bridges for his electric train and stone buildings and even stone barracks for his one thousand and five hundred toy soldiers. Hubert also had a circus with every kind of wooden, jointed animal and clowns and tightrope

From Mrs. *Piggle-Wiggle,* first volume published by J. B. Lippincott Company. Copyright, 1947, by Betty Bard MacDonald.

walkers and trapeze artists. He had a little typewriter, and a real desk, and a little radio, and two automobiles. He had about a hundred or more airplanes and little cars. He had a fire engine with real sirens and lights and hook and ladders; and so many books that he had to have two bookcases in his room.

Hubert liked all of his toys and he was moderately generous about letting other children play with them, but he never put his things away. When his mother made his bed she had to pick her way around and in and out and over the electric train and track. She had to take circus performers off the bureau and the bedposts. She had to pick up books that had been thrown face down on the floor and she was continually gathering up the Little-Builder set. It used to take her about three hours to do Hubert's room and about one hour to do the rest of her housework.

She would send Hubert up to put his toys away, but all he ever did was to stuff them under the bed or into the closet and in the morning when his mother cleaned his room, there they were for her to pick up.

Mrs. Prentiss was getting a little bored with this.

One rainy Saturday Hubert invited all of his little friends to play up in his room. He had Dicky and Charlie and Billy and Tommy and Bobby. They got out every single toy that Hubert owned and played with them and then, just before dinner, they all went home and left the mess. Hubert's mother didn't know a thing about this until the next morning when she went in to make Hubert's bed. Then she just stood in the doorway and looked. The electric train track went under the bed five times and under the bureau and under the chairs and around the desk and into the closet. All along the track were bridges and buildings of the stone blocks and whole towns built from the Little-Builder set. On the bed and under the bed and on the bureau were the circus tent, the animals, the clowns, the tight-rope walkers, and the trapeze artists. The floor was littered with books and little automobiles and airplanes and painting sets and chemical sets and woodburning sets and crayons and coloring books and the little typewriter and the printing set and teddy bears and balls and jacks and parchesi games and jigsaw puzzles and soldiers, soldiers, soldiers.

Perspiration broke out on Hubert's mother's forehead and she began to feel faint, so she closed the door and slowly went downstairs.

She took two aspirin tablets and then telephoned her friend, Mrs. Bags. She said, "Hello, Mrs. Bags, this is Hubert's mother, and I am so disappointed in Hubert. He has such lovely toys—his grandfather sends them to him every Christmas, you know—but he does not take care of them at all. He just leaves them all over his room for me to pick up every morning."

Mrs. Bags said, "Well, I'm sorry, Mrs. Prentiss, but I can't help you because you see, I think it is too late."

"Why, it's only nine-thirty," said Hubert's mother.

"Oh, I mean late in life," said Mrs. Bags. "You see, we started Ermintrude picking up her toys when she was six months old. 'A place for everything and everything in its place,' we have always told Ermintrude. Now, she is so neat that she becomes hysterical if she sees a crumb on the floor."

"Well, I certainly hope she never sees Hubert's room," said Mrs. Prentiss dryly. "She'd probably have a fit." And she hung up the phone.

Then she called Mrs. Moohead. "Good morning, Mrs. Moohead," she said. "Does Gregory pick up his toys?"

"Well, no, he doesn't," said Mrs. Moohead. "But you know Gregory is rather delicate and I feel that just playing with his toys tires him so much that I personally see that all of his little friends put the toys away before they go home."

"That is a splendid idea," said Hubert's mother, "but I am trying to train Hubert, not his playmates."

"Well, of course, Hubert is very strong and healthy, but Gregory is intelligent," said Mrs. Moohead.

"Is he?" said Mrs. Prentiss crossly, because she resented this inference that her son was all brawn and no brain.

"Oh, dear," squealed Mrs. Moohead, "I think Gregory is running a temperature. I must go to him." She hung up the phone.

138

Mrs. Prentiss then called Mrs. Grapple. "Hello, Marge," she said. "How's Susan?"

Mrs. Grapple said, "I've spanked her seven times since breakfast and I just heard a crash so she is probably getting ready for another. How's Hubert?"

"That's what I called about," said Mrs. Prentiss. "Can you suggest a way to make Hubert *want* to pick up his toys? His room looks like a toy store after an earthquake."

"Why don't you call this Mrs. Piggle-Wiggle? I have heard she is perfectly wonderful. All the children in town adore her and she has a cure for everything. As soon as I spank Susan, I'm going to call her."

Hubert's mother said, "Thank you very much, Marge. That is just what I'll do. I had forgotten about Mrs. Piggle-Wiggle, but I just know she can help me."

So she called Mrs. Piggle-Wiggle and said, "Mrs. Piggle-Wiggle, I hate to bother you, but you seem always to know what to do about children and I'll confess that I don't know what to do to make Hubert put his toys away."

Mrs. Piggle-Wiggle said, "Hubert is the sweet little boy with all the wonderful toys that his grandfather sends him, isn't he?"

Mrs. Prentiss said, "Why, yes, but I didn't know that you knew him."

"Oh, yes," said Mrs. Piggle-Wiggle. "Hubert and I are old friends. In fact, he is building an automobile in my back yard out of orange crates and empty tomato cans. Hubert is a very good carpenter."

Hubert's mother thought of the two little automobiles with rubber tires, real horns, leather seats big enough for two boys and lights that turned on with a switch, that Hubert's grandfather had given him; and she wondered why in the world he would want to build an automobile out of old orange crates and tomato cans. She said, however, "So that is where he and Dicky go every afternoon. I certainly hope he behaves himself."

"Oh, he does," said Mrs. Piggle-Wiggle. "We are all very fond of Hubert. But this problem of his toys. Let me see." Mrs. Piggle-Wiggle was quiet for some time. Then she said, "I think

that the best thing for you to use is my old-fashioned Won't-Pick-Up-Toys cure. Starting now, don't pick up any of Hubert's toys. Don't make his bed. In fact, do not go into his room. When his room becomes so messy he can't get out of it, call me." Mrs. Piggle-Wiggle said good-bye and hung up the phone.

Hubert's mother, looking very relieved, went gaily about her housework, baked a chocolate cake for dinner, and did not say a word to Hubert when he came home with ten little boys and they all trailed upstairs to play in Hubert's room.

The next morning when Hubert came downstairs for breakfast his mother noticed that he had a little pan of water-color paint stuck in his hair and his shirt had purple ink from the printing set on one shoulder. She said nothing but tripped upstairs after breakfast and quickly shut the door of his room.

The next morning Hubert's mother had a little trouble shutting the door of his room and she noticed that Hubert had circles under his eyes as though he had not slept very well.

The next morning Hubert was very late coming downstairs and before he opened his door his mother heard a great clatter and scraping as though he were moving furniture. He had Little-Builder bolts stuck to his sweater and two paint pans in his hair. He was so sleepy he could barely keep his eyes open and he had a red mark on one cheek. His mother looked at it closely and saw that it was the shape and size of one of his

140

stone blocks. He must have slept with his head on one of the bridges.

On the seventh day after Hubert's mother stopped putting away his toys, he did not come down to breakfast at all. About eleven o'clock his mother became worried and called up Mrs. Piggle-Wiggle.

She said, "Good morning, Mrs. Piggle-Wiggle. This is the seventh day of the old fashioned Won't-Pick-Up-Toys cure, and I am worried. Hubert has not come downstairs at all this morning."

Mrs. Piggle-Wiggle said, "Let me see! The seventh day—it usually takes ten days—but Hubert has so many toys he would naturally be quicker."

"Quicker at what?" asked Hubert's mother anxiously.

"Quicker at getting trapped in his room," said Mrs. Piggle-Wiggle. "You see, the reason Hubert hasn't come downstairs is that he cannot get out of his room. Have you noticed anything different about him lately?"

"Well," said Hubert's mother, "he looks as though he hadn't been sleeping well and on the fourth morning he had a red blotch on his cheek just the shape of one of his stone blocks."

"Hmmmmm," said Mrs. Piggle-Wiggle. "He probably can't get at his bed and is sleeping with his head on his blocks for a pillow."

"But what will I do?" asked Hubert's mother. "How will I feed him?"

"Wait until he calls for food, then tell him to open the window and you put a piece of rather dry bread and peanut butter on the garden rake. He will have to drink out of the hose. Tie it to the rake and poke it up to him."

When Hubert's mother hung up the telephone she heard a muffled shouting from the direction of Hubert's room. She hurried upstairs and listened outside the door. Hubert was shouting, "Mother, I'm hungry!"

His mother said, "Go over and open the window, dear. I will send something up to you on the rake."

Mrs. Prentiss took the crusty piece of a very old loaf of bread, spread some peanut butter on it and took it around to the side of the house. Pretty soon Hubert's window was raised about a foot and a hand and arm appeared. His mother stuck the bread on one of the tines of the rake and poked it up at the window. The hand groped around for a while and then found the bread and jerked it off. The window banged shut.

That night when Hubert's father came home his mother told him all about Mrs. Piggle-Wiggle's treatment. Hubert's father said, "Mrs. Piggle-Wiggle sounds all right, but none of this would have happened if Hubert's grandfather hadn't given him so many toys. When I was a boy all I needed to have a good time was a little piece of string and a stick. Why, I—"

Mrs. Prentiss said, "Not that old string-and-stick routine again, John. Anyway now that Hubert has the toys the picture is changed."

Mr. Prentiss hid his face behind the evening paper and said, "Something smells delicious. Is it Irish stew, I hope?"

"Yes, dear," said Hubert's mother worrying about how she was going to serve Irish stew to Hubert on a rake. She finally put a potato on one prong, a carrot on another, an onion on another and pieces of meat on the last three. The window was opened only about three inches but the hand grabbed the food. After dinner Hubert's father tied the hose to the rake and held it up while Hubert put his mouth to the window opening and tried to get a drink of water. It was not very successful but he managed to get a few drops.

Mrs. Prentiss was worried. The next morning she knocked on Hubert's door and said, "Hubert, what are you doing in there?"

Hubert said, "I've got a bear pen made out of bureau drawers and my bed's the mother bear's house and my train runs under my bed thirteen times now."

"Hubert, dear, don't you think you should try and come out soon?" asked his mother.

Hubert said, "I don't wanna come out. I like it in here. All my toys are out, and I can play with them any old time I wanna. This is fun."

142

His mother went downstairs and called Mrs. Piggle-Wiggle. Mrs. Piggle-Wiggle said, "Oh, but he will want to come out. Wait and see."

That afternoon about two o'clock there was music on the street and children's voices laughing and calling and pretty soon, right past Hubert's house, marched Mrs. Piggle-Wiggle and all the children and right behind them came the circus parade. Hubert managed, by putting one foot in a bureau drawer and the other in a freight car of his train, to get up to the window and look out. He waved to Mrs. Piggle-Wiggle and she called, "Hurry, hurry, Hubert! We are going to march all over town and then we are all going to the circus."

Hubert turned around quickly with the idea of getting to the door and joining the fun, but the freight car went scooting under the bed and the bureau drawer tipped over and hit him smartly on the shins. Hubert began to cry and to try and kick his way to the door. But everything he kicked seemed to hit back. He kicked a building, and a big block fell on his toe. He kicked at a Little-Builder office building, and it fell over and clouted him on the back of the head. He kicked a book, and it hit a lamp which fell and knocked a heavy wooden elephant off the bedpost onto Hubert's shoulder. He could hear the music of the circus parade growing fainter and fainter and so he bawled louder and louder.

Then he heard a tapping at his window. He crawled over and reached out. It was the rake with a note on it. He took the note and opened it. It said:

The only way you can get out of that trap
is to put everything away where it belongs.
If you hurry we will wait for you.
                    Your friend,
                        Mrs. Piggle-Wiggle

Hubert began by finding the Little-Builder box. He took down an office building and put each piece in its right place. Then he put away the stone blocks, then the train tracks, the circus, the soldiers, the paints, the chemical set, the printing press, the books, the fire engines, the automobiles. He played little games, pretending that he was racing someone to see who could find the most parts of a game the quickest.

He had to take off the bedclothes and shake them in order to find the soldiers and the circus and then he thought that as long as the bedclothes were off anyway, he might as well make his bed. It was so lumpy when he finished he thought he had left some airplanes in it and took the covers off again and shook them. He made the bed again, and this time it was neat and smooth. Hubert was proud.

He was under the desk finding the last piece of the Little-Builder when he heard the music again. He put the piece in the box, put the box in the closet, and tore down the stairs and out the front door.

There they came, Mrs. Piggle-Wiggle, all the children and the CIRCUS! Hubert ran out to meet them and nobody said anything about the pan of orange paint stuck in his hair or the word XYPGUN printed on his cheek in purple ink.

Away they went down the street, Hubert carrying the flag and yelling the loudest.

Peter Wells

THE CAMEL IS A MAMMAL

The camel is a mammal
   Which Arabs dearly prize.
I rode him once just like a dunce
   And got a rude surprise.

It looked so easy, cool and breezy—
   Camels must be fun—
So up I got and let it trot
   Under the desert sun.

Oh, rocklike hump! With every jump
   My pants did rise in air,
Till hard aground myself I found!
   (The camel went elsewhere.)

The camel is a mammal
   By Arabs highly prized . . .
Well, *let* them ride! I'm satisfied
   To just be *mechanized*.

Eleanor Estes

THE FIRST DAY OF SCHOOL

ILLUSTRATED BY
Beatrice Derwinski

THIS morning what a hustle-bustle in the yellow house! And no wonder! It was the first day of school. Not only was it the first day of school for Sylvie, Jane, and Joey, it was also the very first day of school for Rufus. Rufus had never been to school before except for one day last year when Jane brought him to her class for Visiting Day. That day had been more like a party than school, with cookies and oranges, singing games and a spelling bee, instead of lessons. Aside from that day, Rufus had never been to school before. Why should he have been? He was only five and a half. In spite of this, though, he could already print his name RUFUS MOFFAT and count very rapidly up to twenty.

Rufus was so happy he was going to start school, his face was shining. Jane was going to take him this first day. She was going to show him where Room One was and introduce him to the first grade teacher, Miss Andrews. Rufus was radiant as Mama gave him a final going-over, jerking his red tie in place, pulling his stockings up tight, and tying his shoelaces in a double bow.

"There," she said. "Be a good boy. Do as the teacher says and wait for Jane when school is over."

Then she kissed them both good-bye and watched them from the window in the Grape Room all the way down the street. She waved her blue checked apron after Jane and Rufus, the smallest and last of her children to be starting off to school.

"My, my, it'll be lonesome here without any baby around the house," she said as she started to wind the bobbin on the sewing machine.

Rufus and Jane walked hand in hand. They each had a shiny red apple to eat during recess. When they reached Mr. Brooney's delicatessen store at the end of New Dollar Street, a lively sight greeted them. There was Hughie Pudge, kicking his feet against the big bread-box in front of the store, screaming and yelling, "Won't go, won't go!"

His older brother, Chester, was doing his best to quiet him and to pull him away.

"Come on," said Chet. "School's not bad. You know what Mother said. You don't want to grow up to be a dunce, do you? Oh, well, if you do, all right." And with this, Chet shrugged his shoulders and pretended he was going to go off and leave Hughie, hoping his little brother would follow him. But no. Hughie merely howled the louder. So Chet came back and stood beside him helplessly.

"What's the matter?" asked Jane, while Rufus tugged at her arm, impatient to be on his way.

"Aw—Hughie doesn't want to go to school. It's his first day. He did the same thing last year, howled like this, and it ended by his staying home the whole year. Now he's got to go, Mother says, or else he'll grow up a dunce."

Rufus examined Hughie in amazement. Not want to go to school! Imagine! Why, he had looked forward to this day for years, it seemed to him.

Jane tried to take Hughie's hand. "Look," she urged, "Rufus is going to school. You could go with him. You'll be in the same room. Maybe you can sit together. The teacher's nice. Sometimes she has cookies," said Jane.

"Sure," said Rufus, holding out his chubby hand. "Everybody has to go to school. Even God had to go to school."

For a moment Hughie surveyed Rufus with a trace of interest. Hopefully the three others grabbed him by the arm, thinking victory was certain. But Hughie shook them free and started running back towards home. Way down the street they could see Mrs. Pudge shooing with her apron and making gestures with her arms that meant "Go on, go on!" Jane, Chester, and Rufus soon caught up with Hughie. Jane grabbed one arm firmly and Chet the other, and they started to drag him igno-miniously in the right direction.

"School is nice," pleaded Jane.

"No, no," screamed Hughie.

"Well," said Jane, dropping his arm in disgust, "if he doesn't want to, he doesn't want to. We might as well leave him, Rufe, or else we'll be late for school."

"What's this, what's this?" a voice boomed behind them. They turned around. Mr. Pennypepper, the new Superintendent of Schools!

"What seems to be the trouble?" asked Mr. Pennypepper, rocking from heel to toe and clinking the keys in his pocket.

"Hughie doesn't want to go to school, sir," answered Chester, red as a beet.

Mr. Pennypepper put on his glasses and examined Hughie critically. Hughie stopped his blubbering and hung his head.

"Nonsense," said Mr. Pennypepper with an air of finality. "We're all going to school."

He took Hughie by one arm and Rufus by the other. Jane took Rufus' other arm and Chester took Hughie's. In this man-ner, they all proceeded until they reached the boys' schoolyard.

Here Mr. Pennypepper left them. His last words were, "Now then, Hughie, I see you have changed your mind. That's fine. But," he said, leaning down and whispering in Rufus' ear, "in case he changes his mind again and runs away from school, I want you to bring him back. Yes, I want you to watch out for him today; your responsibility until twelve o'clock."

With that he tipped his hat to the four children and marched up the front steps of the school.

Jane, Rufus, and Hughie stood together for a while watching boys and girls arriving in ones, twos, and threes. Rufus felt rather confused and was glad Jane was there. But now someone appeared in one of the windows and rang a bell vigorously.

"First bell," said Jane, speaking from experience. "Now I'll have to go into the girls' schoolyard until it's time to go in. But, Rufus, then I'll show you and Hughie where Room One is."

And so she left.

For a moment Rufus had a rather queer feeling. All alone. None of the other Moffats. Not Mama, Sylvie, not Joey or Jane. Yes, even Rufus felt a slight impulse to run home and play as he used to. Play what? he asked himself. Mud pies? he asked himself sarcastically. Pooh! He was too old for all that business now. He was going to school. Soon he would be going home to lunch with all those throngs he'd always envied. With something to show Mama too, maybe. Moreover, he had to mind Hughie.

He looked at Hughie who was still a bit stunned at the turn of events. The loud voice of authority that had brought him here was evidently holding him as in a spell which the second pealing of the bell did not even break. And he did not think of rebelling when Rufus grasped his hand firmly and led him into that hated school.

Jane met them in the hall as she had promised. In no time at all she introduced them to Miss Andrews, the first grade teacher, and Rufus took such a liking to her he immediately handed her his red apple.

Room One was filled with boys and girls but Rufus didn't recognize any of them except Nelly Cadwalader who lived across the street from the Chief of Police. Rufus was glad Hughie was there, sitting right behind him. He was glad their seats were on the aisle by the window. They could look out on the railroad tracks. He could count the trains in the freighters better from here than he could from the hitching post in front of the yellow house. But of course he wouldn't have much time for watching trains, he chuckled, if he ever wanted to catch up with Joey in school.

First the teacher asked all the boys and girls what their names were. Then she passed books around to all of them. Readers, they were. Rufus opened his. He liked the smell of the shiny printed pages. He liked the pictures, but goodness! would he ever be able to read those words? Now the teacher was writing on the blackboard. Occasionally the white chalk would squeak. She was making the letters of the alphabet. That Rufus knew.

149

Oh, he was enjoying himself hugely. All the new smells! First his new book, then the chalk dust whenever the teacher made lines on the board. And best of all this desk! All his own! Rufus liked it here. He turned around to see if Hughie wasn't liking it too.

The whisper he was going to say, "Gee, it's great, isn't it?" froze on his lips. Hughie wasn't there. The seat back of Rufus where Hughie should have been was empty.

Rufus looked at the teacher. NOPQ she wrote in firm strokes. And at that moment, Hughie Pudge, who had been standing behind the big chart that had a picture of Little Bo-Peep on it, walked out the door. Miss Andrews didn't see him, for her back was to the door. Many of the children saw him, but they thought nothing of it. Lots of them had the idea you could get up and go outdoors or even go home if you felt like it. Imagine! Of course they soon learned differently, but anyway, today—the first day of school—they saw nothing strange in a boy simply walking out of the classroom.

But Rufus, along with several others who had older brothers and sisters at school, knew more of what was expected of you. And he knew that Hughie shouldn't have left until the teacher said to leave. What would that man with the loud voice say? He had told Rufus to see to it that Hughie came to school. True, Hughie had come to school. But now he'd left. Did that big man mean that he was supposed to see to it that Hughie stayed in school too? He supposed he did—but where had Hughie gone anyway?

At this moment the bell rang for recess. The teacher carefully explained that recess meant they were all to go out and play in the schoolyard. It did not mean that they should go home. And after a while the bell would ring again. When it did, they were all to come back to Room One. That's what Miss Andrews said.

"Class, stand," she said.

The class stood up. Then they all had to sit down again because they all hadn't stood up together.

"Class, stand," said Miss Andrews again.

This time they all stood up the way she wanted them to. Rufus stood in the aisle by the window. He looked out, for he heard a train. The train whizzed past.

"Class, march," said the teacher.

But Rufus was so absorbed with something else he saw down by the railroad tracks that he forgot to march, and the boy in back stepped on his heels.

The class had to go back to its seats and again the teacher said, "Class, march!"

This time Rufus marched right past the desks, out the door, down the steps, and into the schoolyard with his classmates. But he didn't stop there. He kept right on marching out the schoolyard gate and across Wood Street to the railroad tracks, for what he had seen up there from the classroom window was Hughie Pudge climbing into a freight car stopped on a sidetrack.

It wasn't easy, what Rufus was going to do, because Mama had warned all the Moffats never to go onto the railroad tracks. But that important man had told Rufus he must see to it that Hughie came to school. He hoped Mama would understand. He would be very careful. Besides, the freight car he had seen

151

Hughie climb into wasn't on the regular tracks. It was on the sidetrack and would be quite safe. Maybe it was an old thing they weren't going to use again, this freight car.

Rufus climbed up. Panting, he looked around. Sure enough! There he was, that Hughie, sitting on a crate in the corner. When he saw Rufus, he stuck out his lower lip and glowered.

"No, I'm not going back," he said.

"Aw, come on," said Rufus impatiently.

"No," said Hughie.

Rufus sat down in another corner and regarded Hughie with a mixture of admiration and contempt.

"What are you goin' to do here?" he finally asked.

"Watch the trains—maybe take one," replied Hughie.

"Are you goin' to watch the trains forever?"

"Well, maybe until it's dark, anyway."

Rufus glared at him. From across the street he could hear the boys and girls shouting and playing in the schoolyard. Soon the bell would ring and recess would be over. He didn't know what to do. Should he go back without Hughie? Or should he stay here with him and try to make him change his mind? Of course if he stayed here with Hughie, he might miss something very important in school. Everyone would get ahead of him. They might start reading in the shiny book.

"Don't you like the shiny book?" he asked Hughie.

Hughie merely shrugged his shoulders. In sudden exasperation Rufus jumped up and yanked Hughie off the crate. But Hughie fought back and yelled so loudly everyone in school would have heard him if an engine hadn't come chugging along—

Choo-Choo-Choo. Choo-Choo-Choo. Choo-Choo-Choo.

To Rufus it was saying, "Go to school. Go to school. Go to school."

It was an engine and it didn't have any cars attached to it. Just an engine all alone.

It was slowing up. Now it was stopping just a little way in front of the freight car Rufus and Hughie were sitting in. A lot of steam went hissing up into the air, and then the engine started

152

backing up with its bell clapping back and forth. Now, CHOO-choo, CHOO-choo; making a great effort, it backed off the main tracks, backed—CHOO-choo, CHOO-choo, right back to the old car where Rufus and Hughie were. A slight jar sent the two boys spinning on the floor. A few heavy jerks and a harsh grating noise and Rufus realized what was happening.

"Criminenty!" he yelled, using a word he'd heard that morning in the schoolyard. "We're movin'. Let's jump."

But Hughie shook his head. "Let's go for a ride," he said.

"We'll get lost," screamed Rufus. "We don't know where this train is goin'. Might be goin' to Boston. We'll be lost."

But Hughie was looking over the side of the freight car happily watching the schoolhouse disappear.

"Lost," repeated Rufus to himself. And a prickly feeling ran up his spine at the word "lost." "Rufus Moffat, 27 New Dollar Street," he muttered to himself. This is what Mama always made him repeat to her when he went shopping in the city with her just in case he might get lost. "Age, five-and-a-half years," he continued and counted up to twenty.

That's what he would do and say if there were anyone to say it to.

However, he soon forgot to be afraid. He forgot about school and the shiny new reader and he began to enjoy the ride.

"You must be the engineer, and I'll be the conductor," he said to Hughie.

The two boys looked back. They had left the brown schoolhouse, Wood Street, and Brooney's delicatessen store far behind. They were crossing the marshes that separated Cranbury from New Haven. Now they were crossing the long trestle over Mill River that emptied into the harbor.

The train was only jogging along—but already they were on the outskirts of New Haven. They could see West Rock, East Rock, and the Sleeping Giant. Now they could see the tall buildings. And now they were chugging down the tracks under the viaduct. Up top, on the viaduct, the trolley from Cranbury ran. So far Rufus knew where he was, for he had often seen these railroad tracks from the trolley car. He knew that soon

they should be at the New Haven depot.

But would they stop there? Perhaps they would go right through to Boston.

An express train bound for New York suddenly flew past them, whistles screaming. Rufus's heart pounded with excitement. Hughie's eyes shone. The two boys laughed out loud, jumped up and down and waved their hats.

"Next stop New York!" Rufus cried.

"New York to Boston!" Hughie yelled louder.

They were entering the New Haven station now. Would they stop? Or would they have to go to Boston? Riding on trains was fun, but Rufus hoped they'd stop. In Boston they'd be lost—Rufus Moffat, 27 New Dollar Street. The engine was slowing up—Puff—It was stopping—a few violent spasms and the train stopped.

"C'mon," said Rufus, "we better get out."

Hughie was beginning to feel hungry and tired too, so he nodded his head in agreement, and the two climbed out of the freight train. There was a man in blue overalls carrying a sooty old lantern and examining the wheels.

"Well, well, well," he said, "what's this? Where did you come from?" The man smelled like kerosene. Rufus thought he looked nice.

"Rufus Moffat, 27 New Dollar Street, five and a half years old. Hughie and me have to get back to school."

The man pushed his cap back and scratched his head.

"Lost?" he asked.

"Not exactly," replied Rufus. "Not yet anyhow. But we have to get back to school."

"You say you live on New Dollar Street? Don't know of any New Dollar Street."

"Sure, Number 27. Chief Mulligan lives on one end."

"Never heard of the man."

"Well, if we could only get back to Cranbury, I could find it," said Rufus.

"Oh—Cranbury. Is that where you come from?" the man asked in astonishment.

"Yes, New Dollar Street," Rufus said.

"Well, I don't see how you got here without no one seein' you. But if that's where you come from, that's where you better go back to."

"If only we could go back on a train, we'd be right at school," said Rufus. "Only trouble is *he* doesn't want to go to school."

The man looked at Hughie. He clicked his tongue against his teeth and shook his head.

"I never," he said. "They ain't many locals to Cranbury this time o' day. But come along, I'll find out."

The man left them for a minute and came back with a time-table.

"Ain't no local for three hours," he said. "Only westbound train is the Bay State Express, comin' in in three minutes."

As if to confirm this statement, a mysterious voice called out, "Bay State Express—On time. Bay State Express—On time. Track 9. 11:45. Track 9."

"Doesn't the Bay State ever stop in Cranbury?" asked Rufus.

"Never," said the man.

"All aboard Bay State Express! ALL ABOARD Bay State. Track 9."

"Never," repeated the man in overalls. "But who knows? C'mon."

With that he grabbed Hughie and Rufus by the arm, tore down the tracks to Track 9, where the engine of the Bay State Express was hissing and steaming, just itching to be off.

"Hey, Dick," called the trackman to the engineer.

"Hey yourself, Bob," answered the engineer, grinning and leaning out of the cab.

"Listen, Dick; here are two kids—lost—come on a freight train from Cranbury—they gotta be returned. How about stopping thirty seconds to let them off?"

"Couldn't be done," answered the engineer. "Bay State never stops in Cranbury—straight through to New York."

Rufus's heart sank. So did Hughie's. However, they both had faith in this man, Bob, of theirs.

Bob said, "Well, the New York, New Haven and Hartford got them here. The way I look at it, they ought to git 'em back."

"M-m-m," said the engineer, "ask the Station-Master."

"Wait here," said Bob to Rufus and Hughie.

Then Bob tore down to the station and it seemed only a second before he was back.

Inside the station, that voice could be heard,

"Last call for Bay State Express—Track 9. Bay State Express —Track 9."

" 'Board," cried the conductors.

156

"He says yup," said Bob, boosting Rufus and Hughie into the engine cab.

Then whistles sounded, a huge blast of steam went up into the sky—the train was off. Hughie and Rufus waved their caps after Bob whom they could see for a second waving his cap after them.

Goodness, this train was just speeding along. Of course, Rufus and Hughie couldn't stand too close to the engineer. But they could watch the fireman and they saw enough to see that running an engine was a marvelous job.

The express whizzed over the tracks the freight train had taken so long to cross a little while before. Rufus and Hughie could hardly tell where they were. And in exactly three minutes after leaving the New Haven station, the express train came to a stop—the fireman lifted the two boys down—the engineer grinned and waved to them, and off the train went with everybody aboard staring out the window to find out why the express, that wasn't supposed to stop until it reached New York, had stopped in this funny little town.

Rufus and Hughie waved after the train until it was just a speck in the distance. Then Rufus thought about school again.

"Come on now," he said, "we better get back to school."

"Do you have to go to school to be an engineer?" asked Hughie.

"Of course you do. That engineer named Dick, well, once't he was in Room One too," replied Rufus, thinking this out laboriously.

"All right then, I'll go to school." Hughie finally gave in.

And the two boys returned to Miss Andrews' room. They took their places just in time to be dismissed to go home to lunch.

"Class, stand," the teacher was saying.

DR. DOLITTLE lives with a lot of animals and knows how to talk their language, but when the monkeys brought him a pushmi-pullyu he got a surprise. This was the rarest animal of all.

Hugh Lofting

DR. DOLITTLE
AND THE PUSHMI-PULLYU

ILLUSTRATED BY THE AUTHOR

PUSHMI-PULLYUS are now extinct. That means, there aren't any more. But long ago, when Doctor Dolittle was alive, there were some of them still left in the deepest jungles of Africa; and even then they were very, very scarce. They had no tail, but a head at each end, and sharp horns on each head. They were very shy and terribly hard to catch. The black men get most of their animals by sneaking up behind them while they are not looking. But you could not do this with the pushmi-pullyu—because, no matter which way you came towards him, he was always facing you. And besides, only one half of him slept at a time. The other head was always awake—and watching. This was why they were never caught and never seen in Zoos. Though many of the greatest huntsmen and the cleverest menagerie-keepers spent years of their lives searching through the jungles in all weathers for pushmi-pullyus, not a single one had ever been caught. Even then, years ago, he was the only animal in the world with two heads.

Well, the monkeys set out hunting for this animal through the forest. And after they had gone a good many miles, one of them found peculiar footprints near the edge of a river; and they knew that a pushmi-pullyu must be very near that spot.

Then they went along the bank of the river a little way and they saw a place where the grass was high and thick; and they guessed that he was in there.

158

So they all joined hands and made a great circle round the high grass. The pushmi-pullyu heard them coming; and he tried hard to break through the ring of monkeys. But he couldn't do it. When he saw that it was no use trying to escape, he sat down and waited to see what they wanted.

They asked him if he would go with Doctor Dolittle and be put on show in the Land of the White Men.

But he shook both his heads hard and said, "Certainly not!"

They explained to him that he would not be shut up in a menagerie but would just be looked at. They told him that the Doctor was a very kind man but hadn't any money; and people would pay to see a two-headed animal, and the Doctor would get rich and could pay for the boat he had borrowed to come to Africa in.

But he answered, "No. You know how shy I am—I hate being stared at." And he almost began to cry.

Then for three days they tried to persuade him.

And at the end of the third day he said he would come with them and see what kind of a man the Doctor was, first.

So the monkeys traveled back with the pushmi-pullyu. And when they came to where the Doctor's little house of grass was, they knocked on the door.

The duck, who was packing the trunk, said, "Come in!"

And Chee-Chee very proudly took the animal inside and showed him to the Doctor.

"What in the world is it?" asked John Dolittle, gazing at the strange creature.

"Lord save us!" cried the duck. "How does it make up its mind?"

"It doesn't look as though it had any," said Jip, the dog.

"This, Doctor," said Chee-Chee, "is the pushmi-pullyu—the rarest animal of the African jungles, the only two-headed beast in the world! Take him home with you, and your fortune's made. People will pay any money to see him."

"But I don't want any money," said the Doctor.

"Yes, you do," said Dab-Dab, the duck. "Don't you remember how we had to pinch and scrape to pay the butcher's bill in

159

Puddleby? And how are you going to get the sailor the new boat you spoke of—unless we have the money to buy it?"

"I was going to make him one," said the Doctor.

"Oh, do be sensible!" cried Dab-Dab. "Where would you get all the wood and the nails to make one with?—And besides, what are we going to live on? We shall be poorer than ever when we get back. Chee-Chee's perfectly right: take the funny-looking thing along, do!"

"Well, perhaps there is something in what you say," murmured the Doctor. "It certainly would make a nice new kind of pet. But does the er—what-do-you-call-it really want to go abroad?"

"Yes, I'll go," said the pushmi-pullyu who saw at once, from the Doctor's face, that he was a man to be trusted. "You have been so kind to the animals here—and the monkeys tell me that I am the only one who will do. But promise me that if I do not like it in the Land of the White Men you will send me back."

"Why, certainly—of course, of course," said the Doctor. "Excuse me, you are related to the Deer Family, are you not?"

"Yes," said the pushmi-pullyu—"to the Abyssinian Gazelles and the Asiatic Chamois—on my mother's side. My father's great-grandfather was the last of the Unicorns."

"Most interesting!" murmured the Doctor; and he took a book out of the trunk which Dab-Dab was packing and began turning the pages. "Let us see if Buffon says anything—"

"I notice," said the duck, "that you only talk with one of your mouths. Can't the other head talk as well?"

"Oh, yes," said the pushmi-pullyu. "But I keep the other mouth for eating—mostly. In that way I can talk while I am eating without being rude. Our people have always been very polite."

When the packing was finished and everything was ready to start, the monkeys gave a grand party for the Doctor, and all the animals of the jungle came. And they had pineapples and mangoes and honey and all sorts of good things to eat and drink.

After they had all finished eating, the Doctor said,—

"My friends: I am not clever at speaking long words after dinner, like some men; and I have just eaten many fruits and much honey. But I wish to tell you that I am very sad at leaving your beautiful country. Because I have things to do in the Land of the White Men, I must go. After I have gone, remember never to let the flies settle on your food before you eat it; and do not sleep on the ground when the rains are coming. I—er—er—I hope you will all live happily ever after."

When the Doctor stopped speaking and sat down, all the monkeys clapped their hands a long time and said to one another, "Let it be remembered always among our people that he sat and ate with us, here, under the trees. For surely he is the Greatest of Men!"

And the Grand Gorilla, who had the strength of seven horses, rolled a great rock up to the head of the table and said,—

"This stone for all time shall mark the spot."

And even to this day, in the heart of the jungle, that stone still is there. And monkey-mothers, passing through the forest with their families, still point down at it from the branches and whisper to their children, "Sh! There! Look—where the Good White Man ate food with us in the Year of the Great Sickness!"

Then, when the party was over, the Doctor and his pets started out to go back to the seashore. And all the monkeys went with him as far as the edge of their country, carrying his trunk and bags, to see him off.

Carolyn Wells

HOW TO TELL WILD ANIMALS

If ever you should go by chance
To jungles in the east;
And if there should to you advance
A large and tawny beast,
If he roars at you as you're dyin'
You'll know it is the Asian Lion . . .

Or if some time when roaming round,
A noble wild beast greets you,
With black strips on a yellow ground,
Just notice if he eats you.
This simple rule may help you learn
The Bengal Tiger to discern.

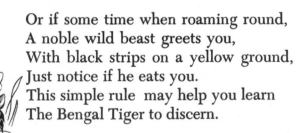

If strolling forth, a beast you view,
Whose hide with spots is peppered,
As soon as he has lept on you,
You'll know it is the Leopard.
'Twill do no good to roar with pain,
He'll only lep and lep again.

If when you're walking round your yard
You meet a creature there,
Who hugs you very, very hard,
Be sure it is a Bear.
If you have any doubts, I guess
He'll give you just one more caress.

Though to distinguish beasts of prey
A novice might nonplus,
The Crocodile you always may
Tell from the Hyena thus:
Hyenas come with merry smiles;
But if they weep they're Crocodiles.

The true Chameleon is small,
A lizard sort of thing;
He hasn't any ears at all,
And not a single wing.
If there is nothing on the tree,
'Tis the chameleon you see.

163

Charles Edward Carryl

A NAUTICAL BALLAD

A capital ship for an ocean trip,
  Was "The Walloping Window-Blind";
No gale that blew dismayed her crew,
  Nor troubled the captain's mind.

The man at the wheel was taught to feel
  Contempt for the wildest blow;
And it often appeared—when the weather had cleared—
  He had been in his bunk below.

The boatswain's mate was very sedate,
  Yet fond of amusement, too;
And he played hopscotch with the starboard watch,
  While the captain tickled the crew.

And the gunner we had was apparently mad,
  For he sat on the after-rail
And fired salutes with the captain's boots
  In the teeth of the booming gale.

The captain sat on the commodore's hat,
  And dined, in a royal way,

Off toasted pigs and pickles and figs
   And gummery bread each day.

The cook was Dutch and behaved as such,
   For the diet he gave the crew
Was a number of tons of hot-cross buns,
   Served up with sugar and glue.

All nautical pride we laid aside,
   And we cast our vessel ashore,
On the Gulliby Isles, where the Poo-Poo smiles
   And the Rumpletum-Bunders roar.

We sat on the edge of a sandy ledge,
   And shot at the whistling bee:
And the cinnamon bats wore waterproof hats,
   As they danced by the sounding sea.

On Rug-gub bark, from dawn till dark,
   We fed, till we all had grown
Uncommonly shrunk—when a Chinese junk
   Came in from the Torriby Zone.

She was stubby and square, but we didn't much care,
   So we cheerily put to sea;
And we left the crew of the junk to chew
   The bark of the Rug-gub tree.

Anne H. White

SERAPINA
PROVES
HERSELF

ILLUSTRATED BY

Tony Palazzo

ONE DAY Serapina entered the Salinus' household. She was an extraordinary cat who did everything but talk. She carried milkbottles with her tail, played ball with the children, tamed fierce Bonzo the dog, made friends with Alexander the parrot, but her unusual powers embarrassed Mrs. Salinus, especially when the neighbors started talking. As rumors about Serapina spread, a reporter came to write about her, but she would not show off. Finally, when the reputation of the Salinus family was at stake because of her, Serapina decided to prove herself.

IN THE meantime Serapina went right on performing her chores in the Salinus household. Every now and then she would add another chore to her collection because the Salinus children were very good and co-operative and she did not find her duties too great. She learned how to turn the lights off and on, to open the refrigerator door, and to pull down the window shades as well as the venetian blinds. She could prepare everything for washing Bobby's face without, we must confess, any help at all from Bobby. Mrs. Salinus thought this disappointed Serapina because she planned her preparations very nicely. By spreading out her toes and then closing them over the stopper, she picked it up and dropped it into place, and then she poked a piece of soap into the wash basin with either tail or paw. The faucets she managed with her paws, and she whipped the washrag off the towel bar with her tail.

166

When the washrag was floating nearly to the edge of the basin, Serapina turned the water off and waited, mostly in vain, for Bobby to come.

So, while all sorts of rumors were flying up and down the block, Serapina was quite happily doing what she had come to the Salinus house to do.

One rainy afternoon, shortly after people had begun to talk about her, Serapina was watching a game of parchesi in the living room. She liked to sit by while games were being played because she had a very keen sense of fair play and a quick eye. If Sally's or Peter's elbow accidentally pushed a checker or a parchesi chip out of its proper place, Serapina could always be counted on to push it back again. She was good at remembering turns and always stood by the player's left hand until he had played and then moved quickly to the next player. Often, with very fast games, she got so dizzy going from player to player she had to lie down afterward, but, fast or slow, she never got bored.

On this particular afternoon the game was going very slowly. Mrs. Salinus was upstairs cleaning the attic, and Bobby was pushing a fire engine in and out under the card table, seeing how near he could come to *not* hitting the legs. As he was not a very good judge of distance he hit them often, which caused a good deal of comment from his brother and sister. So when the front doorbell rang, all three children rushed to answer it, hoping for something more interesting than parchesi. Their hopes were more than fulfilled because into the house and out of the rain stepped something they had never seen before. It turned out to be a reporter-photographer, complete with a camera and flash bulb. He also had chocolate bars in nearly every pocket, which the children thought delightful. He walked right into the hall and then into the living room, asking if Mrs. Salinus was at home. The children said she was, but they were much too fascinated to go call her.

The young man wandered restlessly about, peering everywhere. Then he saw Serapina perched on the arm of a chair, patiently waiting for the game to go on.

"Well, well, so that's the famous cat," he said, and he began to fiddle with his camera and bulbs.

"No," Sally said, "I don't think you can call her famous, because very few people have seen her. I think lots of people have to see you if you are famous."

"Or hear you or read you," the young man said absently, looking around for a good place to take a picture.

"You could certainly hear Serapina if she wanted you to," Peter assured the reporter. "Once we thought she could read—people's minds, you know—but I don't think we were ever sure."

This remark did not startle the young man because almost nothing startles a reporter. He moved some furniture and rearranged two lamps. Serapina remained on the arm of the chair, watching him.

"Now," he said finally to the children, "how about you kiddies and the cat just acting natural for the first shot. You"—he pointed to Sally—"you pick up the kitty and hold it in your lap. And you fine young men—" he turned to the boys.

"Oh," Bobby interrupted, for he thought the reporter was being quite stupid for a grownup, "we aren't men. I'm nearly five and Peter is older."

"Okay. But you are going to be fine young men. Now then—"

"I don't know if you can tell that yet," Peter said thoughtfully. "I might turn out to be dreadful when I grow up and fail in all my exams."

"Or," Bobby added hopefully, "we might be gangsters and have a gang."

"Whatever you like," the reporter said to them and went on with his plans for a picture. When he was satisfied he turned to Sally. "Now then," he said, "just you pick up the kitty and hold it."

"Oh, we never pick up Serapina," Sally told him. "She does not like it, and we think it offends her dignity."

"Just for today," the young man suggested, sounding very tired indeed, "let's pretend we don't care if we do offend her dignity. Now, I want you three kiddies right here," and he placed Sally in an armchair with Peter on one side of her and

Bobby on the floor. "And I will pick up the kitty since no one else is willing to do it."

Sally and Peter had enough confidence in Serapina to let her handle the situation as she wanted to. Bobby was very anxious about the whole thing but he need not have been. Serapina, who preferred never to be unusual in front of strange grownups, had no objection to being both difficult and a nuisance. Perhaps she thought if she could annoy the young man enough he would go away, and the children would finish their game. Serapina was always miserable until she knew who had won. So she sat on the arm of her chair, twitching her tail slightly and waiting.

The reporter, who was not very used to cats, approached the chair and leaned down to pick up the cat. He did not reach for the scruff on the back of the neck, as most people would do, but he reached clumsily under her shoulders, much the way one would reach to pick up a child. Serapina saw her chance and took it. She stood up on her hind legs and did what a child would do. She put her front paws around the young man's neck in a most affectionate manner. At the same time she put one hind paw in his left coat pocket and the other hind paw in his right waistcoat pocket and her nose under his right ear. The reporter looked very pleased at such a show of affection. He grinned at the children over Serapina's head.

"Who said the kitty doesn't like to be picked up!" he crowed. "She sure doesn't act offended."

Sally and Peter and Bobby all looked at Serapina in surprise, and, to tell the truth, they were all a little shocked that she should show so much affection to a stranger. The reporter came over to Sally and started to put Serapina down in Sally's lap. But Serapina had no intention of being put down. She had only begun to be difficult.

"Come, come, puss, this won't do," the young man said. "Let go of me." He reached up to loosen Serapina's paws from around his neck, but Serapina continued to embrace him warmly. He then tried to pry a paw loose, but Serapina gave him a sharp dig through his left coat pocket. The reporter

169

brought both hands down from his neck to his pocket and tried to pry Serapina's right hind foot loose. Serapina promptly dug him in the ribs with her left hind foot, and he grabbed that foot and yanked. But then Serapina nipped his right ear lobe, not very hard, so he let go of her hind foot and reached for her head. So it went for some time. Every time the poor young man started to loosen her grasp in one place, Serapina jabbed him in another, so that he was dancing about the room in great discomfort, his hands flying from coat pocket, to vest pocket, to collar, to ear, as fast as they could. And Serapina, with her head hidden in his neck, was probably laughing fit to kill, only no one could see her expression.

The children were certainly laughing, loudly and delightedly. They made so much noise Mrs. Salinus hurried downstairs to see what all the commotion was about. She stopped in the doorway, astonished beyond words to see a perfectly strange young man waltzing around her living room with Serapina clasped to his chest.

"What on earth is going on here?" she asked.

The young man, whose face was very red from embarrassment and waltzing, said that her horrible cat would not let him go, and all he wanted was a picture of it.

Serapina, seeing Mrs. Salinus, immediately let go of the young man and retired to the window sill. She sat there, grinning broadly at the children with all her whiskers pointed up.

Mrs. Salinus sent Peter for a glass of water for the flustered young man and asked why he wanted a picture of their cat.

"Because there are a lot of stories going around about the cat and I thought I'd write her up, with pictures, for the paper," he explained. "Perhaps," he added hopefully, because reporters never give up, "you will pose with her?"

"But I don't want my picture in the paper, and I'm sure Serapina doesn't want hers either," Mrs. Salinus protested.

"Oh, come, come, Mrs. Salinus," the young man said, laughing. "You can't expect me to believe that. Every woman wants to have her picture in the paper. Just think how all the neighbors will feel when they open the paper Sunday morning and see you and the cat looking out at them. They will be green with envy."

"Oh, no, they won't," Mrs. Salinus contradicted him. "It will be even worse than it is now. Everyone would think I was being very silly, getting my picture in the paper just because of a cat. We have had enough trouble as it is with her."

"Suppose you tell me about the trouble," the reporter wheedled. "There are all sorts of stories going around about this cat, you know. Did you train her? How long did it take? Does she really do any of the things you and the kiddies say she does?"

"Of course she does," Sally replied in a bored tone. "We wouldn't say she does if she doesn't, would we?"

"Okay, okay," the young man said in a tired voice, and then he tried persuading the family once more. "Let's see you make her do a few things for me then."

"No," all four Salinuses answered at once. "I'm sorry," Mrs. Salinus explained, "but you can't *make* Serapina do anything. She does what she thinks she ought to do when she thinks she should. You just have to accept that and take her as she is."

By this time the reporter was so annoyed with this family and their cat he decided not to waste any more words on them. He wished it had been a good day and he had gone to the ball game where everyone loved having their pictures taken and would often fight to get in front of his lens. He picked up his camera, determined for one more try at the cat, but Serapina was too quick for him. As he raised the camera she jumped from the window sill to his feet. The reporter stepped back to get her into focus, and Serapina followed right after him, stepping on his toes. He stepped sideways, and Serapina wove a figure eight around his ankles. He could not possibly take a photograph of her because he could not get her in any sort of focus, which, Serapina could have told you, was the idea.

"I give up," the young man exclaimed angrily, and he picked up all his equipment and started for the door. "I wish I had never heard of your cat."

"Oh, so do I—often." Mrs. Salinus sighed wistfully. "She

171

really doesn't make sense, and I do so like things to make sense!"

"Sense!" shouted the reporter. "I don't think any of you make sense!" And he left in a great hurry.

"I do hope," Mrs. Salinus said anxiously to the children, "that he won't put anything in his paper about us."

It was a very foolish hope because reporters have to put things in their papers or stop being reporters. So there was a story about Serapina in the Sunday paper, but there were no pictures. Instead there were some rather poor sketches of three children and a large speckled cat that did not look anything like Serapina. The story was a collection of rumors that the young man had picked up here and there from people on the block. It said that there was a mysterious animal living at the house of Mr. and Mrs. James Salinus that looked like a cat but was probably not a cat but a baby lion or a jaguar or a monkey or possibly a combination of all these animals. It said that the owners of this creature told extraordinary stories about what it could do, and it added that people found these stories a little hard to swallow.

Mr. Salinus had a good laugh when he read this account, but Mrs. Salinus did not even smile. "It is all very well for you, James," she said. "You're at your office all day long. You don't have people looking at you as if you were crazy or telling lies."

"Oh, pooh!" Mr. Salinus said. "You exaggerate, my dear. No one will pay any attention to such nonsense as this." And he waved the paper at his wife. "Serapina is no lion cub or jaguar or monkey. She is simply a cat genius, and any sort of genius always causes a certain amount of trouble and attention. People will just have to get used to her."

Serapina rolled her clearest, loudest, and most complicated drums at these words, but Mrs. Salinus remained very depressed.

"I wish you were right," she said dolefully, "but I'm perfectly sure that you're wrong."

. . . .

Mrs. Amanda MacPherson could hardly wait until the Dorcas Society Sewing Social met for their weekly tea and cakes. She

172

was the first to arrive at Mrs. Polly Potts's house, and she was full of impatience to tell her story about the cat who sat. But she was not going to tell it until everyone had arrived.

"I hope to goodness," Polly Potts remarked, "that no one will mention that drat cat of Jane Salinus's this afternoon. I am tired to death of hearing Betsy talk about it."

"I told my children flatly," declared Mrs. Timmins, "that I would not listen to another absurd story about the things that cat does. I suggested they choose some other animal to talk about, but they simply said no other animal was as clever as that silly Serapina."

Mrs. MacPherson looked around and saw that everyone had arrived except Jane Salinus, who was unable to come that day. She drew a deep breath and rapped on the table for silence.

"It is my opinion," Mrs. MacPherson boomed, "that there is something even sillier than that cat in the Salinus household."

The ladies all said "What?" in one breath.

"What would any of you think of a woman whose *sitter* was a cat?" she asked, and paused dramatically. It took the Dorcas Society members some time to grasp exactly what Mrs. Mac-Pherson meant by this question, so she explained about her call and her discovery of the sitting Serapina. After her explanation the entire Sewing Social threw itself into a regular "buzzer," which happens when all the ladies in a group talk very fast and nobody listens to anybody.

"I always said there was something very funny about Jane

173

since she got that cat," Mrs. Timmins said, forgetting that she had never said anything of the kind. "I think she really believes all those stories the children make up about that cat, and I think she ought to have her head examined."

"What I think of Jane Salinus and the cat and her children, everyone knows," twittered Mrs. Fowler. Everyone did know about the mice plague and Serapina's refusal to help, but no one knew how the mice could have gotten into Mrs. Fowler's house. It was a secret both Mrs. Fowler and the Salinus children were willing to keep.

"You can't blame Jane entirely," Mrs. Munson remarked. "I think there is something weird about the cat. Our Daisy would never see ordinary cats carrying milk bottles."

"There is no question of its being an ordinary cat," Mrs. MacPherson stated. "I think it's some kind of witch cat that puts spells on people."

The ladies then plunged into the possibilities of there being such a thing as a witch cat, and, if there were such possibilities, was Serapina one? The buzzer became a bigger buzzer, which is something exceedingly deafening. The ladies formed a committee to discuss what should be done about Serapina.

"Certainly she should be removed to another neighborhood at once," Mrs. MacPherson said.

All the mothers agreed that this was an excellent idea. No ordinary, routine block of houses, full of ordinary, routine

174

families, ought to have such an unroutine thing as Serapina in its midst. Finally, after oceans of tea and mountains of cake had been devoured, it was voted to send the committee to the Salinus house to request Jane Salinus, very politely, to please be so kind as to get rid of that cat at once.

The next afternoon at three o'clock Mrs. Potts, Mrs. Mac-Pherson, and Mrs. Timmins came to call on Mrs. Salinus.

Mrs. Salinus was very surprised to see the ladies. She knew something was up right away because they all wore hats and gloves and special "committee" expressions. So she put a special "and-what-can-I-do-for-you?" look on her face, ignored the few butterflies and elevators in her stomach, and asked the ladies in.

"Well, Jane," boomed Mrs. MacPherson, "I will wager you wonder why we are here." Mrs. MacPherson always "wagered" when anyone else would have "bet." "It's about that cat. It has to go."

Long ago Mrs. MacPherson had decided that putting things tactfully was a sign of weakness. Mrs. Salinus looked so startled and so puzzled that Mrs. Potts felt sorry for her.

"The thing is, Jane, we think it would be better for the community if you could find a nice home for Serapina."

"But I couldn't possibly find a home for Serapina," Mrs. Salinus protested. "The children adore her and James considers her a member of the family. Also, I must confess, although I do

175

not think she makes sense as a cat, I rely on her quite a lot myself." Mrs. Salinus blushed with embarrassment as she admitted this fact.

"That's just it," Mrs. Timmins said. "We can't feel that it makes sense to rely on a cat. It should be the other way around."

"No normal cat gets itself so much talked about," complained Mrs. Potts. "I know because I was raised with them."

"So we think it would be better for you, and we know it would be for the neighbors, if you got rid of this one and got a more usual cat," Mrs. MacPherson announced, "which Big Boy will kill, I warn you," she added.

"But I don't want a usual cat," Mrs. Salinus protested, almost in tears. "I never wanted any cat. I am not fond of cats as a rule, but I have become used to Serapina, even if she isn't a rule."

"If she was a rule," Mrs. Timmins said, "we certainly would have no objection to her. But she is so strange, it's hard to be sure she *is* a cat."

"We want to be sure," Mrs. MacPherson boomed, summing everything up in a nutshell, "that on our block people are people, dogs are dogs, cats are cats, and so on."

Mrs. Salinus sighed and made little sounds of despair and misery, and she promised to talk it over with Mr. Salinus. She also said she knew it would do no good because Mr. Salinus and the children would rather move away than part with Serapina. The ladies left with many assurances to Mrs. Salinus that it would make very good sense to get rid of a cat that made no sense at all.

Mrs. Salinus did discuss the matter with her husband that night. Mr. Salinus, backed by his three children, promptly said that he would rather move to another block than part with Serapina. Mr. Salinus was madder than Sally or Peter or Mrs. Salinus had ever seen him. What he said about the committee not only cannot be put in print but should never have been heard by his delighted children. It hardly was heard, as a matter of fact, because Serapina, who was sitting on his feet to keep him from hitting the ceiling, was rolling her drums in ec-

176

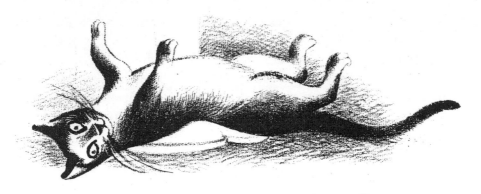

static approval of his words. After Mr. Salinus had calmed down, his wife sighed and said she did not think they would have any friends on the block any more, and probably the children would have no one to play with.

"We will have Serapina," the children said loyally.

Mrs. Salinus shook her head sadly and said that everyone would think they were crazier than ever to be satisfied with just a cat to play with.

"But we couldn't give her up after all she's done for us," Sally declared. "Could we?"

Everyone agreed they could not.

The next day when the committee came to call again, Mrs. Salinus met them at the door.

"You need not waste any time," she said, "trying to change our minds. We cannot part with Serapina and we will not think of sending her away. You will just have to accept her."

"We might be willing to do that," Mrs. Potts said cautiously, "if you could prove to us, before our very eyes, that she actually does do the things the children say she does. But really, Jane, it's asking a great deal to expect us to believe something none of us has seen any sign of."

"Occasionally," Mrs. Timmins said, "one likes to have proof."

Mrs. Salinus sighed deeply and said she was terribly sorry but she did not see how anyone could make Serapina show proof if she did not feel like doing so, which she obviously did not. So the committee departed to report that afternoon to the Dorcas Society Sewing Social that Serapina was going to remain on the block and that was that. The ladies all went home and told their husbands that the Salinuses were keeping their cat that there was so much talk about. The husbands said, oh, yes, that cat, the one that did such strange things for a cat. The ladies then looked very mysterious and suspicious and told their husbands that was just the point. Did the cat do such strange things? And, if it did, why hadn't the ladies ever seen it doing any of these things? Mr. MacPherson said probably none of the ladies was around at the time, but no one heard him say so. Everyone continued to talk about witch cats and to advise everyone else to avoid the Salinus family and their cat from now on. I'm sorry to say everyone acted upon this advice. Mr. and Mrs. Salinus were not asked out after supper any more, and the two little Timminses and Betsy Potts did not come over to play.

"I don't care about Betsy Potts and I love Serapina," Bobby said. But Betsy Potts cried all day long that she wanted to go and play with "Sarah."

"We can play by ourselves," Sally and Peter said. "We don't have to play with the two little Timminses." But the two little Timminses told their mother that they could not play by themselves and they wanted to go and play with Sally and Peter and Serapina. Mrs. Timmins then said quite a lot of things under her breath about the Salinus family.

Of course the news about everyone's avoiding the Salinus household soon got about to Daisy and Maisie and they were very indignant.

"Mean, that's what I call it," Daisy said to Maisie. "All these here grownups being so snooty about Serapina. Why she's smarter than the whole pack of 'em." And Daisy's pastries got heavier and heavier.

"And why should they all pick on her 'cause she doesn't like mice?" Maisie asked. "They don't either." And she put less and less sugar into her sweet puddings.

"She sure is somep'n," the plumber's nephew said to Daisy and Maisie, of whom he was very fond. "I wisht I could buy her and show her off."

178

Very shortly the block became divided into two camps, the Fors and the Againsts Serapina. Matters grew worse every day of the week, because, unfortunately, the Againsts were much stronger than the Fors, being more in number and in years and in authority. The Authority was the hardest to bear because there was nothing to be done but obey it.

The three Salinus children, in the meantime, played with Serapina by themselves and knew nothing of what went on up and down the block. Finally, one Saturday evening, as the three children were sitting on the back porch waiting for the frosting pan and spoon, they began to find out. So did Serapina, who was dozing under the porch steps where any conversation above her could be heard if it seemed worth the effort. Daisy appeared on the Munsons' back porch all of a sudden and burst into tears.

"Why, Daisy," Sally called to her, "I thought you never worked on Saturdays."

"I don't," Daisy sniveled. "Neither does Maisie, and neither does the plumber's nephew. But today we have to, and there is a square dance tonight."

"How come?" asked Peter sympathetically.

It seemed that recently Daisy and Maisie had had their minds more on Serapina and the injustices done her than on their pastries and puddings. The plumber's nephew's mind had also been on Serapina and the possibility, maybe, of buying her. The long and the short of this matter was that these three young people had to work on Saturday to make up for their absent-mindedness during the week. Or, Daisy hinted, they would have to be finding other jobs.

"My!" exclaimed Sally, quite horrified at such cruelty. "Would they fire you?"

"And all because you love Serapina!" Peter said in a dramatic voice.

"Well, not quite that," Daisy confessed, because nothing had really been said by anyone about finding other jobs. "But," she continued, unable to resist the drama in Sally's suggestion, "I'm afraid they *might* fire us."

179

"They probably would," Peter remarked wisely. "But you would still love Serapina, wouldn't you?"

"Oh, yes," Daisy promised earnestly. "We all would. The two little Timminses and Betsy Potts, they suffer a lot, just like us," Daisy went on. "They are kept locked up."

"Locked up?" Peter and Sally exclaimed together in shocked tones.

"Well, they suffer," Daisy insisted, "and they are kept home."

"We are all suffering quite a lot for Serapina," Sally observed. "But, of course, she had done a great deal for us and we couldn't very well let her down by sending her away."

"I should really like to see the two little Timminses again," Peter said wistfully.

"You won't though," Daisy assured him. "Their mother thinks Serapina is a witch cat. She won't believe anything we say about her till she sees her doing some of her tricks herself."

"I wish Betsy would come and play with me." Bobby sighed.

"Well, she won't," Sally told him, "because her mother thinks just the same as everybody else about Serapina."

At this moment Mrs. Salinus stepped out onto the porch with the frosting pan and spoon.

"Gracious, Daisy! What is that awful smell?" she asked.

Daisy sniffed. "My upside-down cake!" she shrieked and disappeared.

"Now she'll have to work on Sunday too," Sally remarked. "It's my turn for the spoon."

"Where is Serapina?" Mrs. Salinus asked.

But no one had seen her.

Serapina was just as glad they hadn't. The conversation embarrassed her, and she was blushing painfully to herself under the steps. Modest as she was about her talents in front of grownups, she realized that there was something more important than modesty, and that was loyalty. Her friends were loyal to her in spite of the fun it cost them, and, she thought, it was about time she repaid them.

There was, she reluctantly decided, only one way to do this. Serapina sighed and swallowed her modesty.

The next morning, which was a bright and cheerful Sunday, there sounded up and down the block a call the like of which was never heard before or since in that neighborhood. It was Serapina, and there was no mistaking what she wanted and when she wanted it. She wanted attention and she wanted it right away. She was walking up and down the ridgepole of the Salinus house, and, after two turns up and down, she had attention. Most of the people on the block had come out into their yards to see who was killing whom. When they saw Serapina they decided she must have turned dangerous, as everyone said she would, and they hoped Mr. Salinus had a gun.

Serapina, as soon as she roused the attention of the neighbors, slid down the gutterpipe to the yard. She trotted smartly to the back door, wrapped her tail firmly around a quart of milk she had left there earlier, and shot out the front gate with it. She kept to the grass to avoid breaking the bottle, which she deposited on the Munsons' front steps.

"Good gracious!" exclaimed Mr. Munson.

Serapina picked up the bottle again just to be sure the Munsons saw her do it.

They did. "Well," gasped Mrs. Munson with relief, "Daisy

181

isn't touched after all. I shall go straight and apologize to her."

Serapina flourished her tail and sped on down the block, followed first by the cheering children and then by the gaping grownups. She made straight for Mrs. MacPherson's yard, just stopping to duck up the front paths to open the front door of every house she passed. Once in the MacPherson frontyard she slowed down.

"Shoo, cat," Mrs. MacPherson said, not very heartily, but Serapina paid no attention. Gloating over every step of the way, she advanced slowly toward Bonzo, who was standing obediently beside his mistress. With each step she took, Bonzo trembled more and more. He turned his pleading eyes on his mistress, but Mrs. MacPherson didn't even look at him. Serapina came on with her whiskers turned definitely up. She walked under the trembling dog's nose, tickled it with her tail, passed under his stomach, giving him a playful poke as she did so, and then looped her tail through the ring in his collar. Leading him after her, she walked him twice around Mrs. MacPherson, who was much too mortified to open her mouth.

Serapina then released Bonzo and stepped briskly over into Mrs. Fowler's yard. Before Mrs. Fowler had time to faint, Serapina vanished into the house and came back with Alex-

182

ander riding happily on her back. Alexander was saying loudly that he liked it, yes, he did. Accompanied by Alexander, who refused to leave her back, Serapina dropped into the Pottses' yard, where she rummaged around until she found Betsy's ball. Bobby and Betsy, who were with the other children behind her, understood at once what she wanted and came forward to have a game with her. Serapina, to her apparent annoyance, discovered then that it was difficult to play ball with Alexander clinging to her back. He was heavy and threw her off her balance, but he would not take the hint and go home. Serapina left the ball game and returned to her own yard. She went quickly up the apple tree and hung by her tail. Alexander plopped into the sandpile, where he swore violently, watching Serapina swinging lazily to and fro above his head. After a while she righted herself and eyed the group of gaping grownups and cheering children below her. Then she came down from the tree, pulled Bobby's express cart across to Alexander, who promptly got into it. If Alexander thought he was going to get

a ride home, however, he was mistaken. Serapina was rapidly getting bored with this show-off business. At last she ran up her own front steps, rang her bell twice, and disappeared indoors.

After she had finished proving to everyone that she could do everything everyone said no cat could do, the grownups said nothing for a long time. Betsy Potts and the two little Timminses, Daisy and Maisie and the plumber's nephew, and the three Salinus children said exactly what you or I would have said. They said, "We told you so."

Then the grownups found their tongues, and they said over and over again, "Goodness gracious!" and "Oh, my! Oh, my!" and "I don't believe it!" But, of course, they had to believe it. So they mumbled rather sheepishly to Mr. and Mrs. Salinus, except Amanda MacPherson, who did not know how to mumble.

"You could knock me right down with a feather," she boomed. "With a small feather at that!"

Then everyone began to drift home, muttering and shaking his head, because he had seen the cat doing all those things he had heard she did. That meant that either the cat had bewitched them all or that she was a most extraordinary cat. It hardly seemed likely that they were all bewitched, so they decided that Serapina was an extraordinary cat.

"Not at all selfish like most cats," Polly Potts said.

"Such a dear pussy," cooed Mrs. Fowler. "So good with my little friends, *and* my big friend."

"Not at all a common cat," was as far as Mrs. MacPherson would go.

"Real smart cat, that," the plumber said to his nephew and gave him a half-dollar for the movies.

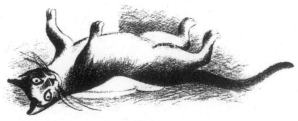

Miriam E. Mason

CAKE FOR COMPANY DINNER

ILLUSTRATED BY *Janet Ross*

MOTHER was a fine hand at getting up a company dinner.

"There is not a woman in Kenton County who can beat Mother at getting up a good company dinner," Pa always said. "I am not ashamed to have anybody come home for dinner with me whether they are expected or not."

Even the preacher always liked best of all to eat his Sunday dinners at Mother's house. Mother knew how to fry chicken so that you could hardly know when to stop eating it; and she knew how to boil chicken and make dumplings which were as soft and light as little feather pillows.

But Mother's cakes were the pride of the family. Mother could make a dozen different kinds of cakes. She could make pound cake, sponge cake, fruit cake, layer cake, ginger cake, and many other kinds. Whenever there was a church supper, everybody looked for Mother's cake. They would have been disappointed if she had not had two or three cakes on the table.

Whenever there was company to sit around the big buckeye-wood table, Mother always had one or two kinds of cake. For a Sunday dinner when the preacher was there, she usually had two kinds of cake. For an ordinary company dinner, she always had at least one cake, covered with fine, thick sugar frosting.

Reprinted by permission of the publishers, J. B. Lippincott Company, from *O, Happy Day*, by Miriam Mason. Copyright, 1939, by J. B. Lippincott Company.

Of course in those times no company dinner would seem right without at least one large frosted cake. A woman who did not have cake for her company dinner would feel ashamed. It would be like leaving off part of your clothes when you are dressed up to go someplace. It would be like leaving off your hat when you were going to church on Sunday.

Miney had learned to bake cake now. She could make a fine buttermilk spice cake. When she wanted to have a very fancy cake, she would make a marble buttermilk spice cake with red frosting.

To make a marble cake, you put your cake batter into two bowls when it was mixed. You put spices in one bowl and made the batter brown. You left the other just plain colored. Then you poured the batter into the pan turn-about; first the plain and then the brown, then the plain and then the brown. When the cake was baked, it was brown and cream-colored in streaks, like the top of Mother's stand table in the parlor.

To make the cake frosting red, you put beet juice in it. Miney just loved to make red cake frosting.

"Even a plain cake has an elegant look when it is covered with red frosting," she said. "If a cake has plenty of red frosting on the outside, it does not matter so much about the taste of the inside!"

These days, however, Mother did not get quite so many big company dinners.

"With Pa and so many of the men away at the War, it does not seem right," she said.

The day was Wednesday.

"I must go over and see about Auntie Rayl today," said Mother, as the family sat at the breakfast table. "Her rheumatism has been bad for a good while, and Uncle Jake is poorly, too. I will go over after the breakfast work is done and spend the day with Auntie."

"Can I go along as far as Grandmother Preston's and spend the day with her?" asked Miney.

"No, you had better stay at home. You will need to shut up the little chickens and help see after things. I will try to be home

186

in time to help get supper. Tonight is prayer-meeting night. Maybe I will bring Auntie Rayl and Uncle Jake home with me and they can go to prayer-meeting afterwards."

"Shall I fix up a company supper, then?" asked Miney. "Bob could kill a chicken, and I could boil it with dumplings and make a marble cake."

Mother shook her head. "There is plenty of fresh pieplant sauce in the upground cellar," she said, "and there is a jar half full of those ginger cookies I made last Saturday. You will not need to make the cake. I will kill and dress an old rooster before I go, and you can boil it all day and have dumplings. Auntie Rayl and Uncle Jake can eat the dumplings even if they cannot eat the chicken."

So Mother got the old rooster ready to boil before she drove off with Old Kit and the buggy. She took the baby with her.

"We will have a long, quiet day, with plenty of time to play in the playhouse," said Sairy. "All we need for dinner is just a snack."

The girls had a nice time that forenoon. After they had finished their morning work, they still had a long time to play in their playhouse. The old rooster was boiling in the black iron kettle on the back of the stove. Bob and Silas went down to the creek to fish. It was a quiet day.

When dinnertime came, the girls went up to the house to look after the chicken and get a snack for dinner. They found that the boys had taken all the rest of the ginger cookies down to the creek with them, as they always liked to eat while they were fishing.

"Never mind, though," said Miney. "With the boys gone, we will not even need to set the table. We will just eat a piece out of our hands. Then we will not have any dishes to wash."

So the girls ate bread and apple butter and dill pickles and a part of a blackberry pie that was left from day before yesterday. The nice part of that dinner was that there were no dishes to wash after it. When they finished eating, all they had to do was to put another big chunk of wood in the stove, put some more water on the chicken and go back to play some more.

187

About the middle of the afternoon they saw a surrey drive up and stop in front of their gate. Jip began to bark. Sairy said, "Oh, look; there is company!"

"Company!" said Miney. "Great, bright, heavenly day! Who could be coming at this time of day to see us? And riding in a surrey, too?"

"They will be staying for supper, too," said Sairy. "Oh, dear, I do hope Mother gets home right away. What will we do with Mother gone, and company here for supper?"

"I am not worried," said Miney, hurrying up to the house. "I can get as good a company supper as anybody. I can cook chicken. I can make dumplings. I can make a marble cake with red frosting."

The girls hurried to the house. The company were standing on the front porch, just getting ready to knock at the door. It was the Warrens, and there were five of them. There were old Mr. Warren, Mrs. Warren, their married daughter, Jennie, and their old-maid daughter, Jessie. There was also the married daughter's daughter, Josie, who was a fine young lady from Dayton.

The girls said hello to all the company. "Come in," said Miney, opening the front door. "I suppose you have come for supper, haven't you?"

"Mother has gone over to Uncle Jake Rayl's house to spend the day," said Sairy, as they went into the house. "But she will be back in time to get supper."

"Do not mention that," said Mrs. Warren. "We do not want to put your ma to any trouble getting supper for us. Jennie was visiting, and she wanted to be sure and see your ma. But we do not want your ma going to any trouble for us."

"Come on into the parlor," said Miney, leading the company into Mother's best room. It was very clean and dark in there, with the window blinds pulled down, and the fresh white tidies on the back of the chairs. "Just make yourselves at home," said Miney, raising the blinds.

The Warrens sat down, and they all talked for a while about the weather, the corn crop, the War, and other things. Mr. Warren was too old to be in the War, but their married daughter's husband was in the War. His name was Mr. Lemons, and he was an officer. He was a Corporal.

Every now and then Miney would say, "Please excuse me while I go see about my supper," then she would go out to the kitchen and stir the fire and look into the kettle to see if the chicken was getting tender.

About an hour passed by.

"Mother will not be home in time to get a good company supper," thought Miney. "It would be a disgrace for Mother to have company and not have a nice supper for them. I am going ahead and get the supper. I am going to surprise Mother by having the supper ready when she comes home."

So she went back into the parlor and told the Warrens, "If you will please excuse me, I will be going ahead with the supper. Just make yourselves at home, and I will soon have the supper ready."

She got out Mother's autograph album for the company to look at. She got out the red plush photograph album which Pa had bought Mother for Christmas last year. It did not have any photographs in it yet, but it was pretty to look at. She got out the singing-school book and gave it to Miss Josie Lemons.

"Here is a book of songs," she said. "It will be all right for

189

you to play the melodeon as much as you want to."

"We will help you get the supper, Miney," said Mrs. Warren and her married daughter.

But Miney said, "Oh, no, not at all. There is hardly anything to do. You have on your good silk dress. Mother would not like it if I let you help with the cooking."

Miney and Sairy went out to get the supper while the Warrens made themselves at home in the parlor.

"I am so glad we have a melodeon and a songbook," said Miney, as they heard the sound of *Darling Nellie Gray* coming from the parlor.

Sairy said, "Oh, Miney, I am so afraid Mother will not be home in time to get supper for all this company, and how will it look to have only a snack when the Warrens come, dressed in their silk dresses, especially since Mrs. Lemons' husband is an officer in the War?"

"This is no time to cry over spilt milk," said Miney. "Go out to the barnyard and call the boys. Call them until they answer. Tell them to hurry home. When they get here, tell them to catch two more chickens and kill them."

Sairy did as she was told, and at last the boys came in with the two chickens. They did not like it because they had to take the feathers from the chickens and help to dress them. They did not want to leave their fishing. But they were afraid not to do as Miney told them, because she sounded just like Grandmother Preston.

"If you do not help, I will see that you get switched with a hickory switch when Pa gets home from the War," she said.

So Bob and Silas got the chickens ready to put on while Miney peeled potatoes, and stirred up the dumplings, and mixed buttermilk biscuits. Sairy set the table with the best blue dishes.

"We will have boiled rooster with dumplings, and fried hens with gravy," said Miney. "We will have mashed potatoes and sauerkraut and canned tomatoes and pickles and several kinds of jelly and sorghum and honey and hot biscuits and butter and one of my marble cakes with red sugar frosting."

"That ought to be enough to keep the Warrens from starving," said Silas, looking cross as he cut open a chicken and took out the insides.

Miney began to get things ready for her marble cake. She got buttermilk and spices and sugar and eggs and lard. The flour box in the butt'ry was nearly empty.

"You go out to the flour barrel in the smokehouse and get me a panful of flour," she said to Sairy. Mother always kept the big flour barrel out in the smokehouse, where it was cooler. "Hurry now. I will be stirring up the eggs and sugar."

Soon Sairy came back with an empty pan. "The flour barrel is empty," she said. "There is not even a half a cupful of flour."

Miney's cheeks turned pale. "Empty? The flour barrel empty? . . ."

Then she remembered hearing Mother say that the flour was nearly gone, and they would soon need to be taking some more wheat to the mill.

"I already knew that," said Silas, looking cross as he cleaned the gizzard of the chicken. "I could have told you. I scraped out the last of the flour for Mother last week."

Miney wanted to cry. "What will we do?" she said. "It will be time to eat in an hour. What will we do without a cake for our company supper? Mother will be ashamed. The Warrens

191

will talk about it. Oh, if I had only known before I used all the flour to make biscuits."

"The Warrens will have to eat biscuits," said Bob, finishing the second chicken. "They will have to eat biscuits and play like they are eating cake."

"Think of Mother," said Miney, putting the chickens on to fry. She had to dip them in cornmeal because there was no flour. "It will be a disgrace to Mother. The Warrens will tell other people that she did not have any cake for her company supper."

Sairy said, "If only the boys had not eaten all the ginger cookies. . . . If they had only not been such pigs. If they had only left even one apiece."

"It is too late to cry over spilt milk," said Miney. She thought for awhile. "We will have to have lots of other things to eat. Silas, go to the smokehouse and get a ham. Get a can of that sausage. Bring in some eggs."

Silas was cross, but he did as he was told because he was afraid not to, and besides he had eaten most of the ginger cookies.

"You go to the cellar," said Miney to Sairy. "Get some of nearly everything. Get some piccalilli. Get some watermelon preserves. Get some crab-apple preserves. Get some cider apple sauce. Get some corn relish. Get something to go in every one of Mother's glass dishes."

Sairy did as she was told.

"There are more ways of killing a dog than by choking it on hot butter," said Miney. "I am not going to have people talking about my mother because she has company for supper and there is no cake!"

Miney went into the butt'ry. She made a big loaf of corn bread in the cake pan. She had eggs and buttermilk and sugar in it. It was just about like cake except that it was corn bread instead of cake. She baked it in the oven. It looked just like a big round loaf cake.

When the corn bread was cool, she made red frosting to go on it. She put plenty of beet juice in the frosting so it was nice and red. Then she put it on the big cake plate and set it over on the shelf where Mother always put her cakes. It was beautiful.

"But what will the Warrens say when they taste the cake?" asked Sairy. "Oh, Miney, I am so afraid they will know it is only corn bread."

"They will not taste it," said Miney. "Nobody will taste it. I will not cut it. . . . Wait and see. And be sure to say, 'No, thank you,' when I ask you if you want any cake!"

She told Silas and Bob the same thing. Then she called the Warrens out to supper. All the Warrens looked happy when they saw the supper on the table.

The long table was just as full as it could be. It took two dishes and two platters to hold the chicken. It took three platters to hold the ham and sausage and eggs. Every dish that Mother had was on the table with something in it.

"Take chairs, folks," said Miney, in a company voice. "Mr. Warren, you can sit in Pa's chair at the head of the table and ask the Blessing. The rest of you can sit wherever you want to."

They all took chairs, and Mr. Warren asked the Blessing. Then everybody began to eat.

Miney waited on the table. She kept saying to all the Warrens,

"Do have some more chicken. Do have some more ham. Do have some sausage. Do eat some of this pickle and some of this preserve. Have another hot biscuit."

The Warrens kept on eating and eating. At first they ate fast, as if they were hungry, and then they ate more slowly, but Miney kept begging them to keep eating.

"Why, you have hardly had enough to keep a bird alive," she said. "You have hardly touched a bite. Have some more of everything. Do sit up and eat hearty."

At last nobody could eat anything else. Miney waited for a minute. Then she jumped up as if she had suddenly remembered something.

"Mercy gracious!" she cried. "What do you suppose? What do you think? Guess what I did not do?"

Nobody could guess. Miney went over to the shelf where the beautiful big red loaf of corn bread was sitting.

"You see?" she said, pointing to it. "I did not cut my cake! I had a cake ready, covered with frosting and everything, and then I did not cut it! Oh, how careless of me. . . . For now I am sure you are all too full to eat any of my cake!"

"It looks like a fine cake," said Mr. Warren, who was very fond of cake. "I wish I had seen it a little sooner."

"To think a person would make a cake and then not cut it!" said Miney. "But I was so busy getting the other things on the table . . . I suppose you are all too full to eat any now . . . even the boys. Do you want any cake, boys?"

Silas said he did not want any cake. Bob just laughed.

"It is too bad for you to have all that trouble for nothing, Miney," said Mrs. Warren. She looked as if she would really like to try a piece of the cake. Sairy was worried. She said, "Oh, Miney, I am so afraid—"

"Yes, I am afraid for you, too," said Miney, looking at her. "I am afraid you would have a stomach-ache if you tried to eat any cake after all the other things you have eaten. It would serve you right for being a pig, too. . . . Would you like for me to cut the cake and give you some, Mrs. Lemons?"

Mrs. Lemons said she guessed not, and all the other Warrens

194

said they guessed they did not care for any of the cake this evening.

So Miney took a long breath and sat down. Sairy looked scared, and Bob kept laughing to himself, but everybody thought it was just because he was so bashful.

Mother came home just as the Warrens were pushing their chairs back from the supper-table. She was surprised to see the Warrens, and she was surprised to see what a fine, big supper the girls had fixed.

"You have two very smart girls, Mrs. Glossbrenner," said Mr. Warren to Mother. "I can see they take after their mother. I bet there is not a pair of girls in Kenton County that could get up a supper like this!"

Mother looked at the table. She hardly knew what to say. She looked at the fine red cake on the shelf.

"But you have not finished supper," she said. "You have not had any cake."

Mrs. Lemons sat back down. "I would not want more than a small piece," she said. Bob began to laugh. Mother looked at him. "What on earth is the matter?" she asked. Bob's face was very red.

"Such a joke, Mother," said Miney. "I made a cake, and then I did not cut it, and everybody ate so much that they could not

195

eat any cake after all. Of course, nobody wanted to be a pig. . . .
Not even the boys."

"Maybe you will feel like eating a piece before you go home,"
said Mother. Sairy looked worried. Bob laughed to himself.

Mrs. Warren offered to stay out in the kitchen and help wash
the dishes, but Miney said, "Thank you kindly, Mrs. Warren.
We will wash the dishes after you go. We will not mind washing a few dishes, since we know we will not have to bake a cake
for tomorrow."

Miney was very, very thankful when the Warrens finally
drove away in their surrey, after saying what a lovely supper
they had had.

"Come back again," said Mother.

"Come back for supper another time," Miney said. "I will
bake another cake, and I will not forget to cut it the next time."

Then she went in and looked at the table with all the dishes.

"It will take a long time to wash all those dishes," she said
to Sairy. "It will take us a long time to eat up those left-over
preserves and pickles. I am sorry we had to cut the last ham
and open Mother's best sausage."

She looked at the beautiful red loaf of corn bread.

"But, anyway, they cannot talk about us," she said in a proud
voice. "They cannot talk about the Glossbrenners. Nobody can
say that we had company for supper and did not offer them
any cake!"

She took another piece of chicken and began to sing *The
Star Spangled Banner.*

THE JUGGLER

J. G. Francis

An elephant sat on some kegs
And juggled glass bottles and eggs.
And he said, "I surmise
This occasions surprise——
But oh, how it tires one's legs!"

196

Paul T. Gilbert

BERTRAM AND THE
MUSICAL CROCODILE

ILLUSTRATED BY *Clarence Biers*

AS A REWARD for learning to like his oatmeal mush, Bertram's daddy had given him a dime. Bertram had bought an ocarina with the dime and had learned to play on it. He learned to play "Old Black Joe" and "Blue Bells of Scotland" and "My Wild Irish Rose." He played the ocarina so much that he neglected his piano exercises. He went "Toodle-oodle-oo" all day, and the sharp noise nearly drove his mamma distracted. Sharp noises always gave her a headache.

"I've stood this as long as I'm going to," she said finally, as she stuffed her fingers in her ears. "That sounds like the tune the old cow died to."

"What old cow?" asked Bertram.

"I don't know!" exclaimed his mamma. "For heaven's sake, give us some peace. If you *must* play, go and practice your piano exercises. You haven't touched the piano for a week."

"That's 'Old Black Joe,' the tune I was playing," said Bertram. "Don't you think it's kinda gay?"

"Gay? Well, a crocodile might think so. That's all I can say."

"Do crocodiles like music, Mamma?" asked Bertram, who was always interested in wild animals.

"How should I know?" said his mamma. "What I meant was that any creature who bites people and then cries and pretends to be sorry for them *might* think that tune of yours was gay."

"Oh!" said Bertram. "Is that the way crocodiles do?"

"That isn't the point," said Bertram's mamma. "We are getting off the subject. What I'm trying to tell you is that you're wasting your time and driving me mad with that ocarina when you ought to be practicing on the piano. I should think you'd get sick and tired of that everlasting tooting."

"But it's *lots* of fun, Mamma," replied Bertram. "And I don't get tired of it at all. It's lots more fun than practicing those stupid old piano exercises."

Bertram's mamma sighed. "Well, go out in the backyard and play your ocarina then if you have to. Only *do* give us a little peace."

So Bertram went out to the backyard and began to play "Old Black Joe." He played it seventeen times, and had about decided that he'd quit and see if George Fish wanted to go swimming, when he felt something cold and clammy against his legs.

Bertram looked down and there at his feet lay a great, big, monstrous *crocodile*. The crocodile was grinning up at Bertram in a sickly sort of way, but oddly enough, his eyes were filled with tears, and tears were running down his cheeks.

Bertram was scared at first and started to run away. But the crocodile said, in a low, croaky sort of voice, "Don't go. Play that tune again. It's such a gay tune that it makes me cry."

"Do gay tunes make you cry?" asked Bertram. "My mamma says that was the tune the old cow died to, but that probably you'd like it."

"Oh, I do," said the crocodile, "and talking of old cows—but no matter. I could listen to that tune forever." And the crocodile sobbed and dried his eyes with his pocket handkerchief.

So Bertram played "Old Black Joe" again for the crocodile. He was quite pleased that somebody, at least, liked his music.

"Boo-hoo-hoo. No wonder I feel like crying," said the crocodile. " 'Old Black Joe.' No wonder! Boo-hoo-hoo. I knew a black Joe once—not an old one, but a young and tender one—like you. I bit him a little. Oh, dear! But it was sad."

And the crocodile burst into another flood of tears. Bertram felt almost like crying himself, only he didn't know whether to feel sorry for poor little Joe or for the crocodile.

"Don't cry," said Bertram. "I'll play you 'My Wild Irish Rose.' That's a sad one. It will make you laugh."

198

So Bertram got his ocarina and played . . . and the Crocodile cried.

"Yes, do," said the crocodile. "I knew a little girl named Rose once, and a sweet little thing she was, too. Tasted like a chocolate drop. She was making mud pies on the river bank and came too close. I bit her. Not enough to hurt—it just tickled really. Yes, play me the tune about Rose."

Bertram didn't exactly like the trend the conversation was taking. It made him a little uneasy. But he played the tune, and the crocodile cried as if his heart would break.

"Do you know any more tunes?" asked the crocodile. "For if you do, I'd like to hear them."

"Oh, I can play 'Blue Bells of Scotland,' " said Bertram, "only I don't know it very well yet."

"Just do the best you can then," said the crocodile. "I knew a little girl named Belle, too. But she wasn't blue exactly. More what you'd called black. Poor little Belle! How she *did* wiggle when I bit her!"

"Do you always feel sorry for the people you bite?" asked Bertram.

"Why, of course. I don't really hurt much, or at least I try not to—but of course it tickles, and they wiggle," said the crocodile.

"That doesn't do them much good, does it?" said Bertram. "I mean your feeling sorry for them, not their wiggling."

"No, I don't suppose so," said the crocodile, and he grinned at Bertram.

Bertram was beginning to feel more and more uneasy. There was something in that grin he didn't like. But he played "Blue Bells of Scotland," and when he had finished, he said, "I will have to go in now and practice my piano exercises."

"Oh, dear!" said the crocodile. "I was afraid of that. Well, I'll go with you then, and when you get through playing the piano, you can play your ocarina for me. All those tunes about Old Black Joe and Rose and Belle. I can live under the porch."

"Well, that will be all right," said Bertram doubtfully. "Only I think you ought to wear a muzzle or something."

"Oh! *That*," said the crocodile, snicking his teeth. "Don't let that bother you. I'll promise to be good. Don't you worry about me."

But when Bertram's mamma saw the crocodile, she disapproved. "I'm not going to have that creature around here unmuzzled," she declared. "Especially with Baby Sam under foot and getting into everything! It would be a mercy. If you're going to keep that crocodile under the porch, I'll have to fasten his mouth shut with sticking plaster."

So Bertram's mamma fastened the crocodile's mouth shut with sticking plaster, and Bertram went indoors to practice his piano exercises. He had been practicing for about fifteen minutes, and his mamma was thinking what a good boy he was, when the crocodile began to make a fuss.

Bertram went out to the back porch. "What are you making such a fuss for?" he demanded. "You will wake up Baby Sam."

"Oh, here you are," mumbled the crocodile, who couldn't talk very plain through the sticking plaster. "I thought you were never coming. Play me those tunes about all the people I bit."

So Bertram got his ocarina and played "Old Black Joe" and "My Wild Irish Rose" and "Blue Bells of Scotland," and the crocodile cried.

200

"Play them again," said the crocodile. "I like them so!"

Bertram played the tunes again, but he was getting tired of them by this time. The crocodile, however, wanted more, and after Bertram had played them twenty-seven times—until his cheeks ached and his breath was all gone, he said, "Oh, I forgot. I've got to go in and practice."

So he went in and practiced until suppertime. And his mamma said, "How Bertram is improving!"

But that night, after he was sound asleep, he heard the crocodile making a fuss under his window. And he looked out and said, "Stop making that fuss. Are you crazy?"

"All right, then," said the crocodile. "Come down and play me some more tunes."

So Bertram went down in his nightgown and played tunes for the crocodile. He played for more than an hour, and all the time the crocodile just grinned and cried. Then Bertram said, "Oh, I forgot. I've got to do my practicing." That was the only way he could get rid of the crocodile.

And he started practicing with the soft petal. But his mamma heard him and came down to see what he was doing. And she said, "When I told you to practice, I didn't mean that you had to practice all night. What's the matter with you? Keeping the whole house awake! You can practice all day tomorrow if you want to. Go upstairs immediately and get into bed."

Right after breakfast next morning, Bertram began practicing like fury. And his mamma said, "I never saw a boy so crazy about practicing all of a sudden. I wonder what's got into him."

And Julia Krause said, "I wonder, too."

But Bertram wasn't crazy about practicing at all. He was only doing it so he wouldn't have to play the ocarina for the crocodile. He had been at it about half an hour when the crocodile began to carry on and make a fuss.

But Bertram's mamma went to the back door and said, "Stop that noise. Bertram is practicing. He doesn't want to be disturbed."

So the crocodile quieted down. Only as soon as Bertram's

mamma wasn't looking, he nudged the screen door open and sneaked into the house and stuck his ugly old head up on the piano keys.

And Bertram said, "You don't belong here. Go away." And he kept right on practicing.

But the crocodile said, "No, no. Not that bang-bang music. Play the toodle-oo music on that sweet potato thing."

So Bertram had to go outdoors and play his ocarina for the crocodile. He played for him until his mamma called him in to dinner. Then, as soon as dinner was over, he sat down at the piano and began to practice. Bertram knew his lesson by heart now, and he was tired of playing the same thing over and over, but it was a lot better than playing tunes for that old crocodile.

He had been practicing for about two hours when George Fish came to the back door to see if Bertram was at home. But the crocodile said, "What do you want? If you want Bertram to go swimming with you, he can't, because he's got to practice.

And when he gets through practicing, he's going to play the ocarina for me."

Then George went to the front door. But Bertram's mamma said, "No, Bertram is practicing now. He can't go swimming today."

So George went home.

Poor Bertram wanted to go swimming awfully. And he wished he didn't have to practice any more. Only he knew that if he stopped, the crocodile would make a fuss, and he would have to play the ocarina. He just *hated* the ocarina by this time.

So he felt sorry for himself and began to cry. And his eyes were so full of tears that at first he didn't see the crocodile, who had sneaked into the house again and crawled into the parlor.

The crocodile said, "Boo!" and Bertram jumped. Then he noticed that the crocodile had licked off the sticking plaster and was grinning at him as if he would split right in two.

"Go away," said Bertram, "and quit bothering me."

"Come on out then," said the crocodile. And he looked a little as if he were beginning to feel sorry for Bertram.

"I won't," said Bertram. And he kept on practicing.

"Oh, all right for *you* then," said the crocodile. And he snicked his teeth and opened his mouth *wide*.

But just as the crocodile went for Bertram, Bertram jumped up on top of the piano and raised the lid and crawled inside. Bertram's mamma heard the fuss and came running in from the kitchen. And she called out, "Bertram! Where are you?"

"I'm in here, Mamma," said Bertram from the inside of the piano, and his voice sounded as hollow as if it had come from a tomb.

"Where?" asked Bertram's mamma. "I can't see you."

"Right in here," said Bertram.

His mamma thought, of course, that he was inside of the crocodile, and she went all green. Luckily though, she kept her wits about her, and she grabbed the crocodile by the tail. And she got up on a chair and held the crocodile at arm's length and began to thump him. And my, but didn't he squirm and wiggle and squeak!

"Ouch! That hurts!" said the crocodile. "Cheese it!" And he began to cry in earnest.

Just then Bertram stuck his head up out of the piano and said, "Here I am, Mamma. I'm all right."

"Oh, *there* you are," said Bertram's mamma. "Thank goodness! What a relief!"

Then Bertram's mamma boxed the crocodile's ears *soundly*. And the crocodile said, "Ouch!"

"I'll give you something to cry about," said Bertram's mamma. "Take *that* and *that* and *that*!" And she boxed the crocodile's ears again.

Then she took the crocodile over her knee and gave him a good, sound spanking, until he howled like a regular cry-baby. And after that she took the poker and shooed the crocodile out of the house, and a dog chased him down Elm Street all the way to Kelley's Greasing Palace.

"All right, Bertram," said his mamma, when the crocodile was gone, "you can go on with your practicing."

And Bertram went on with his practicing.

Lewis Carroll

THE WALRUS AND THE CARPENTER

The sun was shining on the sea, shining with all his might:
He did his very best to make the billows smooth and bright—
And this was odd, because it was the middle of the night.

The moon was shining sulkily, because she thought the sun
Had got no business to be there after the day was done—
"It's very rude of him," she said, "to come and spoil the fun!"

The sea was wet as wet could be, the sands were dry as dry,
You could not see a cloud, because no cloud was in the sky:
No birds were flying overhead—there were no birds to fly.

The Walrus and the Carpenter were walking close at hand:
They wept like anything to see such quantities of sand:
"If this were only cleared away," they said, "it would be grand!"

"If seven maids with seven mops swept it for half a year,
Do you suppose," the Walrus said, "that they could get it clear?"
"I doubt it," said the Carpenter, and shed a bitter tear.

"O Oysters, come and walk with us!" the Walrus did beseech.
"A pleasant walk, a pleasant talk, along the briny beach:
We cannot do with more than four, to give a hand to each."

The eldest Oyster looked at him, but never a word he said:
The eldest Oyster winked his eye, and shook his heavy head—
Meaning to say he did not choose to leave the oyster bed.

But four young Oysters hurried up, all eager for the treat:
Their coats were brushed, their faces washed,
   their shoes were clean and neat—
And this was odd, because, you know, they hadn't any feet.

Four other Oysters followed them, and yet another four;
And thick and fast they came at last, and more, and more,
   and more—
All hopping through the frothy waves, and scrambling
   to the shore.

The Walrus and the Carpenter walked on a mile or so,
And then they rested on a rock conveniently low:
And all the little Oysters stood and waited in a row.

"The time has come," the Walrus said, "to talk of many things:
Of shoes—and ships—and sealing wax—of cabbages—and kings—
And why the sea is boiling hot—and whether pigs have wings."

"But wait a bit," the Oysters cried, "before we have our chat;
For some of us are out of breath, and all of us are fat!"
"No hurry!" said the Carpenter; they thanked him much for that.

"A loaf of bread," the Walrus said, "is what we chiefly need:
Pepper and vinegar besides are very good indeed—
Now, if you're ready, Oysters dear, we can begin to feed."

"But not on us!" the Oysters cried, turning a little blue.
"After such kindness, that would be a dismal thing to do!"
"The night is fine," the Walrus said; "Do you admire the view?

"It was so kind of you to come! And you are very nice!"
The Carpenter said nothing but "Cut us another slice.
I wish you were not quite so deaf—I've had to ask you twice!"

"It seems a shame," the Walrus said, "to play them such a trick.
After we've brought them out so far, and made them trot so
    quick!"
The Carpenter said nothing but "The butter's spread too thick!"

"I weep for you," the Walrus said: "I deeply sympathize."
With sobs and tears he sorted out those of the largest size,
Holding his pocket-handerchief before his streaming eyes.

"O Oysters," said the Carpenter, "you've had a pleasant run!
Shall we be trotting home again?" But answer came there none—
And this was scarcely odd, because they'd eaten every one.

Hugh Lofting

DR. DOLITTLE
MEETS A LONDONER IN PARIS

ILLUSTRATED BY THE AUTHOR

HERE is another adventure of Dr. Dolittle, the man who could talk to animals.

ONE day John Dolittle was walking alone
in the Tuileries Gardens. He had been
asked to come to France by some French
naturalists who wished to consult him on certain new features
to be added to the zoo in the *Jardin des Plantes*. The Doctor
knew Paris well and loved it. To his way of thinking it was the
perfect city—or would be, if it were not so difficult to get a
bath there.

It had been raining all day, but now the sun was shining,
and the gardens, fresh and wet, looked very beautiful. As the
Doctor passed one of the many shrubberies he came upon a
sparrow wallowing in a puddle in the middle of the gravel path.

"Why, I declare!" he muttered to himself, hurrying forward.
"It's Cheapside!"

The small bird, evidently quite accustomed to human traffic,
was far too busy with his bathing to notice anyone's approach.

"How do you do, Cheapside?" said the Doctor in sparrow
language. "Who on earth would ever have thought of finding
you here?"

The sparrow stopped his fluttering and wallowing and looked
up through the water that ran down in big drops off his tousled
head-feathers.

"Jiminy Crickets!" he exclaimed. "It's the Doc himself!"

"How do you come to be in Paris?" asked John Dolittle.

"Oh, it's all Becky's doing," grumbled Cheapside, hopping
out of the puddle and fluttering his wings to dry them. "I'm

satisfied to stay in London, goodness knows. But every Spring it's the same way: 'Let's take a hop over the Continong,' says she. 'The horse-chestnuts will just be budding.' 'We got horse-chestnut trees in Regent's Park,' I says to 'er. 'Ah,' says she, 'but not like the ones in the Twiddle-didee Gardens. Oh, I love Paris in the Spring,' she says . . . It's always the same way: every year she drags me over 'ere. Sentiment, I reckon it is. You see, Doc, me and Becky met one another first 'ere—right 'ere in the Twiddle-didee Gardens. I recognized 'er as a London Sparrow—you can tell 'em the world over—and we got talkin'. You know the way those things 'appen. She wanted to build our first nest up there in the Lufer Palace. But I says, 'No,' hemphatic. 'Let's go back to St. Paul's', I says. 'I know a place in St. Edmund's left ear what 'as all the stonework in Paris beat 'ollow as a nestin' place. Besides,' I says, 'we don't want our children growing up talkin' no foreign language! We're Londoners,' I says: 'let's go back to London.' "

"Yes," said the Doctor. "Even I guessed you were a London sparrow, before I recognized you, because—"

"Because I was washin'," Cheapside finished. "That's true: these 'ere foreign birds don't run to water much."

"That's a fine puddle you have there," said the Doctor. "I've half a mind to ask you to lend it to me. You know, I've been trying to get a bath myself ever since I've been in Paris—without success so far. After all, even a puddle is better than nothing. When I asked them at the *pension* where I'm staying could I have a bath, they seemed to think I was asking for the moon."

"Oh, I can tell you where you can get a bath, Doctor, a good one," said the sparrow. "Just the other side of that shrubbery over there there's an elegant marble pond, with a fountain and statues in the middle. You can hang your bath-towel on the statue and use the fountain for a shampoo. Just helegant!—But of course you'd have to do it after dark. You could manage a tub in the marble pond late at night, easy—because there's hardly anybody in the gardens then."

"My gracious! I've a good mind to try it, Cheapside," said the Doctor. "I haven't had a bath in over a week."

"Well," said the Cockney sparrow, "you meet me here at midnight and me and Becky will guide you to the pond and keep a lookout while you get a wash."

There was a half moon that night. And when, a few minutes before twelve o'clock, John Dolittle came into the Tuileries Gardens with a bath-towel over his arm, the first person he saw was a French policeman. Not wishing to be taken for a suspicious character, he thrust the bath-towel beneath his coat and hurried past the shrubbery as though bent on important business.

But he had not gone very far before he was overtaken by Cheapside and his wife, Becky.

"Don't get worried, Doc, don't get worried," said the sparrow. "That bobby only goes by about once every 'alf-hour. 'E won't be back for a while. Come over 'ere and we'll show you your dressing-room."

John Dolittle was thereupon conducted to a snug retreat in the heart of a big shrubbery.

"Nobody can see you 'ere," said Cheapside. "And as soon as you're ready all you've got to do is to 'op round that privet-'edge, sprint across the little lawn and there's your bath waitin' for you. Me and Becky will keep a lookout. And if any danger comes along we'll whistle."

Five minutes later the famous naturalist was wallowing luxuriously in the marble pond. The night was softly brilliant with moonlight, and the statues in the center of the pool stood out palely against the dark mass of the trees behind.

John Dolittle had paused a moment with a cake of soap uplifted in his hand, utterly enchanted by the beauty of the scene, when he heard Cheapside hoarsely whispering to him from a branch overhead.

"Look out! Hide quick! Someone coming!"

Now the Doctor had left his bath-towel on the base of the statue. At Cheapside's warning he splashed wildly out to get it before attempting to retreat to the shrubbery. Breathless, he finally reached the fountain. But just as he was about to

HUGH LOFTING

grasp the towel Becky called from the other side of the pond:

"Cheapside! There is another party coming in at the other gate! The Doctor can never make it in time."

John Dolittle, waist-deep in the water at the foot of the statue, looked about him in despair.

"Gracious! What shall I do then?" he cried, drawing the bath-towel over his shoulders.

"You'll have to be a statue," hissed Cheapside the quick thinker. "Hop up on to the pedestal. They'll never know the

213

difference in this light. When they go by you can come down. Hurry! They're quite close. I can see their heads over the top of the hedge."

Swiftly winding his bath-towel about him, John Dolittle sprang up on to the pedestal and crouched in a statuesque pose. The marble group was of Neptune the sea-god and several attendant figures. John Dolittle, M.D., became one of the attendant figures. His hand raised to shade his eyes from an imaginary sun, he gazed seaward with a stony stare.

"Fine!" whispered Cheapside, flying on to the base of the statue. "No one could tell you from the real thing. Just keep still and you'll be all right. They won't stay, I don't expect. Here they come. Don't get nervous, now. Bless me, I believe they're English too!—Tourists. Well, did you ever?"

A man and a woman, strolling through the gardens by one of the many crossing paths, had now paused at the edge of the pond and, to John Dolittle's horror, were gazing up at the statue in the center of it. They were both elderly; they both carried umbrellas; and they both wore spectacles.

"I'll bet they're short-sighted, Doc," whispered Cheapside comfortingly. "Don't worry."

"Dear me, Sarah," sighed the man. "What a beautiful night! The moon and the trees and the fountain. And such an imposing statue!—The sea-god Neptune with his mermaids and mermen."

"Lancelot," said the woman shortly, "let us hurry home. You'll get your bronchitis worse in this damp air. I don't like the statue at all. I never saw such fat creatures. Just look at that one on the corner there—the one with his hand up scanning the horizon. Why, he's stouter than the butcher at home!"

"Humph!" muttered Cheapside beneath his breath. "It don't seem to me as though *you* 'ave any figure to write 'ome about, Mrs. Scarecrow."

At this moment a large flying beetle landed on the Doctor's neck and nearly spoiled everything.

"Good gracious, Sarah!" cried the man. "I thought I saw one of the figures move, the fat one."

The tourist adjusted his spectacles and, coming a little closer

214

to the edge of the pond, stared very hard. But Cheapside, to add a touch of convincing realism, flew up on to the merman's shoulder, kicked the beetle into the pond with a secret flick of his foot and burst into a flood of carefree song.

"No, Sarah," said the man. "I was mistaken. See, there is a bird sitting on his shoulder. How romantic! Must be a nightingale."

"*Will* you come home, Lancelot?" snapped the woman. "You won't feel so romantic when your cough comes back. It must be after midnight."

"But you know, Sarah," said the man, as he was almost forcibly dragged away, "*I* don't think he's too fat. They had to be stout, those marine people: they floated better that way. Dear me, Paris is a beautiful city!"

As the footsteps died away down the moonlit path, John Dolittle sighed a great sigh of relief and came to life.

"Cheapside," said he, stretching his stiff arms, "you could never guess who those people were. My sister Sarah and her husband, the Reverend Lancelot Dingle. It's funny, Cheapside, but whenever I am in an awkward or ridiculous situation Sarah seems bound to turn up. Of course she and her husband would just *have* to come touring Paris at the exact hour when I was taking a bath in the Tuileries Gardens. Ah well, thank goodness the pond kept them off from getting any closer to me!"

"Well, listen, Doc," said the London sparrow, "I think you had better be gettin' along yourself now. It's about time for that bobby to be coming round again."

"Yes, you're right," said the Doctor. And he slid back into the water, waded to the edge and stepped out on to dry ground.

But John Dolittle's troubles were not over yet. While he was still no more than half way to his "dressing-room" there came another warning shout from Cheapside.

"Look out!—Here he comes!"

This time flight seemed the only course. The policeman had seen the culprit disappear into the shrubbery. Breaking into a run, he gave chase.

"Don't stop, Doc!" cried Cheapside. "Grab your clothes and

215

get out the other side—Becky! Hey, Becky! Keep that policeman busy a minute."

The Doctor did as he was told. Seizing his clothes in a pile as he rushed through the shrubbery, he came out at the other end like an express train emerging from a tunnel. Here Cheapside met him and led him across a lawn to another group of bushes. Behind this he hurriedly got into his clothes. Meanwhile Becky kept the policeman busy by furiously pecking him in the neck and making it necessary for him to stop and beat her off.

However, she could not of course keep this up for long. And if John Dolittle had not been an exceptionally quick dresser he could never have got away. In one minute and a quarter, collar and tie in one hand, soap and towel in the other, he left his second dressing-room on the run and sped for the gate and home.

The loyal Cheapside was still with him; but the sparrow was now so convulsed with laughter that he could scarcely keep up, even flying.

"I don't see what you find so funny about it," panted the Doctor peevishly as he slowed down at the gate and began putting on his collar. "I had a very narrow escape from getting arrested."

"Yes, and you'd have gone to jail, too," gasped Cheapside. "It's no light offense, washing in this park. But that wasn't what I was laughing at."

"Well, what was it, then?" asked the Doctor, feeling for a stud in his pocket.

"The Reverend Dingle took me for a nightingale!" tittered the Cockney sparrow. "I must go back and tell Becky that. So long, Doc! You'll be all right now. That bobby's lost you altogether. . . . After all, you got your bath. See you in Puddleby next month."

CAROL BIRD, a little invalid, has invited all the Ruggles children to a
wonderful Christmas dinner-party. At
last the great day comes.

Kate Douglas Wiggin

THE RUGGLESES' CHRISTMAS DINNER

ILLUSTRATED BY *Janet Smalley*

BEFORE the earliest Ruggles could wake
and toot his five-cent tin horn, Mrs. Ruggles was up and stirring
about the house, for it was a gala day in the family. Gala day!
I should think so! Were not her nine "children" invited to a
dinner-party at the great house, and weren't they going to sit
down free and equal with the mightiest in the land? She had
been preparing for this grand occasion ever since the receipt
of Carol Bird's invitation, which, by the way, had been speedily
enshrined in an old photograph frame and hung under the
looking glass in the most prominent place in the kitchen, where
it stared the occasional visitor directly in the eye and made him
livid with envy:

BIRDS' NEST, *December* 17, 188—
DEAR MRS. RUGGLES—I am going to have a dinner-party on
Christmas Day, and would like to have all your children come.
I want them every one, please, from Sarah Maud to Baby
Larry. Mamma says dinner will be at half past five, and the

217

Christmas tree at seven; so you may expect them home at nine o'clock. Wishing you a Merry Christmas and a Happy New Year, I am

Yours truly

Carol Bird

Breakfast was on the table promptly at seven o'clock, and there was very little of it, too; for it was an excellent day for short rations, though Mrs. Ruggles heaved a sigh as she reflected that the boys, with their India-rubber stomachs, would be just as hungry the day after the dinner-party as if they had never had any at all.

As soon as the scanty meal was over, she announced the plan of the campaign: "Now, Susan, you an' Kitty wash up the dishes; an' Peter, can't yer spread up the beds, so't I can git ter cuttin' out Larry's new suit? I ain't satisfied with his clo'es, an' I thought in the night of a way to make him a dress out o' my old red plaid shawl—kind o' Scotch style, yer know, with the fringe 't the bottom.—Eily, you go find the comb an' take the snarls out the fringe, that's a lady! You little young ones clear out from under foot! Clem, you an' Con hop into bed with Larry while I wash yer underflannins; 'twon't take long to dry 'em.—Yes, I know it's bothersome, but yer can't go int' s'ciety 'thout takin' some trouble, 'n' anyhow I couldn't git round to 'em last night.—Sarah Maud, I think 'twould be perfeckly han'som' if you ripped them brass buttons off yer uncle's *policeman's* coat 'n' sewed 'em in a row up the front o' yer green skirt. Susan, you must iron out yours 'n' Kitty's apurns; 'n' there, I come mighty near forgettin' Peory's stockin's! I counted the whole lot last night when I was washin' of 'em, 'n' there ain't but nineteen anyhow yer fix 'em, 'n' no nine pairs mates nohow; 'n' I ain't goin' ter have my childern wear odd stockin's to a dinner-comp'ny, fetched up as I was!—Eily, can't you run out an' ask Mis' Cullen ter lend me a pair o' stockin's for Peory, 'n' tell her if she will, Peory'll give Jim half her candy when she gets home. Won't yer, Peory?"

Peoria was young and greedy and thought the remedy so out of all proportion to the disease that she set up a deafening howl

218

at the projected bargain—a howl so rebellious and so entirely out of season that her mother started in her direction with flashing eye and uplifted hand; but she let it fall suddenly, saying, "No, I vow I won't lick ye Christmas Day, if yer drive me crazy; but speak up smart, now, 'n' say whether yer'd ruther give Jim Cullen half yer candy or go bare-legged ter the party?" The matter being put so plainly, Peoria collected her faculties, dried her tears, and chose the lesser evil, Clem having hastened the decision by an affectionate wink that meant he'd go halves with her on his candy.

"That's a lady!" cried her mother. "Now, you young ones that ain't doin' nothin', play all yer want ter before noontime, for after ye git through eatin' at twelve o'clock me 'n' Sarah Maud's goin' ter give yer sech a washin' 'n' combin' 'n' dressin' as yer never had before 'n' never will ag'in likely, 'n' then I'm goin' to set yer down 'n' give yer two solid hours trainin' in manners; 'n' 'twon't be no foolin' neither."

"All we've got ter do's go eat!" grumbled Peter.

"Well, that's enough," responded his mother; "there's more'n one way of eatin', let me tell yer, 'n' you've got a heap ter learn about it, Peter Ruggles. Land sakes, I wish you children could see the way I was fetched up to eat. I never took a meal o' vittles in the kitchen before I married Ruggles; but yer can't keep up that style with nine young ones 'n' yer Pa always off ter sea."

The big Ruggleses worked so well, and the little Ruggleses kept from "under foot" so successfully, that by one o'clock nine complete toilets were laid out in solemn grandeur on the beds. I say, "complete"; but I do not know whether they would be called so in the best society. The law of compensation had been well applied: he that had necktie had no cuffs; she that had sash had no handkerchief, and *vice versa*, but they all had shoes and a certain amount of clothing, such as it was, the outside layer being in every case quite above criticism.

"Now, Sarah Maud," said Mrs. Ruggles, her face shining with excitement, "everything's red up an' we can begin. I've got a boiler 'n' a kettle 'n' a pot o' hot water. Peter, you go into the back bedroom, 'n' I'll take Susan, Kitty, Peory, 'n' Cornelius; 'n' Sarah Maud, you take Clem, 'n' Eily, 'n' Larry, one to a time. Scrub 'em 'n' rinse 'em, or, 'tany rate, git's fur's yer can with 'em, 'n' then I'll finish 'em off while you do yerself."

Sarah Maud couldn't have scrubbed with any more decision and force if she had been doing floors, and the little Ruggleses bore it bravely, not from natural heroism, but for the joy that was set before them. Not being satisfied, however, with the "tone" of their complexions and feeling that the number of freckles to the square inch was too many to be tolerated in the highest social circles, she wound up operations by applying a little Bristol brick from the knife-board, which served as the proverbial "last straw," from under which the little Ruggleses issued rather red and raw and out of temper. When the clock struck four they were all clothed, and most of them in their right minds, ready for those last touches that always take the most time.

Kitty's red hair was curled in thirty-four ringlets, Sarah Maud's was braided in one pig-tail, and Susan's and Eily's in two braids apiece, while Peoria's resisted all advances in the shape of hair oils and stuck out straight on all sides, like that of the Circassian girl of the circus—so Clem said; and he was sent into the bedroom for it, too, from whence he was dragged

out forgivingly, by Peoria herself, five minutes later. Then, exciting moment, came linen collars for some and neckties and bows for others—a magnificent green glass breastpin was sewed into Peter's purple necktie—and Eureka! the Ruggleses were dressed, and Solomon in all his glory was not arrayed like one of these!

A row of seats was then formed directly through the middle of the kitchen. Of course, there were not quite chairs enough for ten, since the family had rarely wanted to sit down all at once, somebody always being out or in bed, or otherwise engaged, but the wood-box and the coal hod finished out the line nicely, and nobody thought of grumbling. The children took their places according to age, Sarah Maud at the head and Larry on the coal hod, and Mrs. Ruggles seated herself in front, surveying them proudly as she wiped the sweat of honest toil from her brow.

"Well," she exclaimed, "if I do say so as shouldn't, I never see a cleaner, more stylish mess o' children in my life! I do wish Ruggles could look at ye for a minute!—Larry Ruggles, how many times have I got ter tell yer not ter keep pullin' at yer sash? Haven't I told yer if it comes ontied, yer waist 'n' shirt'll part comp'ny in the middle, 'n' then where'll yer be?—Now, look me in the eye, all of yer! I've of'en told yer what kind of a family the McGrills was. I've got reason to be proud, goodness knows! Your uncle is on the *po*lice force o' New York City; you can take up the paper most any day an' see his name printed right out—James McGrill—'n' I can't have my children fetched up common, like some folks'; when they go out they've got to have clo'es, and learn to act decent! Now, I want ter see how yer goin' to behave when yer git there tonight. 'Tain't so awful easy as you think 'tis. Let's start in at the beginnin' 'n' act out the whole business. Pile into the bedroom, there, every last one o' ye, 'n' show me how yer goin' to go int' the parlor. This'll be the parlor, 'n' I'll be Mis' Bird."

The youngsters hustled into the next room in high glee, and Mrs. Ruggles drew herself up in the chair with an infinitely haughty and purse-proud expression that much better suited a descendant of the McGrills than modest Mrs. Bird.

The bedroom was small, and there presently ensued such a clatter that you would have thought a herd of wild cattle had broken loose. The door opened, and they straggled in, all the younger ones giggling, with Sarah Maud at the head, looking as if she had been caught in the act of stealing sheep; while Larry, being last in line, seemed to think the door a sort of gate of heaven which would be shut in his face if he didn't get there in time; accordingly he struggled ahead of his elders and disgraced himself by tumbling in head foremost.

Mrs. Ruggles looked severe. "There, I knew yer'd do it in some sech fool way! Now, go in there an' try it over ag'in, every last one o' ye, 'n' if Larry can't come in on two legs he can stay ter home—d'yer hear?"

The matter began to assume a graver aspect; the little Ruggleses stopped giggling and backed into the bedroom, issuing presently with lock-step, Indian file, a scared and hunted expression on every countenance.

"No, no, no!" cried Mrs. Ruggles, in despair. "That's worse yet; yer look for all the world like a gang o' pris'ners! There ain't no style ter that: spread out more, can't yer, 'n' act kind o' carelesslike—nobody's goin' ter kill ye! That ain't what a dinner-party is!"

The third time brought deserved success, and the pupils took their seats in the row. "Now, yer know," said Mrs. Ruggles impressively, "there ain't enough decent hats to go round, 'n' if there was I don' know's I'd let yer wear 'em, for the boys would never think to take 'em off when they got inside, for they never do—but, anyhow, there ain't enough good ones. Now, look me in the eye. You're only goin' jest round the corner; you needn't wear no hats, none of yer, 'n' when yer get int' the parlor, 'n' they ask yer ter lay off yer hats, Sarah Maud must speak up 'n' say it was sech a pleasant evenin' 'n' sech a short walk that yer left yer hats to home. Now, can yer remember?"

All the little Ruggleses shouted, "Yes, marm!" in chorus.

"What have *you* got ter do with it?" demanded their mother; "did I tell *you* to say it? Warn't I talkin' ter Sarah Maud?"

222

The little Ruggleses hung their diminished heads. "Yes, marm," they piped, more discreetly.

"Now, we won't leave nothin' to chance; git up, all of ye, an' try it.—Speak up, Sarah Maud."

Sarah Maud's tongue clove to the roof of her mouth.

"Quick!"

"Ma thought—it was—sech a pleasant hat that we'd—we'd better leave our short walk to home," recited Sarah Maud, in an agony of mental effort.

This was too much for the boys. An earthquake of suppressed giggles swept all along the line.

"Oh, whatever shall I do with yer?" moaned the unhappy mother; "I s'pose I've got to learn it to yer!"—which she did, word for word, until Sarah Maud thought she could stand on her head and say it backwards.

"Now, Cornelius, what are *you* goin' ter say ter make yerself good comp'ny?"

"Do? Me? Dunno!" said Cornelius, turning pale, with unexpected responsibility.

"Well, ye ain't goin' to set there like a bump on a log 'thout sayin' a word ter pay for yer vittles, air ye? Ask Mis' Bird how she's feelin' this evenin', or if Mr. Bird's hevin' a busy season, or how this kind o' weather agrees with him, or somethin' like that.—Now, we'll make b'lieve we've got ter the dinner—that won't be so hard, 'cause yer'll have somethin' to do—it's awful bothersome to stan' round an' act stylish.—If they have napkins, Sarah Maud down to Peory may put 'em in their laps, 'n' the rest of ye can tuck 'em in yer necks. Don't eat with yer fingers—don't grab no vittles off one 'nother's plates; don't reach out for nothin', but wait till yer asked, 'n' if you never *git* asked don't git up an' grab it.—Don't spill nothin' on the tablecloth, or like's not Mis' Bird'll send yer away from the table—'n' I hope she will if yer do! (Susan! keep your handkerchief in your lap where Peory can borry it if she needs it, 'n' I hope she'll know when she does need it, though I don't expect it.) Now, we'll try a few things ter see how they'll go! Mr. Clement, do you eat cramb'ry sarse?"

"Bet yer life!" cried Clem, who in the excitement of the moment had not taken in the idea exactly and had mistaken this for an ordinary bosom-of-the-family question.

"Clement McGrill Ruggles, do you mean to tell me that you'd say that to a dinner-party? I'll give ye one more chance. Mr. Clement, will you take some of the cramb'ry?"

"Yes, marm, thank ye kindly, if you happen ter have any handy."

"Very good, indeed! But they won't give yer two tries tonight —yer just remember that!—Miss Peory, do you speak for white or dark meat?"

"I ain't perticler as ter color—anything that nobody else wants will suit me," answered Peory with her best air.

"First-rate! Nobody could speak more genteel than that. Miss Kitty, will you have hard or soft sarse with your pudden?"

"Hard or soft? Oh! A little of both, if you please, an' I'm much obliged," said Kitty, bowing with decided ease and grace; at which all the other Ruggleses pointed the finger of shame at her, and Peter *grunted* expressively, that their meaning might not be mistaken.

"You just stop your gruntin', Peter Ruggles; that warn't greedy, that was all right. I wish I could git it inter your heads that it ain't so much what yer say, as the way you say it. An' don't keep starin' cross-eyed at your necktie pin, or I'll take it out 'n' sew it on to Clem or Cornelius: Sarah Maud'll keep her eye on it, 'n' if it turns broken side out she'll tell yer. Gracious! I shouldn't think you'd ever seen nor worn no jool'ry in your life.—Eily, you an' Larry's too little to train, so you just look at the rest an' do's they do, 'n' the Lord have mercy on ye 'n' help ye to act decent! Now, is there anything more ye'd like to practice?'

"If yer tell me one more thing, I can't set up an' eat," said Peter gloomily; "I'm so cram full o' manners now, I'm ready ter bust, 'thout no dinner at all."

"Me, too," chimed in Cornelius.

"Well, I'm sorry for yer both," rejoined Mrs. Ruggles sarcastically; "if the 'mount o' manners yer've got on hand now troubles ye, you're dreadful easy hurt! Now, Sarah Maud, after dinner, about once in so often, you must git up 'n' say, 'I guess we'd better be goin',' 'n' if they say, 'Oh, no, set a while longer,' yer can set; but if they don't say nothin', you've got ter get up 'n' go.—Now, hev yer got that int' yer head?"

About once in so often! Could any words in the language be fraught with more terrible and wearing uncertainty?

"Well," answered Sarah Maud mournfully, "seems as if this whole dinner-party set right square on top o' me! Mebbe I could manage my own manners, but to manage nine mannerses is worse'n staying to home!"

"Oh, don't fret," said her mother, good-naturedly, now that the lesson was over; "I guess you'll git along. I wouldn't mind if folks would only say, 'Oh, childern will be childern'; but they won't. They'll say, 'Land o' Goodness, who fetched them childern up?'—It's quarter past five, 'n' yer can go now:—remember 'bout the hats—don't all talk ter once—Susan, lend yer han'k-'chief ter Peory—Peter, don't keep screwin' yer scarf-pin—Cornelius, hold yer head up straight—Sarah Maud, don't take yer eyes off o' Larry, 'n', Larry, you keep holt o' Sarah Maud 'n' do jest as she says—'n' whatever you do, all of yer, never forgit for one second that yer mother was a McGrill."

225

The children went out of the back door quietly and were presently lost to sight, Sarah Maud slipping and stumbling along absent-mindedly, as she recited rapidly under her breath, "Itwassuchapleasantevenin'n'suchashortwalk,   thatwethought-we'dleaveourhatstohome. —Itwassuchapleasantevenin'n'sucha-shortwalk, thatwethoughtwe'dleaveourhatstohome."

Peter rang the doorbell, and presently a servant admitted them, and, whispering something in Sarah's ear, drew her downstairs into the kitchen. The other Ruggleses stood in horror-stricken groups as the door closed behind their commanding officer; but there was no time for reflection, for a voice from above was heard, saying, "Come right upstairs, please!"

> "Theirs not to make reply,
> Theirs not to reason why,
> Theirs but to do or die."

Accordingly they walked upstairs, and Elfrida, the nurse, ushered them into a room more splendid than anything they had ever seen. But, oh, woe! where was Sarah Maud! and was it Fate that Mrs. Bird should say, at once, "Did you lay your hats in the hall?" Peter felt himself elected by circumstance the head of the family, and, casting one imploring look at tongue-tied Susan, standing next him, said huskily, "It was so very pleasant—that—that——" "That we hadn't good hats enough to go 'round," put in little Susan, bravely, to help him out, and then froze with horror that the ill-fated words had slipped off her tongue.

However, Mrs. Bird said, pleasantly, "Of course you wouldn't wear hats such a short distance—I forgot when I asked. Now, will you come right in to Miss Carol's room? She is so anxious to see you."

Just then Sarah Maud came up the back stairs, so radiant with joy from her secret interview with the cook that Peter could have pinched her with a clear conscience; and Carol gave them a joyful welcome. "But where is Baby Larry?" she cried, looking over the group with searching eye. "Didn't he come?"

"Larry! Larry!" Good gracious, where was Larry? They were all sure that he had come in with them, for Susan remembered scolding him for tripping over the doormat. Uncle Jack went into convulsions of laughter. "Are you sure there were nine of you?" he asked, merrily.

"I think so, sir," said Peoria timidly; "but anyhow, there was Larry." And she showed signs of weeping.

"Oh, well, cheer up!" cried Uncle Jack. "Probably he's not lost —only mislaid. I'll go and find him before you can say Jack Robinson!"

"I'll go, too, if you please, sir," said Sarah Maud, "for it was my place to mind him, an' if he's lost I can't relish my vittles!"

The other Ruggleses stood rooted to the floor. Was this a dinner-party, forsooth; and if so, why were such things ever spoken of as festive occasions?

Sarah Maud went out through the hall, calling, "Larry! Larry!" and without any interval of suspense a thin voice piped up from below, "Here I be!"

The truth was that Larry, being deserted by his natural guardian, dropped behind the rest, and wriggled into the hat-

tree to wait for her, having no notion of walking unprotected
into the jaws of a fashionable entertainment. Finding that she
did not come, he tried to crawl from his refuge and call somebody, when—dark and dreadful ending to a tragic day—he
found that he was too much intertwined with umbrellas and
canes to move a single step. He was afraid to yell (when I have
said this of Larry Ruggles I have pictured a state of helpless
terror that ought to wring tears from every eye); and the sound
of Sarah Maud's beloved voice, some seconds later, was like a
strain of angel music in his ears. Uncle Jack dried his tears,
carried him upstairs, and soon had him in breathless fits of
laughter, while Carol so made the other Ruggleses forget themselves that they were presently talking like accomplished
diners-out.

Carol's bed had been moved into the farthest corner of the
room, and she was lying on the outside, dressed in a wonderful
dressing-gown that looked like a fleecy cloud. Her golden hair
fell in fluffy curls over her white forehead and neck, her cheeks
flushed delicately, her eyes beamed with joy, and the children
told their mother afterwards that she looked as beautiful as the
angels in the picture books.

There was a great bustle behind a huge screen in another part
of the room, and at half-past five this was taken away, and the

Christmas dinner-table stood revealed. What a wonderful sight it was to the poor little Ruggles children, who ate their sometimes scanty meals on the kitchen table! It blazed with tall colored candles, it gleamed with glass and silver, it blushed with flowers, it groaned with good things to eat; so it was not strange that the Ruggleses, forgetting altogether that their mother was a McGrill, shrieked in admiration of the fairy spectacle. But Larry's behavior was the most disgraceful, for he stood not upon the order of his going, but went at once for a high chair that pointed unmistakably to him, climbed up like a squirrel, gave a comprehensive look at the turkey, clapped his hands in ecstasy, rested his fat arms on the table, and cried with joy, "I beat the hull lot o' yer!" Carol laughed until she cried, giving orders, meanwhile—"Uncle Jack, please sit at the head, Sarah Maud at the foot, and that will leave four on each side; Mamma is going to help Elfrida, so that the children need not look after each other, but just have a good time."

A sprig of holly lay by each plate, and nothing would do but each little Ruggles must leave his seat and have it pinned on by Carol, and as each course was served, one of them pleaded to take something to her. There was hurrying to and fro, I can assure you, for it is quite a difficult matter to serve a Christmas dinner on the third floor of a great city house; but if it had been necessary to carry every dish up a rope ladder the servants would gladly have done so. There were turkey and chicken, with delicious gravy and stuffing, and there were half a dozen vegetables, with cranberry jelly, and celery, and pickles; and as for the way these delicacies were served, the Ruggleses never forgot it as long as they lived.

Peter nudged Kitty, who sat next him, and said, "Look, will yer, ev'ry feller's got his own partic'lar butter; I s'pose that's to show you can eat that 'n' no more. No, it ain't either, for that pig of a Peory's just gettin' another helpin'!"

"Yes," whispered Kitty, "an' the napkins is marked with big red letters! I wonder if that's so nobody'll nip 'em; an' oh, Peter, look at the pictures stickin' right on ter the dishes! Did yer ever?"

"The plums is all took out o' my cramb'ry sarse an' it's friz to

229

a stiff jell'l!" whispered Peoria, in wild excitement.

"Hi—yah! I got a wishbone!" sang Larry, regardless of Sarah Maud's frown; after which she asked to have his seat changed, giving as excuse that he "gen'ally set beside her, an' would feel strange"; the true reason being that she desired to kick him gently, under the table, whenever he passed what might be termed "the McGrill line."

"I declare to goodness," murmured Susan, on the other side, "there's so much to look at I can't scarcely eat nothin'!"

"Bet yer life I can!" said Peter, who had kept one servant busily employed ever since he sat down; for, luckily, no one was asked by Uncle Jack whether he would have a second helping, but the dishes were quietly passed under their noses, and not a single Ruggles refused anything that was offered him, even unto the seventh time.

Then, when Carol and Uncle Jack perceived that more turkey was a physical impossibility, the meats were taken off and the dessert was brought in—a dessert that would have frightened a strong man after such a dinner as had preceded it. Not so the Ruggleses—for a strong man is nothing to a small boy—and they kindled to the dessert as if the turkey had been a dream and the six vegetables an optical delusion. There were plum-pudding, mince-pie, and ice cream; and there were nuts, and raisins, and oranges. Kitty chose ice cream, explaining that she knew it "by sight, though she hadn't never tasted none"; but all the rest took the entire variety, without any regard to consequences.

"My dear child," whispered Uncle Jack, as he took Carol an orange, "there is no doubt about the necessity of this feast, but I do advise you after this to have them twice a year, or quarterly perhaps, for the way these children eat is positively dangerous; I assure you I tremble for that terrible Peoria. I'm going to run races with her after dinner."

"Never mind," laughed Carol; "let them have enough for once; it does my heart good to see them, and they shall come oftener next year."

The feast being over, the Ruggleses lay back in their chairs

230

And there stood the brilliantly lighted Christmas tree.

languidly, like little gorged boa constrictors, and the table was cleared in a trice. Then a door was opened into the next room, and there, in a corner facing Carol's bed, which had been wheeled as close as possible, stood the brilliantly lighted Christmas tree, glittering with gilded walnuts and tiny silver balloons, and wreathed with snowy chains of popcorn. The presents had been bought mostly with Carol's story-money, and were selected after long consultations with Mrs. Bird. Each girl had a blue knitted hood, and each boy a red crocheted comforter, all made by Mamma, Carol, and Elfrida. ("Because if you buy everything, it doesn't show so much love," said Carol.) Then every girl had a pretty plaid dress of a different color, and every boy a warm coat of the right size. Here the useful presents stopped, and they were quite enough; but Carol had pleaded to give them something "for fun." "I know they need the clothes," she had said, when they were talking over the matter just after Thanksgiving, "but they don't care much for them, after all. Now, Papa, won't you *please* let me go without part of my presents this year, and give me the money they would cost, to buy something to amuse the Ruggleses?"

"You can have both," said Mr. Bird, promptly. "Is there any need of my little girl's going without her own Christmas, I should like to know? Spend all the money you like."

"But that isn't the thing," objected Carol, nestling close to her father; "it wouldn't be mine. What is the use? Haven't I almost everything already, and am I not the happiest girl in the world this year, with Uncle Jack and Donald at home? You know very well it is more blessed to give than to receive; so why won't you let me do it? You never look half as happy when you are getting your presents as when you are giving us ours. Now, Papa, submit, or I shall have to be very firm and disagreeable with you!"

"Very well, your Highness, I surrender."

"That's a dear Papa! Now what were you going to give me? Confess!"

"A bronze figure of Santa Claus; and in the 'little round belly that shakes when he laughs like a bowlful of jelly,' is a wonderful clock—oh, you would never give it up if you could see it!"

"Nonsense," laughed Carol; "as I never have to get up to breakfast, nor go to bed, nor catch trains, I think my old clock will do very well! Now, Mamma, what were you going to give me?"

"Oh, I hadn't decided. A few more books, and a gold thimble, and a smelling-bottle, and a music-box, perhaps."

"Poor Carol," laughed the child, merrily, "she can afford to give up these lovely things, for there will still be left Uncle Jack, and Donald, and Paul, and Hugh, and Uncle Rob, and Aunt Elsie, and a dozen other people to fill her Christmas stocking!"

So Carol had her way, as she generally did; but it was usually a good way, which was fortunate, under the circumstances; and Sarah Maud had a set of Miss Alcott's books, and Peter a modest silver watch, Cornelius a tool-chest, Clement a doghouse for his lame puppy, Larry a magnificent Noah's ark, and each of the younger girls a beautiful doll.

You can well believe that everybody was very merry and very thankful. All the family, from Mr. Bird down to the cook, said that they had never seen so much happiness in the space of three hours; but it had to end, as all things do. The candles flickered and went out, the tree was left alone with its gilded ornaments, and Mrs. Bird sent the children downstairs at half past eight, thinking that Carol looked tired.

"Now, my darling, you have done quite enough for one day," said Mrs. Bird, getting Carol into her little nightgown. "I'm afraid you will feel worse tomorrow, and that would be a sad ending to such a charming evening."

"Oh, wasn't it a lovely, lovely time," sighed Carol. "Everything was just right. I shall never forget Larry's face when he looked at the turkey; nor Peter's when he saw his watch; nor Kitty's smile when she kissed her dolly; nor the tears in poor Sarah Maud's eyes when she thanked me for her books; nor——"

"But we mustn't talk any longer about it tonight," said Mrs. Bird, anxiously; "you are too tired, dear."

"I am not so very tired, Mamma. I have felt well all day; not a bit of pain anywhere. Perhaps this has done me good."

"Perhaps; I hope so. There was no noise or confusion; it was just a merry time. Now, may I close the door and leave you

alone, dear? Papa and I will steal in softly by and by to see if
you are all right; but I think you need to be very quiet."

"Oh, I'm willing to stay by myself; but I am not sleepy yet,
and I am going to hear the music, you know."

"Yes, I have opened the window a little, and put the screen
in front of it, so that you won't feel the air."

"Can I have the shutters open? and won't you turn my bed,
please? This morning I woke ever so early, and one bright,
beautiful star shone in that eastern window. I never noticed it
before, and I thought of the Star in the East, that guided the
wise men to the place where the baby Jesus was. Good night,
Mamma. Such a happy, happy day!"

"Good night, my Carol—mother's blessed Christmas child."

"Bend your head a minute, mother dear," whispered Carol,
calling her mother back. "Mamma, dear, I do think that we have
kept Christ's birthday just as He would like it. Don't you?"

"I am sure of it," said Mrs. Bird softly.

Hilaire Belloc

THE BIG BABOON

The Big Baboon is found upon
    The plains of Cariboo:
He goes about with nothing on
    (A shocking thing to do).
But if he dressed respectably
    And let his whiskers grow,
How like this Big Baboon would be
    To Mister So-and-so!

Hilaire Belloc

THE GNU

G. stands for Gnu, whose weapons of defense
Are long, sharp, curling horns, and commonsense.
To these he adds a name so short and strong,
That even hardy Boers pronounce it wrong.
How often on a bright autumnal day
The pious people of Pretoria say,
"Come, let us hunt the—" then no more is heard,
But sounds of strong men struggling with a word;
Meanwhile the distant Gnu with grateful eyes
Observes his opportunity and flies.

234

Hilaire Belloc

THE YAK

As a friend to the children commend me the Yak.
 You will find it exactly the thing:
It will carry and fetch, you can ride on its back,
 Or lead it about with a string.

The Tartar who dwells on the plains of Tibet
 (A desolate region of snow)
Has for centuries made it a nursery pet,
 And surely the Tartar should know!

Then tell your papa where the Yak can be got,
 And if he is awfully rich
He will buy you the creature—or else he will not.
 (I cannot be positive which.)

235

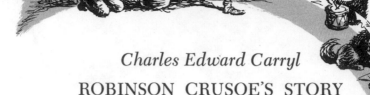

Charles Edward Carryl

ROBINSON CRUSOE'S STORY

The night was thick and hazy
  When the "Piccadilly Daisy"
Carried down the crew and captain in the sea;
  And I think the water drowned 'em;
  For they never, never found 'em,
And I know they didn't come ashore with me.

Oh! 'twas very sad and lonely
  When I found myself the only
Population on this cultivated shore;
  But I've made a little tavern
  In a rocky little cavern
And I sit and watch for people at the door.

I spent no time in looking
  For a girl to do my cooking,
As I'm quite a clever hand at making stews;
  But I had that fellow Friday,
  Just to keep the tavern tidy,
And to put a Sunday polish on my shoes.

I have a little garden
  That I'm cultivating lard in,
As the things I eat are rather tough and dry;
  For I live on toasted lizards,
  Prickly pears, and parrot gizzards,
And I'm really very fond of beetle-pie.

236

The clothes I had were furry,
And it made me fret and worry
When I found the moths were eating off the hair;
And I had to scrape and sand 'em,
And I boiled 'em and I tanned 'em,
Till I got the fine morocco suit I wear.

I sometimes seek diversion
In a family excursion
With the few domestic animals you see;
And we take along a carrot
As refreshment for the parrot,
And a little can of jungleberry tea.

Then we gather as we travel,
Bits of moss and dirty gravel,
And we chip off little specimens of stone;
And we carry home as prizes
Funny bugs, of handy sizes,
Just to give the day a scientific tone.

If the roads are wet and muddy,
We remain at home and study,—
For the Goat is very clever at a sum,—
And the Dog, instead of fighting,
Studies ornamental writing,
While the Cat is taking lessons on the drum.

We retire at eleven,
And we rise again at seven;
And I wish to call attention, as I close,
To the fact that all the scholars
Are correct about their collars,
And particular in turning out their toes.

Robert McCloskey

THE CASE OF THE COSMIC COMIC

ILLUSTRATED BY THE AUTHOR

ONE Saturday afternoon Homer and Freddy and Freddy's little brother Louis were listening to the State College football game on the radio.

After the game Homer said, "I'm feeling sort of hungry. Come on, Freddy, come on, Louis. Let's go down to the kitchen and get something to eat."

They went downstairs and Homer poured out three glasses of milk, and Homer's mother brought out the cookie jar.

"Don't eat too many cookies," she cautioned, "because it's almost dinnertime."

"No, Ma'm, we won't," said Freddy. Then he said to Homer, "Has tonight's newspaper come yet?"

"I think so," said Homer. "Yes, there it is, on top of the refrigerator."

"Oh, boy!" said Freddy as he opened it to the comic page. "Let's see what happened to the 'Super-Duper'."

So Freddy and little brother Louis and Homer gathered around the paper to see how the Super-Duper was going to get out of the big steel box filled with dynamite, where the villain had put him and dropped him into the middle of the ocean from an airship.

There in the first picture, the Super-Duper was saying, "Haw, Haw! That villain thinks he can get rid of me, but he's mistaken!" Then in the next picture the dynamite exploded and blew the steel box to bits. But that didn't hurt the Super-Duper because the Super-Duper is *so* tough (tougher than steel) that *nothing* can hurt *him*!

"Just look at those muscles and that chest the Super-Duper's got!" said Freddy before going on to the next picture. In the next picture the Super-Duper bounded up from the bottom of the ocean and went whizzing through the air. He caught the airship by the tail and broke it off with a loud *crack!* In the last picture the villain was trying to escape in an airplane, and was machine-gunning the Super-Duper, but the bullets were just bouncing off his chest because he was so tough. Then it said, "Continued on Monday."

"Boy!" said Freddy, "the Super-Duper can do anything!"

"Yeh, but it's only a story," said Homer. "And the story's always the same. The Super-Duper always hits things and breaks them up, and a villain always tries to bomb him, or shoot him with a cannon or a gun or an electric ray. Then he always rescues the pretty girl and gets the villain in the end."

"Well, it isn't just a story," said Freddy, "because Super-Duper's in the movies too. They really take *movies* of him lifting battleships with one hand and even flying through space."

"Aw," said Homer, "I read a book once that said they do that sort of thing with wires and mirrors. It's just trick photography, that's all it is."

Then little brother Louis, who had been eating cookies all this time said, "Read it to me!"

So Freddy had to read it all over again, out loud, and explain the story to little Louis.

"Freddy," called Homer's mother, "your mother just phoned and wants you to bring little Louis right home."

"O.K. C'mon, Louis, finish your milk. Good-bye, Homer, and thank you for the cookies."

The next time Freddy came over to visit Homer he brought along some of his Super-Duper comic magazines.

"Say, Homer, I thought you might like to look at these," said Freddy.

"Gosh, Freddy, you certainly have a lot of those comic magazines," said Homer.

"They don't cost much," said Freddy. "Only ten cents apiece. Here, read this one, Homer, it's the most exciting."

Homer took the comic magazine and started to read, while Freddy looked over his shoulder.

At the beginning of the story the Super-Duper was dressed in ordinary clothes, just like any other man. Then after the villain appeared on the second page, the Super-Duper slipped behind a tree and changed into red tights and a long blue cape.

"Why does he always change his clothes like that?" asked Homer.

"That's because he is so modest," said Freddy in a knowing way. Homer started reading again: After the Super-Duper had changed his clothes he started flying through space and smashing things. He picked up automobiles and tossed them over cliffs, and he even carried a train across a river, after the villain had blown up the bridge. Then finally he saved the pretty girl from a horrible death and caught the villain, who turned out to be a very notorious criminal.

"Gosh, Freddy, these Super-Duper stories are all the same," said Homer.

"No, they're not!" said Freddy. "Sometimes the Super-Duper smashes airships and sometimes he smashes ocean liners. Then, other times he just breaks up mountains."

"But he always rescues the pretty girl and catches the villain on the last page," said Homer.

"Of course," said Freddy. "That's to show that crime does not pay!"

"Shucks!" said Homer. "Let's go pitch horseshoes."

"O.K.," said Freddy.

Freddy won two games out of three and then he said, "Guess it's almost suppertime, see you tomorrow, Homer."

"Yep! G'by, Freddy," said Homer, and Freddy gathered up his comic magazines and went up the road home.

After supper when Homer was doing his homework the phone rang. "Hello!" said Homer.

"Hello, that you, Homer? This is Freddy. Say! Did you see in the paper tonight that there is going to be a Super-Duper movie over at the Centerburg theater next Saturday afternoon?"

Before Homer could say, "No, I didn't." Freddy shouted, "And guess what! The Super-Duper in person is going to be there! And, Homer," Freddy went on, "Mother has a box from the mail-order house over at the Centerburg Railroad station. So Dad says that little Louis and I can take the horse and wagon and drive to Centerburg on Saturday. We can get the box, and then go to see the Super-Duper! I thought you might like to come along."

"Sure thing!" said Homer.

"O.K. We'll stop by for you," said Freddy. "G'by, Homer."

On Saturday Freddy and little Louis drove up to Homer's house with old Lucy hitched to the wagon, just as Homer was finishing his lunch.

"I thought we had better get an early start," said Freddy, "because it takes old Lucy about an hour to go as far as Centerburg."

"I'll be ready in just a second," said Homer. Then after Homer had climbed in, Freddy said "Giddap!" to old Lucy, and they started off to see the Super-Duper in person.

When they arrived in Centerburg the first thing they did was go to the station and load the box from the mail-order house onto the back of the wagon.

"Gosh, that's heavy!" said Homer as they lifted it on.

"Yeah," said Freddy, "but I betcha the Super-Duper could lift it with his little finger."

"Mebby so," said Homer. "Let's stop over at Uncle Ulysses' lunchroom and get some doughnuts to eat in the movie."

Freddy and little Louis both thought that was a good idea so they drove old Lucy around to the lunchroom to get some doughnuts.

Then Freddy and little Louis and Homer walked across the town square to the movie.

241

The Super-Duper's super-streamlined car was standing in front of the theater. It was long and red, with chromium trimmings, and it had the Super-Duper's monogram on the side. After they had admired the car, they bought three tickets and went inside. There in the lobby was the *real honest-to-goodness* Super-Duper. He shook hands with Freddy and Homer and little brother Louis, and he autographed a card for Freddy, too.

"Mr. Super-Duper, would you please do a little flying through space for us, or mebbe just bend a few horseshoes?" asked Freddy.

"I'm sorry, boys, but I haven't time today," said the Super-Duper with a smile.

So Homer and Freddy and little Louis found three good seats and ate doughnuts until the picture began.

The picture was called "THE SUPER-DUPER and the ELECTRIC RAY." That was because the villain had a machine that produced an electric ray, and every time he shined it on a skyscraper, or an airplane, the skyscraper or the airplane would explode! He turned the ray on Super-Duper, too, but of course the Super-Duper was so tough that it didn't hurt *him*.

Little Louis got so excited, though, that he choked on a doughnut, and Homer had to take him to the lobby for a drink of water. But finally the Super-Duper broke the villain's headquarters to bits, and lifted the ray-machine (which must have weighed several tons) and tossed it over a cliff. *Then*, he caught the villain and rescued the pretty girl. But at the very end, the villain slipped away again, and then these words appeared on the screen: "NEXT INSTALLMENT NEXT SATURDAY AFTERNOON!"

"Why did the Super-Duper let the villain get away again?" asked little Louis on the way out.

"I guess that's because he wants to chase him again next Saturday," said Homer.

Outside they admired the Super-Duper's car once more and then started home in the wagon.

It was evening by the time old Lucy, pulling the wagon with Freddy and little Louis and Homer on it, had reached the curve

242

in the road just before you come to Homer's father's filling station.

A car honked from behind, and Freddy pulled old Lucy over to the edge of the road. Then, "SWOOOSH!" around from the rear sped a long red car with chromium trimmings.

"Gosh! It's the Super-Duper!" said Freddy.

"Well, he shouldn't drive so fast around this curve," said Homer, sort of doubtful-like.

Almost before Homer had finished speaking there was a loud screech of brakes, and then a loud crash!

"Giddup! Lucy," said Freddy, "we better hurry up and see what happened!"

"Gee, there weren't any cars coming the other way," said Homer, "I wonder what happened?"

"Golly," said Freddy in a quavery voice, "do you suppose . . . the electric ray? . . . Whoow, Lucy, WHOO, LUCY! . . . we better park here!"

"Oh, shucks!" said Homer in his bravest voice, "I'm going to see what happened."

Little Louis began to cry, and Homer tried to comfort him. "Louis, that electric ray business was just part of a movie, and it couldn't have anything to do with this." Homer tried hard to make it sound convincing.

Then Homer and Freddy and little Louis got out of the wagon and crept along the side of the road.

There, around the curve, was the Super-Duper's car, down in a ditch. All three boys stopped crawling along and lay down on their stomachs to watch.

"Oh, Boy!" whispered Freddy. "Now we'll get to see the Super-Duper lift it back on the road with one hand!"

There was a flash of light and little Louis cried, "Is that the electric ray?"

"It's only the headlights of a car," said Homer. "Come on, let's go a little closer."

They crept a little closer . . . They could see the Super-Duper now, sitting there in the twilight with his head in his hands.

"I wonder if he got hurt?" asked Homer.

"Naaw!" whispered Freddy. "Nothing can hurt the Super-Duper because he's too tough."

"Well, if he isn't hurt, why doesn't he lift the car back on the road?" asked Homer.

"Sh-h-h!" said Freddy, "he's an awful modest fellow." So they waited and watched from the bushes.

The Super-Duper sighed a couple of times, and then he got up and started walking around his car.

"Now watch!" said Freddy in a loud whisper. "Oh, boy! Oh, boy!" The Super-Duper didn't lift the car, no, not yet. He looked at the dent that a fence post had made in his shiny red fender, and *then*, the incredible happened. That colossal-osal, gigantic-antic, Super-Duper, that same Super-Duper who defied the elements, who was so strong that he broke up battleships like toothpicks, who was so tough that cannon balls bounced off his chest, yes, who was *tougher* than steel, he stooped down and said . . . "Ouch!" Yes, there could be no mistake, he said it again, louder . . . "OUCH!"

The great Super-Duper had gotten himself caught on a barbed-wire fence!

"Well . . . well, for crying out loud!" said Freddy.

"What happened?" asked little Louis. "Did he get himself rayed by the villain?"

"Come on, Freddy, let's go and untangle him," said Homer. Then Freddy and little Louis and Homer unsnagged the Super-Duper and he sighed again and said, "Thank you boys. Do you know if there's a garage near here? It looks as though it will take a wrecking car to get my car out of this ditch."

"Sure, my father has a garage down at the crossing," said Homer. "And we have a horse right up there on the road. We can pull your car out of the ditch!" said Freddy.

"Well, now, isn't that lucky!" said the Super-Duper with a smile.

So they hitched old Lucy to the car and she pulled and everybody pushed until the car was back on the road.

Little Louis sat with the Super-Duper in his car, and Homer and Freddy rode on old Lucy's back while she towed the car

toward Homer's father's filling station.

"What happened, Mr. Super-Duper, did the villain ray you?" asked little Louis.

"No," said the Super-Duper, and he laughed. "When I drove around that curve, there was a skunk right in the middle of the road. I didn't want to hit him and get this new car all smelled up, so I went into the ditch. Ha! Ha!"

When they had reached the filling station they put some iodine on the scratches that the barbed wire had made on the Super-Duper. (He made faces, just like anybody else, when it was daubed on.) Then he ate a hamburger, and by that time Homer's father had the car fixed, except for the dent in the fender. Before the Super-Duper drove away, he thanked the boys and made them a present of a large stack of Super-Duper

comic books. After he'd gone, Homer and Freddy went back
with old Lucy to get the wagon.

"Well, anyway, Freddy, we've got a complete set of Super-
Duper Comic Books," said Homer.

"Yeah," said Freddy. Then he said, "Say, Homer, do me a
favor, will you, and don't tell anybody about the Super-Duper
and the barbed wire and the ditch and the iodine, especially
Artie Bush. If he doesn't hear about this I might be able to
trade my comic books for that baseball bat of his, the Louisville
Slugger that's only slightly cracked."

"O.K." said Homer. "Come to think of it, his cousin, Skinny,
has a pretty good ball, too. This is a good time to get even for
the time Skinny traded me a bicycle bell that wouldn't ring, for
my nearly new bugle."

O. Henry

THE RANSOM
OF RED CHIEF

ILLUSTRATED BY *Kay Lovelace*

I T LOOKED like a good thing; but wait till I tell you. We were down South, in Alabama—Bill Driscoll and myself—when this kidnaping idea struck us. It was, as Bill afterwards expressed it, "during a moment of temporary mental apparition"; but we didn't find that out till later.

There was a town down there, as flat as a flannel cake, and called Summit, of course. It contained inhabitants of as undeleterious and self-satisfied a class of peasantry as ever clustered around a Maypole.

Bill and me had a joint capital of about six hundred dollars, and we needed just two thousand dollars more to pull off a fraudulent town-lot scheme in western Illinois with. We talked it over on the front steps of the hotel. Philoprogenitiveness, says we, is strong in semi-rural communities; therefore, and for other reasons, a kidnaping project ought to do better there than in the radius of newspapers that send reporters out in plain-clothes to stir up talk about such things. We knew that Summit couldn't get after us with anything stronger than constables and, maybe, some lackadaisical bloodhounds and a diatribe or two in the *Weekly Farmers' Budget*. So, it looked good.

We selected for our victim the only child of a prominent citizen named Ebenezer Dorset. The father was respectable and tight, a mortgage fancier and a stern, upright collection-plate passer and forecloser. The kid was a boy of ten, with bas-relief freckles, and hair the color of the cover of the magazine you buy at the newsstand when you want to catch a train. Bill and me figured that Ebenezer would melt down for a ransom of two thousand dollars to a cent. But wait till I tell you.

About two miles from Summit was a little mountain, covered

with a dense cedar brake. On the rear elevation of this mountain was a cave. There we stored provisions.

One evening after sundown, we drove in a buggy past old Dorset's house. The kid was in the street, throwing rocks at a kitten on the opposite fence.

"Hey, little boy!" says Bill, "would you like to have a bag of candy and a nice ride?"

The boy catches Bill neatly in the eye with a piece of brick.

"That will cost the old man an extra five hundred dollars," says Bill, climbing over the wheel.

That boy put up a fight like a welterweight cinnamon bear; but, at last, we got him down in the bottom of the buggy and drove away. We took him up to the cave, and I hitched the horse in the cedar brake. After dark I drove the buggy to the little village, three miles away, where we had hired it, and walked back to the mountain.

Bill was pasting court plaster over the scratches and bruises on his features. There was a fire burning behind the big rock at the entrance of the cave, and the boy was watching a pot of boiling coffee, with two buzzard feathers stuck in his red hair. He points a stick at me when I come up, and says:

"Ha! cursed paleface, do you dare to enter the camp of Red Chief, the terror of the plains?"

"He's all right now," says Bill, rolling up his trousers and examining some bruises on his shins. "We're playing Indian. We're making Buffalo Bill's show look like magic-lantern views of Palestine in the town hall. I'm Old Hank, the Trapper, Red Chief's captive, and I'm to be scalped at daybreak. By Geronimo! that kid can kick hard."

Yes, sir, that boy seemed to be having the time of his life. The fun of camping out in a cave had made him forget that he was a captive himself. He immediately christened me Snake-eye, the Spy, and announced that, when his braves returned from the warpath, I was to be broiled at the stake at the rising of the sun.

Then we had supper; and he filled his mouth full of bacon and bread and gravy, and began to talk. He made a during-dinner speech something like this:

"I like this fine. I never camped out before; but I had a pet 'possum once, and I was nine last birthday. I hate to go to school. Rats ate up sixteen of Jimmy Talbot's aunt's speckled hen's eggs. Are there any real Indians in these woods? I want some more gravy. Does the trees moving make the wind blow? We had five puppies. What makes your nose so red, Hank? My father has lots of money. Are the stars hot? I whipped Ed Walker twice, Saturday. I don't like girls. You dassent catch toads unless with a string. Do oxen make any noise? Why are oranges round? Have you got beds to sleep on in this cave? Amos Murray has got six toes. A parrot can talk, but a monkey or a fish can't. How many does it take to make twelve?"

Every few minutes he would remember that he was a pesky redskin and pick up his stick rifle and tiptoe to the mouth of the cave to rubber for the scouts of the hated paleface. Now and then he would let out a war whoop that made Old Hank, the Trapper, shiver. That boy had Bill terrorized from the start.

"Red Chief," says I to the kid, "would you like to go home?"

"Aw, what for?" says he. "I don't have any fun at home. I hate to go to school. I like to camp out. You won't take me back home again, Snake-eye, will you?"

"Not right away," says I. "We'll stay here in the cave awhile."

"All right!" says he. "That'll be fine. I never had such fun in all my life."

We went to bed about eleven o'clock. We spread down some wide blankets and quilts and put Red Chief between us. We weren't afraid he'd run away. He kept us awake for three hours, jumping up and reaching for his rifle and screeching: "Hist! pard," in mine and Bill's ears, as the fancied crackle of a twig or the rustle of a leaf revealed to his young imagination the stealthy approach of the outlaw band. At last I fell into a troubled sleep, and dreamed that I had been kidnaped and chained to a tree by a ferocious pirate with red hair.

Just at daybreak I was awakened by a series of awful screams from Bill. They weren't yells, or howls, or shouts, or whoops, or yawps, such as you'd expect from a manly set of vocal organs— they were simply indecent, terrifying, humiliating screams, such

250

as women emit when they see ghosts or caterpillars. It's an awful thing to hear a strong, desperate, fat man scream incontinently in a cave at daybreak.

I jumped up to see what the matter was. Red Chief was sitting on Bill's chest, with one hand twined in Bill's hair. In the other he had the sharp case knife we used for slicing bacon; and he was industriously and realistically trying to take Bill's scalp, according to the sentence that had been pronounced upon him the evening before.

I got the knife away from the kid and made him lie down again. But, from that moment Bill's spirit was broken. He laid down on his side of the bed, but he never closed an eye again in sleep as long as that boy was with us. I dozed off for a while, but along toward sun-up I remembered that Red Chief had said I was to be burned at the stake at the rising of the sun. I wasn't nervous or afraid; but I sat up and lit my pipe and leaned against a rock.

"What you getting up so soon for, Sam?" asked Bill.

"Me?" says I. "Oh, I got a kind of a pain in my shoulder. I thought sitting up would rest it."

"You're a liar!" says Bill. "You're afraid. You was to be

251

burned at sunrise, and you was afraid he'd do it. And he would, too, if he could find a match. Ain't it awful, Sam? Do you think anybody will pay out money to get a little imp like that back · home?"

"Sure," said I. "A rowdy kid like that is just the kind that parents dote on. Now, you and the Chief get up and cook breakfast, while I go up on the top of this mountain and reconnoiter."

I went up on the peak of the little mountain and ran my eye over the contiguous vicinity. Over toward Summit I expected to see the sturdy yeomanry of the village armed with scythes and pitchforks beating the countryside for the dastardly kidnapers. But what I saw was a peaceful landscape dotted with one man plowing with a dun mule. Nobody was dragging the creek; no couriers dashed hither and yon, bringing tidings of no news to the distracted parents. There was a sylvan attitude of somnolent sleepiness pervading that section of the external outward surface of Alabama that lay exposed to my view. "Perhaps," says I to myself, "it has not yet been discovered that the wolves have borne away the tender lambkin from the fold. Heaven help the wolves!" says I, and I went down the mountain to breakfast.

When I got to the cave, I found Bill backed up against the side of it, breathing hard, and the boy threatening to smash him with a rock half as big as a coconut.

"He put a red-hot boiled potato down my back," explained Bill, "and then mashed it with his foot; and I boxed his ears. Have you got a gun about you, Sam?"

I took the rock away from the boy and kind of patched up the argument.

"I'll fix you," says the kid to Bill. "No man ever yet struck the Red Chief but what he got paid for it. You better beware!"

After breakfast the kid takes a piece of leather with strings wrapped around it out of his pocket and goes outside the cave unwinding it.

"What's he up to now?" says Bill, anxiously. "You don't think he'll run away, do you, Sam?"

"No fear of it," says I. "He don't seem to be much of a home body. But we've got to fix up some plan about the ransom. There don't seem to be much excitement around Summit on account of his disappearance; but maybe they haven't realized yet that he's gone. His folks may think he's spending the night with Aunt Jane or one of the neighbors. Anyhow, he'll be missed today. Tonight we must get a message to his father demanding the two thousand dollars for his return."

Just then we heard a kind of war whoop, such as David might have emitted when he knocked out the champion Goliath. It was a sling that Red Chief had pulled out of his pocket, and he was whirling it around his head.

I dodged, and heard a heavy thud and a kind of a sigh from Bill, like a horse gives out when you take his saddle off. A rock the size of an egg had caught Bill just behind his left ear. He loosened himself all over and fell in the fire across the frying pan of hot water for washing the dishes. I dragged him out and poured cold water on his head for half an hour.

By and by, Bill sits up and feels behind his ear and says: "Sam, do you know who my favorite Biblical character is?"

"Take it easy," says I. "You'll come to your senses presently."

"King Herod," says he. "You won't go away and leave me here alone, will you, Sam?"

I went out and caught that boy and shook him until his freckles rattled.

"If you don't behave," says I, "I'll take you straight home. Now, are you going to be good, or not?"

"I was only funning," says he, sullenly. "I didn't mean to hurt Old Hank. But what did he hit me for? I'll behave, Snake-eye, if you won't send me home, and if you'll let me play the Black Scout today."

"I don't know the game," says I. "That's for you and Mr. Bill to decide. He's your playmate. I'm going away for a while, on business. Now, you come in and make friends with him and say you are sorry for hurting him, or home you go, at once."

I made him and Bill shake hands, and then I took Bill aside and told him I was going to Poplar Cove, a little village three miles from the cave, and find out what I could about how the kidnaping had been regarded in Summit. Also, I thought it best to send a peremptory letter to old man Dorset that day, demanding the ransom and dictating how it should be paid.

"You know, Sam," says Bill, "I've stood by you without batting an eye in earthquakes, fire, and flood—in poker games, dynamite outrages, police raids, train robberies, and cyclones. I never lost my nerve yet till we kidnaped that two-legged sky-rocket of a kid. He's got me going. You won't leave me long with him, will you, Sam?"

"I'll be back some time this afternoon," says I. "You must keep the boy amused and quiet till I return. And now we'll write the letter to old Dorset."

Bill and I got paper and pencil and worked on the letter while Red Chief, with a blanket wrapped around him, strutted up and down, guarding the mouth of the cave. Bill begged me tearfully to make the ransom fifteen hundred dollars instead of two thousand. "I ain't attempting," says he, "to decry the celebrated moral aspects of parental affection, but we're dealing with humans, and it ain't human for anybody to give up two thousand dollars for that forty-pound chunk of freckled wildcat. I'm willing to take a chance at fifteen hundred dollars. You can charge the difference up to me."

So, to relieve Bill, I acceded, and we collaborated a letter that ran this way:

Ebenezer Dorset, Esq.:

We have your boy concealed in a place far from Summit. It is useless for you or the most skillful detectives to attempt to find him. Absolutely, the only terms on which you can have him restored to you are these: We demand fifteen hundred dollars in large bills for his return; the money to be left at midnight at the same spot and in the same box as your reply—as hereinafter described. If you agree to these terms, send your answer in writing by a solitary messenger tonight at half-past eight o'clock. After crossing Owl Creek, on the road to Poplar Cove, there are three large trees about a hundred yards apart, close to the fence of the wheat field on the right-hand side. At the bottom of the fence post opposite the third tree will be found a small pasteboard box.

The messenger will place the answer in this box and return immediately to Summit.

If you attempt any treachery or fail to comply with our demand as stated, you will never see your boy again.

If you pay the money as demanded, he will be returned

to you safe and well within three hours. These terms are final, and if you do not accede to them, no further communication will be attempted.

TwO DESPERATE MEN.

I addressed this letter to Dorset, and put it in my pocket. As I was about to start, the kid comes up to me and says:

"Aw, Snake-eye, you said I could play the Black Scout while you was gone."

"Play it, of course," says I. "Mr. Bill will play with you. What kind of game is it?"

"I'm the Black Scout," says Red Chief, "and I have to ride to the stockade to warn the settlers that the Indians are coming. I'm tired of playing Indian myself. I want to be the Black Scout."

"All right," says I. "It sounds harmless to me. I guess Mr. Bill will help you foil the pesky savages."

"What am I to do?" asks Bill, looking at the kid suspiciously.

"You are the hoss," says Black Scout. "Get down on your hands and knees. How can I ride to the stockade without a hoss?"

256

"You'd better keep him interested," said I, "till we get the scheme going. Loosen up."

Bill gets down on his all fours, and a look comes in his eye like a rabbit's when you catch it in a trap.

"How far is it to the stockade, kid?" he asks, in a husky manner of voice.

"Ninety miles," says the Black Scout. "And you have to hump yourself to get there on time. Whoa, now!"

The Black Scout jumps on Bill's back and digs his heels in his side.

"For heaven's sake," says Bill, "hurry back, Sam, as soon as you can. I wish we hadn't made the ransom more than a thousand. Say, you quit kicking me, or I'll get up and warm you good."

I walked over to Poplar Cove and sat around the post office and store, talking with the chawbacons that come in to trade. One whiskerando says that he hears Summit is all upset on account of Elder Ebenezer Dorset's boy having been lost or stolen. That was all I wanted to know. I bought some smoking tobacco, referred casually to the price of blackeyed peas, posted my letter surreptitiously, and came away. The postmaster said the mail carrier would come by in an hour to take the mail on to Summit.

When I got back to the cave, Bill and the boy were not to be found. I explored the vicinity of the cave, and risked a yodel or two, but there was no response.

So I lighted my pipe and sat down on a mossy bank to await developments.

In about half an hour I heard the bushes rustle, and Bill wabbled out into the little glade in front of the cave. Behind him was the kid, stepping softly like a scout, with a broad grin on his face. Bill stopped, took off his hat, and wiped his face with a red handkerchief. The kid stopped about eight feet behind him.

"Sam," says Bill, "I suppose you'll think I'm a renegade, but I couldn't help it. I'm a grown person with masculine proclivities and habits of self-defense, but there is a time when all sys-

257

tems of egotism and predominance fail. The boy is gone. I have sent him home. All is off. There was martyrs in old times," goes on Bill, "that suffered death rather than give up the particular graft they enjoyed. None of 'em ever was subjugated to such supernatural tortures as I have been. I tried to be faithful to our articles of depredation; but there came a limit."

"What's the trouble, Bill?" I asks him.

"I was rode," says Bill, "The ninety miles to the stockade, not barring an inch. Then, when the settlers was rescued, I was given oats. Sand ain't a palatable substitute. And then, for an hour I had to try to explain to him why there was nothin' in holes, how a road can run both ways, and what makes the grass green. I tell you, Sam, a human can only stand so much. I takes him by the neck of his clothes and drags him down the mountain. On the way he kicks my legs black-and-blue from the knees down; and I've got to have two or three bites on my thumb and hand cauterized.

"But he's gone," continues Bill, "gone home. I showed him the road to Summit and kicked him about eight feet nearer there at one kick. I'm sorry we lose the ransom; but it was either that or Bill Driscoll to the madhouse."

Bill is puffing and blowing, but there is a look of ineffable peace and growing content on his rose-pink features.

"Bill," says I, "no heart disease in your family, is there?"

"No," says Bill, "nothing chronic except malaria and accidents. Why?"

"Then you might turn around," says I, "and have a look behind you."

Bill turns and sees the boy, and loses his complexion, and sits down plump on the ground, and begins to pluck aimlessly at grass and little sticks. For an hour I was afraid of his mind. And then I told him that my scheme was to put the whole job through immediately and that we would get the ransom and be off with it by midnight if old Dorset fell in with our proposition. So Bill braced up enough to give the kid a weak sort of smile and a promise to play the Russian in a Japanese war with him as soon as he felt a little better.

I had a scheme for collecting that ransom without danger of being caught by counterplots that ought to commend itself to professional kidnapers. The tree under which the answer was to be left—and the money later on—was close to the road fence with big, bare fields on all sides. If a gang of constables should be watching for anyone to come for the note they could see him a long way off crossing the fields or in the road. But no, sirree! At half-past eight I was up in that tree as well hidden as a tree toad, waiting for the messenger to arrive.

Exactly on time, a half-grown boy rides up the road on a bicycle, locates the pasteboard box at the foot of the fence post, slips a folded piece of paper into it, and pedals away again back toward Summit.

I waited an hour and then concluded the thing was square. I slid down the tree, got the note, slipped along the fence till I struck the woods, and was back at the cave in another half an hour. I opened the note, got near the lantern, and read it to Bill. It was written with a pen in a crabbed hand, and the sum and substance of it was this:

Two Desperate Men.

GENTLEMEN: I received your letter today by post, in regard to the ransom you ask for the return of my son. I think you are a little high in your demands, and I hereby make you a counterproposition, which I am inclined to believe you will accept. You bring Johnny home and pay me two hundred and fifty dollars in cash, and I agree to take him off your hands. You had better come at night, for the neighbors believe he is lost, and I couldn't be responsible for what they would do to anybody they saw bringing him back.

Very respectfully,

EBENEZER DORSET.

"Great pirates of Penzance!" says I; "of all the impudent——"

But I glanced at Bill, and hesitated. He had the most appealing look in his eyes I ever saw on the face of a dumb or a talking brute.

"Sam," says he, "what's two hundred and fifty dollars, after all? We've got the money. One more night of this kid will send me to a bed in Bedlam. Besides being a thorough gentleman, I think Mr. Dorset is a spendthrift for making us such a liberal offer. You ain't going to let the chance go, are you?"

"Tell the truth, Bill," says I, "this little he ewe lamb has somewhat got on my nerves, too. We'll take him home, pay the ransom, and make our get-away."

We took him home that night. We got him to go by telling him that his father had bought a silver-mounted rifle and a pair of moccasins for him, and we were going to hunt bears the next day.

It was just twelve o'clock when we knocked at Ebenezer's front door. Just as the moment when I should have been abstracting the fifteen hundred dollars from the box under the tree, according to the original proposition, Bill was counting out two hundred and fifty dollars into Dorset's hand.

When the kid found out we were going to leave him at home, he started up a howl like a calliope and fastened himself as tight as a leech to Bill's leg. His father peeled him away gradually, like a porous plaster.

"How long can you hold him?" asks Bill.

"I'm not as strong as I used to be," says old Dorset, "but I think I can promise you ten minutes."

"Enough," says Bill. "In ten minutes I shall cross the Central, Southern, and Middle Western States, and be legging it trippingly for the Canadian border."

And, as dark as it was, and as fat as Bill was, and as good a runner as I am, he was a good mile and a half out of Summit before I could catch up with him.

MAYBE

Mildred Plew Meigs

Maybe it's wondrous, thrilling, and thunderous
   Down in the deeps of the sea;
Maybe they've fiddles and rollicky riddles
   And scallopy tarts for tea;
Maybe the oysters come out of their cloisters
   And mock at the ones that won't;
Maybe tra-loo, they d-d-d-do,
   And maybe they d-d-d-don't!
Maybe it's glimmery, shining, and shimmery
   Down in the dim and the damp,
Whenever the terrapin starts up a larrupin'
   Under the phosphor lamp;
Maybe the turtles flip out in their kirtles
   And flirt with the octopuzownt;
Maybe tra-loo, they d-d-d-do,
   And maybe they d-d-d-don't!

Lucretia P. Hale

THE LADY WHO PUT SALT
IN HER COFFEE

ILLUSTRATED BY

H. I. Bacharach AND *Frances Eckart*

THIS was Mrs. Peterkin. It was a mistake. She had poured out a delicious cup of coffee, and, just as she was helping herself to cream, she found she had put in salt instead of sugar! It tasted bad. What should she do? Of course she couldn't drink the coffee; so she called in the family, for she was sitting at a late breakfast all alone. The family came in; they all tasted and looked, and wondered what should be done, and all sat down to think.

At last Agamemnon, who had been to college, said, "Why don't we go over and ask the advice of the chemist?" (For the chemist lived over the way and was a very wise man.)

Mrs. Peterkin said, "Yes," and Mr. Peterkin said, "Very well," and all the children said they would go too. So the little boys put on their india-rubber boots, and over they went.

Now the chemist was just trying to find out something which should turn everything it touched into gold; and he had a large glass bottle into which he put all kinds of gold and silver, and many other valuable things, and melted them all up over the fire, till he had almost found what he wanted. He could turn things into almost gold. But just now he had used up all the gold that he had around the house, and gold was high. He had used up his wife's gold thimble and his great-grandfather's gold-bowed spectacles; and he had melted up the gold head of his great-great-grandfather's cane; and, just as the Peterkin family came in, he was down on his knees before his wife, asking her to let him have her wedding ring to melt up with all the rest, because this time he knew he should succeed, and should

. . . the little old woman . . . began to stir in the different herbs.

be able to turn everything into gold; and then she could have a new wedding ring of diamonds, all set in emeralds and rubies and topazes, and all the furniture could be turned into the finest of gold.

Now his wife was just consenting when the Peterkin family burst in. You can imagine how mad the chemist was! He came near throwing his crucible—that was the name of the melting pot—at their heads. But he didn't. He listened as calmly as he could to the story of how Mrs. Peterkin had put salt in her coffee.

At first he said he couldn't do anything about it; but when Agamemnon said they would pay in gold if he would only go, he packed up his bottles in a leather case, and went back with them all.

First he looked at the coffee, and then stirred it. Then he put in a little chlorate of potassium, and the family tried it all around; but it tasted no better. Then he stirred in a little bichlorate of magnesia. But Mrs. Peterkin didn't like that. Then he added some tartaric acid and some hypersulphate of lime. But no; it was no better. "I have it!" exclaimed the chemist— "a little ammonia is just the thing!" No, it wasn't the thing at all.

Then he tried, each in turn, some oxalic, cyanic, acetic, phosphoric, chloric, hyperchloric, sulphuric, boracic, silicic, nitric, formic, nitrous nitric, and carbonic acids. Mrs. Peterkin tasted each and said the flavor was pleasant, but not precisely that of coffee. So then he tried a little calcium, aluminum, barium, and strontium, a little clear bitumen, and a half of a third of a sixteenth of a grain of arsenic. This gave rather a pretty color; but still Mrs. Peterkin ungratefully said it tasted of anything but coffee. The chemist was not discouraged. He put in a little belladonna and atropine, some granulated hydrogen, some potash, and a very little antimony, finishing off with a little pure carbon. But still Mrs. Peterkin was not satisfied.

The chemist said that all he had done ought to have taken out the salt. The theory remained the same, although the experiment had failed. Perhaps a little starch would have some effect. If not, that was all the time he could give. He should like to be paid, and go. They were all much obliged to him, and willing to give him $1.37½ in gold. Gold was now 2.69¾, so Mr. Peterkin found in the newspaper. This gave Agamemnon a pretty little sum. He set himself down to do it. But there was the coffee! All sat and thought a while, till Elizabeth Eliza said, "Why don't we go to the herb-woman?" Elizabeth Eliza was the only daughter. She was named after her two aunts—Elizabeth, from the sister of her father; Eliza, from her mother's sister. Now the herb-woman was an old woman who came around to sell herbs, and knew a great deal. They all shouted with joy at the idea of asking her, and Solomon John and the younger children agreed to go and find her too. The herb-woman lived down at the very end of the street; so the boys put on their india-rubber boots again, and they set off. It was a long walk through the village, but they came at last to the herb-woman's house, at the foot of a high hill. They went through her little garden. Here she had marigolds and hollyhocks, and old maids and tall sunflowers, and all kinds of sweet-smelling herbs, so that the air was full of tansy tea and elderblow. Over the porch grew a hop vine, and a brandy cherry tree shaded the door, and a luxuriant cranberry vine flung its delicious fruit across the window. They went into a small parlor, which smelt very spicy. All around hung little bags full of catnip, and peppermint, and all kinds of herbs; and dried stalks hung from the ceiling; and on the shelves were jars of rhubarb, senna, manna, and the like.

But there was no little old woman. She had gone up into the woods to get some more wild herbs, so they all thought they would follow her—Elizabeth Eliza, Solomon John, and the little boys. They had to climb up over high rocks, and in among huckleberry bushes and blackberry vines. But the little boys had their india-rubber boots. At last they discovered the little old woman. They knew her by her hat. It was steeple-crowned, without any vane. They saw her digging with her trowel around a sassafras bush. They told her their story—how their mother had put salt in her coffee, and how the chemist had made it worse instead of better, and how their mother couldn't drink it, and wouldn't she come and see what she could do? And she said she would and took up her little old apron, with pockets all around, all filled with everlasting and pennyroyal, and went back to her house.

There she stopped and stuffed her huge pockets with some of all the kinds of herbs. She took some tansy and peppermint, and caraway seed and dill, spearmint and cloves, pennyroyal and sweet marjoram, basil and rosemary, wild thyme and some of the other time—such as you have in clocks—sappermint and oppermint, catnip, valerian, and hop; indeed, there isn't a kind of herb you can think of that the little old woman didn't have done up in her little paper bags, that had all been dried in her little Dutch oven. She packed these all up, and then went back with the children, taking her stick.

Meanwhile Mrs. Peterkin was getting quite impatient for her coffee.

As soon as the little old woman came she had it set over the fire, and began to stir in the different herbs. First she put in a little hop for the bitter. Mrs. Peterkin said it tasted like hop tea, and not at all like coffee. Then she tried a little flagroot and snakeroot, then some spruce gum, and some caraway and some dill, some rue and rosemary, some sweet marjoram and sour, some oppermint and sappermint, a little spearmint and peppermint, some wild thyme, and some of the other tame time, some tansy and basil, and catnip and valerian, and sassafras, ginger, and pennyroyal. The children tasted after each mixture but made up dreadful faces. Mrs. Peterkin tasted and did the same. The more the old woman stirred, and the more she put in, the worse it all seemed to taste.

So the old woman shook her head, and muttered a few words, and said she must go. She believed the coffee was bewitched. She bundled up her packets of herbs, and took her trowel and her basket and her stick, and went back to her root of sassafras, that she had left half in the air and half out. And all she would take for pay was five cents in currency.

Then the family were in despair, and all sat and thought a great while. It was growing late in the day, and Mrs. Peterkin hadn't had her cup of coffee. At last Elizabeth Eliza said, "They say that the lady from Philadelphia, who is staying in town, is very wise. Suppose I go and ask her what is best to be done." To this they all agreed, it was a great thought, and off Elizabeth Eliza went.

She told the lady from Philadelphia the whole story—how her mother had put salt in the coffee; how the chemist had been called in; how he tried everything but could make it no better; and how they went for the little old herb-woman, and how she had tried in vain, for her mother couldn't drink the coffee. The lady from Philadelphia listened very attentively, and then said, "Why doesn't your mother make a fresh cup of coffee?" Elizabeth Eliza started with surprise. Solomon John shouted with joy; so did Agamemnon, who had just finished his sum; so did the little boys, who had followed on. "Why didn't we think of that?" said Elizabeth Eliza; and they all went back to their mother, and she had her cup of coffee.

NONSENSE LIMERICKS

Edward Lear

There was an old lady whose folly
Induced her to sit in a holly;
   Whereon by a thorn
   Her dress being torn,
She quickly became melancholy.

There was an old man of the Cape,
Who made himself garments of crêpe.
   When asked, "Do they tear?"
   He replied, "Here and there,
But they're perfectly splendid for shape."

Wallace Irwin

A NAUTICAL EXTRAVAGANZA

I stood one day by the breezy bay
    A-watching the ships go by,
When a tired tar said, with a shake of his head:
    "I wisht I could tell a lie!"

"I've seen some sights as would jigger yer lights,
    And they've jiggered me own, in sooth,
But I ain't wuth a darn at spinnin' a yarn
    What wanders away from the truth.

"We were out in the gig, the Rigagajig,
    Jest a mile and a half to sea,
When Capting Snook, with a troubled look,
    He came and he says to me:

" 'O Bos'n Smith, make haste forthwith
    And hemstitch the fo'ard sail;
Accordeon pleat the dory sheet,
    For there's going to be a gale.'

"I straightway did as the capting bid—
    No sooner the job was through
When the north wind, whoof, bounced over the roof,
    And, murderin' lights, she blew!

"She blew the tars right off the spars,
　　And the spars right off the mast,
Sails and pails and anchors and nails
　　Flew by on the wings o' the blast.

"The galley shook as she blew our cook
　　Straight out o' the porthole glim,
While pots and pans, kettles and cans
　　Went clatterin' after him.

"She blew the fire from our gallant stove
　　And the coal from our gallant bin,
She whistled apace past the capting's face
　　And blew the beard off his chin!

" 'O wizzel me dead!' the capting said
　　(And the words blew out of his mouth);
'We're lost, I fear, if the wind don't veer
　　And blow a while from the south.'

" 'And wizzel me dead,' no sooner he'd said
　　Them words that blew from his mouth,
Than the wind switched round with a hurricane sound
　　And blew straight in from the south.

"We opened our eyes with a wild surprise,
　　And never a word to say—
In changin' her tack the wind blew back
　　The things that she'd blew away!

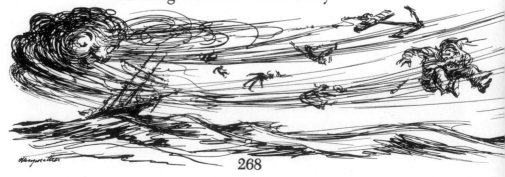

268

"She blew the tars back onto the spars,
  And the spars back onto the mast;
Back flew the pails, the sails and the nails,
  Which into the ship stuck fast.

"And 'fore we could look she blew back the cook
  Straight into the galley coop,
Back dropped the pans, kettles and cans,
  Without even spillin' the soup.

"She blew the fire back into the stove
  Where it burnt in its proper place—
And all of us cheered as she blew the beard
  Back on the capting's face.

"There's more o' me tale," said the sailor hale,
  "As would jigger yer lights, in sooth,
But I ain't wuth a darn at spinnin' a yarn
  What wanders away from the truth."

269

Russell Carpenter

YOU NEVER SAW SUCH AN EGG

ILLUSTRATED BY *Seymour Fleishman*

WHEN the new science prof hit Central High last fall, my twin brother Bud got the urge to start experiments with animal life at home. A biological listening post he called it. Before he got through, we heard plenty!

It didn't work out too well. In fact, I guess we're about washed up on home biology. But now we have a jalopy instead —only I'll have to explain why.

First Mom got kind of sore about some little jelly-bean things we put down in the cellarway for observation. They turned into frog peepers and set up a yodeling that would take your ear off. Mom said, "Goodness gracious! What's that?" She started down and upset the works. You never saw such a place so full of slippery things and stuff in your life.

A few nights later at supper, Bud asked if we could keep white mice. Mom landed on him with both feet.

"William!" she hollered, hanging on to the table. "Don't you DARE bring such things into this house!—You *haven't*, have you?"

"Just these two I got from Al Benson," Bud answered, when Mom whooped again. Instead of climbing up Bud's arm, the mice streaked across the table and took off, with the cat waiting. No more mice—and fifty cents shot!

Mom fanned the air, breathing hard. She glared at us and

270

then lit into Dad. "Walter," she said, kind of slow and cold, "I will not have my house turned into a creeping, *crawling* NIGHTMARE!"

He screwed his face straight and scowled at us. "Hear that, you fellows? No more shenanigans. Suppose you try turkeys for a change. Go over to Hagenberger's and buy yourselves a pair. Only, no more funny stuff."

So that's how we got Henry.

Mr. Hagenberger wanted to know how much money we had. When we counted out our last dime, he shook his head. "You boys better start with one good husky specimen. That'll put you on the road to riches and fame. Then, soon as you've saved up, you can get its mate. Now, here's a prize winner!"

Bud went big for that riches-and-fame stuff, so we closed the deal and put the crate in the wheelbarrow. We'd fixed up a coop down by the old cow barn that hasn't been used since Grampa died. Mister Turkey gobbled a couple of times as if he didn't feel so good and squatted down like an old pillow.

"Holy smoke!" I said. "Do you suppose he's all right?"

"Sure he is," said Bud. "Just lonesome. Mr. Hagenberger said he's a thoroughbred bird and very highstrung. He may pine for a while until we're able to get his wife over here to keep him company."

"We'd better get busy and earn some money quick, then," I said. "Right now it looks to me as if he isn't long for this world."

Bud decided to call him Henry, which is our science prof's first name.

The Saturday after we got Henry, Prof put on a Field Excursion, Science III, down at the old limestone quarry to look for fossils. When the class got to the quarry, he announced a surprise. During the winter, the frost had cracked off a big rock slab that had slid down a few feet. Up top, out of sight, Prof had discovered a hole leading inside. We climbed in with our flashlights and ropes and hammers and stuff and found a cave about twenty feet square, all cold and clammy, with rock formations hanging from the ceiling and bulging up from the floor. Prof began sounding off about Paleozoic limestones and the fossils we might find. His voice echoed like a loud-speaker in a bass drum.

My feet were getting frozen, so I was ready to shove when Bud eased up beside me. "Don't look now," he whispered, "but I've spotted another opening. Let's see where it goes."

We slid away from the gang and squirmed behind a sort of rock screen. Sure enough, there was an inky black shadow like the mouth of a well. One quick flashlight beam showed it slanted downward.

"Come on," said Bud. "You're not scared?"

He popped inside. I shivered. The air that came up was icier than a blast from the big walk-in cooler at the co-op packing plant. Only I wouldn't let him dare me.

The passage didn't go far, but plenty far enough. I was petrified. And when I bumped against Bud at the bottom and found us dead-ended in a blind hole, I started right off to climb back out again—but fast. Brrr! Believe it or not, there was thick ice under foot. Goodness only knows how long it had been there.

Bud was hunkered down prying something loose just where the ice floor met the rock wall. "Hey, Ben!" he said, his voice gone tight, "grab this!"

Before I could get clear, he handed me a smooth, gray, oval thing the size of a small football. It was exactly like a rounded beach stone, without the solid heft.

I started to kick, but he cut me off. "Get going, it's cold down here. We've got ourselves a souvenir, that's all. A souvenir egg maybe a million years old!"

That sure sounded crazy, but still he might be on the beam. It was either an egg or a mighty good imitation, and I couldn't see why anybody'd plant a fake.

We smuggled the egg out in my packsack. On the way home we took another squint. I was disappointed. It was just dirty gray and still icy.

"What kind could it be?" I asked Bud. "A condor, or an emu? Or just a *roc?*"

I don't think he got the joke. "At this stage I'd rather not guess," he said solemnly, sounding more like a professor than Prof himself. "It remains to be seen."

"I'll say it does," I agreed. "But whatever it is, I bet Mom won't like it."

"We'll park it in that pile of moldy hay in the cowbarn, where it's all hot and steamy," he announced. "That'll be like an incubator."

"You don't expect the thing to hatch?"

"I didn't expect to find it in the first place, did I?" he said, starting to get sore. So in the hay it went.

But it seems we had other things to worry about. During the next three or four days Henry kept acting sicker and sicker, and less like a prize winner. We asked Mom what she thought. She was still touchy about the mice and things.

"Huh!" she sniffed, while Henry cocked one sad eye. "A lot you biologists know about poultry. This bird is broody, that's all. She thinks she wants to set. Let her mope until she gets over it."

"*Henry?*" I said, once she'd gone. "Pining for his *wife?*"

"Well, Henrietta, then," Bud said impatiently. "The question now is how to get some setting eggs. They cost money."

"Don't look at me," I told him. "I've got exactly four cents left."

"Wait a minute!" he busted out suddenly. "I know the answer." And he high-tailed it for where we'd buried the antique

273

egg. I got the idea right away. It would be like one of those glass eggs you use in a chicken-house as a come-on.

Bud was all smiles again. "See," he said, "it's thawed out nice and warm. This is going to be a pushover. We make Henrietta happy, and—well, our troubles are under control."

That's what *he* thought. If we'd only known!

I wouldn't have believed one phony looking old cold-storage egg—if it was really an egg—could make so much difference to a turkey. Not even if she did want to raise a family. The minute we rolled it inside the coop, Henrietta got all excited. She began to talk to it and push it around lovingly and stick her feathers out and do everything but turn somersaults. She almost did that, too, trying to climb aboard and stay put. By the time we left her, to go to supper, she was balanced on top, swelled up like a balloon, her eyes tight shut and her voice cooed down to a gargly gurgle. Boy, was she happy!

Four or five nights later, things began to pop. As they say in the newspapers, the lid blew off. The levee done bust! Bud and I had been in bed about half an hour, talking, when all of a sudden—WHAM!—there was a loud bang behind the house. In the stillness it sounded like a cannon. We bounced up, and at that same instant Henrietta let loose, screeching the top of her head off.

We yanked on pants and sneakers and lit out for the coop. At first we couldn't see anything but the turkey's head bobbing and weaving round and round. You couldn't hear yourself think for the squawking. At least she was alive. Then Dad put the flashlight on us and said, "What tomfoolery have you boys been up to now?" and Mom hollered from upstairs to know what was wrong.

We didn't know, any more than they did. Henrietta looked as if she'd been hit by a cyclone. We tried to get her calmed down, and pretty soon Dad growled something about morons and practical jokes and told us to scram back to bed.

At the first chance, Bud grabbed my arm hard and hissed, *"Did you see the egg?"*

"No, but she'll find it as soon as she gets over being scared."

"No, she won't either. I hunted but it isn't there any more. I tell you, our million-year-old egg has gone!"

I said, "Who'd want to take that?" but all Bud did was look sort of wild-eyed and mutter that we'd see in the morning.

When Mom called me, Bud was already on the job.

"How's Henrietta?" I asked. "And did you find the egg?"

Naturally, the turkey was still all ruffled and wrought up, as nervous as a cat, and I thought Bud would be hot and bothered about it. Instead, he just said, "Aw, she's all right." Then he held out his hand. In it were two or three scraps of shell. "That," he said impressively, "is all I can find. BUT—there's a lizard somewhere in the coop! A gray one about six inches long."

"Great Guns!" I said. "The lizard ate the egg right out from under Henrietta."

He stared at me, eyes half closed. "I wonder. Then what about the explosion?"

"The shot? Somebody trying to bop the lizard," I explained. "He's probably been raising cain around the neighborhood lately, eating eggs."

"Well," said Bud grimly, "I want to see that lizard, close up, that's all."

About eleven-thirty that morning, a message came down from the principal's office that Bud was to go home at noon hour. Something about a sick turkey, the girl said. That didn't sound too good, so we borrowed a bike and lit out, riding double.

Mom saw us come into the yard. "Your turkey has sounded very strange today," she called from the kitchen window. "I haven't been down to look, but I thought you'd better know."

One minute later I got the biggest shock of my life. Bud didn't because he'd been suspicious from the start.

No. Henrietta wasn't sick. She was making funny noises, all right, clucking and gobbling, up and down the scale. And she was acting crazy just like a proud old mother hen. But you'd never in the world imagine what she was making such a fuss over. It was the lizard! No kidding. And as if that wasn't enough, you should have seen her child.

Maybe he was only six inches long when Bud first spotted him, but by now he was a good eighteen or twenty. The middle part was mainly belly, round and fat, sprouting four short legs. They wobbled so that he scraped along the ground. His hinder end tapered off into a thick, pointed tail. But up front—wow! There was a long, thin neck that could twist around in all directions, and at the top a puny little head with gentle brown eyes about three sizes too big and a long, red tongue that kept sliding in and out. He didn't look like any lizard I ever saw.

When Bud and I tiptoed near, he stuck his head up as high as it would go, then scooted under Henrietta while she clucked and fussed anxiously. His tail still hung out on the side nearest us, but those big eyes came peeking up through her back feathers on the other side. They were all soft and begging like a spaniel's.

I guess I stood there like a dumfounded idiot. At last I goggled at Bud. It was another shock to find him absolutely beaming. I licked my lips and tried to swallow. "What is it?" I croaked, feeling weak.

"Just exactly as I thought," said Bud. "It's in the Mesozoic chapter—about page seventy-five, I think. I'll look it up when we go back."

"What is?" I said. "What are you talking about?"

"A picture of this thing," he said calmly. "In our science book. I'd say it's either of the family Diplodocus or the family

276

Iguanodon, of the order Dinosauria. Prehistoric, you know. It hatched out of our egg. I think we'll call him Egbert."

I felt as if we were both completely goofy. But just then Mom called us for lunch.

"We'd better keep this under our hats for now," warned Bud. Gosh, you couldn't have pried a word out of me!

The afternoon classes had only started when Bud signaled "seventy-two." I got out my science book, and there, by golly, was a picture of Henrietta's young one, grown up. But it looked about the size of our house, with a neck long enough to see right over the silo or even maybe the Episcopal Church steeple. At that rate we were going to have a sweet time keeping Egbert under our hats or anywhere else.

On the way home I said to Bud, "Say, how big do you think Egbert will grow?"

He looked a little startled. "I don't know. I hadn't thought much about it."

"You'd better," I advised. "And what does he eat?"

"Most dinosaurs lived on grass and stuff. I guess Egbert will, too." But he sounded pretty uneasy.

Henrietta seemed tired and bewildered. Her son Egbert had kept right on growing all afternoon. He almost filled the wire coop now. When he curled up to be with his mother, he reached around three sides, with her in the middle. He'd licked the turkey yard as slick as if it had been swept. Henrietta's house, too, was clean as a whistle. No mash, no corn, no water, no straw, no nothing. And I almost fell over backward when his little head came gliding in the door on its long rubberneck, searching around for one more scrap to eat. That was some neck! When Henrietta clucked at him to come back outside, he just popped his head out of the window to see what she wanted.

But he did have the gentlest brown eyes. And he liked to have us scratch him with sticks or a nail. Then he'd close his eyes the way a kitten does and squeak with happiness. That was the only sound he ever made, just a squeak.

Bud and I got busy. We mixed a whole bushel of mash in

277

the rusty washboiler. We pulled two cabbages from the field and picked up three bagfuls of windfall apples. Egbert gulped it all down, drank four buckets of water, and then peered around for something to fill up on.

I could tell that Bud was worried. He was very quiet during supper and went to bed early with a slight headache.

About daybreak next morning Bud and I woke at the same second, listening. Somewhere out back there was a creaking of wire and the cracking, splintering sound of wood, followed by drowsy gobbles from Henrietta. We got dressed fast and climbed down over the porch roof because the stairs squeak and Mom wakes up.

Henrietta was sitting in the middle of the yard, exhausted. The backyard, not the turkey run. Her house was tipped over, the coop just a crumpled mess of wire and broken sticks, and Egbert nowhere to be seen.

"He's run away!" whispered Bud. "What'll we do?"

"I'd say to start cheering, except that I bet he hasn't run away far enough to get himself lost," I answered. I was disgusted. But just then, ker-*thump* CRASH! went something in the cow barn. Egbert's head stuck out of one of the little square windows behind the stalls and his tongue pulled down ten feet of ivy, vines and all.

I bellowed, "GET OUT OF THAT!" and hit for the barn.

Egbert wanted to play. He'd just had himself a light breakfast, what with dumping over the grain bin and a barrel of potatoes, and he felt good. When I ran in, he galloped down the barn, fell over Grampa's old sleigh and squashed it flat. Then he made little rushes at me just like a puppy would. First his head would be right down to the floor and next he'd peek at me around a post from about ten feet up. He was still growing. What I mean, his body alone now was the size of a tractor.

I didn't know how to make him stop fooling around. It was Henrietta who came to the rescue. She walked in, gobbling and scolding and talking baby talk, so Egbert flopped down with a thud that made the barn bounce and let his tongue hang out. Then she scrambled up on his neck, and they both went to sleep.

278

I nailed the barn door shut, hoping for the best. After which I
looked at Bud, who was pale.

That afternoon, we were almost afraid to go home. But we
finally screwed up enough courage. It wasn't too bad, considering. Henrietta and Egbert were both taking another snooze, so
Bud and I set to work and salvaged as much of the wreckage as
we could. Most of the potatoes and all the turnips were gone.
So were two bushels of eating apples. Egbert had also cleaned
up every wisp of moldy hay, the sleigh cushions, and an old
horse blanket, as well as munched on quite a lot of the wood-
work. He had grown a lot more since morning.

We collected as much fodder as we could lay hands on,
making a big pile on the barn floor. Then we nailed the door
shut again, using spikes this time. In the back of my mind I
kept seeing that picture in the science book.

The next morning we were up very early, working like mad
to get together another pile of grass and weeds and junk to last
through the day. When we opened the barn door to put it inside,
the place was completely shot. Henrietta tottered out with a
frantic yelp and hit for cover in the raspberry bushes. I guess

she'd had enough. Right behind her loomed Egbert's foolish smile, his brown eyes the size of saucers.

"Get back in there, *you!*" I ordered, and I cuffed him alongside the head, which hurt my fingers. He put his cheek down on the floor and rolled one eye at me lovingly, coaxing to be fed. Good grief! By now his back arched up higher than the cow stalls, and as far as I could tell, his tail reached the other end of the building.

"Start forking!" I told Bud. Hay began to fly in the doorway. "More!" I hollered. "More!" but the faster Bud worked, the faster Egbert's long, red tongue baled up the forkfuls and tucked them out of sight. To him it was only a snack. By the time we nailed up again he was just getting interested and the grub was all gone.

"Whew!" groaned Bud, mopping the sweat. "This is getting me down."

"Well," I said, giving him a dirty look, "you asked for it, and we are certainly getting it." And all the way to school I kept wondering how we could possibly dig up enough food to keep Egbert satisfied.

Our first period that day was Science. Bud could hardly wait to ask Prof how long prehistoric animals could live under present-day conditions.

Prof peered over his glasses and said, "Do you mean after surviving for millions of years?"

"No," said Bud, squirming. "How long could one live if he hatched out now?"

Prof took off his glasses with a lunge. "Quite impossible!" he snorted. "Utterly fantastic! What makes you ask such a ridiculous question?"

As if in answer, a kid bounced into the room from the principal's office, all out of breath, and said, "Bud and Ben Travis are wanted home at once. Their barn fell down."

At the same moment somebody's car horn came blaring past the school like Paul Revere, traveling a mile a minute. Then a wagon sailed by, keeping right behind the car. High above the racket you could hear the driver telling the horse, "GIDDAP!"

Some women screeched, the way they do on murder mystery radio programs. I looked at Bud to find him looking at me, both of us green around the gills.

This was it! Egbert had followed us because he was still hungry.

I jumped over a row of desks trying to beat Prof to the window, just as he pushed up the sash. It couldn't have been timed better. Egbert's moon face rose just outside, making it a threesome. Before Prof could get his weak eyes focused, Egbert's friendly wet tongue went *slurp*.

"GET OUT'A HERE!" I howled, and cuffed Egbert. He blinked at me, looking surprised, and sank slowly out of sight. Bud and I raced down the stairs. Two girls and three teachers had fainted, besides the one who got hysterics.

We found Egbert very busy and happy in a field out back, trying to get filled up. When we ran at him, hollering and waving, he wanted to play, the way he did with me in the barn. Throwing stones didn't do any good. They just bounced off his hide and he'd chase after them, thinking it was a game. But when our yells of *"G'wan home!"* got good and mad, he finally tumbled to the idea. His head drooped, his brown eyes got sad and reproachful, and he slunk off dejectedly as if nobody loved him, walking right through a fence and knocking a big signboard flat.

281

Before we could follow and chase him home, Prof sneaked out from behind the Gym with two State Troopers, so we had to answer their questions. They said we'd have to round Egbert up and turn him in. That was what we wanted, anyway, and we got going.

Egbert's tracks weren't hard to follow because he broke so many things. In the dirt road were great big footprints. Between them ran a deep furrow where he'd dragged his tail. I'd noticed before that he did that whenever he got bawled out and felt bad.

I began to get sorry for the poor little fella. "Gosh, Bud," I said, "we were pretty hard on Egbert. He doesn't know any better, and we've hurt his feelings."

"I was just thinking that, too," Bud admitted. "He's affectionate and sensitive."

But we'd realized it too late. We never had a chance to let him know that we understood how he felt.

You remember the place where the L. M. & O. tracks cross route 96A? There's a swale of long, tender grass, fringed all around with young birch saplings. Yes, that's where we found him. He was completely overstuffed, his tail curled round for a pillow, a look of contentment on his face. And he was dead as a doorpost. Poor old Egbert!

The County got Dad on the phone and threatened to sue him into the Poor Farm. But all that fell through because none of the laws said anything about dinosaurs. As for Prof, he wired to some natural history museum people he knows and arranged to sell poor Egbert for enough money to put up a new turkey shed, buy a mate for Henrietta, and get Bud and me a good second-hand car—which is what I started to tell you about in the first place.

How do you know it's the truth? Well, you've been to the Museum, haven't you?

Frank R. Stockton

MRS. LECKS AND MRS. ALESHINE
ARE SHIPWRECKED

ILLUSTRATED BY *George Richards*

I WAS on my way from San Francisco to Yokohama when in a very desultory and gradual manner I became acquainted with Mrs. Lecks and Mrs. Aleshine. The steamer on which I was making a moderately rapid passage toward the land of the legended fan and the lacquered box carried a fair complement of passengers, most of whom were Americans; and among these, my attention was attracted from the very first day of the voyage to two middle-aged women who appeared to me very unlike the ordinary traveler or tourist. At first sight they might have been taken for farmers' wives who for some unusual reason had determined to make a voyage across the Pacific; but on closer observation one would have been more apt to suppose that they belonged to the families of prosperous tradesmen in some little country town where, besides the arts of rural housewifery, there would be opportunities of becoming acquainted in some degree with the ways and manners of the outside world. They were not of that order of persons who generally take first-class passages on steamships, but the stateroom occupied by Mrs. Lecks and Mrs. Aleshine was one of the best in the vessel; and although they kept very much to themselves and showed no desire for the company or notice of the other passengers, they evidently considered themselves quite as good as anyone else, and with as much right to voyage to any part of the world in any manner or style which pleased them.

Mrs. Lecks was a rather tall woman, large-boned and muscular, and her well-browned countenance gave indications of that conviction of superiority which gradually grows up in the minds of those who for a long time have had absolute control of the destinies of a state or the multifarious affairs of a country household. Mrs. Aleshine was somewhat younger than her friend, somewhat shorter, and a great deal fatter. She had the same air of reliance upon her individual worth that characterized Mrs. Lecks, but there was a certain geniality about her which indicated that she would have a good deal of forbearance for those who never had had the opportunity or the ability of becoming the thoroughly good housewife which she was herself.

These two worthy dames spent the greater part of their time on deck, where they always sat together in a place at the stern of the vessel which was well sheltered from wind and weather. As they sat thus they were generally employed in knitting, although this occupation did not prevent them from keeping up what seemed to me, as I passed them in my walks about the deck, a continuous conversation. From a question which Mrs. Lecks once asked me about a distant sail, our acquaintance began. There was no one on board for whose society I particularly cared; and as there was something quaint and odd about these countrywomen on the ocean which interested me, I was glad to vary my solitary promenades by an occasional chat with them. They were not at all backward in giving me information about themselves. They were both widows, and Mrs. Aleshine was going out to Japan to visit a son who had a position there in a mercantile house. Mrs. Lecks had no children and was accompanying her friend because, as she said, she would not allow Mrs. Aleshine to make such a voyage as that by herself, and because, being quite able to do so, she did not know why she should not see the world as well as other people.

These two friends were not educated women. They made frequent mistakes in their grammar and a good deal of Middle States provincialism showed itself in their pronunciation and expressions. But although they brought many of their rural ideas to sea with them, they possessed a large share of that common sense which is available anywhere, and they frequently made use of it in a manner which was very amusing to me. I think also, that they found in me a quarry of information concerning nautical matters, foreign countries, and my own affairs, the working of which helped to make us very good ship friends.

Our steamer touched at the Sandwich Islands; and it was a little more than two days after we left Honolulu that about nine o'clock in the evening we had the misfortune to come into collision with an eastern-bound vessel. The fault was entirely due to the other ship, the lookout on which, although the night was rather dark and foggy, could easily have seen our lights in time to avoid collision if he had not been asleep or absent from his post. Be this as it may, this vessel, which appeared to be a small steamer, struck us with great force near our bows and then, backing, disappeared into the fog, and we never saw or heard of her again. The general opinion was that she was injured very much more than we were and that she probably sank not very long after the accident; for when the fog cleared away about an hour afterward, nothing could be seen of her lights.

As it usually happens on occasions of accidents at sea, the damage to our vessel was at first reported to be slight; but it was soon discovered that our injuries were serious and, indeed, disastrous. The hull of our steamer had been badly shattered on the port bow, and the water came in at a most alarming rate. For nearly two hours the crew and many of the passengers worked at the pumps, and everything possible was done to stop the enormous leak; but all labor to save the vessel was found to

285

be utterly unavailing, and a little before midnight the captain announced that it was impossible to keep the steamer afloat and that we must all take to the boats. The night was now clear, the stars were bright, and as there was but little wind the sea was comparatively smooth. With all these advantages the captain assured us that there was no reason to apprehend danger, and he thought that by noon of the following day we could easily make a small inhabited island where we could be sheltered and cared for until we should be taken off by some passing vessel.

There was plenty of time for all necessary preparations, and these were made with much order and subordination. Some of the ladies among the cabin passengers were greatly frightened and inclined to be hysterical. There were pale faces also among the gentlemen. But everybody obeyed the captain's orders, and all prepared themselves for the transfer to the boats. The first officer came among us and told each of us what boats we were to take and where we were to place ourselves on deck. I was assigned to a large boat which was to be principally occupied by steerage passengers; and as I came up from my stateroom, where I had gone to secure my money and some portable valuables, I met on the companionway Mrs. Lecks and Mrs. Aleshine, who expressed considerable dissatisfaction when they found that I was not going in the boat with them. They, however, hurried below and I went on deck, where in about ten minutes I was joined by Mrs. Lecks, who apparently had been looking for me. She told me she had something very particular to say to me, and conducted me toward the stern of the vessel, where behind one of the deckhouses we found Mrs. Aleshine.

"Look here," said Mrs. Lecks, leading me to the rail and pointing downward; "do you see that boat there? It has been let . down, and there is nobody in it. The boat on the other side has just gone off, full to the brim. I never saw so many people crowded into a boat. The other ones will be just as packed, I expect. I don't see why we shouldn't take this empty boat, now we've got a chance, instead of squeezin' ourselves into those crowded ones. If any of the other people come afterward, why, we shall have our choice of seats, and that's considerable of a p'int, I should say, in a time like this."

"That's so," said Mrs. Aleshine; "and me and Mrs. Lecks would 'a' got right in when we saw the boat was empty if we hadn't been afraid to be there without any man, for it might have floated off and neither of us don't know nothin' about rowin'. And then Mrs. Lecks she thought of you, supposin' a young man who knew so much about the sea would know how to row."

"Oh yes," said I; "but I cannot imagine why this boat should have been left empty. I see a keg of water in it, and the oars and some tin cans, and so I suppose it has been made ready for somebody. Will you wait here a minute until I run forward and see how things are going on there?"

Amidships and forward I saw that there was some confusion among the people who were not yet in their boats, and I found that there was to be rather more crowding than at first was expected. People who had supposed that they were to go in a certain boat found there no place and were hurrying to other boats. It now became plain to me that no time should be lost in getting into the small boat which Mrs. Lecks had pointed out, and which was probably reserved for some favored persons, as the officers were keeping the people forward and amidships, the other stern boat having already departed. But as I acknowledged no reason why anyone should be regarded with more favor than myself and the two women who were waiting for me, I slipped quietly aft and joined Mrs. Lecks and Mrs. Aleshine.

"We must get in as soon as we can," said I, in a low voice, "for this boat may be discovered, and then there will be a rush for it. I suspect it may have been reserved for the captain and some of the officers, but we have as much right in it as they."

"And more too," replied Mrs. Lecks; "for we had nothin' to do with the steerin' and smashin'."

"But how are we goin' to get down there?" said Mrs. Aleshine. "There's no steps."

"That is true," said I. "I shouldn't wonder if this boat is to be taken forward when the others are filled. We must scramble down as well as we can by the tackle at the bow and stern. I'll get in first and keep her close to the ship's side."

"That's goin' to be a scratchy business," said Mrs. Lecks, "and I'm of the opinion we ought to wait till the ship has sunk a little more so we'll be nearer to the boat."

"It won't do to wait," said I, "or we shall not get in it at all."

"And goodness gracious!" exclaimed Mrs. Aleshine, "I can't stand here and feel the ship sinkin' cold-blooded under me till we've got where we can make an easy jump!"

"Very well, then," said Mrs. Lecks, "we won't wait. But the first thing to be done is for each one of us to put on one of these life preservers. Two of them I brought from Mrs. Aleshine's and my cabin, and the other one I got next door, where the people had gone off and left it on the floor. I thought if anythin' happened on the way to the island, these would give us a chance to look about us; but it seems to me we'll need 'em more gettin' down them ropes than anywhere else. I did intend puttin' on two myself to make up for Mrs. Aleshine's fat; but you must wear one of 'em, sir, now that you are goin' to join the party."

As I knew that two life preservers would not be needed by Mrs. Lecks and would greatly inconvenience her, I accepted the one offered me, but declined to put it on until it should be necessary, as it would interfere with my movements.

"Very well," said Mrs. Lecks, "if you think you are safe in gettin' down without it. But Mrs. Aleshine and me will put ours on before we begin sailor-scramblin'. We know how to do it, for we tried 'em on soon after we started from San Francisco. And now, Barb'ry Aleshine, are you sure you've got everythin' you want? for it'll be no use thinkin' about anythin' you've forgot after the ship has sunk out of sight."

"There's nothin' else I can think of," said Mrs. Aleshine; "at least, nothin' I can carry; and so I suppose we may as well begin, for your talk of the ship sinkin' under our feet gives me a sort o' feelin' like an oyster creepin' up and down my back."

Mrs. Lecks looked over the side at the boat, into which I had

already descended. "I'll go first, Barb'ry Aleshine," said she, "and show you how."

The sea was quiet, and the steamer had already sunk so much that Mrs. Leck's voice sounded frightfully near me, although she spoke in a low tone.

"Watch me," said she to her companion. "I'm goin' to do just as he did, and you must follow in the same way."

So saying, she stepped on a bench by the rail; then, with one foot on the rail itself, she seized the ropes which hung from one of the davits to the bow of the boat. She looked down for a moment and then she drew back.

"It's no use," she said. "We must wait until she sinks more, and I can get in easier."

This remark made me feel nervous. I did not know at what moment there might be a rush for this boat, nor when, indeed, the steamer might go down. The boat amidships on our side had rowed away some minutes before, and through the darkness I could distinguish another boat, near the bows, pushing off. It would be too late now for us to try to get into any other boat, and I did not feel that there was time enough for me to take this one to where the two women could more easily descend to her. Standing upright, I urged them not to delay.

"You see," said I, "I can reach you as soon as you swing yourself off the ropes, and I'll help you down."

"If you're sure you can keep us from comin' down too sudden we'll try it," said Mrs. Lecks; "but I'd as soon be drowned as to get to an island with a broken leg. And as to Mrs. Aleshine, if she was to slip she'd go slam through that boat to the bottom of the sea. Now then, be ready! I'm comin' down."

So saying, she swung herself off, and she was then so near me that I was able to seize her and make the rest of her descent comparatively easy. Mrs. Aleshine proved to be a more difficult subject. Even after I had a firm grasp of her capacious waist she refused to let go the ropes, for fear that she might drop into the ocean instead of the boat. But the reproaches of Mrs. Lecks and the downward weight of myself made her loosen her nervous grip; and although we came very near going overboard together, I safely placed her on one of the thwarts.

I now unhooked the tackle from the stern; but before casting off at the bow I hesitated, for I did not wish to desert any of those who might be expecting to embark in this boat. But I could hear no approaching footsteps, and from my position close to the side of the steamer I could see nothing. Therefore I cast off and, taking the oars, pushed away and rowed to a little distance, where I could get whatever view was possible of the deck of the steamer. Seeing no forms moving about, I called out; and receiving no answer, I shouted again at the top of my voice. I waited for nearly a minute and, hearing nothing and seeing nothing, I became convinced that no one was left on the vessel.

"They are all gone," said I, "and we will pull after them as fast as we can."

And I began to row toward the bow of the steamer, in the direction which the other boats had taken.

"It's a good thing you can row," said Mrs. Lecks, settling herself comfortably in the stern-sheets, "for what Mrs. Aleshine and me would ha' done with them oars I am sure I don't know."

"I'd never have got into this boat," said Mrs. Aleshine, "if Mr. Craig hadn't been here."

"No indeed," replied her friend. "You'd ha' gone to the bottom, hangin' for dear life to them ropes."

When I had rounded the bow of the steamer, which appeared to me to be rapidly settling in the water, I perceived at no great distance several lights which of course belonged to the other boats, and I rowed as hard as I could, hoping to catch up with them or at least to keep sufficiently near. It might be my duty to take off some of the people who had crowded into the other boats, probably supposing that this one had been loaded and gone. How such a mistake could have taken place I could not divine, and it was not my business to do so. Quite certain that no one was left on the sinking steamer, all I had to do was to row after the other boats and to overtake them as soon as possible. I thought it would not take me very long to do this, but after rowing for half an hour Mrs. Aleshine remarked that the lights seemed as far off, if not farther, than when we first started after them. Turning, I saw that this was the case and was greatly surprised. With only two passengers I ought soon to have come up with those heavily laden boats. But after I had thought over it a little I considered that as each of them was probably pulled by half a dozen stout sailors, it was not so very strange that they should make as good or better headway than I did.

It was not very long after this that Mrs. Lecks said that she thought that the lights on the other boats must be going out, and that this most probably was due to the fact that the sailors had forgotten to fill their lanterns before they started. "That sort of thing often happens," she said, "when people leave a place in a hurry."

But when I turned around and peered over the dark waters,

291

it was quite plain to me that it was not want of oil but increased distance which made those lights so dim. I could now perceive but three of them, and as the surface was agitated only by a gentle swell I could not suppose that any of them were hidden from our view by waves. We were being left behind, that was certain, and all I could do was to row on as long and as well as I could in the direction which the other boats had taken. I had been used to rowing, and thought I pulled a good oar, and I certainly did not expect to be left behind in this way.

"I don't believe this boat has been emptied out since the last rain," said Mrs. Aleshine, "for my feet are wet, though I didn't notice it before."

At this I shipped my oars and began to examine the boat. The bottom was covered with a movable floor of slats, and as I put my hand down I could feel the water welling up between the slats. The flooring was in sections, and lifting the one beneath me, I felt under it and put my hand into six or eight inches of water.

The exact state of the case was now as plain to me as if it had been posted up on a bulletin-board. This boat had been found to be unseaworthy and its use had been forbidden, all the people having been crowded into the others. This had caused confusion at the last moment, and of course we were supposed to be in some one of the other boats.

And now here was I in the middle of the Pacific Ocean, in a leaky boat, with two middle-aged women! ·

"Anythin' the matter with the floor?" asked Mrs. Lecks.

I let the section fall back into its place and looked aft. By the starlight I could see that my two companions had each fixed upon me a steadfast gaze. They evidently felt that something was the matter and wanted to know what it was. I did not hesitate for a moment to inform them. They appeared to me to be women whom it would be neither advisable nor possible to deceive in a case like this.

"This boat has a leak in it," I said. "There is a lot of water in her already, and that is the reason we have got along so slowly."

"And that is why," said Mrs. Aleshine, "it was left empty.

292

We ought to have known better than to expect to have a whole boat just for three of us. It would have been much more sensible, I think, if we had tried to squeeze into one of the others."

"Now, Barb'ry Aleshine," said Mrs. Lecks, "don't you begin findin' fault with good fortune when it comes to you. Here we've got a comfortable boat, with room enough to set easy and stretch out if we want to. If the water is comin' in, what we've got to do is to get it out again just as fast as we can. What's the best way to do that, Mr. Craig?"

"We must bail her out, and lose no time about it," said I. "If I can find the leak I may be able to stop it."

I now looked about for something to bail with, and the two women aided actively in the search. I found one leather scoop in the bow; but as it was well that we should all go to work, I took two tin cans that had been put in by someone who had begun to provision the boat and proceeded to cut the tops from them with my jackknife.

"Don't lose what's in 'em," said Mrs. Lecks: "that is, if it's anythin' we'd be likely to want to eat. If it's tomatoes, pour it into the sea, for nobody ought to eat tomatoes put up in tins."

I hastily passed the cans to Mrs. Lecks and I saw her empty the contents of one into the sea and those of the other on a newspaper which she took from her pocket and placed in the stern.

I pulled up the movable floor and threw it overboard and then began to bail.

"I thought," said Mrs. Aleshine, "that they always had pumps for leaks."

"Now, Barb'ry Aleshine," said Mrs. Lecks, "just gether yourself up on one of them seats and go to work. The less talkin' we do, and the more scoopin', the better it'll be for us."

I soon perceived that it would have been difficult to find two more valuable assistants in the bailing of a boat than Mrs. Lecks and Mrs. Aleshine. They were evidently used to work and were able to accommodate themselves to the unusual circumstances in which they were placed. We threw out the water very rapidly, and every little while I stopped bailing and felt about to see if I could discover where it came in. As these attempts met with no success, I gave them up after a time and set about bailing with new vigor, believing that if we could get the boat nearly dry I should surely be able to find the leak.

But after working half an hour more I found that the job would be a long one; and if we all worked at once we would all be tired out at once, and that might be disastrous. Therefore I proposed that we should take turns in resting, and Mrs. Aleshine was ordered to stop work for a time. After this Mrs. Lecks took a rest, and when she went to work I stopped bailing and began again to search for the leak.

For about two hours we worked in this way, and then I concluded it was useless to continue any longer this vain exertion. With three of us bailing we were able to keep the water at the level we first found it; but with only two at work it slightly gained upon us, so that now there was more water in the boat than when we first discovered it. The boat was an iron one and the leak in it I could neither find nor remedy. It had probably been caused by the warping of the metal under a hot sun, an accident which I am told frequently occurs to iron boats. The little craft, which would have been a lifeboat had its air-boxes remained intact, was now probably leaking from stem to stern; and in searching for the leak without the protection of the flooring, my weight had doubtless assisted in opening the seams, for it was quite plain that the water was now coming in more rapidly than it did at first. We were very tired, and even Mrs. Lecks, who had all along counseled us to keep at work and not to waste one breath in talking, now admitted that it was of no use to try to get the water out of that boat.

It had been some hours since I had used the oars, but whether we had drifted or remained where we were when I stopped rowing, of course I could not know; but this mattered very little; our boat was slowly sinking beneath us, and it could make no difference whether we went down in one spot or another. I sat and racked my brain to think what could be done in this fearful emergency. To bail any longer was useless labor, and what else was there that we could do?

"When will it be time," asked Mrs. Lecks, "for us to put on the life preservers? When the water gets nearly to the seats?"

I answered that we should not wait any longer than that, but in my own mind I could not see any advantage in putting them on at all. Why should we wish to lengthen our lives by a few hours of helpless floating upon the ocean?

"Very good," said Mrs. Lecks; "I'll keep a watch on the water. One of them cans was filled with lobster, which would be more than likely to disagree with us, and I've throwed it out; but the other had baked beans in it, and the best thing we can do is to eat some of these right away. They are mighty nourishin' and will keep up strength as well as anythin', and then, as you said there's a keg of water in the boat, we can all take a drink of that and it'll make us feel like new cre'tur's. You'll have to take the beans in your hands, for we've got no spoons nor forks."

Mrs. Lecks and Mrs. Aleshine were each curled up out of reach of the water, the first in the stern and the other on the aft thwart. The day was now beginning to break and we could see about us very distinctly. Before reaching out her hands to

295

receive her beans, Mrs. Aleshine washed them in the water in the boat, remarking at the same time that she might as well make use of it since it was there. Having then wiped her hands on some part of her apparel, they were filled with beans from the newspaper held by Mrs. Lecks, and these were passed over to me. I was very hungry, and when I had finished my beans I agreed with my companions that although they would have been a great deal better if heated up with butter, pepper, and salt, they were very comforting as they were. One of the empty cans was now passed to me, and after having been asked by Mrs. Lecks to rinse it out very carefully, we all satisfied our thirst from the water in the keg.

"Cold baked beans and lukewarm water ain't exactly company vittles," said Mrs. Aleshine, "but there's many a poor wretch would be glad to get 'em."

I could not imagine any poor wretch who would be glad of the food together with the attending circumstances; but I did not say so.

"The water is just one finger from the bottom of the seat," said Mrs. Lecks, who had been stooping over to measure, "and it's time to put on the life preservers."

"Very good," said Mrs. Aleshine; "hand me mine."

Each of us now buckled on a life preserver, and as I did so I stood up upon a thwart and looked about me. It was quite light now, and I could see for a long distance over the surface of the ocean, which was gently rolling in wide, smooth swells. As we rose upon the summit of one of these I saw a dark spot upon the water, just on the edge of our near horizon. "Is that the steamer?" I thought; "and has she not yet sunk?"

At this there came to me a glimmering of courageous hope. If the steamer had remained afloat so long, it was probable that on account of water-tight compartments or for some other reason her sinking had reached its limit, and that if we could get back to her we might be saved. But alas, how were we to get back to her? This boat would sink long, long before I could row that distance.

However, I soon proclaimed the news to my companions,

whereupon Mrs. Aleshine prepared to stand upon a thwart and see for herself. But Mrs. Lecks restrained her.

"Don't make things worse, Barb'ry Aleshine," said she, "by tumblin' overboard. If we've got to go into the water, let us do it decently and in order. If that's the ship, Mr. Craig, don't you suppose we can float ourselves to it in some way?"

I replied that by the help of a life preserver a person who could swim might reach the ship.

"But neither of us can swim," said Mrs. Lecks, "for we've lived where the water was never more'n a foot deep, except in time of freshets, when there's no swimmin' for man or beast. But if we see you swim, perhaps we can follow, after a fashion. At any rate, we must do the best we can, and that's all there is to be done."

"The water now," remarked Mrs. Aleshine, "is so near to the bottom of my seat that I've got to stand up, tumble overboard or no."

"All right," remarked Mrs. Lecks; "we'd better all stand up, and let the boat sink under us. That will save our jumpin' overboard, or rollin' out any which way, which might be awkward."

"Goodness gracious me!" exclaimed Mrs. Aleshine. "You set the oysters creepin' over me again! First you talk of the ship sinkin' under us, and now it's the boat goin' to the bottom under our feet. Before any sinkin' is to be done I'd ruther get out."

"Now, Barb'ry Aleshine," said Mrs. Lecks, "stand up straight and don't talk so much. It'll be a great deal better to be let down gradual than to flop into the water all of a bunch."

"Very well," said Mrs. Aleshine; "it may be best to get used to it by degrees, but I must say I wish I was home."

As for me, I would have much preferred to jump overboard at once, instead of waiting in this cold-blooded manner; but as my companions had so far preserved their presence of mind I did not wish to do anything which might throw them into a panic. I believed there would be no danger from the suction caused by the sinking of a small boat like this, and if we took care not to entangle ourselves with it in any way we might as well follow Mrs. Lecks's advice as not. So we all stood up,

297

Mrs. Lecks in the stern, I in the bow, and Mrs. Aleshine on a thwart between us. The last did not appear to have quite room enough for a steady footing; but as she remarked, it did not matter very much, as the footing, broad or narrow, would not be there very long.

I am used to swimming and have never hesitated to take a plunge into river or ocean, but I must admit that it was very trying to my nerves to stand up this way and wait for a boat to sink beneath me. How the two women were affected I do not know. They said nothing, but their faces indicated that something disagreeable was about to happen and that the less that was said about it the better.

The boat had now sunk so much that the water was around Mrs. Aleshine's feet, her standing-place being rather lower than ours. I made myself certain that there were no ropes nor any other means of entanglement near my companions or myself, and then I waited. There seemed to be a good deal of buoyancy in the bow and stern of the boat and it was a frightfully long time in sinking. The suspense became so utterly unendurable that I was tempted to put one foot on the edge of the boat and by tipping it put an end to this nerve-rack; but I refrained, for I probably would throw the women off their balance, when they might fall against some part of the boat and do themselves a hurt. I had just relinquished this intention, when two little waves seemed to rise one on each side of Mrs. Aleshine, and gently flowing over the side of the boat, they flooded her feet with water.

"Hold your breath!" I shouted. And now I experienced a sensation which must have been very like that which comes to a condemned criminal at the first indication of the pulling of the drop. Then there was a horrible sinking, a gurgle, and a swash, and the ocean over which I had been gazing appeared to rise up and envelop me.

In a moment, however, my head was out of the water, and looking hastily about me, I saw, close by, the heads and shoulders of Mrs. Lecks and Mrs. Aleshine. The latter was vigorously winking her eyes and blowing from her mouth some sea-

298

water that had got into it; but as soon as her eyes fell upon me she exclaimed, "That was ever so much more suddint than I thought it was goin' to be!"

"Are you both all right?"

"I suppose I am," said Mrs. Aleshine, "but I never thought that a person with a life preserver on would go clean under the water."

"But since you've come up again, you ought to be satisfied," said Mrs. Lecks. "And now," she added, turning her face toward me, "which way ought we to try to swim? and have we got everythin' we want to take with us?"

"What we haven't got we can't get," remarked Mrs. Aleshine; "and as for swimmin', I expect I'm goin' to make a poor hand at it."

I had a hope, which was not quite strong enough to be a belief, that supported by their life preservers the two women might paddle themselves along; and that by giving them in turn a helping hand I might eventually get them to the steamer. There was a strong probability that I would not succeed, but I did not care to think of that.

I now swam in front of my companions and endeavored to instruct them in the best method of propelling themselves with their arms and their hands. If they succeeded in this, I thought I would give them some further lessons in striking out with their feet. After watching me attentively, Mrs. Lecks did manage to move herself slowly through the smooth water, but poor Mrs. Aleshine could do nothing but splash.

"If there was anythin' to take hold of," she said to me, "I might get along; but I can't get any grip on the water, though you seem to do it well enough. Look there!" she added in a higher voice. "Isn't that an oar floatin' over there? If you can get that for me I believe I can row myself much better than I can swim."

This seemed an odd idea, but I swam over to the floating oar and brought it to her. I was about to show her how she could best use it, but she declined my advice.

"If I do it at all," she said, "I must do it in my own way." And

299

taking the oar in her strong hands, she began to ply it on the water very much in the way in which she would handle a broom. At first she dipped the blade too deeply, but, correcting this error, she soon began to paddle herself along at a slow but steady rate.

"Capital!" I cried. "You do that admirably!"

"Anybody who's swept as many rooms as I have," she said, "ought to be able to handle anythin' that can be used like a broom."

"Isn't there another oar?" cried Mrs. Lecks, who had now been left a little distance behind us. "If there is I want one."

Looking about me, I soon discovered another floating oar and brought it to Mrs. Lecks, who after holding it in various positions so as to get "the hang of it," as she said, soon began to use it with as much skill as that shown by her friend. If either of them had been obliged to use an oar in the ordinary way, I fear they would have had a bad time of it; but considering the implement in the light of a broom, its use immediately became familiar to them, and they got on remarkably well.

I now took a position a little in advance of my companions, and as I swam slowly they were easily able to keep up with me. Mrs. Aleshine, being so stout, floated much higher out of the water than either Mrs. Lecks or I, and this permitted her to use her oar with a great deal of freedom. Sometimes she would give such a vigorous brush to the water that she would turn herself almost entirely around, but after a little practice she learned to avoid undue efforts of this kind.

I was not positively sure that we were going in the right direction, for my position did not allow me to see very far over the water; but I remembered that when I was standing up in the boat and made my discovery the sun was just about to rise in front of me, while the dark spot on the ocean lay to my left. Judging, therefore, from the present position of the sun, which was not very high, I concluded that we were moving toward the north and therefore in the right direction. How far off the steamer might be I had no idea, for I was not accustomed to judging distances at sea; but I believed that if we were careful of our strength and if the ocean continued as smooth as it now was, we might eventually reach the vessel, provided she were yet afloat.

"After you are fairly in the water," said Mrs. Aleshine as she swept along, although without the velocity which that phrase usually implies, "it isn't half so bad as I thought it would be. For one thing, it don't feel a bit salt, although I must say it tasted horribly that way when I first went into it."

"You didn't expect to find pickle-brine, did you?" said Mrs. Lecks. "Though if it was, I suppose we could float on it settin'."

"And as to bein' cold," said Mrs. Aleshine, "the part of me that's in is actually more comfortable than that which is out."

"There's one thing I would have been afraid of," said Mrs. Lecks, "if we hadn't made preparations for it, and that's sharks."

"Preparations!" I exclaimed. "How in the world did you prepare for sharks?"

"Easy enough," said Mrs. Lecks. "When we went down into our room to get ready to go away in the boats we both put on black stockin's. I've read that sharks never bite colored people, although if they see a white man in the water they'll snap him up as quick as lightnin'; and black stockin's was the nearest we could come to it. You see, I thought as like as not we'd have some sort of an upset before we got through."

"It's a great comfort," remarked Mrs. Aleshine, "and I'm very glad you thought of it, Mrs. Lecks. After this I shall make it a rule: Black stockin's for sharks."

"I suppose in your case," said Mrs. Lecks, addressing me, "dark trousers will do as well."

To which I answered that I sincerely hoped they would.

"Another thing I'm thankful for," said Mrs. Aleshine, "is that I thought to put on a flannel skeert."

"And what's the good of it," said Mrs. Lecks, "when it's soppin' wet?"

"Flannel's flannel," replied her friend, "whether it's wet or dry; and if you'd had the rheumatism as much as I have you'd know it."

301

To this Mrs. Lecks replied with a sniff, and asked me how soon I thought we would get sight of the ship; for if we were going the wrong way and had to turn round and go back it would certainly be very provoking.

I should have been happy indeed to be able to give a satisfactory answer to this question. Every time that we rose upon a swell I threw a rapid glance around the whole circle of the horizon; and at last, not a quarter of an hour after Mrs. Lecks's question, I was rejoiced to see, almost in the direction in which I supposed it ought to be, the dark spot which I had before discovered. I shouted the glad news, and as we rose again my companions strained their eyes in the direction to which I pointed. They both saw it and were greatly satisfied.

"Now, then," said Mrs. Aleshine, "it seems as if there was somethin' to work for"; and she began to sweep her oar with great vigor.

"If you want to tire yourself out before you get there, Barb'ry Aleshine," said Mrs. Lecks, "you'd better go on in that way. Now, what I advise is that we stop rowin' altogether and have somethin' to eat; for I'm sure we need it to keep up our strength."

"Eat!" I cried. "What are you going to eat? Do you expect to catch fish?"

"And eat 'em raw?" said Mrs. Lecks. "I should think not. But do you suppose, Mr. Craig, that Mrs. Aleshine and me would go off and leave that ship without takin' somethin' to eat by the way? Let's all gether here in a bunch, and see what sort of a meal we can make. And now, Barb'ry Aleshine, if you lay your oar down there on the water, I recommend you to tie it to one of your bonnet-strings, or it'll be floatin' away, and you won't get it again."

As she said this, Mrs. Lecks put her right hand down into the water, and fumbled about, apparently in search of a pocket. I could not but smile as I thought of the condition of food when for an hour or more it had been a couple of feet under the surface of the ocean; but my ideas on the subject were entirely changed when I saw Mrs. Lecks hold up in the air two Ger-

man sausages, and shake the briny drops from their smooth and glittering surfaces.

"There's nothin'," she said, "like sausages for shipwreck and that kind o' thing. They're very sustainin', and bein' covered with a tight skin, water can't get at 'em, no matter how you carry 'em. I wouldn't bring these out in the boat, because, havin' the beans, we might as well eat them. Have you a knife about you, Mr. Craig?"

I produced a dripping jackknife, and after the open blade had been waved in the air to dry it a little, Mrs. Lecks proceeded to divide one of the sausages, handing the other to me to hold meanwhile.

"Now don't go eatin' sausages without bread, if you don't want 'em to give you dyspepsy," said Mrs. Aleshine, who was tugging at a submarine pocket.

"I'm very much afraid your bread is all soaked," said Mrs. Lecks.

To which her friend replied that that remained to be seen, and forthwith produced with a splash a glass preserve-jar with a metal top.

"I saw this nearly empty as I looked into the ship's pantry, and I stuffed into it all the soft biscuits it would hold. There was some sort of jam left at the bottom, so that the one who gets the last biscuit will have somethin' of a little spread on it. And now, Mrs. Lecks," she continued triumphantly, as she unscrewed the top, "that rubber ring has kept 'em as dry as chips. I'm mighty glad of it, for I had trouble enough gettin' this jar into my pocket, and gettin' it out, too, for that matter."

Floating thus, with our hands and shoulders above the water, we made a very good meal from the sausages and soft biscuit.

"Barb'ry Aleshine," said Mrs. Lecks, as her friend proceeded to cut the second sausage, "don't you lay that knife down, when you've done with it, as if 'twas an oar; for if you do it'll sink, as like as not, about six miles. I've read that the ocean is as deep as that in some places."

"Goodness gracious me!" exclaimed Mrs. Aleshine, "I hope we are not over one of them deep spots."

"There's no knowin'," said Mrs. Lecks, "but if it's more comfortin' to think it's shallerer, we'll make up our minds that way. Now then," she continued, "we'll finish off this meal with a little somethin' to drink. I'm not given to takin' spirits, but I never travel without a little whisky, ready mixed with water, to take if it should be needed."

So saying, she produced from one of her pockets a whisky-flask tightly corked, and of its contents we each took a sip, Mrs. Aleshine remarking that, leaving out being chilled or colicky, we were never likely to need it more than now.

Thus refreshed and strengthened, Mrs. Lecks and Mrs. Aleshine took up their oars, while I swam slightly in advance as before. When, with occasional intermissions of rest and a good deal of desultory conversation, we had swept and swam for about an hour, Mrs. Lecks suddenly exclaimed,—

"I can see that thing ever so much plainer now, and I don't

believe it's a ship at all. To me it looks like bushes."

"You're mighty long-sighted without your specs," said Mrs. Aleshine, "and I'm not sure but what you're right."

For ten minutes or more I had been puzzling over the shape of the dark spot, which was now nearly all the time in sight. Its peculiar form had filled me with a dreadful fear that it was the steamer, bottom upward, although I knew enough about nautical matters to have no good reason to suppose that this could be the case. I am not far-sighted, but when Mrs. Lecks suggested bushes, I gazed at the distant object with totally different ideas, and soon began to believe that it was not a ship, either right side up or wrong side up, but that it might be an island. This belief I proclaimed to my companions, and for some time we all worked with increased energy in the desire to get near enough to make ourselves certain in regard to this point.

"As true as I'm standin' here," said Mrs. Lecks, who, although she could not read without spectacles, had remarkably good sight at long range, "them is trees and bushes that I see before me, though they do seem to be growin' right out of the water."

"There's an island under them; you may be sure of that!" I cried. "Isn't this ever so much better than a sinking ship?"

"I'm not so sure about that," said Mrs. Aleshine. "I'm used to the ship, and as long as it didn't sink I'd prefer it. There's plenty to eat on board of it, and good beds to sleep on, which is more than can be expected on a little bushy place like that ahead of us. But then, the ship might sink all of a suddint, beds, vittles, and all."

"Do you suppose that is the island the other boats went to?" asked Mrs. Lecks.

This question I had already asked of myself. I had been told that the island to which the captain intended to take his boats lay about thirty miles south of the point where we left the steamer. Now I knew very well that we had not come thirty miles, and had reason to believe, moreover, that the greater part of the progress we had made had been toward the north. It was not at all probable that the position of this island was

305

unknown to our captain; and it must therefore have been considered by him as an unsuitable place for the landing of his passengers. There might be many reasons for this unsuitableness: the island might be totally barren and desolate; it might be the abode of unpleasant natives; and, more important than anything else, it was in all probability a spot where steamers never touched.

But whatever its disadvantages, I was most wildly desirous to reach it; more so, I believe, than either of my companions. I do not mean that they were not sensible of their danger and desirous to be freed from it; but they were women who had probably had a rough time of it during a great part of their lives, and on emerging from their little circle of rural experiences accepted with equanimity and almost as a matter of course the rough times which come to people in the great outside world.

"I do not believe," I said in answer to Mrs. Lecks, "that that is the island to which the captain would have taken us; but whatever it is, it is dry land, and we must get there as soon as we can."

"That's true," said Mrs. Aleshine, "for I'd like to have ground nearer to my feet than six miles; and if we don't find anything to eat and any place to sleep when we get there, it's no more than can be said of the place where we are now."

"You're too particular, Barb'ry Aleshine," said Mrs. Lecks, "about your comforts. If you find the ground too hard to sleep on when you get there, you can put on your life preserver and go to bed in the water."

"Very good," said Mrs. Aleshine, "and if these islands are made of coral, as I've heard they are, and if they're as full of small p'ints as some coral I've got at home, you'll be glad to take a berth by me, Mrs. Lecks."

I counseled my companions to follow me as rapidly as possible, and we all pushed vigorously forward. When we had approached near enough to the island to see what sort of place it really was, we perceived that it was a low-lying spot apparently covered with verdure and surrounded, as far as we could see as we rose on the swells, by a rocky reef against which a tolerably high surf was running.

I knew enough of the formation of these coral islands to suppose that within this reef was a lagoon of smooth water, into which there were openings through the rocky barrier. It was necessary to try to find one of these, for it would be difficult and perhaps dangerous to attempt to land through the surf.

Before us we could see a continuous line of white-capped breakers, and so I led my little party to the right, hoping that we would soon see signs of an opening in the reef.

We swam and paddled, however, for a long time, and still the surf rolled menacingly on the rocks before us. We were now as close to the island as we could approach with safety, and I determined to circumnavigate it if necessary before I would attempt, with these two women, to land upon that jagged reef. At last we perceived at no great distance before us a spot where there seemed to be no breakers; and when we reached it we found to our unutterable delight that here was smooth water flowing through a wide opening in the reef. The rocks were piled up quite high, and the reef, at this point at least, was a wide one, but as we neared the opening we found that it narrowed very soon and made a turn to the left, so that from the outside we could not see into the lagoon.

I swam into this smooth water, followed closely by Mrs. Lecks and Mrs. Aleshine, who, however, soon became unable to use their oars, owing to the proximity of the rocks. Dropping these useful implements, they managed to paddle after me with their hands, and they were as much astonished as I was when, just after making the slight turn, we found stretched across the narrow passage a great iron bar about eight or ten inches above the water. A little farther on, and two or three feet above the water, another iron bar extended from one rocky wall to the other. Without uttering a word I examined the lower bar and found one end of it fastened by means of a huge padlock to a great staple driven into the rock. The lock was securely wrapped in tarred canvas. A staple through an eyehole in the bar secured the other end of it to the rocks.

307

"These bars were put here," I exclaimed, "to keep out boats, whether at high or low water. You see they can only be thrown out of the way by taking off the padlocks."

"They won't keep us out," said Mrs. Lecks, "for we can duck under. I suppose whoever put 'em here didn't expect anybody to arrive on life preservers."

Adopting Mrs. Lecks's suggestion, I "ducked" my head under the bar, and passed to the other side of it. Mrs. Lecks with but little trouble followed my example; but Mrs. Aleshine, who by reason of her stoutness floated so much higher out of the water than her friend and I, found it impossible to get herself under the bar. In whatever manner she made the attempt, her head or her shoulders were sure to bump and arrest her progress.

"Now Barb'ry Aleshine," said Mrs. Lecks, who had been watching her, "if you ever want to get out of this salt water, you've got to make up your mind to take some of it into your mouth and into your eyes; that is, if you don't keep 'em shut. Get yourself as close to that bar as you can, and I'll come and put you under." So saying, Mrs. Lecks returned to the other side of the bar, and having made Mrs. Aleshine bow down her head and close her eyes and mouth, she placed both hands upon her companion's broad shoulders and threw as much weight as possible upon them. Mrs. Aleshine almost disappeared beneath the water, but she came up sputtering and blinking on the other side of the bar, where she was quickly joined by Mrs. Lecks.

"Merciful me!" exclaimed Mrs. Aleshine, wiping her wet face with her still wetter sleeve, "I never supposed the heathens would be up to such tricks as makin' us do that!"

I had waited to give any assistance that might be required, and while doing so had discovered another bar under the water which proved that entrance at almost any stage of the tide had been guarded against. Warning my companions not to strike their feet against this submerged bar, we paddled and pushed ourselves around the turn in the rocky passage and emerged into the open lagoon.

This smooth stretch of water which separated the island from its encircling reef was here about a hundred feet wide; and the first thing that arrested our attention as we gazed across it was a little wharf or landing-stage erected upon the narrow beach of the island, almost opposite to us.

"As sure as I stand here," exclaimed Mrs. Lecks, who never seemed to forget her upright position, "somebody lives in this place!"

"And it isn't a stickery coral island, either," cried Mrs. Aleshine, "for that sand's as smooth as any I ever saw."

"Whoever does lives here," resumed Mrs. Lecks, "has got to take us in, whether they like it or not, and the sooner we get over there the better."

Mrs. Aleshine now regretted the loss of her oar and suggested that some one of us who could get under bars easily should go back after it. But Mrs. Lecks would listen to no such proposition.

"Let the oars go," she said. "We won't want 'em again, for I'll never leave this place if I have to scoop myself out to sea with an oar."

I told the two women that I could easily tow them across this narrow piece of water; and instructing Mrs. Lecks to take hold of the tail of my coat, while Mrs. Aleshine grasped her companion's dress, I began to swim slowly toward the beach, towing my companions behind me.

"Goodnessful gracious me!" suddenly exclaimed Mrs. Aleshine, with a great bounce and a splash, "look at the fishes!"

The water in the lagoon was so clear that it was almost transparent, and beneath us and around us we could see fish, some large and some small, swimming about as if they were floating in the air, while down below the white sandy bottom seemed to sparkle in the sunlight.

"Now don't jerk my skeert off on account of the fishes," said Mrs. Lecks. "I expect there was just as many outside, though we couldn't see 'em. But I must say that this water looks as if it had been boiled and filtered."

If any inhabitant of the island had then been standing on

the wharf, he would have beheld on the surface of the lagoon the peculiar spectacle of a man's head surmounted by a wet and misshapen straw hat and followed by two other heads, each wearing a dripping and bedraggled bonnet, while beneath, among the ripples of the clear water, would have been seen the figures belonging to these three heads, each dressed in the clothes ordinarily worn on land.

As I swam I could see before me on the island nothing but a mass of low-growing tropical vegetation behind which rose some palms and other trees. I made for the little wharf, from which steps came down into the water, and as soon as we reached it we all clambered rapidly up and stood dripping upon the narrow platform, stamping our feet and shaking our clothes.

"Do you see that house?" said Mrs. Lecks. "That's where they live, and I wonder which way we must go to get there."

From this somewhat elevated position I could plainly see, over the tops of the bushes and low trees, the upper part of the roof of a house. When I found the bars across the passage in the reef, I had easily come to the conclusion that the inhabitants of this island were not savages; and now since I had seen the wharf and the roof of this house I felt quite convinced that we had reached the abode of civilized beings. They might be pirates or some other sort of sea miscreants, but they were certainly not savages or cannibals.

Leaving the wharf, we soon found a broad path through the bushes and in a few moments reached a wide open space in which stood a handsome modern-built house. It was constructed after the fashion of tropical houses belonging to Europeans, with jalousied porches and shaded balconies; the grounds about it were neatly laid out and behind it was a walled inclosure, probably a garden.

"Upon my word," exclaimed Mrs. Aleshine, "I'd like to be less drippin' before I make a call on genteel folks!"

"Genteel folks!" exclaimed Mrs. Lecks, indignantly. "If you're too proud to go in as you are, Barb'ry Aleshine, you can go dry in the sun. As for me, I'm goin' to ask for the lady of the

310

house, and if she don't like me she can lump me, so long as she
gives me somethin' to eat and a dry bed to get into."

I was too much amazed to speak, but my companions took
everything as a matter of course. They had expected to see
strange things in the outer world and they were not surprised
when they saw them. My mind was not capable of understand-
ing the existence of an establishment like this on a little island
in mid-ocean. But it was useless for me to attempt to reason on
this apparent phenomenon; and, indeed, there was no time for
it, for Mrs. Lecks walked boldly up to the front door and plied
the knocker, stepping back immediately so that she might not
drip too much water on the porch.

"When they come," she said, "we'll ask 'em to let us in the back way so that we shan't slop up their floors any more than we can help."

We waited for a couple of minutes, and then I, as the member of the party who dripped the least, went up on the porch and knocked again.

"It's my belief they're not at home," said Mrs. Lecks, after we had waited some time longer, "but perhaps we'll find some of the servants in," and she led the way to the back part of the house.

As we passed the side of the mansion I noticed that all the window shutters were closed, and my growing belief that the place was deserted became a conviction after we had knocked several times at a door at the back of the building without receiving any answer.

"Well, they're all gone out, that's certain!" said Mrs. Lecks.

"Yes, and they barred up the entrance to the island when they left," I added.

"I wonder if there's another house in the neighborhood," said Mrs. Aleshine.

"I don't believe," said I, "that the neighborhood is very thickly settled; but if you will wait here a few minutes I will run around this wall and see what there is beyond. I may find the huts of some natives or work-people."

I followed a path by the side of the garden wall, but when I reached the end of the inclosure I could see nothing before me but jungle and forest, with paths running in several directions. I followed one of these and very soon came out upon an open beach, with the reef lying beyond it. From the form of the beach and the reef and from the appearance of things generally, I began to think that this was probably a very small island and that the house we had seen was the only one on it. I returned and reported this belief to my companions.

Now that Mrs. Aleshine had no fear of appearing in an untidy condition before "genteel folks," her manner changed very much.

"If the family has gone into the country," said she, "or whatever else they've done, I want to get into this house as soon as I can. I expect we can find something to eat. At any rate, we can get ourselves dry and lay down somewhere to rest, for not a wink has one of us slept since night before last."

"I should think," said Mrs. Lecks, addressing me, "that if you could manage to climb up to them second-story windows, you might find one of them that you could get in, and then come down and open the door for us. Everybody is likely to forget to fasten some of the windows on the upper floors. I know it isn't right to force our way into other people's houses, but there's nothin' else to be done and there's no need of our talkin' about it."

I agreed with her perfectly and, taking off my coat and shoes, I climbed up one of the columns of the veranda and got upon its roof. This extended nearly the whole length of two sides of the house. I walked along it and tried all the shutters and I soon came to one in which some of the movable slats had been broken. Thrusting my hand and arm through the aperture thus formed, I unhooked the shutters and opened them. The sash was fastened down by one of the ordinary contrivances used for such purposes, but with the blade of my jackknife I easily pushed the bolt aside, raised the sash, and entered. I found myself in a small hall at the head of a flight of stairs. Down these I hurried and, groping my way through the semi-darkness of the lower story, I reached a side door. This was fastened by two bolts and a bar, and I quickly had it open.

Stepping outside, I called Mrs. Lecks and Mrs. Aleshine.

"Well," said the latter, "I'm sure I'll be glad to get in, and as we've squeezed most of the water out of our clothes we won't make so much of a mess, after all."

We now entered and I opened one of the shutters.

"Let's go right into the kitchen," said Mrs. Lecks, "and make a fire. That's the first thing to do."

But Mrs. Lecks soon discovered that this mansion was very different from a country dwelling in one of our Middle States. Externally and as far as I had been able to observe its internal arrangements, it resembled the houses built by English resi-

313

dents which I had seen in the West Indies. It was a dwelling in which modern ideas in regard to construction and furnishing adapted themselves to the requirements of a tropical climate. Apparently there was no kitchen. There were no stairs leading to a lower floor and the darkened rooms into which my companions peered were certainly not used for culinary purposes.

In the meantime I had gone out of the door by which we had entered, and soon discovered on the other side of the house a small building with a chimney to it, which I felt sure must be the kitchen. The door and shutters were fastened, but before making any attempt to open them I returned to announce my discovery.

"Door locked, is it?" said Mrs. Aleshine. "Just wait a minute."

She then disappeared, but in a very short time came out, carrying a bunch of large keys.

"It's always the way," said she as the two followed me round the back of the house, "when people shut up a house and leave it, to put all the door keys in the back corner of some drawer in the hall and to take only the front-door key with them. So you see I knew just where to go for these."

"It's a poor hen," said Mrs. Lecks, "that begins to cackle when she's goin' to her nest; the wise ones wait till they're comin' away. Now we'll see if one of them keys fit."

Greatly to the triumph of Mrs. Aleshine, the second or third key I tried unlocked the door. Entering, we found ourselves in a good-sized kitchen with a great fireplace at one end of it. A door opened from the room into a shed where there was a pile of dry twigs and firewood.

"Let's have a fire as quick as we can," said Mrs. Lecks, "for since I went into that shet-up house I've been chilled to the bones."

"That's so," said Mrs. Aleshine; "and now I know how a fish keeps comfortable in the water and how dreadfully wet and flabby it must feel when it's taken out."

I brought in a quantity of wood and kindling and, finding matches in a tin box on the wall, I went to work to make a fire, and was soon rewarded by a crackling blaze. Turning around, I was amazed at the actions of Mrs. Lecks and Mrs Aleshine. I had expected to see them standing shivering behind me, waiting for the fire to be made; but instead of that they were moving rapidly here and there, saying not a word but going as straight to cupboard, closet, and pantry as the hound follows the track of the hare. From a wild chaos of uncongenial surroundings, these two women had dropped into a sphere in which they were perfectly at home. The kitchen was not altogether like those to which they had been accustomed, but it was a well-appointed one and their instincts and practice made them quickly understand where they would find what they wanted. I gazed on them with delight while one filled a kettle from a little pump in the corner which brought water from a cistern and the other appeared from the pantry, carrying a tea-caddy and a tin biscuit-box.

"Now then," said Mrs. Lecks, hanging the kettle on a crane over the fire and drawing up a chair, "by the time we've got a little dried off, the kettle will bile and we'll have some hot tea, and then the best thing to do is to go to bed."

"We'll take time to have a bite first," said Mrs. Aleshine, "for I was never so near famished in my life. I brought out a box nearly full of biscuits, and there's sardines in this, Mr. Craig, which you can easy open with your knife."

I piled on more wood and we gathered close around the genial heat. The sunshine was hot outside, but that did not prevent the fire from being most comforting to us.

As soon as the kettle began to simmer, up jumped Mrs. Aleshine. A sugar-bowl and some cups were placed upon a table and in a short time we were cheered and invigorated by hot tea, biscuits, and sardines.

"This isn't much of a meal," said Mrs. Aleshine, apologetically, "but there's no time to cook nothin', and the sooner we get off our wet things and find some beds, the better."

"If I can once get into bed," said Mrs. Lecks, "all I ask is that the family will not come back till I have had a good long nap. After that they can do what they please."

We now went back to the house and ascended the main stairway, which led up to a large central hall.

"We won't go into the front rooms," said Mrs. Lecks, "for we don't want to make no more disturbance than we can help; but if we can find the smallest kind of rooms in the back with beds in 'em, it is all we can ask."

The first chamber we entered was a good-sized one, neatly furnished, containing a bedstead with uncovered mattress and pillows. Opening a closet door, Mrs. Lecks exclaimed:

"This is a man's room, Mr. Craig, and you'd better take it. Look at the trousers and coats! There's no bedclothes in here, but I'll see if I can't find some."

In a few minutes she returned, bearing blankets, sheets, and a pillowcase. With Mrs. Aleshine on one side of the bedstead and Mrs. Lecks on the other, the sheets and blankets were laid with surprising deftness and rapidity and in a few moments I saw before me a most inviting bed.

While Mrs. Aleshine held a pillow in her teeth as she pulled on the pillowcase with both hands, Mrs. Lecks looked around the room with the air of an attentive hostess.

"I guess you'll be comfortable, Mr. Craig," she said, "and I advise you to sleep just as long as you can. We'll take the room on the other side of the hall; but I'm first goin' down to see if the kitchen fire is safe, and to fasten the doors."

I offered to relieve her of this trouble, but she promptly declined my services. "When it's rowin' or swimmin', you can do it, Mr. Craig, but when it's lockin' up and lookin' to fires, I'll attend to that myself."

My watch had stopped, but I suppose it was the middle of the afternoon when I went to bed, and I slept steadily until some hours after sunrise the next morning, when I was awakened by a loud knock at the door.

"It's time to get up," said the voice of Mrs. Lecks, "and if your clothes are not entirely dry you'd better see if there isn't somethin' in that closet you can put on. After a while I'll make a big fire in the kitchen and dry all our things."

I found my clothes were still very damp, and after investi-

316

gating the contents of the closet and bureau, I was able to supply myself with linen and a light summer suit which fitted me fairly well. I even found socks and a pair of slippers.

When I entered the kitchen, I first opened wide my eyes with delight and then I burst out laughing. Before me was a table covered with a white cloth, with plates, cups, and everything necessary upon it; at one end was a steaming teapot and at the other a dish of some kind of hot meat, and Mrs. Aleshine was just taking a pan of newly baked biscuits from a small iron oven.

"I don't wonder you laugh," said Mrs. Lecks, "but our clothes was still wet and we had to take just what we could find. I'm not in the habit of goin' about in a white muslin wrapper with blue-ribbon trimmin's, and as for Mrs. Aleshine, I did think we'd never find anything that she could get into; but there must be one stout woman in the family, for that yeller frock with black buttons fits her well enough, though I must say it's a good deal short."

"I never thought," said Mrs. Aleshine, as she sat down at the teapot, "that the heathens had so many conveniences, specially bakin'-powders and Dutch ovens. For my part, I always supposed that they used their altars for bakin' when they wasn't offerin' up victims on 'em."

"Have you got it into your head, Barb'ry, Aleshine," said Mrs. Lecks, looking up from the dish of potted beef she was serving, "that this house belongs to common heathen? I expect that most of the savages who live on these desert islands has been converted by the missionaries, but they'd have to take 'em from Genesis to Revelations a good many times before they'd get 'em to the p'int of havin' force pumps in their kitchens and spring-mattresses on their beds. As far as I've seen this house, it looks as if the family had always been Christians, and probably either Catholics or Episcopalians."

"On account of the cross on the mantelpiece in our room, I suppose," said Mrs. Aleshine. "But whether they're given to idols or prayer books, I know they've got a mighty nice house; and considerin' the distance from stores, there's a good deal

317

more in that pantry than you'd expect to find in any house I know of, when the family is away."

"It is my opinion," said I, "that this house belongs to some rich man, probably an American or European merchant, who lives on one of the large islands not far away and who uses this as a sort of summer residence."

"I thought it was always summer in this part of the world," said Mrs. Lecks.

"So it is in effect," I replied, "but there are some seasons when it is very unpleasant to remain in one of those towns which are found on the larger islands, and so the owner of this house may come up here sometimes for fresh sea air."

"Or it's just as like," said Mrs. Aleshine, "that he lives somewhere up in the iceberg regions and comes here to spend his winters. It would do just as well. But whichever way it is, I can't help thinkin' it's careless not to leave somebody in the house to take care of it. Why, for all the family would know about it, tramps might break in and stay as long as they like."

"That's just what's happenin' now," said Mrs. Lecks, "and for my part I ain't goin' to find no fault. I don't suppose the people would have been so hard-hearted as to turn us away from their doors, but I've seen enough of folks in this world not to be too sure about that."

"How do you suppose," said Mrs. Aleshine, addressing me, "that the family gets here and goes back? Do they keep a private steamboat?"

"Of course they have a private vessel of some kind," I answered, "probably a yacht. It is quite certain that ordinary steamers never touch here."

"If that's the case," said Mrs. Lecks, "all we can do is to wait here till they come, and get them to send us away in their ship. But whether they've just gone or are just a-comin' back depends, I suppose, on whether they live in a freezin' or a burnin' country; and if they don't like our bein' here when they come back, there's one thing they can make up their minds to and that is that I'm never goin' to leave this place on a life preserver."

318

"Nor me nuther," said Mrs. Aleshine, finishing with much complacency her third cup of tea.

When breakfast was over, Mrs. Lecks pushed back her chair but did not immediately rise. With an expression of severe thought upon her face, she gazed steadfastly before her for a minute and then she addressed Mrs. Aleshine, who had begun to gather together the cups and the plates.

"Now, Barb'ry Aleshine," said she, "don't you begin to clear off the table, nor touch a single thing to wash it up, till we've been over this house. I want to do it now, before Mr. Craig goes out to prospect around and see what else is on the island, which I suppose he'll be wantin' to do."

I replied that I had that intention, but I was quite willing to go over the house first.

"It's come to me," said Mrs. Lecks, speaking very gravely, "that it's no use for us to talk of the family bein' here or bein' there, till we've gone over this house. If we find that they have, as far as we know, gone away in good health and spirits, that's all well enough; but if anything's happened in this house, I don't want to be here with what's happened—at least, without knowin' it—and when we do go over the house I want a man to go with us."

"If you'd talked that way last night, Mrs. Lecks," exclaimed Mrs. Aleshine, "I'd never slept till after sunup and then got up and gone huntin' round among them frocks and petticoats to find somethin' that would fit me, with the quiet pulse I did have, Mrs. Lecks!"

To this remark Mrs. Lecks made no reply, but rising, she led the way out of the kitchen and into the house.

The rooms on the first floor were very well furnished. There was a large parlor and back of it a study or library, while on the other side of the hall was a dining room and an apartment probably used as a family room. We found nothing in these which would indicate that anything untoward had happened in them. Then we went upstairs, I leading the way, Mrs. Lecks following, and Mrs. Aleshine in the rear. We first entered one of the front chambers, which was quite dark, but Mrs. Lecks un-

fastened and threw open a shutter. Then with a rigid countenance and determined mien she examined every part of the room, looked into every closet and even under the bed. It was quite plain that it was in one of the chambers that she expected to find what had happened, if anything had happened.

The room on the other side of the hall was very like the one we first examined, except that it had two beds in it. We next visited the chamber recently occupied by my two companions, which was now undergoing the process of "airing."

"We needn't stop here," remarked Mrs. Aleshine.

But Mrs. Lecks instantly replied, "Indeed we will stop; I'm going to look under the bed."

"Merciful me!" exclaimed Mrs. Aleshine, putting her hand on her friend's shoulder. "Supposin' you should find somethin', and we sleepin' here last night! It curdles me to think of it!"

"It's my duty," said Mrs. Lecks, "and I shall do it."

And do it she did, rising from the task with a sigh of relief.

My room was subjected to the same scrutiny as the others, and then we visited some smaller rooms at the extreme back of the house which we had not before noticed. A garret or loft was reached by a steep stairway in one of these rooms, and into its dusky gloom I ventured by myself.

320

"Now, don't come down, Mr. Craig," said Mrs. Lecks, "till you're sure there's nothin' there. Of all places in the house, that cockloft, after all, is the most likely."

I had none of the fears which seemed to actuate the two women, but I had a very unpleasant time of it groping about in the darkness and heat and, as the place was only partly floored, running the continual risk of crashing down through the lath and plaster. I made myself quite sure, however, that nothing had happened in that loft, unless someone had suffocated there and had dried up and become the dust which I raised at every step.

"Now, then," said Mrs. Lecks, when I descended, "as there is no cellar, we'll go wash up the breakfast things; and if you want to take a walk, to see if there's any genuwine heathens or anybody else a-livin' in this island, we're not afraid to be left alone."

For the whole of the rest of the morning I wandered about the island. I investigated the paths that I had before noticed, and found that each of them led, after a moderate walk, to some wide and pleasant part of the beach. At one of these points I found a rustic bench; and stuffed in between two of the slats which formed the seat I found a book. It had been sadly wet and discolored by rain and dried and curled up by the wind and sun. I pulled it out and found it to be a novel in French. On one of the flyleaves was written "Emily." Reasoning from the dilapidated appearance of this book, I began to believe that the family must have left this place some time ago, and that therefore their return might be expected at a proportionately early period. On second thoughts, however, I considered that the state of this book was of little value as testimony. A few hours of storm, wind, and sun might have inflicted all the damage it had sustained. The two women would be better able to judge by the state of the house and the condition of the provisions how long the family had been away.

I then started out on a walk along the beach, and in little more than an hour I had gone entirely around the island. Nowhere did I see any sign of habitation except at the house which had given us shelter, nor any opening through the reef except the barred passageway through which we had come.

When I returned to the house, I found that Mrs. Lecks and Mrs. Aleshine had been hard at work all the morning. They had, so to speak, gone regularly and systematically to housekeeping and had already divided the labors of the establishment between them. Mrs. Aleshine, who prided herself on her skill in culinary matters, was to take charge of the cooking, while Mrs. Lecks assumed the care of the various rooms and the general management of the household. This arrangement was explained to me at length, and when I remarked that all this seemed to indicate that they expected to remain here for a long time, Mrs. Lecks replied:

"In my part of the country I could tell pretty close, by the dust on the tables and on the top of the pianner, how long a family had been out of a house; but dust in Pennsylvany and dust on a sea island, where there's no wagons nor carriages, is quite different. This house has been left in very good order, and though the windows wants washin' and the floors and stairs brushin'—which will be easy considerin' that none of 'em has carpets—and everything in the house a reg'lar cleanin' up and airin', it may be that the family hasn't been gone away very long, and so it may be a good while before they come back again. Mrs. Aleshine and me has talked it over and we've made up our minds that the right thing to do is just to go along and attend to things as if we was a-goin' to stay here for a month or two; and it may be even longer than that before the people come back. And I don't think they'll have anything to complain of when they find their house in apple-pie order, their windows washed, their floors clean, and not a speck of dust anywhere."

"For my part," said Mrs. Aleshine, "I don't see what they've got to find fault with, anyway. I look on this as part of the passage. To be sure, we ain't movin' a bit on our way to Japan, but that's not my fault, nor yet yours, Mrs. Lecks, nor yours, Mr. Craig. We paid our passage to go to Japan, and if the ship was steered wrong and got sunk, we hadn't anything to do with it. We didn't want to come here, but here we are, and I'd like to know who's got any right to find fault with us."

"And bein' here," said Mrs. Lecks, "we'll take care of things."

"As far as I'm concerned," added Mrs. Aleshine, "if this island was movin' on to Japan, I'd a great deal rather be on it than on that ship, where to my way of thinkin' they didn't know much more about housekeepin' than they did about steerin'."

"I think your plans and arrangements are very good," I said. "But how about the provisions? Are there enough to hold out for any time?"

"There's pretty nigh a barrel of flour," said Mrs. Aleshine, "a good deal of tea and coffee and sugar, and lots of things in tins and jars. There's a kind of cellar outside where they keep things cool and there's more than half a keg of butter down there. It's too strong to use, but I can take that butter and wash it out and work it over and salt it, and make it just as good butter as any we got on board the ship."

"But," said I, "you have given me nothing to do. I shall not be content to stand about idle and see you do all the work."

"There's nothin' in the house," said Mrs. Lecks, "which you need put your hand to; but if you choose to go out into that garden and see if there's anything can be done in it or got out of it—that is, if you know anything about garden work—I'm sure we'd be very glad of any fresh vegetables we could get."

I replied that I had been accustomed to garden work in an amateur way and would be glad to do anything that was possible in that direction.

"I never seed into that garden," said Mrs. Aleshine, "but of all the foolish things that ever came under my eye, the buildin' a wall around a garden when a picket fence would do just as well is the foolishest."

I explained that in these countries it was the fashion to use walls instead of fences.

"If it's the fashion," said Mrs. Aleshine, "I suppose there's no use sayin' anything ag'in' it; but if the fashion should happen to change they'd find it a good deal easier to take down a barbed-wire fence than a stone wall."

This conversation took place in the large lower hall, which Mrs. Lecks had been "putting to rights" and where Mrs. Aleshine had just entered from the kitchen. Mrs. Lecks now sat down upon a chair, and, dustcloth in hand, she thus addressed me:

"There's another thing, Mr. Craig, that me and Mrs. Aleshine has been talkin' about. We haven't made up our minds about it, because we didn't think it was fair and right to do that before speakin' to you and hearin' what you had to say on one side or another of it. Mrs. Aleshine and me has had to bow our heads to afflictions and to walk sometimes in roads we didn't want to; but we've remembered the ways in which we was brought up and have kept in them as far as we've been able. When our husbands died, leavin' Mrs. Aleshine with a son and me without any, which perhaps is just as well, for there's no knowin' how he might have turned out—"

"That's so," interrupted Mrs. Aleshine, "for he might have gone as a clerk to Roosher, and then you and me would 'a' had to travel different ways."

"And when our husbands died," continued Mrs. Lecks, "they left us enough and plenty to live on, and we wasn't the women to forget them and their ways of thinkin', any more than we'd forget the ways of our fathers and mothers before us."

"That's so!" said Mrs. Aleshine, fervently.

"And now, Mr. Craig," continued Mrs. Lecks, "we don't know how you've been brought up, nor anything about you in fact, except that you've been as kind to us as if you was some sort of kin and that we never would have thought of comin' here without you, and so me and Mrs. Aleshine has agreed to leave this whole matter to you and to do just as you say. When us two started out on this long journey we didn't expect to find it what you call the path of roses, and dear only knows we haven't found it so."

"That's true!" ejaculated Mrs. Aleshine.

"And what we've had to put up with," continued Mrs. Lecks, "we have put up with. So, Mr. Craig, whether you say dinner in the middle of the day at twelve as we've always been used to, or at six o'clock in the afternoon as they had it on board that ship—and how people ever come to turn their meals hind part foremost in that way, I can't say—we are goin' to do it; if you've been brought up to six o'clock, you won't hear no complainin' from us, think what we may."

I was on the point of laughing aloud at the conclusion of this speech, but a glance at the serious faces of the two women, who with so much earnest solicitude awaited my reply, stopped me, and I hastened to assure them that dinner in the middle of the day would be entirely in accordance with my every wish.

"Good!" exclaimed Mrs. Aleshine, her eyes sparkling amid the plumpness of her face, while an expression of calm relief passed over the features of Mrs. Lecks.

"And now I'll be off and get us somethin' to eat in less than no time," said Mrs. Aleshine. "We didn't know whether to make it lunch or dinner till we had seen you, so you can't expect much today, but tomorrow we'll begin and have everything straight and comfortable. I'm goin' to get up early in the mornin' and bake a batch of bread, and you needn't be afraid, Mr. Craig, but what I'll have you a bit of hot meat every night for your supper."

In the afternoon we all visited the garden, which, although a good deal overgrown with luxuriant weeds, showed marks of fair cultivation. Some of the beds had been cleared out and left to the weeds, and we found some "garden truck," as my companions called it, with which we were not familiar. But there were tomato-vines loaded with fruit, plenty of beans of various kinds, and a large patch of potatoes, many of which had been dug.

From the lower end of the garden, Mrs. Aleshine gave a shout of delight. We went to her and found her standing before a long asparagus bed.

"Well!" she exclaimed. "If there's anything that settles it firm in my mind that these people is Christians, it's this bed of grass. I don't believe there ever was heathens that growed grass."

"I thought that was all settled when we found the bakin'-powders," said Mrs. Lecks.

"But this clinches it," answered her companion. "I can't tell from a sparrowgrass bed what church they belong to, but they're no idolaters."

The next morning I delivered to the genial Mrs. Aleshine a large basket full of fresh vegetables, and we had a most excellent dinner. Somewhat to my surprise, the table was not set in the kitchen but in the dining room.

"Me and Mrs. Aleshine have made up our minds," said Mrs. Lecks in explanation, "that it's not the proper thing for you to be eatin' in the kitchen, nor for us neither. Here's tablecloths, and good glass and china, and spoons and forks which although they're not solid silver are plated good enough for anybody. Neither you nor us is servants, and a kitchen is no place for us."

"That's so!" said Mrs. Aleshine. "We paid our money for first-class passages, and it was understood that we'd have everything as good as anybody."

"Which I don't see as that has anything to do with it, Barb'ry Aleshine," said Mrs. Lecks, "for the steamship people don't generally throw in desert islands as part of the accommodation."

"We didn't ask for the island," retorted Mrs. Aleshine, "and if they'd steered the ship right we shouldn't have wanted it."

When we had finished our dinner, Mrs. Lecks pushed back her chair and sat for a few moments in thought, as was her wont before saying anything of importance.

"There's another thing," said she, "that I've been thinkin' about, though I haven't spoke of it yet even to Mrs. Aleshine. We haven't no right to come here and eat up the victuals and use the things of the people that own this house, without payin' for 'em. Of course we're not goin' to sleep on the bare ground and starve to death while there's beds and food close to our hands. But if we use 'em and take it, we ought to pay the people that the place belongs to—that is, if we've got the money to do it with—and Mrs. Aleshine and me has got the money. When we went down into our cabin to get ready to leave the ship, the first thing we did was to put our purses in our pockets, and we've both got drafts wrapped up in oil silk and sewed inside our frock-bodies; and if you didn't think to bring your money along with you, Mr. Craig, we can lend you all you need."

I thanked her for her offer, but stated that I had brought with me all my money.

"Now," continued Mrs. Lecks, "it's my opinion that we ought to pay our board regular every week. I don't know what is commonly charged in a place like this, but I know you can get very good board where I come from for six dollars a week."

"That is for two in a room," said Mrs. Aleshine; "but havin' a room to himself would make it more for Mr. Craig."

"It ain't his fault," said Mrs. Lecks, somewhat severely, "that he ain't got a brother or some friend to take part of the room and pay part of the expense. But anyway the room isn't a large one, and I don't think he ought to pay much more for havin' a room to himself. Seven dollars is quite enough."

"But then you've got to consider," said Mrs. Aleshine, "that we do the cookin' and housework, and that ought to be counted."

"I was comin' to that," said Mrs. Lecks. "Now, if me and Mrs. Aleshine was to go out to service, which you may be sure we wouldn't do unless circumstances was very different from what they are now—"

"That's true!" earnestly ejaculated Mrs. Aleshine.

"But if we was to do it," continued Mrs. Lecks, "we wouldn't go into anybody's family for less than two dollars a week. Now,

I've always heard that wages is low in this part of the world, and the work isn't heavy for two of us; so, considering the family isn't here to make their own bargain, I think we'd better put our wages at that, so that'll make four dollars a week for each of us two to pay."

"But how about Mr. Craig?" said Mrs. Aleshine. "He oughtn't to work in that garden for nothin'."

"Fifty cents a day," said Mrs. Lecks, "is as little as any man would work for, and then it oughtn't to take all his time. That will make three dollars to take out of Mr. Craig's board, and leave it four dollars a week the same as ours."

I declared myself perfectly satisfied with these arrangements, but Mrs. Aleshine did not seem to be altogether convinced that they were just.

"When a woman goes out to service," said she, "she gets her board and is paid wages besides, and it's the same for gardeners."

"Then I suppose, Barb'ry Aleshine," said Mrs. Lecks, "that we ought to charge these people with our wages and make 'em pay it when they come back!"

This remark apparently disposed of Mrs. Aleshine's objections, and her friend continued:

"There's a jar on the mantelpiece there, of the kind the East Indy ginger comes in. It's got nothin' in it now but some brown paper in which fishhooks is wrapped. We came here on a Wednesday, and so every Tuesday night we'll each put four dollars in that jar, under the fishhook paper; then if, by night or by day, the family comes back and makes a fuss about our bein' here, all we have to say is, 'The board money's in the ginger-jar,' and our consciences is free."

Mrs. Lecks's plan was adopted as a very just and proper one, and at the expiration of the week we each deposited four dollars in the ginger-jar.

While occupying this house I do not think that any of us endeavored to pry into the private concerns of the family who owned it, although we each had a very natural curiosity to know something about said family. Opportunities of acquiring such knowledge, however, were exceedingly scarce. Even if we had been willing to look into such receptacles, the several desks and secretaries that the house contained were all locked, and nowhere could Mrs. Lecks or Mrs. Aleshine find an old letter or piece of wrapping paper with an address on it. I explained to my companions that letters and packages were not likely to come to a place like this, but they kept a sharp lookout for anything of the kind, asserting that there could be no possible harm in reading the names of the people whose house they were in.

In some of the books in the library, which were English and French in about equal proportions, with a few volumes in German, I found written on the blank pages the names "Emily" and "Lucille," and across the title pages of some French histories was inscribed in a man's hand, "A. Dusante." We discussed these names, but could not make up our minds whether the family were French or English. For instance, there was no reason why an English woman might not be called Lucille, and even such a surname as Dusante was not uncommon either among English or Americans. The labels on the boxes and tins of provisions showed that most of them came from San Francisco, but this was likely to be the case no matter what the nationality of the family.

The question of the relationship of the three persons of whose existence we had discovered traces was a very interesting one to Mrs. Lecks and Mrs. Aleshine.

"I can't make up my mind," said the latter, "whether Emily is the mother of Lucille or her daughter, or whether they are both children of Mr. Dusante, or whether he's married to Lucille and Emily is his sister-in-law, or whether she's his sister and not hers, or whether he's the uncle and they're his nieces, or whether Emily is an old lady and Mr. Dusante and Lucille are both her children, or whether they are two maiden ladies and Mr. Dusante is their brother, or whether Mr. Dusante is only a friend of the family and boards here because no two women ought to live in such a lonely place without a man in the house."

"Well," said Mrs. Lecks, "whether Mr. Dusante comes back

with two nieces, or a wife and daughter, or Mrs. Dusante and a mother-in-law, or a pair of sisters, all we've got to say is, 'The board money's in the ginger-jar,' and let 'em do their worst."

In my capacity as gardener I do not think I earned the wages which my companions had allotted to me, for I merely gathered and brought in such fruits and vegetables as I found in proper condition for use. In other ways, however, I made my services valuable to our little family. In a closet in my chamber I found guns and ammunition and frequently I was able to bring in a few birds. Some of these were pronounced by Mrs. Aleshine as unsuitable for the table, but others she cooked with much skill, and they were found to be very good eating.

Not far from the little wharf which has been mentioned there stood, concealed by a mass of low-growing palms, a boathouse in which was a little skiff hung up near the roof. This I let down and launched, and found great pleasure in rowing it about the lagoon. There was fishing-tackle in the boathouse, which I used with success, the lagoon abounding in fish. Offerings of this kind were much more acceptable to Mrs. Aleshine than birds.

"There's some kinds of fishes that's better than others," said she, "but as a gen'ral rule a fish is a fish, and if you catch 'em you can eat 'em; but it's a very different thing with birds. When you've never seen 'em before, how are you goin' to tell but what they're some kin to an owl, or a crow? And if I once get it into my head that there's any of that kind of family blood in 'em, they disagree with me just the same as if there really was."

One afternoon, as I was returning in the boat from the point on the other side of the island where I had found the rustic seat and Emily's book, I was surprised to see Mrs. Lecks and Mrs. Aleshine standing on the end of the little wharf. This was an unusual thing for them to do, as they were very industrious women and seldom had an idle moment, and it seemed to be one of their greatest pleasures to discuss the work they were going to do when they had finished that on which they were then engaged. I was curious, therefore, to know why they should be standing thus idly on the wharf, and pulled toward them as rapidly as possible.

When I had rowed near enough to hear them, Mrs. Aleshine remarked with cheerful placidity, "The Dusantes are comin'."

The tide was quite low, and I could not see over the reef; but in a few moments I had grounded the skiff and had sprung upon the wharf. Out on the ocean, about a mile away, I saw a boat, apparently a large one, approaching the island.

"Now then, Barb'ry Aleshine," said Mrs. Lecks, "you'll soon see whether it's his two nieces, or his daughters, wife and sister-in-law, or whatever of them other relationships which you've got so pat."

"Yes," said Mrs. Aleshine; "but, what's more, we'll find out if he's goin' to be satisfied with the board money we've put in the ginger-jar."

When the boat which we saw approaching the island had come near enough for us to distinguish its occupants, we found that it contained five persons. Three sat in the stern and two were rowing. Of those in the stern, we soon made out one to be a woman, and after putting our eyesight to its very best efforts we were obliged to admit that there was only one female on board.

"Now, that's disapp'intin'," said Mrs. Aleshine, "for I've wondered and wondered which I should like best, Emily or Lucille, and now that only one of 'em has come, of course I can't tell."

The boat came on, almost directly toward the passageway in the reef, and it was not long before the two women had been able to decide that Mr. Dusante was an elderly man, and that the lady was moderately young and in all probability his daughter.

"It may be," said Mrs. Aleshine, "that the mother, whether she was Emily or whether she was Lucille, has died and for that reason they are comin' back sooner than they expected."

"Well, I hope you're wrong there, Barb'ry Aleshine," said Mrs. Lecks, "for they'll see lots of things here that will freshen up their affliction, and that won't make 'em any too lively people to be with."

"On the other hand," said Mrs. Aleshine, "it may be that Emily, or else Lucille, has got married and has gone away with her

331

husband to travel, and by the time she's got a little baby she'll come here to live on account of the sea air for the child, and that'll make the house pleasant, Mrs. Lecks."

"I'd like to know how long you expect to live here," said Mrs. Lecks, regarding her friend with some severity.

"That's not for me to say," replied Mrs. Aleshine, "knowin' nothin' about it. But this I will say, that I hope they have brought along with them some indigo blue, for I nearly used up all there was the last time I washed."

During this dialogue I had been thinking that it was a very strange thing for the owners of this place to visit their island in such a fashion. Why should they be in an open boat? And where did they come from? Wherever they might live, it was not at all probable that they would choose to be rowed from that point to this. From the general character and appointments of the house in which we had found a refuge, it was quite plain that its owners were people in good circumstances, who were in the habit of attending to their domestic affairs in a very orderly and proper way. It was to be presumed that it was their custom to come here in a suitable vessel and to bring with them the stores needed during their intended stay. Now, there could be little or nothing in that boat, and on the whole I did not believe it contained the owners of this island.

It would not do, however, to assume anything of the kind. There might have been a disaster; in fact, I knew nothing about it, but it was my immediate duty to go and meet these people at the passage, for if they were unable to unlock the bars their boat could not enter, and I must ferry them across the lagoon. Without communicating my doubts to my companions, I hurried into the skiff and pulled as far as possible into the passage through the reef. The bars, of which there were more than I at first supposed, were so arranged that it was impossible for a boat to go in or out at any stage of the tide.

I had been there but a few minutes when the boat from without came slowly in between the rocks; and almost as soon as I saw it, its progress was suddenly stopped by a sunken bar.

"Hello!" cried several men at once.

"Hello!" cried I, in return. "Have you the key to these bars?"

A stout man with a red beard stood up in the stern. "Key?" said he, "what key?"

"Then you do not belong here?" said I. "Who are you?"

At this the gentleman who was sitting by the lady arose to his feet. He was a man past middle age, rather tall and slim, and when he stood up the slight rolling of the boat made him stagger and he came near falling.

"You'd better sit down, sir," said the man with the red beard, who I saw was a sailor. "You can talk better that way."

The gentleman now seated himself, and thus addressed me:

"I am, sir, the Reverend Mr. Enderton, lately missionary to Nanfouchong, China, and this is my daughter, Miss Enderton. We are returning to the United States by way of the Sandwich Islands, and took passage in a sailing-vessel for Honolulu. About two weeks ago this vessel, in some way which I do not understand, became disabled—"

"Rotten forem'st," interrupted the man with the red beard, "which give way in a gale; strained and leaky besides."

"I did not know that the mast was rotten," said the gentleman, "but since the occasion of our first really serviceable wind she has been making very unsatisfactory progress. And, more than that, the whole force of seamen was employed night and day in endeavoring to keep the water out of the tea, thereby causing such a thumping and pounding that sleep was out of the question. Add to this the fact that our meals became very irregular, and were sometimes entirely overlooked—"

"Prog was gettin' mighty short," interpolated the red-bearded man.

"You can easily discern, sir," continued the gentleman, "that it was impossible for myself and my daughter to remain longer on that vessel, on which we were the only passengers. I therefore requested the captain to put us ashore at the nearest land, and after more than a week of delay and demur he consented to do so."

"Couldn't do it," said the man, "till there was land nigh enough."

333

"The captain informed me," continued the gentleman, "that this island was inhabited, and that I could find shelter and repose here until a vessel could be sent from Honolulu to take me off. He furnished me with this boat and three seamen, one of whom," pointing to the red-bearded man, "is a coxswain. We have been rowing ever since early this morning, with but a very moderate quantity of food and much discomfort. Now, sir, you have heard my story; and I ask you as one man to another, if you still intend to bar your water-gates against us?"

"I did not bar the gates," I said, "and I would gladly unlock them if I could. I belong to a shipwrecked party who took refuge here some two weeks ago."

"And how did you get in?" hastily inquired the red-bearded coxswain.

"Our boat sunk when we were within sight of the island, and we came here on life preservers and so got under the bars."

The two men who had been rowing now turned suddenly and looked at me. They both had black beards, and they both exclaimed at the same moment, "By George!"

"I won't stop here to tell any more of our story," said I. "The great point now is to get you all ashore and have you cared for."

"That's so!" said the coxswain. And the two sailors murmured, "Aye-aye, sir."

The bar which stopped the progress of the larger boat was just under the surface of the water, while another a foot above the water kept my skiff about six feet distant from the other boat. There was some loose flooring in the bottom of the coxswain's boat, and he ordered two of the boards taken out, and with them a bridge was made, one end resting on the bow of the larger boat and the other on the iron bar by my skiff.

"Now," said the coxswain, "let the lady go first."

The elderly gentleman arose as if he would prefer to take the lead, but his daughter, who had not yet spoken a word, was passed forward by the coxswain, steadied over the bridge by one of the sailors, and assisted by me into the skiff. Then her father came aboard, and I rowed with them to the wharf.

Mrs. Lecks and Mrs. Aleshine came forward most cordially.

"Mr. Dusante, I suppose?" said Mrs. Lecks, while Mrs. Aleshine hurriedly whispered in my ear, "Is it Lucille or Emily?"

As quickly as possible I explained the situation. For a few moments Mrs. Lecks and Mrs. Aleshine stood speechless. Nothing which had happened to them—the wreck of the steamer, the sinking of the boat, or our experience with life preservers— affected them so much as this disappointment in regard to the problem of the Dusante family. Travel by sea was all novel and strange to them, and they had expected all sorts of things to which they were not accustomed, but they had never imagined that Fate would be so hard upon them as to snatch away the solution of this mystery just as they were about to put their hands upon it. But in spite of this sudden blow, the two good women quickly recovered themselves, and with hearty and kindly words hurried the missionary and his daughter to the house while I went to bring over the men.

I found the three sailors busy in securing their boat so that it would not be injured by the rocks during the rising and falling of the tide. When they had finished this job, they had to do a good deal of scrambling before they reached my skiff.

"We thought at first, sir," said the coxswain, as I rowed them across the lagoon, "that it was all gammon about your not livin' here and havin' no keys to them bars; but we've come to the 'pinion that if you'd been able to unlock 'em you'd have done it sooner than take all this trouble."

I now related my story more fully, and the men were greatly astonished when they heard that my companions in this adventure were two women. Upon my asking the coxswain why he had come to this island, he replied that his captain had heard that people lived on it, although he knew nothing about them; and that, as it would be almost impossible to get his brig here with the wind that was then prevailing and as he did not wish to go out of his course anyway, he made up his mind that he would rather lose the services of three men than keep that missionary on board a day longer.

"You see, sir," said the coxswain, as we went ashore, "the parson wouldn't never take it into account that we were short of prog and leakin' like Sam Hill; and because things were uncomfortable he growled up and he growled down, till he was wuss for the spirits of the men than the salt water comin' in or the hardtack givin' out, and there was danger, if he wasn't got rid of, that he'd be pitched overboard and left to take his chances for a whale. And then by sendin' us along, that give the crew three half-rations a day extry, and that'll count for a good deal in the fix they're in."

When I reached the house I took the men into the kitchen, where Mrs. Aleshine already had the table spread. There were bread and cold meat, while the teakettle steamed by the fire. In a very short time three happy mariners sat round that table, while Mrs. Aleshine with beaming face attended to their wants and plied them with innumerable questions. They had not finished eating when Mrs. Lecks entered the kitchen.

"I put that minister and his daughter in the two front bedrooms," said she to me after hospitably greeting the three men, "which me and Mrs. Aleshine had run and got ready for the Dusantes as soon as you went in your boat to meet 'em. The young lady was mighty nigh worn out, and glad enough of the tea and things and to get into bed. But the gentleman he wanted a soft-boiled egg, and when I told him I hadn't come across no henhouse yet on this island, he looked at me as if he didn't half believe me and thought I was keepin' the eggs to sell."

"Which it would be ridiculous to do," said Mrs. Aleshine, "in the middle of an ocean like this."

"If he lets you off with soft-b'iled eggs, ma'am," said the coxswain, very respectfully, "I think you may bless your stars."

"Aye-aye, sir," said the two sailors with black beards.

Miss Ruth Enderton and her father did not make their appearance until the next morning at breakfast-time. I found the young lady a very pleasant person. She was rather slight in figure, inclined to be pretty, and was what might be called a warm-colored blonde. Her disposition was quite sociable and she almost immediately stepped into the favor of Mrs. Lecks and Mrs. Aleshine.

Mr. Enderton, however, was a person of another sort. He was

336

a prim and somewhat formal man and appeared to be entirely self-engrossed, with very vague notions in regard to his surroundings. He was not by any means an ill-tempered man, being rather inclined to be placid than otherwise; but he gave so little attention to circumstances and events that he did not appear to understand why he should be incommoded by the happenings of life. I have no doubt that he made existence on board the disabled brig a hundred times more unsatisfactory than it would otherwise have been. With his present condition he seemed very well satisfied, and it was quite plain that he looked upon Mrs. Lecks, Mrs. Aleshine, and myself as the proprietors of the establishment, having forgotten or paid no attention to my statement in regard to our coming here.

As soon as she thought it fit and proper—and this moment arrived in the course of the first forenoon—Mrs. Lecks spoke to Mr. Enderton on the subject of the board which should be paid to the Dusantes. She stated the arrangements we had made in the matter, and then told him that as he and his daughter had the best accommodations in the house, each occupying a large, handsome room, she thought that he should pay fifteen dollars a week for the two.

"Now, if your daughter," she continued, "can do anything about the house which will be of real help, though for the life of me I don't see what she can find to do, with me and Mrs. Aleshine here, somethin' might be took off on account of her services; but of course you, sir, can't do nothin', unless you was to preach on Sunday; and not knowin' what denomination the Dusantes belong to, it wouldn't be fair to take their money to pay for the preachin' of doctrines which perhaps they don't believe in."

This financial proposal aroused Mr. Enderton's opposition. "When I came here, madam," he said, "I did not expect to pay any board whatever, and I think, moreover, that your rates are exorbitant. In Nanfouchong, if I remember rightly, the best of board did not cost more than two or three dollars a week."

"I don't want to say anything, sir," said Mrs. Lecks, "which might look disrespectful, but as long as I've got a conscience in-

337

side of me I'm not goin' to stay here and see the Dusantes lose money by Chinese cheapness."

"I don't know anything about the Dusantes," said Mr. Enderton, "but I am not going to pay fifteen dollars a week for board for myself and daughter."

The discussion lasted for some time, with considerable warmth on each side, and was at last ended by Mr. Enderton agreeing to pay board at the same rate as the two women and myself and each week to deposit in the ginger-jar eight dollars for himself and daughter.

"You may not care to remember, sir," said Mrs. Lecks, with cold severity, "that Mr. Craig and me and Mrs. Aleshine puts in services besides, although, to be sure, they don't go into the jar."

"I only remember," said Mr. Enderton, "that I am paying an unjustifiable price as it is."

Mrs. Lecks and Mrs. Aleshine, however, were not at all of this opinion and they agreed that if it should be in their power they would see to it that the Dusantes lost nothing by this close-fisted missionary.

After dinner—and I may remark that the newcomers were not consulted in regard to the hours for meals—Mrs. Lecks had an interview with the coxswain on the subject of board for himself and his two companions. This affair, however, was very quickly settled, for the three mariners had among them only one dollar and forty-three cents, and this, the coxswain explained, they would like to keep for tobacco. It was therefore settled that as the three sailors could pay no money, as much work as possible should be got out of them, and to this plan they agreed heartily and cheerfully.

"There's only one thing we'll ask, ma'am," said the coxswain to Mrs. Lecks, "and that is that we be put in a different mess from the parson. We've now eat two meals with the passengers, and me and my mates is agreed that that's about as much as we can go."

After this, therefore, the three men had their meals in the kitchen, where they were generally joined by Mrs. Aleshine, who much delighted in their company. But she made it a point sometimes to sit down with us in the dining room, merely to show that she had as much right there as anybody.

"As to the work for them sailormen," said Mrs. Aleshine, "I don't see what they're goin' to do. Of course they don't know nothin' about gardenin', and it seems to me that the best thing to be done is to put 'em to fishin'.'"

Mrs. Lecks considered this a good suggestion and accordingly the coxswain and his companions were told that thereafter they would be expected to fish for eight hours a day, Sundays excepted. This plan, however, did not work very well. During the first two days the sailors caught so many fish that, although the fishermen themselves had excellent appetites for such food, it was found utterly impossible to consume what they brought in. Consequently it was ordered that thereafter they should catch only as many fish as should be needed and then make themselves useful by assisting Mrs. Aleshine and Mrs. Lecks in any manner they might direct.

I found it quite easy to become acquainted with Miss Ruth Enderton, as she was very much inclined to conversation.

"It's ever so long," she said, "since I've had anybody to talk to."

She had left the United States when she was quite a little girl, and had since seen nothing of her native land. She was, consequently, full of questions about America, although quite willing to talk of her life in China. Society, at least such kind as she had ever cared for, had been extremely scarce in the little missionary station at which she had lived so long, and now, coming from a wearisome sojourn on a disabled sailing-vessel, with no company but the crew and a preoccupied father, she naturally was delighted to get among people she could talk to. With Mrs. Lecks, Mrs. Aleshine, and myself she soon became very friendly and showed herself to be a most lively and interesting young person.

I did all that I could to make Miss Ruth's time pass agreeably. I rowed with her on the lagoon, taught her to fish, and showed her all the pleasant points on the island which could be easily reached by walking. Mr. Enderton gave us very little of his company, for having discovered that there was a library in the house, he passed most of his time in that room.

"You have made a very fair selection of books, sir," he remarked to me, "but it may readily be conceived from the character of the works that your tastes are neither ecclesiastic nor scientific."

Several times I explained to him the ownership of the library and the house, but he immediately forgot what I had said or paid no attention to it. When he paid his board at the end of the week, he handed the money to Mrs. Lecks; and although before his eyes she put it into the ginger-jar, beneath the paper of fishhooks, I know very well that he considered he was paying it to her for her own use and behoof. He was comfortably lodged, he had all that he needed—and very nearly all that he wanted—to eat, and I do not know that I ever saw a man more contented with his lot.

As for the coxswain and the two ·sailors, they had a very pleasant time of it, but Mrs. Lecks and Mrs. Aleshine would not think of such a thing as allowing them to eat in idleness the bread of the Dusantes. After they had been with us a few days Mrs. Lecks told me that she thought she could show the coxswain and his mates how to dig and gather the garden-stuff which was daily needed.

"To be sure," said she, "that work goes ag'in part of your board, but fishin' and bringin' in firewood don't take up quarter of the time of them sailors, and so that the garden work is done, I don't suppose it matters to the Dusantes who does it. And that'll give you more time to make things pleasant for Miss Ruth, for as far as I can see there isn't a thing for her to do even if she knows how to do it."

The three mariners were more than willing to do anything desired by Mrs. Lecks or Mrs. Aleshine, to whom they looked up with great admiration and respect. The latter was their favorite, not only because she was with them a great deal during their meals, and at other times, but because of her genial nature and easy sociability. The men were always trying to lighten her

labors and to do something that would please her.

One of them climbed to the top of what she called a "palm-leaf-fan tree," and brought therefrom some broad leaves, which he cut and trimmed and sewed in true nautical fashion until he made some fans which were heavy and clumsy, but, as he said, they would stand half a gale of wind if she chose to raise it. The coxswain caught or trapped two sea-birds, and having clipped their wings, he spent days in endeavoring to tame them, hoping to induce them, as far as the power in them lay, to take the place of the barnyard fowls whose absence Mrs. Aleshine continually deplored. Every evening the two black-bearded sailors would dance hornpipes for her, much to her diversion and delight.

"I've often heard," she remarked, "that in these hot coconut countries the tricks of the monkeys was enough to keep everybody on a steady laugh, but I'm sure sailormen is a great deal better. When you get tired of their pranks and their tomfooleries you can tell 'em to stop, which with monkeys you can't."

It was about ten days after the arrival of the missionary's party that, as I was going to get ready the boat in which Miss Ruth and myself generally rowed in the cool of the evening, I saw Mrs. Lecks and Mrs. Aleshine sitting on the beach in the shade of some low-growing trees. They were evidently waiting for me and as soon as I appeared Mrs. Lecks beckoned to me; whereupon I joined them.

"Sit down," said Mrs. Lecks; "there's somethin' I want to talk to you about. Mrs. Aleshine and me have made up our minds that you ought to be hurried up a little about poppin' the question to Miss Ruth."

This remark astounded me. "Popping the question!" I exclaimed.

"Yes," continued Mrs. Lecks, "and me and Mrs. Aleshine know very well that you haven't done it yet, for both of us havin' been through that sort of thing ourselves, we know the signs of it after it has happened."

"And we wouldn't say nothin' to hurry you," added Mrs. Aleshine, "if it wasn't that the groceries, especially the flour, is a-gettin' low. We've been talkin' to them sailormen, and they're pretty well agreed that there's no use now in expectin' their captain to send for 'em; for if he was a-goin' to do it at all, he'd a' done it before this. And perhaps he never got nowhere himself, in which case he couldn't. And they say the best thing we can all do when the victuals has nearly give out, provided the Dusantes don't come back in time, is to take what's left and all get into their big boat and row away to that island, which I don't know just how far it is, that the captain of our ship was goin' to. There we can stay pretty comfortable till a ship comes along and takes us off."

"But what has all that to do," I asked, "with Miss Ruth and me?"

"Do?" cried Mrs. Lecks. "It has everything to do. When it's all settled and fixed between you and Miss Ruth, there'll be nothin' to hinder us from gettin' ready to start when we please."

"But, my dear friends," I said with much earnestness, "I have

342

not the slightest idea of proposing to Miss Enderton."

"That's just what I said to Mrs. Aleshine," said Mrs. Lecks, "and that's the reason we let our irons cool and come out here to talk to you. It's just like a young man to keep puttin' off that sort of thing, but this can't be put off."

"That's so!" cried Mrs. Aleshine; "and I'll just let you see how the matter stands. There is housekeepers who allows a pint of flour a day to each person, but this is for farm hands and people who works hard and eats hearty, and I've found that three quarters of a pint will do very well if the dough is kneaded conscientious and made up light so that it'll rise well when it's put into the oven. Now, I've measured all the flour that's left, and me and Mrs. Lecks we've calculated that, allowin' three-quarters of a pint of flour a day to each one of us, there's just eight days more that we can stay here—that is, if the Dusantes don't come back before that time, which of course can't be counted on. So you can see for yourself, Mr. Craig, there's no time to be lost, even considerin' that she hasn't to make up anything to be married in."

"No," said Mrs. Lecks; "just for us and three sailors, that wouldn't be needed."

I looked from one to the other in dumb astonishment. Mrs. Lecks gave me no time to say anything.

"In common cases," said she, "this might all be put off till we got somewhere; but it won't do now. Here you are, with everythin' in your own hands, but just get away from here and there's an end of that. She's as pretty a girl as you'll see in a month of Sundays, and if she leaves here without your gettin' her, there's no knowing who'll snap her up. When we've got to that island, you may see her once a week, but maybe you won't. She may go away in one ship and you in another, and there may be somebody right there—a missionary, for all I know—who'll have her before you have a chance to put in a word."

"And that's not the worst of it," said Mrs. Aleshine. "Supposin' them Dusantes come back before we go. There's no knowin' what that Mr. Dusante is. He may be a brother of Emily and Lucille. And what sort of a chance would you have then, I'd like to know, with Miss Ruth right here in his own house, and he ownin' the rowboat, and everythin'? Or it may be he's a widower, and that'll be a mighty sight worse, I can tell you."

"No matter whether they're widowers or never been married," said Mrs. Lecks, "there'll be plenty that'll want her as soon as they see her and if it isn't for the girl's own pretty face, it'll be for her father's money."

"Her father's money!" I exclaimed. "What are you talking of?"

"There's no good tellin' me anything about that," said Mrs. Lecks, very decidedly. "There never was a man as close-fisted as Mr. Enderton who hadn't money."

"And you know as well as we do," said Mrs. Aleshine, "that in them countries where he's been, the heathens worship idols of silver and idols of gold, and when them heathens is converted, don't you suppose the missionaries get any of that? I expect that Mr. Enderton has converted thousands of heathens."

At this suggestion I laughed outright. But Mrs. Lecks reproved me.

"Now, Mr. Craig," said she, "this is no laughin' matter. What me and Mrs. Aleshine is sayin' is for your good, and for the good of Miss Ruth along with you. I haven't much opinion of her father, but his money is as good as anybody else's, and though they had to leave their trunks on board their ship, what little they brought with them shows that they've been used to havin' the best there is. Mrs. Aleshine and me has set up till late into the night talkin' over this thing and we are both of one mind that you two need never expect to have the same chance again that you've got now. The very fact that the old gentleman is a preacher and can marry you ought to make you tremble when you think of the risks you are runnin' by puttin' it off."

"I've got to go into the house now to see about supper," said Mrs. Aleshine, rising, "and I hope you'll remember, Mr. Craig, when your bread is on your plate and Miss Ruth is sittin' opposite to you, that three quarters of a pint of flour a day is about as little as anybody can live on, and that time is flyin'."

Mrs. Lecks now also rose. But I detained the two for a moment.

"I hope you have not said anything to Miss Enderton on this subject," I said.

"No," replied Mrs. Aleshine, "we haven't. We are both agreed that as you're the one that's to do what's to be done, you are the one that's to be spoke to. And havin' been through it ourselves, we understand well enough that the more a woman don't know nothin' about it, the more likely she is to be ketched if she wants to be."

The two women left me in an amused but also somewhat annoyed state of mind. I had no intention whatever of proposing to Miss Ruth Enderton. She was a charming girl, very bright and lively, and withal, I had reason to believe, very sensible. But it was not yet a fortnight since I first saw her, and no thought of marrying her had entered into my head. Had Mrs. Lecks and Mrs. Aleshine, or, more important than all, had Miss Enderton, any reason to believe that I was acting the part of a lover?

The latter portion of this question was almost immediately answered to my satisfaction by the appearance of Miss Ruth, who came skipping down to me and calling out to me in that free and hearty manner with which a woman addresses a friend or near acquaintance but never a suspected lover. She betrayed no more notion of the Lecks and Aleshine scheme than on the day I first met her.

But as I was rowing her over the lagoon I felt a certain constraint which I had not known before. There was no ground whatever for the wild imaginings of the two women, but the fact that they had imagined interfered very much with the careless freedom with which I had previously talked to Miss Ruth. I do not think, however, that she noticed any change in me, for she chatted and laughed, and showed, as she had done from the first, the rare delight which she took in this novel island life.

When we returned to the house, we were met by Mrs. Aleshine. "I am goin' to give you two your supper," she said, "on

345

that table there under the tree. We all had ours a little earlier than common, as the sailormen seemed hungry; and I took your father's to him in the libr'ry, where I expect he's a-sittin' yet, holdin' a book in one hand and stirrin' his tea with the other till he's stirred out nearly every drop on the floor; which, however, won't matter at all, for in the mornin' I'll rub up that floor till it's as bright as new."

This plan delighted Miss Ruth, but I saw in it the beginning of a deep-laid scheme. I was just about to sit down when Mrs. Aleshine said to me in a low voice as she left us,—

"Remember that the first three quarters of a pint apiece begins now!"

"Don't you think that Mrs. Lecks and Mrs. Aleshine are perfectly charming?" said Miss Ruth, as she poured out the tea. "They always seem to be trying to think of some kind thing to do for other people."

I agreed entirely with Miss Enderton's remark, but I could not help thinking of the surprise she would feel if she knew of the kind thing that these two women were trying to do for her.

"Have you taken any steps yet?" asked Mrs. Lecks of me the next day. On my replying that I had taken no steps of the kind to which I supposed she alluded, she walked away with a very grave and serious face.

A few hours later Mrs. Aleshine came to me. "There's another reason for hurryin' up," said she. "Them sailormen seems able to do without 'most anything in this world except tobacco, and Mrs. Lecks has been sellin' it to 'em out of a big box she found in a closet upstairs, at five cents a teacupful—which I think is awful cheap, but she says prices in islands is always low—and wrapping the money up in a paper, with 'Cash paid by sailormen for tobacco' written on it, and puttin' it into the ginger-jar with the board money. But their dollar and forty-three cents is nearly gone, and Mrs. Lecks she says that not a whiff of Mr. Dusante's tobacco shall they have if they can't pay for it. And when they have nothin' to smoke they'll be wantin' to leave this island just as quick as they can, without waitin' for the flour to give out."

Here was another pressure brought to bear upon me. Not only the waning flour but the rapidly disappearing tobacco money was used as a weapon to urge me forward to the love-making which Mrs. Lecks and Mrs. Aleshine had set their hearts upon.

I was in no hurry to leave the island and hoped very much that when we did go we should depart in some craft more comfortable than a ship's boat. In order, therefore, to prevent any undue desire to leave on the part of the sailors, I gave them money enough to buy a good many teacupfuls of tobacco. By this act I think I wounded the feelings of Mrs. Lecks and Mrs. Aleshine, although I had no idea that such would be the effect of my little gift. They said nothing to me on the subject, but their looks and manners indicated that they thought I had not been acting honorably. For two days they had very little to say to me, and then Mrs. Aleshine came to me to make what I suppose was their supreme effort.

"Mrs. Lecks and me is a-goin' to try," she said—and as she spoke she looked at me with a very sad expression and a watery appearance about the eyes—"to stretch out the time for you a little longer. We are goin' to make them sailormen eat more fish; and as for me and her, we'll go pretty much without bread, and make it up as well as we can on other things. You and Miss Ruth and the parson can each have your three-quarters of a pint of flour a day, just the same as ever, and what we save ought to give you three or four days longer."

This speech moved me deeply. I could not allow these two kind-hearted women to half starve themselves in order that I might have more time to woo, and I spoke very earnestly on the subject to Mrs. Aleshine, urging her to give up the fanciful plans which she and Mrs. Lecks had concocted.

"Let us drop this idea of love-making," I said, "which is the wildest kind of vagary, and all live happily together as we did before. If the provisions give out before the Dusantes come back, I suppose we shall have to leave in the boat; but until that time comes let us enjoy life here as much as we can and be the good friends that we used to be."

I might as well have talked to one of the palm trees which waved over us.

"As I said before," remarked Mrs. Aleshine, "what is saved from Mrs. Lecks's and mine and the three sailormen's three-quarters of a pint apiece ought to give you four days more." And she went into the house.

All this time the Reverend Mr. Enderton had sat and read in the library, or meditatively had walked the beach with a book in his hand; while the three mariners had caught fish, performed their other work, and lain in the shade, smoking their pipes in peace. Miss Ruth and I had taken our daily rows and walks and had enjoyed our usual hours of pleasant converse, and all the members of the little colony seemed happy and contented except Mrs. Lecks and Mrs. Aleshine. These two went gravely and sadly about their work and the latter asked no more for the hornpipes and the sea-songs of her sailormen.

But for some unaccountable reason Mr. Enderton's condition of tranquil abstraction did not continue. He began to be fretful and discontented. He found fault with his food and his accommodations, and instead of spending the greater part of the day in the library, as had been his wont, he took to wandering about the island, generally with two or three books under his arm, sometimes sitting down in one place, and sometimes in another,

348

and then rising suddenly to go grumbling into the house.

One afternoon, as Miss Ruth and I were in the skiff in the lagoon, we saw Mr. Enderton approaching us, walking on the beach. As soon as he was near enough for us to hear him, he shouted to his daughter:

"Ruth, come out of that boat! If you want to take the air, I should think you might as well walk with me as to go rowing round with—with anybody."

This rude and heartless speech made my blood boil, while my companion turned pale with mortification. The man had never made the slightest objection to our friendly intercourse and this unexpected attack was entirely indefensible.

"Please put me ashore," said Miss Ruth, and without a word, for I could not trust myself to speak, I landed her; and petulantly complaining that she never gave him one moment of her society, her father led her away.

An hour later, my soul still in a state of turmoil, but with the violence of its tossings somewhat abated, I entered one of the paths which led through the woods. After a few turns, I reached a point where I could see for quite a long distance to the other end of the path, which opened out upon the beach. There I perceived Mr. Enderton sitting upon the little bench on which I had found Emily's book. His back was toward me and he seemed to be busily reading. About midway between him and myself I saw Miss Ruth slowly walking toward me. Her eyes were fixed upon the ground, and she had not seen me.

Stepping to one side, I awaited her approach. When she came near I accosted her.

"Miss Ruth," said I, "has your father been talking to you of me?"

She looked up quickly, evidently surprised at my being there. "Yes," she said, "he has told me that it is not—suitable that I should be with you as much as I have been since we came here."

There was something in this remark that roused again the turmoil which had begun to subside within me. There was so much that was unjust and tyrannical, and—what perhaps touched me still deeper—there was such a want of consideration and respect in this behavior of Mr. Enderton's that it brought to the front some very incongruous emotions. I had been superciliously pushed aside and I found I was angry. Something was about to be torn from me, and I found I loved it.

"Ruth," said I, stepping up close to her, "do you like to be with me as you have been?"

If Miss Ruth had not spent such a large portion of her life in the out-of-the-world village of Nanfouchong, if she had not lived among those simple-hearted missionaries, where it was never necessary to conceal her emotions or her sentiments, if it had not been that she never had had emotions or sentiments that it was necessary to conceal, I do not believe that when she answered me she would have raised her eyes to me with a look in them of a deep-blue sky seen through a sort of Indian-summer mist, and that, gazing thus, she would have said, "Of course I like it.

"Then let us make it suitable," I said, taking both her hands in mine.

There was another look, in which the skies shone clear and bright, and then in a moment it was all done.

About five minutes after this I said to her, "Ruth, shall we go to your father?"

"Certainly," she answered. And together we walked along the thickly shaded path.

The missionary still sat with his back toward us, and, being so intent upon his book, I found that by keeping my eyes upon him it was perfectly safe to walk with my arm around Ruth until we had nearly reached him. Then I took her hand in mine and we stepped in front of him.

"Father," said Ruth, "Mr. Craig and I are going to be married."

There was something very plump about this remark, and Mr. Enderton immediately raised his eyes from his book and fixed them first upon his daughter and then upon me; then he let them drop and through the narrow space between us he gazed out over the sea.

"Well, Father," said Ruth, "what do you think of it?"

Mr. Enderton leaned forward and picked up a leaf from the ground. This he placed between the open pages of his book and closed it.

"It seems to me," he said, "that on many accounts the arrangement you propose may be an excellent one. Yes," he added more decidedly, "I think it will do very well indeed. I shall not be at all surprised if we are obliged to remain on this island for a considerable time, and for my part I have no desire to leave it at present. And when you shall place yourself, Ruth, in a position in which you will direct the domestic economies of the establishment, I hope that you will see to it that things generally are made more compatible with comfort and gentility, and, as regards the table, I may add with palatability."

Ruth and I looked at each other and then together we promised that as far as in us lay we would try to make the life of Mr. Enderton a happy one, not only while we were on the island but ever afterward.

We were promising a great deal, but at that moment we felt very grateful.

Then he stood up, shook us both by the hand, and we left him to his book.

When Ruth and I came walking out of the woods and approached the house, Mrs. Aleshine was standing outside, not far from the kitchen. When she saw us she gazed steadily at us for a few moments, a strange expression coming over her face. Then she threw up both her hands and without a word she turned and rushed indoors.

We had not reached the house before Mrs. Lecks and Mrs. Aleshine came hurrying out together. Running up to us with a haste and an excitement I had never seen in either of them, first one and then the other took Ruth into her arms and kissed her with much earnestness. Then they turned upon me and shook my hands with hearty vigor, expressing, more by their looks and actions than their words, a triumphant approbation of what I had done.

"The minute I laid eyes on you," said Mrs. Aleshine, "I knowed it was all right. Wasn't no need of askin' questions."

I now became fearful lest, in the exuberance of their satisfaction, these good women might reveal to Ruth the plans they had laid for our matrimonial future, and the reluctance I had shown in entering into them. My countenance must have expressed my apprehensions, for Mrs. Aleshine, her ruddy face glowing with warmth both mental and physical, gave me a little wink and drew me to one side.

"You needn't suppose that we've ever said anything to Miss Ruth, or that we're goin' to. It's a great deal better to let her think you did it all yourself."

I felt like resenting this imputation upon the independence of my love-making, but at this happy moment I did not want to enter into a discussion and therefore merely smiled.

"I'm so glad, I don't know how to tell it," continued Mrs. Aleshine as Mrs. Lecks and Ruth walked toward the house.

I was about to follow, but my companion detained me.

"Have you spoke to the parson?" she asked.

"Oh yes," said I, "and he seems perfectly satisfied. I am rather surprised at this, because of late he has been in such a remarkably bad humor."

"That's so," said Mrs. Aleshine; "there's no gettin' round the fact that he's been a good deal crosser than two sticks. You see, Mr. Craig, that Mrs. Lecks and me we made up our minds that it wasn't fair to the Dusantes to let that rich missionary go on payin' nothin' but four dollars a week apiece for him and his daughter, and if we couldn't get no more out of him one way we'd do it another. It was fair enough that if he didn't pay more he ought to get less; and so we gave him more fish and not so much bread, the same as we did the sailormen; and we weakened his tea, and sent him just so much sugar and no more; and as for openin' boxes of sardines for him, which there was no reason why they shouldn't be left here for the Dusantes, I just wouldn't do it, though he said he'd got all the fresh fish he wanted when he was in China. And then we agreed that it was high time that that libr'ry should be cleaned up, and we went to work at it, not mindin' what he said; for it's no use tellin' me that four dollars a week will pay for a front room and good

352

board, and the use of a libr'ry all day. And as there wasn't no need of both of us cleanin' one room, Mrs. Lecks she went into the parlor, where he'd took his books, and begun there. And then, again, we shut down on Mr. Dusante's dressing-gown. There was no sense includin' the use of that in his four dollars a week, so we brushed it up, and camphored it, and put it away. We just wanted to let him know that if he undertook to be skin-flinty he'd better try it on somebody else besides us. We could see that he was a good deal upset, for if ever a man liked to have things quiet and comfortable around him, and everything his own way, that man is that missionary. But we didn't care if we did prod him up a little. Mrs. Lecks and me we both agreed that it would do him good. Why, he'd got into such a way of shettin' himself up in himself that he didn't even see that his daughter was goin' about with a young man and fixin' her affections on him more and more every day, when he never had no idea, as could be proved by witnesses, of marryin' her."

"Mrs. Aleshine," said I, looking at her very steadfastly, "I believe, after all, that you and Mrs. Lecks had your own way in regard to hurrying up this matter."

"Yes," said she, with happy complacency; "I shouldn't wonder if we had. Stirrin' up the parson was our last chance and it wasn't much trouble to do it."

Mrs. Lecks, whose manner toward me for the last few days had been characterized by cold severity, now resumed her former friendly demeanor, although she was not willing to let the affair pass over without some words of reproach.

"I must say, Mr. Craig," she remarked the next morning, "that I was gettin' pretty well outdone with you. I was beginnin' to think that a young man that couldn't see and wouldn't see what was good for him didn't deserve to have it; and if Miss Ruth's father had just come down with a heavy foot and put an end to the whole business I'm not sure I'd been sorry for you. But it's all right at last, and bygones is bygones. And now what we've got to do is to get ready for the weddin'."

"The wedding!" I exclaimed.

Mrs. Lecks regarded me with an expression in which there

was something of virtuous indignation and something of pity. "Mr. Craig," said she, "if there ever was anybody that wanted a guardeen, it's you. Now, just let me tell you this. That Mr. Enderton ain't to be trusted no further than you can see him, and not so fur, neither, if it can be helped. He's willin' for you to have Miss Ruth now, because he's pretty much made up his mind that we're goin' to stay here, and as he considers you the master of this island, of course he thinks it'll be for his good for his daughter to be mistress of it. For one thing, he wouldn't expect to pay no board then. But just let him get away from this island, and just let him set his eyes on some smooth-faced young fellow that'll agree to take him into the concern and keep him for nothin' on books and tea, he'll just throw you over without winkin'. And Miss Ruth is not the girl to marry you against his will if he opens the Bible and piles texts on her, which he is capable of doin'. If in any way you two should get separated when you leave here, there's no knowin' when you'd ever see each other again, for where he'll take her nobody can tell. He's more willin' to set down and stay where he finds himself comfortable than anybody I've met yet."

"Of course," I said, "I'm ready to be married at any moment; but I don't believe Miss Ruth and her father would consent to anything so speedy."

"Don't you get into the way," said Mrs. Lecks, "of beforehand believin' this or that. It don't pay. Just you go to her father and talk to him about it, and if you and him agree it'll be easy enough to make her see the sense of it. You attend to them and I'll see that everythin' is got ready. And you'd better fix the day for tomorrow, for we can't stay here much longer, and there's a lot of house-cleanin' and bakin' and cookin' to be done before we go."

I took this advice and broached the subject to Mr. Enderton.

"Well, sir," said he, laying down his book, "your proposition is decidedly odd; I may say very odd indeed. But it is perhaps, after all, no odder than many things I have seen. Among the various denominational sects I have noticed occurrences quite as odd; quite as odd, sir. For my part, I have no desire to object

354

to an early celebration of the matrimonial rites. I may say, indeed, that I am of the opinion that a certain amount of celerity in this matter will conduce to the comfort of all concerned. It has been a very unsatisfactory thing to me to see my daughter occupying a subordinate position in our little family, where she has not even the power to turn household affairs into the channels of my comfort. Tomorrow, I think, will do very well indeed. Even if it should rain, I see no reason why the ceremony should be postponed."

The proposition of a wedding on the morrow was not received by Ruth with favor. She was unprepared for such precipitancy. But she finally yielded to arguments; not so much to mine, I fear, as to those offered by Mrs. Lecks and Mrs. Aleshine.

For the rest of that day the three mariners were kept very busy, bringing in green things to deck the parlor and doing every imaginable kind of work necessary to a wedding which Mrs. Aleshine was willing to give into their hands. As for herself and her good friend, they put themselves upon their mettle as providers of festivals. They made cakes, pies, and I never knew half so well as the three sailors how many other kinds of good things. Besides all this, they assisted Ruth to array herself in some degree in a manner becoming a bride. Some light and pretty adornments of dress were borrowed from Emily or Lucille, they knew not which, and, after having them "done up" and fluted and crimped by Mrs. Lecks, were incorporated by Ruth into her costume with so much taste that on the wedding morning she appeared to me to be dressed more charmingly than any bride I had ever seen.

The three sailors had done their own washing and ironing, and appeared in cleanly garb and with hair and beards well wet and brushed. Mrs. Lecks and Mrs. Aleshine put on their best bibs and tuckers, and Mr. Enderton assumed his most clerical air as he stood behind a table in the parlor and married Ruth and me.

"This," said Mr. Enderton, as we were seated at the wedding-feast, "is a most creditable display of attractive viands, but I may say, my dear Ruth, that I think I perceived the influence of the happy event of today even before it took place. I have lately had a better appetite for my food, and have experienced a greater enjoyment of my surroundings."

"I should think so," murmured Mrs. Aleshine in my ear, "for we'd no sooner knowed that you two were to make a match of it than we put an extra spoonful of tea into his pot and stopped scrubbin' the libr'ry."

For the next two days all was bustle and work on the island. Mrs. Lecks and Mrs. Aleshine would not consent to depart without leaving everything in the best possible order, so that the Dusantes might not be dissatisfied with the condition of their house when they returned. It was, in fact, the evident desire of the two women to gratify their pride in their housewifely abilities by leaving everything better than they found it.

Mr. Enderton was much surprised at these preparations for immediate departure. He was very well satisfied with his life on the island and had prepared his mind for an indefinite continuance of it, with the position of that annoying and obdurate Mrs. Lecks filled by a compliant and affectionate daughter. He had no reasonable cause for complaint, for the whole subject of the exhaustion of our supply of provisions and the necessity of an open-boat trip to an inhabited island had been fully discussed before him; but he was so entirely engrossed in the consideration of his own well-being that this discussion of our plans had made no impression upon him. He now became convinced that a conspiracy had been entered into against him, and fell into an unpleasant humor. This, however, produced very little effect upon any of us, for we were all too busy to notice his whims. But his sudden change of disposition made me understand how correct were the opinions of Mrs. Lecks and Mrs. Aleshine concerning him. If I had left that island with my marriage with Ruth depending upon Mr. Enderton's co-operation, my prospects of future happiness would have been at the mercy of his caprices.

Very early on a beautiful morning Ruth and I started out on our wedding journey in the longboat. Mr. Enderton was made as comfortable as possible in the stern, with Ruth near him. Mrs. Lecks and Mrs. Aleshine sat facing each other, each with a brown-paper package by her side, containing the life preserver on which she had arrived. These were to be ever cherished as memorials of a wonderful experience. The three sailors and I took turns at the oars. The sea was smooth and there was every reason to believe that we should arrive at our destination before the end of the day. Mrs. Aleshine had supplied us with an abundance of provisions, and with the exception of Mr. Enderton, who had not been permitted to take away any of the Dusante books, we were a contented party.

"As long as the flour held out," remarked Mrs. Aleshine, "I'd never been willin' to leave that island till the Dusantes came back and we could have took Emily or Lucille, whichever it was that kept house, and showed her everythin' and told her just what we had done. But when they do come back," she added, "and read that letter which Mr. Craig wrote and left for them, and find out all that happened in their country-place while they was away; and how two of us was made happy for life; and how two more of us, meanin' Mrs. Lecks and me, have give up goin' to Japan, intendin', instid of that, writin' to my son to come home to America and settle down in the country he ought to live in—why, then, if them Dusantes ain't satisfied, it's no use of anybody to ever try to satisfy 'em."

"I should think not," said Mrs. Lecks, "with the weddin'-cards on the parlor table, not a speck of dust in any corner, and the board money in the ginger-jar."

Charles E. Carryl

SIR PETER BOMBAZOO

Post-captain at the Needles and commander of a crew
On the "Royal Biddy" frigate was Sir Peter Bombazoo;
His mind was full of music, and his head was full of tunes,
And he cheerfully exhibited on pleasant afternoons.

He could whistle, on his fingers, an invigorating reel,
And could imitate a piper on the handles of the wheel;
He could play in double octaves, too, all up and down the rail,
Or rattle off a rondo on the bottom of a pail.

Then porters with their packages, and bakers with their buns,
And countesses in carriages, and grenadiers with guns,
And admirals and commodores, arrived from near and far
To listen to the music of this entertaining tar.

When they heard the Captain humming, and beheld the danc-
ing crew,
The commodores severely said, "Why, this will never do!"
And the admirals all hurried home, remarking, "This is most
Extraordinary conduct for a captain at his post."

Then they sent some sailing-orders to Sir Peter, in a boat,
And he did a little fifing on the edges of the note;
But he read the sailing-orders, as, of course, he had to do,
And removed the "Royal Biddy" to the Bay of Boohgabooh.

Now, Sir Peter took it kindly, but it's proper to explain
He was sent to catch a pirate out upon the Spanish Main;

358

And he played a little dirge upon a handle of a pike.

And he played, with variations, an imaginary tune
On the buttons of his waistcoat, like a jocular bassoon.

Then a topman saw the Pirate come a-sailing in the bay
And reported to the Captain in the customary way.
"I'll receive him," said Sir Peter, "with a musical salute!"
And he gave some imitations of a double-jointed flute.

Then the Pirate cried derisively, "I've heard it done before!"
And he hoisted up a banner emblematical of gore.
But Sir Peter said serenely, "You may double-shot the guns
While I sing my little ballad of 'The Butter on the Buns.'"

Then the Pirate banged Sir Peter and Sir Peter banged him back,
And they banged away together as they took another tack.
Then Sir Peter said politely, "You may board him, if you like"—
And he played a little dirge upon the handle of a pike.

Then the "Biddies" poured like hornets down upon the Pirate's
     deck,
And Sir Peter caught the Pirate, and he took him by the neck,
And remarked, "You must excuse me, but you acted like a brute
When I gave my imitation of the double-jointed flute."

So they took that wicked Pirate, and they took his wicked crew,
And tied them up with double knots in packages of two;
And left them lying on their backs in rows upon the beach
With a little bread and water within comfortable reach.

Now the Pirate had a treasure (mostly silverware and gold),
And Sir Peter took and stowed it in the bottom of his hold;
And said, "I will retire on this cargo of doubloons,
And each of you, my gallant crew, may have some silver spoons."

Now commodores in coach-and-fours, and corporals in cabs,
And men with carts of pies and tarts, and fishermen with crabs,
And barristers with wigs, in gigs, still gather on the strand—
But there isn't any music save a little German band.

Robert McCloskey

HOMER PRICE AND
THE DOUGHNUTS

ILLUSTRATED BY THE AUTHOR

ONE Friday night in November Homer overheard his mother talking on the telephone to Aunt Agnes over in Centerburg. "I'll stop by with the car in about half an hour, and we can go to the meeting together," she said, because tonight was the night the Ladies' Club was meeting to discuss plans for a box social and to knit and sew for the Red Cross.

"I think I'll come along and keep Uncle Ulysses company while you and Aunt Agnes are at the meeting," said Homer.

So after Homer had combed his hair and his mother had looked to see if she had her knitting instructions and the right size needles, they started for town.

Homer's Uncle Ulysses and Aunt Agnes have a very up and coming lunchroom over in Centerburg, just across from the courthouse on the town square. Uncle Ulysses is a man with advanced ideas and a weakness for laborsaving devices. He equipped the lunchroom with automatic toasters, automatic coffee-maker, automatic dishwasher and an automatic doughnut-maker. All just the latest thing in laborsaving devices. Aunt Agnes would throw up her hands and sigh every time Uncle Ulysses bought a new laborsaving device. Sometimes she became unkindly disposed toward him for days and days. She was of the opinion that Uncle Ulysses just frittered away his spare time over at the barber-shop with the sheriff and the boys, so, what was the good of a laborsaving device that gave you more time to fritter?

When Homer and his mother got to Centerburg they stopped at the lunchroom, and after Aunt Agnes had come out and

360

said, "My, how that boy does grow!" which was what she always said, she went off with Homer's mother in the car. Homer went into the lunchroom and said, "Howdy, Uncle Ulysses!"

"Oh, hello, Homer. You're just in time," said Uncle Ulysses. "I've been going over this automatic doughnut machine, oiling the machinery and cleaning the works . . . wonderful things, these laborsaving devices."

"Yep," agreed Homer, and he picked up a cloth and started polishing the metal trimmings while Uncle Ulysses tinkered with the inside workings.

"Opfwo-oof!!" sighed Uncle Ulysses and, "Look here, Homer, you've got a mechanical mind. See if you can find where these two pieces fit in. I'm going across to the barber-shop for a spell, 'cause there's somethin' I've got to talk to the sheriff about. There won't be much business here until the double feature is over, and I'll be back before then."

Then as Uncle Ulysses went out the door he said, "Uh, Homer, after you get the pieces in place, would you mind mixing up a batch of doughnut batter and put it in the machine? You could turn the switch and make a few doughnuts to have on hand for the crowd after the movie . . . if you don't mind."

"O.K.," said Homer, "I'll take care of everything."

A few minutes later a customer came in and said, "Good evening, Bud."

Homer looked up from putting the last piece in the doughnut machine and said, "Good evening, Sir, what can I do for you?"

"Well, young feller, I'd like a cup o' coffee and some doughnuts," said the customer.

"I'm sorry, Mister, but we won't have any doughnuts for about half an hour, until I can mix some dough and start this machine. I could give you some very fine sugar rolls instead."

"Well, Bud, I'm in no real hurry so I'll just have a cup o' coffee and wait around a bit for the doughnuts. Fresh doughnuts are always worth waiting for is what I always say."

"O.K.," said Homer, and he drew a cup of coffee from Uncle Ulysses's super automatic coffee-maker.

"Nice place you've got here," said the customer.

361

"Oh, yes," replied Homer, "this is a very up and coming lunchroom with all the latest improvements."

"Yes," said the stranger, "must be a good business. I'm in business too. A traveling man in outdoor advertising. I'm a sandwich man. Mr. Gabby's my name."

"My name is Homer. I'm glad to meet you. Mr. Gabby. It must be a fine profession, traveling and advertising sandwiches."

"Oh no," said Mr. Gabby, "I don't advertise sandwiches, I just wear any kind of an ad, one sign on front and one sign on behind, this way . . . Like a sandwich. Ya know what I mean?"

"Oh, I see. That must be fun, and you travel too?" asked Homer as he got out the flour and the baking powder.

"Yeah, I ride the rods between jobs, on freight trains, ya know what I mean?"

"Yes, but isn't that dangerous?" asked Homer.

"Of course there's a certain amount of risk, but you take any method of travel these days, it's all dangerous. Ya know what I mean? Now take airplanes for instance . . ."

Just then a large shiny black car stopped in front of the lunchroom, and a chauffeur helped a lady out of the rear door. They both came inside and the lady smiled at Homer and said, "We've stopped for a light snack. Some doughnuts and coffee would be simply marvelous."

Then Homer said, "I'm sorry, Ma'm, but the doughnuts won't be ready until I make this batter and start Uncle Ulysses's doughnut machine."

"Well now aren't *you* a clever young man to know how to make *doughnuts!*"

"Well," blushed Homer, "I've really never done it before but I've got a receipt to follow."

"Now, young man, you simply must allow me to help. You know, I haven't made doughnuts for years, but I know the best receipt for doughnuts. It's marvelous, and we really must use it."

"But, Ma'm . . ." said Homer.

"Now just *wait* till you taste these doughnuts," said the lady. "Do you have an apron?" she asked, as she took off her fur coat and her rings and her jewelry and rolled up her sleeves. "Charles," she said to the chauffeur, "hand me that baking powder, that's right, and, young man, we'll need some nutmeg."

So Homer and the chauffeur stood by and handed things and cracked the eggs while the lady mixed and stirred. Mr. Gabby sat on his stool, sipped his coffee, and looked on with great interest.

"There!" said the lady when all of the ingredients were mixed. "Just *wait* till you taste these doughnuts!"

"It looks like an awful lot of batter," said Homer as he stood on a chair and poured it into the doughnut machine with the help of the chauffeur. "It's about *ten* times as much as Uncle Ulysses ever makes."

"But wait till you taste them!" said the lady with an eager look and a smile.

Homer got down from the chair and pushed a button on the machine marked *"Start."* Rings of batter started dropping into the hot fat. After a ring of batter was cooked on one side an automatic gadget turned it over and the other side would cook. Then another automatic gadget gave the doughnut a little push and it rolled neatly down a little chute, all ready to eat.

"That's a simply *fascinating* machine," said the lady as she waited for the first doughnut to roll out.

"Here, young man, *you* must have the first one. Now isn't that just *too* delicious? Isn't it simply marvelous?"

"Yes, Ma'm, it's very good," replied Homer as the lady handed doughnuts to Charles and to Mr. Gabby and asked if they didn't think they were simply divine doughnuts.

"It's an old family receipt!" said the lady with pride.

Homer poured some coffee for the lady and her chauffeur and for Mr. Gabby, and a glass of milk for himself. Then they all sat down at the lunch counter to enjoy another few doughnuts apiece.

"I'm so glad you enjoy my doughnuts," said the lady. "But now, Charles, we really must be going. If you will just take this apron, Homer, and put two dozen doughnuts in a bag to take along, we'll be on our way. And, Charles, don't forget to pay the young man." She rolled down her sleeves and put on her jewelry, then Charles managed to get her into her big fur coat.

"Good night, young man, I haven't had so much fun in years. *I really* haven't!" said the lady, as she went out the door and into the big shiny car.

"Those are sure good doughnuts," said Mr. Gabby as the car moved off.

"You bet!" said Homer. Then he and Mr. Gabby stood and watched the automatic doughnut machine make doughnuts.

After a few dozen more doughnuts had rolled down the little chute, Homer said, "I guess that's about enough doughnuts to sell to the after-theater customers. I'd better turn the machine off for a while."

Homer pushed the button marked *"Stop"* and there was a little click, but nothing happened. The rings of batter kept right on dropping into the hot fat, and an automatic gadget kept right on turning them over, and another automatic gadget kept right on giving them a little push, and the doughnuts kept right on rolling down the little chute, all ready to eat.

"That's funny," said Homer, "I'm sure that's the right button!" He pushed it again, but the automatic doughnut-maker kept right on making doughnuts.

"Well I guess I must have put one of those pieces in backwards," said Homer.

"Then it might stop if you pushed the button marked *"Start,"* said Mr. Gabby.

Homer did, and the doughnuts still kept rolling down the little chute, just as regular as a clock can tick.

"I guess we could sell a few more doughnuts," said Homer, "but I'd better telephone Uncle Ulysses over at the barbershop." Homer gave the number and while he waited for someone to answer he counted thirty-seven doughnuts roll down the little chute.

Finally someone answered, "Hello! This is the sarber-bhop, I mean the barber-shop."

"Oh, hello, sheriff. This is Homer. Could I speak to Uncle Ulysses?"

"Well, he's playing pinochle right now," said the sheriff. "Anythin' I can tell 'im?"

"Yes," said Homer. "I pushed the button marked *Stop* on the doughnut machine, but the rings of batter keep right on dropping into the hot fat, and an automatic gadget keeps right on turning them over, and another automatic gadget keeps giving them a little push, and the doughnuts keep right on rolling down the little chute! It won't stop!"

"O.K. Wold the hire, I mean, hold the wire and I'll tell 'im." Then Homer looked over his shoulder and counted another twenty-one doughnuts roll down the little chute, all ready to eat. Then the sheriff said, "He'll be right over . . . Just gotta finish this hand."

"That's good," said Homer. "G'by, sheriff."

The window was full of doughnuts by now, so Homer and

365

Mr. Gabby had to hustle around and start stacking them on plates and trays and lining them up on the counter.

"Sure are a lot of doughnuts!" said Homer.

"You bet!" said Mr. Gabby. "I lost count at twelve hundred and two and that was quite a while back."

People had begun to gather outside the lunchroom window, and someone was saying, "There are almost as many doughnuts as there are people in Centerburg, and I wonder how in tarnation Ulysses thinks he can sell all of 'em!"

Every once in a while somebody would come inside and buy some, but while somebody bought two to eat and a dozen to take home, the machine made three dozen more.

By the time Uncle Ulysses and the sheriff arrived and pushed through the crowd, the lunchroom was a calamity of doughnuts! Doughnuts in the window, doughnuts piled high on the shelves, doughnuts stacked on plates, doughnuts lined up twelve deep all along the counter, and doughnuts still rolling down the little chute, just as regular as a clock can tick.

"Hello, sheriff, hello, Uncle Ulysses, we're having a little trouble here," said Homer.

"Well, I'll be dunked!!" said Uncle Ulysses.

"Dernd ef you won't be when Aggy gits home," said the sheriff.

"Mighty fine doughnuts though. What'll you do with 'em all, Ulysses?"

Uncle Ulysses groaned and said, "What will Aggy say? We'll never sell 'em all."

Then Mr. Gabby, who hadn't said anything for a long time, stopped piling doughnuts and said, "What you need is an advertising man. Ya know what I mean? Ya got the doughnuts, ya gotta create a market . . . Understand? . . . It's balancing the demand with the supply . . . That sort of thing."

"Yep!" said Homer. "Mr. Gabby's right. We have to enlarge our market. He's an advertising sandwich man, so if we hire him, he can walk up and down in front of the theater and get the customers."

"You're hired, Mr. Gabby!" said Uncle Ulysses.

366

Then everybody pitched in to paint the signs and to get Mr. Gabby sandwiched between. They painted "SALE ON DOUGHNUTS" in big letters on the window too.

Meanwhile the rings of batter kept right on dropping into the hot fat, and an automatic gadget kept right on turning them over, and another automatic gadget kept right on giving them a little push, and the doughnuts kept right on rolling down the little chute, just as regular as a clock can tick.

"I certainly hope this advertising works," said Uncle Ulysses, wagging his head. "Aggy'll certainly throw a fit if it don't."

The sheriff went outside to keep order, because there was quite a crowd by now—all looking at the doughnuts and guessing how many thousand there were, and watching new ones roll down the little chute, just as regular as a clock can tick. Homer and Uncle Ulysses kept stacking doughnuts. Once in a while

367

somebody bought a few, but not very often.

Then Mr. Gabby came back and said, "Say, you know there's not much use o' me advertisin' at the theater. The show's all over, and besides almost everybody in town is out front watching that machine make doughnuts!"

"Zeus!" said Uncle Ulysses. "We must get rid of these doughnuts before Aggy gets here!"

"Looks like you will have ta hire a truck ta waul 'em ahay, I mean haul 'em away!!" said the sheriff who had just come in. Just then there was a noise and a shoving out front, and the lady from the shiny black car and her chauffeur came pushing through the crowd and into the lunchroom.

"Oh, gracious!" she gasped, ignoring the doughnuts, "I've lost my diamond bracelet, and I know I left it here on the counter," she said, pointing to a place where the doughnuts were piled in stacks of two dozen.

"Yes, Ma'm, I guess you forgot it when you helped make the batter," said Homer.

Then they moved all the doughnuts around and looked for the diamond bracelet, but they couldn't find it anywhere. Meanwhile the doughnuts kept rolling down the little chute, just as regular as a clock can tick.

After they had looked all around, the sheriff cast a suspicious eye on Mr. Gabby, but Homer said, "He's all right, sheriff, he didn't take it. He's a friend of mine."

Then the lady said, "I'll offer a reward of one hundred dollars for that bracelet! It really *must* be found! . . . it *really* must!"

"Now don't you worry, lady," said the sheriff. "I'll get your bracelet back!"

"Zeus! This is terrible!" said Uncle Ulysses. "First all of these doughnuts and then on top of all that, a lost diamond bracelet . . ."

Mr. Gabby tried to comfort him; and he said, "There's always a bright side. That machine'll probably run outta batter in an hour or two."

If Mr. Gabby hadn't been quick on his feet Uncle Ulysses would have knocked him down, sure as fate.

368

Then while the lady wrung her hands and said, "We must find it, we *must!*" and Uncle Ulysses was moaning about what Aunt Agnes would say, and the sheriff was eyeing Mr. Gabby, Homer sat down and thought hard.

Before twenty more doughnuts could roll down the little chute he shouted, "SAY! I know where the bracelet is! It was lying here on the counter and got mixed up in the batter by mistake! The bracelet is cooked inside one of these doughnuts!"

"Why . . . I really believe you're right," said the lady through her tears. "Isn't that *amazing?* Simply *amazing!*"

"I'll be durn'd!" said the sheriff.

"OhH-h!" moaned Uncle Ulysses. "Now we have to break up all of these doughnuts to find it. Think of the *pieces!* Think of the *crumbs!* Think of what *Aggy* will say!"

"Nope," said Homer. "We won't have to break them up. I've got a plan."

So Homer and the advertising man took some cardboard and some paint and printed another sign. They put this sign in the window, and the sandwich man wore two more signs that said the same thing and walked around in the crowd out front.

FRESH DOUGHNUTS 2 FOR 5¢
WHILE THEY LAST
$100.⁰⁰ PRIZE
FOR FINDING A BRACELET INSIDE A DOUGHNUT
P.S. YOU HAVE TO GIVE THE BRACELET BACK

THEN . . . The doughnuts began to sell! *Everybody* wanted to buy doughnuts, *dozens* of doughnuts!

And that's not all. Everybody bought coffee to dunk the doughnuts in too. Those that didn't buy coffee bought milk or soda. It kept Homer and the lady and the chauffeur and Uncle Ulysses and the sheriff busy waiting on the people who wanted to buy doughnuts.

When all but the last couple of hundred doughnuts had been sold, Rupert Black shouted, "I GAWT IT!!" and sure enough . . . there was the diamond bracelet inside of his doughnut!

Then Rupert went home with a hundred dollars, the citizens of Centerburg went home full of doughnuts, the lady and her chauffeur drove off with the diamond bracelet, and Homer went home with his mother when she stopped by with Aunt Aggy.

As Homer went out of the door he heard Mr. Gabby say, "Neatest trick of merchandising I ever seen," and Aunt Aggy was looking skeptical while Uncle Ulysses was saying, "The rings of batter kept right on dropping into the hot fat, and the automatic gadget kept right on turning them over, and the other automatic gadget kept right on giving them a little push, and the doughnuts kept right on rolling down the little chute just as regular as a clock can tick—they just kept right on a comin', an' a comin', an' a comin', an' a comin'."

Index